GETTING
garbo
A NOVEL OF HOLLYWOOD NOIR

Jerry Ludwig

SOURCEBOOKS LANDMARK™
AN IMPRINT OF SOURCEBOOKS, INC.®
NAPERVILLE, ILLINOIS

Published by Sourcebooks, Inc.
P.O. Box 4410, Naperville, Illinois 60567-4410
(630) 961-3900
FAX: (630) 961-2168
www.sourcebooks.com

Library of Congress Cataloging-in-Publication Data

Ludwig, Jerry.
  Getting Garbo / by Jerry Ludwig.
      p. cm.
  ISBN 1-4022-0223-7 (alk. paper)
  1. Autographs—Collectors and collecting—Fiction. 2. Motion
picture actors and actresses—Fiction. 3. Hollywood (Los Angeles,
Calif.)—Fiction. 4. Fans (Persons)—Fiction. I. Title.
  PS3562.U29G48 2004
  813'.54--dc22

2004013122

Printed and bound in the United States of America
BG 10 9 8 7 6 5 4 3 2 1

For Tobi,
the miracle of my life

part one

"What we are and what we think we are
are really two different things. And the
discovery of who one is is a soul-shaking
experience."

—John Huston

Reva

Do you believe in destiny? Since I was a little kid and I first learned the word, I always thought that it applied only to people who were rich or famous, like Marie Antoinette or Charles Lindbergh. They had a destiny. The rest of us just went through life and things kind of happened with no particular rhyme or reason. But sometimes, when you stop and look back, you see a pattern, maybe even an inevitability.

This is how it started for me.

Back in the late '40s through the mid-'50s, my folks and I were living in this dinky cold-water third-floor walkup in a quasi-slum at the end of the IRT subway line in Brooklyn. Sickly and already undersized as a child, I wasn't allowed by Mother to play with any of the neighborhood kids if they even had a runny nose for fear that I would catch whatever was going around. Not that any of them were clamoring to play with me; mostly whenever they paid any attention to me it was to chant, "Reva *Hess* is a *mess.*" So basically that left me with a grand total of no friends, except for one: it was the pre-television era, and the radio became my best friend. "Who knows what evil lurks in the hearts of men? The Shadow knows!" Fred Allen nasally calling for "Mrs. Nussbauuuum." *Gangbusters* and the *Kate Smith Show.* "Jello everybody, this is Jack Benny…" *Corliss Archer* and *Henry Aldrich.* The stirring *William Tell Overture* that brought the Lone Ranger and Tonto galloping out of the West.

"Tired of the everyday routine? CBS offers you—*Suspense.*"

I feel real sorry for everyone who missed that time. Now, I know what you're gonna say: we got the tube now and isn't it much better to have words *and* pictures? Well, that's just my point. I could hear *and* see. Incredible pictures, in living color, castles and jungles, distant battlefields and planets in other galaxies, bigger and better than even Cecil B. DeMille can afford to actually create for his movies, pictures woven only of words and sound effects, and here's the best part: it was all happening inside my head. Sure, maybe you saw a different picture than me, but that was fine, too, because the only real limit on what you experienced was imagination, and I've always prided myself on having a lot of that.

My top favorite radio show was *Let's Pretend* on Saturday morning. They acted out fairy tales and I was transported to all those make-believe kingdoms. When Jack climbed the beanstalk that reached to the sky, I was right up there with him. I was Rapunzel letting her hair cascade down the length of the tower for the brave knight to ascend, and when the prince awakened Sleeping Beauty with a kiss, that was me, too. I never missed an episode. But I'd begun to notice something. Every Saturday morning, I pictured one familiar face besides mine. Sometimes it belonged to Aladdin or Hansel or even the court jester. My favorite characters. But they'd all have the same voice. *His* voice. Only I didn't know that yet. Not until I persuaded Mother to let me accept the offer made by the announcer at the end of *Let's Pretend* to write away for free tickets to attend a broadcast. Mother finally agreed as a present for my thirteenth birthday. It was 1950 and that was the first trip I'd ever made into Manhattan.

It took over an hour on the subway, but when Mother and I climbed up into the center of Radio City, I didn't know what to look at first. The skyscrapers, the neon signs, the honking traffic, Lindy's famous restaurant (with signed movie star photos in the window), men digging up the gutter with jackhammers, a novelty store where I tried (unsuccessfully) to convince Mother to buy me a pet turtle with the Empire State Building painted on its shell. We stood with a bunch of people in front of a restaurant window where a black cook in a white coat and hat flipped pancakes and omelets in the air and caught them in his frying pan.

Then there was the radio show itself, in a theater on 54th Street, just off Broadway. Unlike the movie houses we had in Brooklyn, it was clean. No wads of gum stuck under the seats or candy wrappers and sticky dried soda pop on the floor. And the floor was carpeted, which none of the theaters in our neighborhood were. Of course, there was no screen in the CBS radio theater. Just a narrow stage with a painted backdrop of fairy tale characters. The actors and actresses, all holding their scripts, sat on folding chairs, chatting quietly. They didn't wear costumes, just ordinary business-type clothes.

While we were waiting for the show to start, this young guy with shaggy chestnut brown hair wandered out. He was wearing a black windbreaker, a white shirt with no tie, and wrinkled khaki pants and brown work boots. I figured he was a stagehand because he looked like he should be pushing a broom. He adjusted the height of a microphone and placed a script on the stand in front of it. He went over to talk to the sound effects engineer, who was sitting at this complicated setup where they do all that stuff like patting their chests with coconut shells to fake a horse's hoof beats or crinkling sheets of cellophane to create the illusion of crackling flames, and they talked so long I thought maybe the shaggy guy was the assistant sound engineer.

The story they were doing was "The Fisherman and His Wife," about the guy who saves the life of the magic fish. The fish thanks him and the fisherman goes home and tells his wife about it and she tells him he should go back and ask for a wish. So he goes and asks for a house, and the fish gives it to them, but the wife still isn't satisfied, so she sends her husband back again to ask for a palace, and it goes on like that, with the wife never content. Finally, the last time she sends him back, the fisherman tells the magic fish that his wife now wants to be queen of the moon and the stars and the sky. The magic fish is really irked by that and he cancels all the other good stuff he already gave them and they're back where they started—with nothing.

Mother said there was a moral to the story. I just thought it was exciting and wished the wife would slip and fall and die in the palace so he could find someone nice who really loved him. But guess who was playing the fisherman? It was him, of course. *The voice.* But big surprise to me: turns out the voice belonged to the shaggy guy in the windbreaker, who wasn't a stagehand or the assistant sound engineer after all. Actually, he acted in a bunch of different voices, as a tiny beggar boy and a witchy old hag and if you weren't watching, you'd never guess they were all him. At the end of the show the announcer rattled off the names of the cast, each actor or actress took a little bow for the audience, and that's how I first found out his name was Roy Darnell.

Afterwards Mother and I strolled down Broadway past the great movie theaters I'd heard of, like the Capitol and the Strand. Just below the Camels billboard with the man's face blowing real smoke rings out into Times Square, we found a Nedicks stand and had hot dogs and orange drinks. Because it was my birthday, Mother broke down and bought me a bag of saltwater taffy for dessert. Then we were on 45th Street and the theaters here weren't movie houses or radio studios. Mother explained that these were the theaters where the hit Broadway shows played with real actors on stage. Some of the names on the marquees I recognized, some I didn't. Ethel Merman. Bobby Clark. Alfred Lunt and Lynn Fontanne. Spencer Tracy. Bert Lahr. Then I spotted Sardi's. A name I know from the weekday radio show they broadcast from there, *Luncheon At Sardi's,* interviewing the stars.

Just when we approached the entrance, something really unusual happened. The fatso uniformed doorman was yelling at us, "Move it, move it, ladies, don't block the way," when who should come sauntering out but Danny Kaye and his daughter. Now, Danny Kaye was absolutely God in our neighborhood. He grew up there and went to the same junior high school I was in at the time. In fact, he was one of only two famous people who ever graduated from J.H.S. 149. The other one was Anthony Esposito, who became a hitman for "Murder, Incorporated," and he went to the electric chair when I was in the seventh grade.

But seeing Danny Kaye in the flesh wasn't the unusual thing.

The sidewalk in front of Sardi's was real crowded, a regular mob scene of theater customers hotfooting it to their matinees, and a bunch of Damon Runyon–type guys blocking the sidewalk and kibbitzing in front of the ticket agency next door, not to mention the horde of other people shoving by in order to get to who knows where. But at the sight of Danny Kaye, a half dozen of the pedestrians loitering on the sidewalk suddenly came out of the crowd and closed in. It was like a squadron of vultures swooping in on their prey. Well, that makes it sound mean—it was more like a coordinated ballet movement. They must have been there all along, those half-dozen, but they'd been invisible until now. They came in all sizes, shapes, and forms, from teenage bobbysoxers to a leathery old woman. But they all had autograph books and pens in their hands now. They formed a circle around Danny Kaye and his daughter—and pushed Mother and me completely aside.

As Danny Kaye began to sign his name for them, Mother poked me to get in there too. We didn't have any paper, but she poured all the salt water taffy into her handbag and gave me the empty paper bag. But by then it was too late. Danny Kaye was about to get into a taxi. I don't know where I got the chutzpah from, but I hollered: "Mr. Kaye, wait, I'm from one-forty-nine!"

He turned and looked back. Right at me. So I repeated what I'd said and he shook his head. "You're too little to be in junior high."

"I skipped a grade," I told him.

"So let me hear the school song."

Everybody was staring at me now. So I started off kind of shaky.

"One-four-nine is the school for me…"

He joined in on the second line and we sang it together:

"Drives away adversity,
Steady and true,
We'll be unto you,
Loyal to one-four-nine,
Rah-rah-rah-h-h-h!"

Then everybody on the pavement clapped and he signed my paper bag. He wrote, "For Reva, Say Hi to 149 for me, Danny Kaye." He drove off and while Mother was admiring the autograph, who else should come out but Roy Darnell with a pretty young lady. By now I was in the swing of things and asked him to sign the other side of my paper bag. The professional autograph hunters all crowded around us.

"Who'zat?" one wanted to know.

"Roy Darnell," I said, proud to be of service to them. "He's the star of *Let's Pretend* on the radio."

"It's nobody," the leathery old lady said. And they all melted away into the crowd again. The pretty girl with Roy Darnell laughed.

"You still want my autograph?" he asked.

"Oh, yeah!" I said. And he wrote, "Thanks for asking, Reva, all the best, Roy Darnell." Imagine that—*he* thanked *me*. That happened six years ago, but I can still hear him just like it was yesterday.

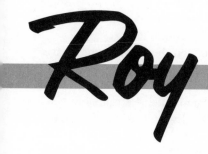

2

Roy

Humphrey Bogart is telling a joke. So, of course, we're all listening. After all, it's Bogie's booth. Second on the left as you descend into the main room at Romanoff's restaurant in Beverly Hills. Where the elite meet to eat lunch and ogle each other. Bogie sits in front of his usual Scotch and soda, dragging on a cigarette in that special cupped-hand way that made smokers of so many of us and killed him two years later. Some of the usual suspects are gathered: genial actor David Niven, high-powered agent Irving Paul Lazar, *Herald Trib* columnist Joe Hyams, plus our imperious host, the royal pretender himself, Prince Mike Romanoff. And don't forget me—Roy Darnell, the kid from South Philly who's finally made it into the big time by way of the small screen. That's us. The guys.

"So there's this man needs a new suit," Bogie begins, "and his friend Harry says, 'C'mon, let's go see Pincus the tailor over on Fairfax Avenue. He's a magician with a needle.' They go over and the man tells Pincus, 'I need a black suit, not navy blue. Black. Black as Joe McCarthy's heart.' Pincus assures him he'll make a great suit. Pincus measures the man, tells him to come back next Tuesday."

Romanoff interrupts. The Oxford-borrowed accent. "Excuse me, Mr. Bogart, is this going to be a very long story?"

"Shut the fuck up, Mike. So on Tuesday, the man and his buddy Harry come back and the suit fits like a dream. But the man holds a sleeve up to the light. 'Whaddayathink, Harry? Looks just like very dark blue to me.' Pincus swears to him it's the blackest suit he ever made."

"Single or double breasted?" Lazar wants to know. Bogie glares. Like he used to at Conrad Veidt in the anti-Nazi flicks. Lazar says no more. Bogie continues.

"So the guy pays Pincus, puts on the suit and they leave. Walking down the street. Still not sure. But here's two nuns coming toward them."

"That's supposed to be real good luck," Hyams says.

"You assholes," Bogie says. "Just forget it. Forget the whole thing."

"Go on, Bogie, finish the story. I'm dying to hear the ending." Niven could be razzing him along with the others. But Bogie enjoys the commotion. Another toke on his unfiltered Chesterfield. Then he goes on.

"So the man rushes up to the younger nun and says, 'Excuse me, sister,' and he holds up the sleeve of his new suit next to her nun's habit. Then he turns to Harry and mumbles something. Now, the two nuns stroll on. After a minute the younger nun says, 'I didn't know persons of the Jewish persuasion could speak Latin.' The older nun asks her what she means. 'Well,' says the younger nun, 'when that gentleman held up his sleeve he said *pincus fuctus.*'"

I laugh. But I'm alone. The rest of the guys just sit there.

"Funny, huh?" Bogie berates Lazar.

"It's anti-Semitic."

"Up yours, Swifty. I'm more Jewish than you'll ever be."

"You're a full-blooded goy," Hyams reminds him.

Bogie focuses on me. "Tell 'em why it's hilarious."

I pick my words carefully. They can all jump on me in a second. Including Bogie. That's how the game is played.

"Don't you guys get it?" I say. "It's about Hollywood—all the people who got screwed and lived to dine and whine about it. See, everybody tells a different story. But they're really all the same. They're all the tales of how Pincus fucked us."

Bogie chuckles in his mirthless way. "The kid's the only one in the joint with a sense of humor."

I bask in my mentor's approval. My punchline echoes inside my head: They're all the tales of how Pincus fucked us.

And this tale happens to be mine.

"Mr. Darnell, your luncheon companion has arrived," Kurt, the maitre d', confides to me in a Kraut accent. Prince Mike, nee Harry Gerguson from Brooklyn, likes to hire people with European accents. Classes up the place. Kurt gestures across the room to where Laszlo the waiter is ceremoniously seating a wind-swept ash blonde wearing oversized sunglasses and a fur coat that a stable of sables died for. Flash of good legs as she scuttles into her seat. She waves to me. I wave to her. In fact, all the guys at Bogie's table wave to her.

"Sheilah, huh?" Bogie says. I shrug nonchalantly. "Sunday story?" he asks. I'm too smart to answer. "She always dangles a Sunday story. Well, don't do anything I wouldn't do."

"Did," Romanoff corrects him.

"Shut the fuck up, Mike. Go get 'er, kid."

I cross the room to the green leather banquette where she's waiting. Step into my parlor.

She'll never see forty again. But from where I'm sitting now, Sheilah Graham seems more like a zaftig aging starlet than one of Hollywood's grand inquisitors. No studio press agent to chaperone. Just she and me and here we go.

"Roy Darnell," she begins. "They say you're the most dangerous man in Hollywood."

So that's how it's going to be. Okay. "Hey, Sheilah, I'm peanuts compared to Sinatra. I slug snotty barroom drunks. He runs his limo over pushy photographers and clobbers columnists. He's my hero."

She laughs and jots on her pad. It's what she came for. Jack Havoc in person.

"You took a swing at Jack Warner."

"Not since last Christmas."

"Do you ever have the urge to hit a columnist?"

"You mean, are you safe?" I shrug. "So far."

She laughs. She jots.

Time was, just three long years ago, no one cared what my opinion was about anything. Since then I've been interviewed by hundreds of publications ranging from *Time* magazine to the *B'nai B'rith Messenger*. They want to know if I sleep in the nude and what I think of Frank Costello and what food I hate the most and if I believe in the death penalty. Actually, they're never talking to me. They're always talking to Jack Havoc. That's also me. *Roy Darnell is Jack Havoc*. That's how the billing reads every week on the main title of my TV show. The press tends to confuse the two of us. Me and Jack. And that's okay. I encourage the confusion. Makes better copy. Bogie taught me that.

"How come you're not in the Army?" Sheilah Graham wonders. "We probably would have won the war if you'd volunteered." It's a compliment with a depth charge attached to it. Simple arithmetic, see? Korea started in 1950, here it is 1956, and I'm 27. So what she wants to know is how I beat the draft.

"Well, I tried to enlist. I begged the Marines but they turned me down. Punctured eardrum. Half deaf on my left side. Souvenir from a gang rumble when I was a kid in South Philly." Actually, a mastoid from when I had the mumps. But how's she ever going to know the difference? "Bunch of my buddies went to Korea. Some of 'em didn't come back. Not in one piece, anyway."

She likes the answer. Jot-jot. She's allowed to hit you with questions only a confessional priest is normally entitled to ask. Rules of the game. Hedda, Louella, and Sheilah are the self-appointed protectors of Hollywood's morals. Big job. Takes three of them to do it.

So go explain that now, on twenty minutes' acquaintanceship, beneath the protective concealment of Romanoff's finest linen tablecloth, Sheilah Graham is playing footsie with me.

"Why haven't we met before?" she says lazily as Laszlo the waiter fusses over us. Pouring straight shots of aquavit from a bottle embedded in a slab of ice. Imagine. I'm matching shots with F. Scott Fitzgerald's last mistress, inspiration for *The Last Tycoon,* which he never finished because he drank himself to death. Another one of my heroes. "Have you been hiding from me?" she wants to know.

She doesn't remember, but our paths actually did cross before. Six years ago. Backstage after a performance of *A Streetcar Named Desire.* I was temporarily understudying a small role, the kid who knocks on the door in Act Two and almost gets seduced by Blanche DuBois. Only one scene, but a winner—except the regular actor was healthy as a packhorse so I hardly ever got to play it for an audience. Anyway, this night, Sheilah Graham and entourage brush past me without a glance and sweep into the star dressing room of Jessica Tandy to be introduced to her costar, Broadway's latest sensation—fellow name of Brando.

Expecting high drama? Better settle for low comedy.

"Marlon, I'd like you to meet someone," Jessica says.

"Well, hello there," Sheilah says.

"So you're Jessica's mother," Marlon says. Smiling boyishly.

Sheilah, two years younger than Jessica Tandy, gapes in horror.

Natural enough mistake, of course. Sheilah's blonde and British, just like Tandy. Marlon is nearsighted, refuses to wear glasses, and has been told that Tandy's mother is in town. It might have been glossed over, explained away. Except for the braying laughter. Coming from the hallway. Coming from me.

Me and my sense of humor.

Sheilah Graham fled. Never printed a pleasant word about Brando after that. So no point reminding her of our chance meeting.

Now she's asking about Bogie and me. This part of the interview I can do in my sleep. Friendly Philly cop arrests street punk. Steers him into acting class. Kid actor. New York radio scene. Kid's voice changes, career's over. Starving in New York. Until. Ta-dah! Bogie to the rescue. Comes to New York for "live" TV production of *The Petrified Forest.* Bogie as

Duke Mantee once again. Kid auditions six times. Nobody wants me. Except Bogie. Makes them hire me as third mobster in the gang. Next gets Hollywood pal to give me a showy bit as a rapist hoodlum in *Blackboard Jungle*. Warner's TV people come to Bogie. Wanna star in a TV series? *Jack Havoc*. Hired gun with a personal code. White knight in a black T-Bird, tilting against injustice. *Have Gun, Will Travel* without the horses. Get Peter Lorre to play your sidekick. How about it, Bogie? Big laugh. I'm too old and too rich. But Bogie recommends this kid. Me. I work cheap, I work hard. A star is born. Show's a smash. Three years in the Top Ten. Blah-blah-blah. The truth with the edges rounded off.

But she likes it.

Sheilah is jotting with her right hand. Probing with her left foot. Shoeless. Her toes up my pants leg. I glance over at Bogie's table. Others yakking. Bogie, munching his usual platter of French toast, grinning at me. Son of a bitch has X-ray vision.

Clink! Another round of icy aquavit. Platter of cracked crab we're sharing stands neglected. *Skaol!* And now *she's* confiding in *me*. Her marriage has hit a bumpy patch. Looks like it's never gonna recover. I don't really give a shit, of course, and I'm not sure she does either. But I sympathize. I pat her hand, she squeezes my thigh. Hey. So what's the big deal here? To boff or not to boff, that is the question. Not like it's Louella the horned toad or Hedda the decrepit dowager queen. A roll in the hay with Miss Graham might be fun. Used to be a London chorus girl, bet she's still got rhythm. Follow in F. Scott's footsteps, what's the matter with that? Damn. It's the aquavit talking. Get a grip on yourself, Roy.

I lean forward. Accentuating the importance of my next words. Tongue's a little thick, but it's straight from my heart.

"Sheilah, can I tell you? I am in love with the most beautiful, wonderful girl in the world—my wife. That's what I wish for you. But with a guy, of course."

She shrugs. "All the good guys are taken." Her sunglasses slip down her nose. She pushes them back up again. Sighs.

Disappointed? Maybe. What she's really after besides my ass is secrets. Exclusives. Hot bulletins for her readers.

We're walking out now. Closing the joint. Last stragglers. Prince Mike kisses Sheilah's hand. Shakes mine. Solemnly. We amble on. Cozy. Arms around each other's waists. Clutching. Because we're both shit-faced. Saunter, don't stagger. Make it to the curb outside Romanoff's. Usual knot of fans still there. Autograph books and flash cameras. The valet parking guy has Sheilah's Rolls-Royce waiting. I bend close to kiss her cheek. She turns her face and I get a mouth full of tongue. Flashes go off. We both laugh. She whispers, "If anything changes in your situation, let me know right away." For her column? For her bedroom? Probably both.

The autograph kids swarm now. Waving pens and albums and 8x10s and candid photos they've shot. A red-haired, freckle-faced boy holds out a folded hunk of paper. New kid. Built like a high school linebacker. Brassy smile. "What's your name?" I ask. Ready to write on his paper.

"Doesn't matter," he says. "You can keep that."

"What?" Having a little difficulty focusing just now.

"That's for you," the new kid says. "You're served."

Unfold the hunk of paper. Legal mumbo jumbo. Subpoena. Fucking subpoena! Words blurry, dancing. Must be Jack Warner, that creep! Ruining my life. I look at the red-haired kid. He's standing there in triplicate. All three faces grinning. What would Jack Havoc do? I take my best shot. Short right-handed jab. Straight from the shoulder. At the face in the middle. But I hit air. And tumble forward. Sprawling on the hood of Sheilah's Rolls. All three red-haired kids snickering at me now. More camera flashes. Sheilah climbing out of the Rolls. Shark smells blood. Asks the red-haired kid what it's all about. Ready to jot. "Divorce papers," he tells her.

I feel a friendly hand. Helping me sway up. I gaze into the sweetest face I know. Little Reva. Reva Hess. My number-one fan. Perky little teenager. Pops up wherever I am. New York. Hollywood. Always there. With that worshipful smile.

"Hi, Reva," I say.

"You okay, Mr. Darnell?" Worshipful-worried.

"Never better," I say.

Reva doesn't look like she believes me.

I tool away in my sporty black T-Bird two-seater. Our sponsor, Ford Motors, gives me a fresh ride every year. For free. I'm a roving ambassador for my show and, of course, their product. Almost two-thirds of those T-Birds in the country are in Southern California. But none of them has the lustrous twenty-six coats of midnight black finish mine has, with the specially designed wire wheels. I change lanes carefully, with the concentrated attention that only the drunk put into their driving. I should go home and sleep it off. But I don't usually do what I should do. God. I'm starting to sound like Jack Havoc—and on my own time.

Rodeo Drive is just another sleepy second-string shopping street. Books, garden supplies, haberdashery. None of the exclusive shops and salons. The action is all a block east on Beverly Drive. But the rents are cheaper on Rodeo. I find a parking space easily in front of Francis Orr Stationers. Adrienne's Emporium is next door. Tasteful window display done in imported-snobby. I sail into the store, still flying from the aquavit and the adrenaline from my Romanoff's adventure. Full of righteous indignation. There are only a couple of shoppers browsing the inventory of expensive furnishings that I've paid for and hardly ever see any return on. But Addie claims that's normal for a startup interior decorator operation. I always ask her, Addie, why don't all the other decorators in town bother with their own showrooms? She says I don't understand. And don't call her Addie around the clients. She's *Adrienne*.

"Where's Addie?" I loudly ask one of the sedate sales biddies.

She looks like I just farted in front of the queen. Hands flutter. "Miss Adrienne is in the office, Mr. Darnell. But she's in a meeting with—"

I turn. Chug to the rear. In passing I give a nod to Benjy, the muscle-bound black security guy, sitting on a sale-priced

Eames chair, reading the *Hollywood Reporter*. "Hey, Roy, how's the man?" he greets. Benjy's after me to help him get his SAG card so he can become the next Sidney Poitier.

Through the glass wall of her office, I can see Addie. She's with Guy Saddler. He's this retired movie set decorator who once won an Oscar for Garbo's *Camille*. Now he's on our payroll as a "consultant." That seems to translate into standing around fingering fabric swatches and reminiscing about "my most recent fortnight in Milano." They spend a lot of time together, Addie and Guy, but he's light in the loafers so I never mind—except for the sarcasm he aims in my direction. As if I'm too much of an animal to even understand I'm being insulted. He gestures in my direction and Addie looks over. He whispers something snively in his Clifton Webb voice and she gives a small laugh and steps out to meet me.

So here she is, folks. The girl that I married. She still looks so much like the first moment I saw her. Shoulder-length chestnut hair. Beverly Hills Tennis Club tan. We used to play together. Good legs, terrific boobs. Hazel eyes that always used to be ready for laughter.

When we met, that's six years ago, she was working her way through Columbia pre-law by writing feature stories for *Film Daily* in New York. I was playing the Prince on CBS-Radio's *Let's Pretend* every Saturday morning. She did the first interview on me. At Sardi's. Gotta love her, right? We were a perfect combination. Opposites attracting. The college chick and the high school dropout. She taught me how to read and I taught her how to fuck. Oversimplified? Sure. The important thing to remember is how close we were then. Two kids out to beat the world. Together. And it worked like a road map. She graduated Columbia University and through a *Film Daily* contact got a job at Columbia Pictures in New York. Negotiating contracts, keeping an eye out for work for me. After Bogie brought me to the Coast, she transferred here, too. Everything was marvelous when we were getting started. It was when I succeeded that the problems began.

She hates Jack Havoc. Resents the heads turning on the street, the fans interrupting dinner at restaurants, calling her

"Mrs. Havoc." She despises that. So she blames me. "It seems you've acquired all the annoyances and none of the advantages of being famous," she likes to say. Nice talk, huh?

Also, she hit a roadblock at Columbia when Harry Cohn made a pass at her. She rebuffed him so vigorously that he canned her. End of one career. Start of another. Addie helped Bogie and Betty decorate their new house in Holmby Hills. Home run! Addie's suddenly in demand as a decorator. Loves being Adrienne. Working the party circuit, trolling for clients. That's when I got left behind. The kid from South Philly snoozing at dinner parties during heated discussions between elegant pansies and snide society bitches about Kurdistan carpeting and fun new fabrics. But at least Addie was making money at it then. When she talked me into backing her store, I thought that'd get us close again. It only got us deeper in hock.

So now I look at her in the office doorway. She is far from smiling.

"I was in the neighborhood, so I thought I'd drop in," I say. "Anything new goin' on?"

"Don't play games, Roy. The process server just phoned."

"What the hell's this all about, Addie? No warning, no discussion—"

She reaches behind her into the office. Guy Saddler hands her an 8x10 envelope. She hands it to me. "I warned you."

"Addie, c'mon, don't be dramatic. Whatever's bothering you, we can talk it out, like always, if you just give me a—"

She gives me a little tired wave. I think she's weakening. But when Benjy grips my elbow, I realize she's signaling him. "This is ridiculous, Addie, you can't just—" I vigorously shake off Benjy. Just like I do on the show. But Benjy's ready for me, twists my arm behind my back.

"Roy," Addie sounds so bored. "Sometimes I think you think you really *are* Jack Havoc." She tosses a dismissive wave of her hand and Benjy starts giving me the bum's rush toward the front door.

"You're gonna be sorry, sweetie, very sorry!" I yell over my shoulder before Benjy propels me bodily out onto the sidewalk.

"No offense, Roy," Benjy says, releasing me, dusting my lapel. "Just my job, y'know?"

Yeah, I think, well, find someone else to get you your SAG card. Benjy goes back inside. I'm left with egg on my face and the 8x10 envelope in my hand.

Feels like photos in the envelope.

That's when a chill runs down my spine.

3

Reva

"It's my fault," I whisper.

"What is?" Podolsky whispers back.

We're hiding in the bushes, watching the driveway portico of Earl Carroll's nightclub on Sunset Boulevard. A special event's being held here tonight, the annual BOOMTOWN show, when all the Hollywoodites dress up in cowboy clothes for some charity. In another few minutes, the driveway's going to be jammed with departing stars. We're perfectly positioned, unless the parking attendants spot us first and chase us away.

"Letting that guy with the subpoena serve Roy," I say. "My fault."

"Grow up," Podolsky says. He's twenty-one, only two years older than I am, but he likes to gives me his condescending George Sanders sneer of disdain (in his Bronx accent). "Reva, you have a deluded sense of the amount of control you exert over the universe."

Barry Podolsky, my best friend and worst critic, is skinny as a string bean and has thick horn-rimmed glasses that fog up when he gets excited. We go back to the New York days.

"No, really, I blame myself," I tell him.

It's been bothering me all day. I feel like I should have left well enough alone when that redheaded kid, at least we thought he was just another kid, strolled up to us collectors outside Romanoff's at lunchtime. He said, "Who you guys waiting for?" and we said "Ginny Sims," as we usually do, because Ginny Sims, the former band singer who's on the radio now, is well-known enough so that her name is recognized, but nobody's ever sufficiently excited to hang around to see her, so they always walk off, which is what we want. But then the redheaded kid smiles his freckled Butch Jenkins smile and says, "Somebody said Roy Darnell was in there," and I, of course, had to say, proudly, as if I were talking to a fellow fan, "As a matter of fact, he is." So I figure I kinda trapped Roy for the subpoena guy.

"You didn't make him go into his Jack Havoc routine and try to take a poke at the process server," Podolsky whispers.

"Roy shouldn't drink so much at lunch," I concede.

Podolsky snickers. "That's like telling a camel not to tank up on water at the oasis."

I worry about Roy's drinking lately. It's where all the Roy the Bad Boy behavior comes from, I'm sure of it.

"Hey, if they didn't serve the papers on him at Romanoff's, they'd've got him somewhere else," Podolsky points out. "So let's not dramatize, dahling."

"Divorce. I never thought it'd happen. I mean, I know Roy fooled around a little—"

Podolsky snorts. "A *little?*"

"Okay, a lot, but I thought he and Addie would stay together forever and—"

Podolsky interrupts. "Heads up, here we go!"

The doors to the nightclub fly open and people start pouring out. The parking attendants race to bring up the cars for the stars. The last thing they have time for is the handful of collectors, who appear out of the darkness and have a field day. It's like shooting fish in a barrel.

That's how autograph collecting is on the West Coast. Not that I'm complaining. Of course, most of the collectors out here look like cornfed surfers. They're nice and all, but the thing of it is, they don't have a sense of history. For instance, if I say to Podolsky, "I vant to be alone," he knows I'm imitating Greta Garbo, but the L.A. collectors are too young to even know who Garbo is, let alone how totally rare her autograph is. Generally speaking, the California collectors have it too soft. The stars live out here, so if you miss someone on Monday, there's always Tuesday, or a week from Tuesday. It's all *mañana*. Go stand outside the studio gates and the stars will come driving right up to you. When there's a premiere, the *L.A. Times* prints alphabetized lists of the celebs who are coming. It's almost too easy.

In New York, you had to be good. Stars might pass through for just a few hours, so you had to be fast, sharp, plugged in. Emergency alert: no one even knew Errol Flynn's in town, but he's boozing at the Stork Club before boarding the Queen Mary. Get a move on! Of course, even back East most of the collectors, they were out of it. They were crumb collectors, operating alone, no organization, hit or miss. I say that with no disrespect, because I was a crumb collector myself, until I was rescued by the Secret Six.

Actually, there were more like ten or eleven of us, but the Secret Six had a nice ring to it. We were like a machine, hardly anyone ever got past us. We always had someone on the pavement at mealtimes at Sardi's and the "21" Club, clocking in the celebs and coordinating intelligence with Arleigh, who was control central at her apartment in Queens; we all checked in with her by phone. At night we covered the Broadway plays, there was one of us standing in the crowded lobby of every hit show, spotting who arrived. Then we'd gather at the Automat on 45th and Sixth and sit at a couple of tables off in a corner and make free lemonade out of the iced tea fixings and pool our information about who's where. General Eisenhower is at *Mr. Roberts,* Judy Garland and Vincente Minnelli are at *Death of a Salesman,* Bing Crosby is at *Brigadoon,* Cary Grant is at *Streetcar,* Sinatra and Ava Gardner are at *South Pacific.* Like that. Of course, we knew the exact times for all the intermissions and when the shows were over. A precision operation.

Our activities extended to the posh hotels and the luxury ships that sailed the Atlantic. In those days, overseas air flights were just beginning, so most stars traveling to and from Europe still went by one of the great Cunard Liners.

We'd find out who was coming in on the Queen Elizabeth and we'd take the subway down to the Customs Office at the Battery a couple days before and get passes to go onto the dock to meet imaginary relatives (they never had the complete passenger lists in advance of arrival) and be there to greet our favorites while they waited for their luggage. A collector working as a file clerk at United Artists used to sneak a peek at *Celebrity Service,* a very expensive, ultra-exclusive information sheet that detailed which hotels the stars were staying at. That simplified life for us.

Mostly we'd just call the stars at the hotels and say we were fans and ask when they were coming out. Some of the hotels we could sneak upstairs; we'd get the room numbers by calling the hotel and asking for reservations. Has Richard Widmark arrived yet? The reservation desk would say, He's already registered, and then they'd click the operator and say, Connect this call with Room Twenty-Two-Twenty. It was that easy in those days, and we had it down to a science.

We were like a shadow army and we knew everything about the stars, often before anyone else. We'd be waiting and watching late at night at the Pierre Hotel for Mario Lanza or the Plaza for Susan Hayward, when two other celebs married to two other people would come smooching out of a cab and into the hotel (sometimes it'd be two guys). Days, maybe weeks or even months later, the gossip columns might pick up the news, but the collectors knew it first. We talked among ourselves, but we never told anyone else. Spencer Tracy would stop off in town and always stay with Katharine Hepburn in her apartment overlooking the East River, then she'd drive him in her station wagon to catch the 20th Century Limited out of Grand Central. We'd be there, but we kept the stars' secrets.

We felt as if we were part of their world. Sure, we knew we were just on the fringes, but everyone else was on the outside. It was kind of our duty, our *responsibility,* to protect them from prying eyes and narrow minds. They were stars and couldn't be judged by the same standards as everybody else.

"Reva, look at that!" Podolsky yells at me across the portico.

I'm just getting Jane Withers's autograph; who knew she was still even alive? But I look in the direction Podolsky is pointing. Another second and I'd've missed the sight of the night: runty little Frank Sinatra, costumed and made-up as a Navajo Indian, hassling and suddenly leaping up to swing a roundhouse right like a tomahawk at mountainous Sheriff John Wayne. He only succeeds in knocking off his ten-gallon hat. Fearless Frank is obviously pissed at the Duke—probably about politics, money, or women, what else would they have to argue about?—but Wayne shoves Sinatra, who falls on his keister, and then dozens of people intervene, making it the second one-punch battle I've seen today.

Later, as he walks me to the bus stop, I tell Podolsky, "You know, I still blame myself."

I'm the lead item in Sheilah's column the next morning—
her on-the-scene exclusive, of course. Roy Darnell swears
eternal love for wife, Adrienne Ballard, chic Beverly Hills
interior decorator to the stars, as process server slaps him
with divorce papers. Darnell, known in Hollywood as Roy
the Bad Boy, mixes it up in street brawl outside Romanoff's.

Okay, Sheilah. Close enough for jazz.

The *New York Daily Mirror* gives me the entire front page
of their tabloid:

WIFE CHARGES ADULTERY!
TV'S JACK HAVOC CAUGHT
WITH HIS PANTS DOWN?

The ratings on my show go up three share points the next
night.

Nathan Curtis Scanlon chortles. You read about people
chortling, but Nate Scanlon is the only person I know who
actually does it. The laughing lawyer. An overstuffed, smallish man with a graying spiky crewcut. Enthroned in his also
overstuffed armchair behind his oversized desk. Not a sheet
of paper on it. Just the small stack of 8x10 glossies Addie
gave me. Nate is leafing.

"Hmmm." He turns one of the photos sideways, then upside down. Really studies it. "Don't you have back trouble?"

"Occasionally."

"I can see why." There he goes again. He's chortling. I'm burning. Waiting for his expert legal opinion. For which I'm paying a fortune per hour.

"No question about it, laddie," he finally pronounces. "The little lady has got you by the gonads."

He isn't talking about the lady in the photos. He means Addie. Addie wants blood. Guess whose? And the thing about Addie is that she always gets what she wants.

"So what do I do?" I ask.

"We can fight her. Every inch of the way. Drag our heels. Withhold tax returns, bank accounts, contractual information. Muddy the financial waters. But…eventually we'll have to go to court. And that, with all due immodesty, is where I shine! I'll make the rafters of the courthouse shake. I'll bring tears to the eyes of the judge."

"Yeah?" Sounding good. "And then?"

"Then we get our heads kicked in." Nate Scanlon chortles. "No question about it. She wins, you lose. And winner takes all in this game."

He explains it to me. The only local grounds for divorce are insanity or adultery.

"Insanity or adultery," I repeat.

"Based on these," Nate Scanlon holds up the photos, "I think you definitely qualify on both counts. What're you, *crazy?* Shacking up in some fleabag motel—"

"—the Hotel Bel-Air, a quiet bungalow, nobody saw us coming or going—"

"Except a hired transom-peeper who snapped candid photos of you and this broad in action!"

"It's blackmail, Nate! Addie's trying to blackmail me. Isn't that a crime?"

"Don't start, laddie. They've got all the cards. Mr. Giesler—" Jerry Giesler, who's representing Addie, and is Nate Scanlon's only real competition in town "—will flash these glossies in the judge's chambers and you are chopped liver."

See? It's worse than I thought. "So I suppose your advice is to—"

"Cave in. I'll tell Giesler we're cooperating in every way, you are repentant and willing to pay for your transgression, blah-blah-blah—"

"Yeah, fine. I've got next to nothing in the bank, thanks to Warners' penny-pinching contract. Even the money I made on the loan-out movie. Warners grabbed it and gave me my usual chicken feed salary, so sure, let her take it all—"

"Plus your royalties."

"Fuck no!" I explode. "She can have the equity in the house, that yappy mutt she loves so much, all the loose change around, but not the royalties!"

"They're not asking, laddie, they're telling. Giesler phoned me. That's the cornerstone of their demands."

Now I'm panicking. Because we're talking about real money. The only real money I've gotten close to in my life. The money that's going to take care of me in my old age— if I live that long. When TV used to broadcast "live" the shows disappeared into the ether. Then Desi and Lucy decided to put their show on film. Since then most of the shows are done on film. Including mine.

Back when we made our deal, Nate tried to get me five hundred dollars per show more. Warners dug in their heels, deal breaker. So instead Nate asked for very hefty royalties, in perpetuity, if the shows are ever rerun off-network. Warners figured that'd never happen, so they gave it to us. Couple months ago, Desi negotiated a multi-million dollar deal for local stations to rerun their old shows. Now there's a new business called Syndication. And I'm in on the ground floor. That's my jackpot. Those royalty payments.

"We give them the royalties," Nate Scanlon says, "and we accept any joint debts and we wrap the whole deal up— lickety-split. Don't waste a moment!"

I stare at him. Which side is this bastard on? Hey. He's grinning like the cat that ate the bird. And it hits me. Something's happened. "Good news to go with the bad?"

"You might say that. Providing our footwork is nimble

enough." He tumbles a pair of Chiclets out of a box, offers me some. I shake my head, he starts to chew, I wait him out. It's worth waiting for.

"I think I've found a way for you to escape from Burbank."

Okay. Before we go any farther, let me tell you some stuff about Jack Warner and his studio, because it's important to my tale.

During the '30s and '40s, they made tons of money with prison pictures like *20,000 Years in Sing Sing, Each Dawn I Die,* and *I Was a Fugitive from a Chain Gang.* Jack Warner liked those movies so much, that's how he ran his studio. Anyway. The studio is located in Burbank, a small town in the San Fernando Valley invented by Warner. The studio guards are like prison guards, and Jack L. Warner himself is the warden. Writers are treated like convicts—locked down in their assigned cells from nine to six on weekdays and a half day Saturday. Rumors of a writers' conspiracy to tunnel out for off-the-lot lunches were part of the Warners legend. Among the actors, long-term contract players felt like lifers—the harder you worked, the farther you were from ever getting out.

You think I'm bullshitting, right?

Well, not much.

You could start out with a seven-year contract and still be there ten, eleven years later. How? Whenever you rejected a script or said no about anything, the studio suspended you. That meant off-salary—and they tacked the suspension time onto your contract. Bette Davis tried to escape by going to England to make movies, but the long arm of Jack Warner kiboshed that. Olivia de Havilland was more successful a couple years later. She sued the studio for involuntary servitude and a high court found in her favor: they could suspend, but they couldn't extend. So now seven years is the longest sentence you can draw in the fair city of Burbank.

I've only done three years. I owe them four more. We've been trying to get a release now while I'm hot in TV and a movie career is possible. Jack L. has personally said no to me in very graphic terms. So I figured that's it. Breaking a Warner Bros. contract is slightly harder than busting out of Alcatraz.

But here's Nathan Curtis Scanlon, Esq. saying he's found a way.

He struts across his spartan office with the ramrod posture of the West Pointer he once was. A decorated WWII and Korean War vet. Major Scanlon. Never mind the Chasen's paunch that Nate has added since then. Nate Scanlon looks out the window down onto the Sunset Strip. Now Hollywood is his battleground.

"It's in the small print," he says. "You know what they say, God is in the details. That's our out."

I still don't get it. Warner Bros. invented small print—Nate taught me that when I first became a client. "They give you on page one of the contract what they take back on pages seventeen, nineteen, and twenty-four." That's why I need Nate. A cop to monitor the robbers.

"They were a day late." He says it like he's revealing the secret of the world.

"A day late—to do what?"

"To pick up your option for the next year of the contract."

"But they started paying me the extra dough anyway, a big hundred-and-fifty dollar a week raise, which brings me to fifty cents above the minimum wage. And I cashed the checks—"

"Doesn't matter!" He pivots to face me. For Nate Scanlon, breaking the Warners contract would be more than just a business coup. He's back at Inchon, trying to free a POW. "They were a day late with their official notification. So the entire contract is no longer binding. It'll take a tussle in court, but we're going to win this one. You'll be a free agent. Count on it. And I've already got an offer in my back pocket from Burt Lancaster's company for you to set up shop over there. You're going to be a great big movie star!"

So far nobody's made the big jump from TV to the movies. I'm ready and willing to be the first. I savor the prospect for a delicious moment.

Then something Scanlon said plays back in my head. "So what's the big hurry—with the divorce, I mean?"

"Everything depends on that. We must get Addie to sign off on final divorce terms before she gets wind of the possibility of a huge movie deal—or she'll wait and go after the money from that, too."

Looking back later, I see that this was one of the key moments that might have changed everything in my life. A get-off point if I'd played it another way. But right then there were only visions of sugar plums and Oscar-winning movies dancing in my head.

"When you explain it that way..." I shrug expansively. "Hell, give her the royalties, give her whatever she wants. Let's get this show on the road!"

He comes closer. Looms over my chair.

"Understand this clearly, Roy my boy. What I just told you is a secret—known only by you and me and my paralegal. That's how it's got to stay. Our secret. If it leaks prematurely, it will cost you a fortune. So tell no one." I nod. He leans into my face. "Not your rabbi, not your barber, not your agents, not your saintly mother. No one. You're a marvelous actor. These next few weeks will be the most important performances you've ever given. Act sad because you are being divorced. Act contrite when you tell people that all you want is for dear Addie to get whatever makes her secure. Act happy to be working at the Warner Brothers studio."

"That's asking a lot." I grin. He doesn't grin back. Okay. Serious. "I got it, Nate."

"I'm not sure you do. You always like to bend the rules. And then there's your temper."

"What temper? Can't believe everything you read in *Confidential*."

I have Nate chortling again.

You're probably wondering where this reputation I have as a tough guy comes from. The answer is Merle Heifetz. Blame it all on him.

Merle is this tiny Jewish leprechaun over in the Warners publicity department. He's the one who dubbed Anne Sheridan "The Oomph Girl" and labeled Lauren Bacall "The Look." They sent me to see him my first day on the lot. He was in his cubbyhole office. Shooting paper clips with a rubber band at a framed photo of Jack L. Warner. His aim was pretty good.

"What's with your schnoz?" he asked.

I touched my nose. Self-conscious as always.

"Slipped on the ice when I was a kid and busted my beak on the curb," I said.

"No, no, you—" he stopped firing paper clips and stared at the ceiling like there was writing up there "—you broke your nose fighting in the Golden Gloves. Yeah, you fought sixteen bouts, seven kayos, quit undefeated."

And that's how it began. The making of the legend of Big Bad Roy.

Merle Heifetz—"No relation to the fiddle player," he used to introduce himself—started putting out press releases and planting column items that this real tough cookie had come to town. He said it fit the Jack Havoc image. Everything that didn't fit, we skipped over. Little boy of seven with a bout of meningitis, bedridden for a year. *Skip.* Glued to the radio, sopping up soap operas. *Make it "The Lone Ranger" and we can use it.* Going to grade school and getting into a fistfight every day. *Definitely use!* Minor scrape with the police. *Great!*

I got the hang of it fast and censored stuff by myself. My nose really got busted by my father, the South Street bookie, who used me as a punching bag whenever he got drunk. *Skip.* Daddy passes out in the gutter on an icy winter night and freezes to death. *Skip.* Just say: *Roy Darnell lost his father, a well-known Philadelphia sportsman, at an early age.* Mother encouraged Roy's youthful dream to act. *Use.* But skip parts about when she was half-bagged and came on to casting directors, stage managers, and anyone else who showed a flicker of interest.

Then Merle and I went beyond the gossip columns and broke into the legit news pages.

A cowboy, half a head taller than me, sashays up during jam-packed cocktail hour at the Polo Lounge and sneers, "So yer the lil' peckerwood from TV who's supposed to be such a badass." He swings and misses. I give him one in the gut and he goes down. In front of the whole damn town. Story moves on both the AP and UPI wires. Merle Heifetz is proud as punch. Tells me *now* that it was a put-up job, he paid the cowboy to pick the fight and take the dive. "If Sinatra's people can hire bobbysox swooners, why can't we use a few barroom brawlers?"

Pretty soon Merle didn't have to hire 'em. I'd joined the select group of he-man actors who are magnets for every saloon blowhard out to show off in front of his girl. It's like being the fastest gun in the west. They all want to test you.

Not that I wasn't kind of fast with my fists when I was a kid in Philly. You had to be to stay alive. Even during my New York days, I got into a scrape or two. For my art. I always thoroughly research my roles, and one time I was going to play a longshoreman on a TV show. So I hung out in some of the waterfront bars, studying the dock wallopers. Two bruisers followed me out onto the street one night. Push led to shove. But I pumped up on adrenaline. Pretended I was my guardian angel, who's absolutely fearless. Really got into it. Like I became him. It had worked for me before and it did this time, too. I creamed those two guys. Definitely put the big one in the hospital with a concussion. So that was the attitude I used on the TV show. Got a good mention from John Crosby in the *Herald Trib* review.

You probably want to know a little more about the guardian angel I just mentioned. Calling him that makes him sound like a cartoon cherub with wings. He's more like a voice inside me. The voice of self-preservation. I only hear him when I'm really in trouble, I mean in deep shit. Then he's there. It started when I was just a scared little kid. Whispering, warning, reassuring, always inspiring me to do what's best for me. Like a survival instinct. But with street savvy. Cool but daring. The idealized me, I guess. He's the last word on whether it's time for fight or flight. Cross him and you've got a problem. I never gave him a name or any-thing. Until Jack Havoc came along.

On the *Jack Havoc* set nobody wants to test me. Everyone is gun-shy. Trying to stay on my good side. I'm ashamed to admit I like it. People running scared of me. From the pro-ducer to the prop man, I win all the arguments. Saves a lot of time and aggravation. I frown and they jump.

In the early days of the show there were a few problems. The lead stunt man was after the same wardrobe gal I was interested in that week. I warned him, but some people just won't take a hint. So when we did the next big fight scene, I screwed up the choreography just slightly. Instead of safely fanning him with a roundhouse right, I flattened him. Broke his jaw in two places. No chance he could get back at me, of course. If I'm damaged, everybody's out of work.

Or the time the studio assigned this British phony-baloney to direct one of the episodes. Used to suck on his pipe, tell backstage stories about "Larry" and "Viv" at the Old Vic. And treat me like this dumbbell ex-radio actor. "Do be aware of your body language, dear boy, the performance can't originate exclusively in your tonsils." I could have reamed him in front of the whole company, but that would have been tacky. Instead, my stand-in arranged a little prac-tical joke with the horse wranglers. This director's pride and joy was a cute MG convertible with wrong-side English steering. He always parked it off to the side near the West-ern street so it wouldn't get dinged. Well, one afternoon, wouldn't you know, an entire truckload of horse dung acci-dentally got dumped on his MG. With the top down. I mean, buried. Everyone was in on the gag, so we all were there to see his face when he went looking for his wheels. It was a hoot. He never could get the smell out of the uphol-stery, wound up selling the car.

But now it's time for a change of pace—here comes Roy the Good Ol' Boy.

5

Roy

This is a dumb thing to do. Every time I do it, that's what I think. Dumb. But it gives the troops a lift. So here goes nothing: I put a cigarette between my lips and turn sideways. So I'm in profile, me and my cigarette, for the man with the bullwhip.

That's Paco Alvarez, our production manager. He's the guy who figuratively cracks the whip to set the tempo and keep track of the bucks on my TV series. But Paco, who began in the business acting as a villainous shtarka in Poverty Row westerns, developed this trick back then. He can take a cigarette out of your mouth. At twenty paces. If you'll let him.

It's the tail end of our lunch break, a time when mischief often prevails on a set. We're shooting on a residential street in Toluca Lake near the studio. Usually I eat my lunch in my custom-fitted trailer, mostly alone. But this is the new me. Standing in the chow line with the troops. Just one of the guys. Making nice. Tossing the football around with the teamsters. Now accepting Paco's offer to perform the cigarette trick.

CRRRRRRRACK!

The bullwhip snaps in the air. Warmup shot to unfurl. Almost everyone in the company—from gaffers to actors to teamsters—is gathered in a circle to watch. A chance to maybe see Roy the Bad Boy get his head handed to him.

Literally. Possible revenge for all the times I've chewed out one of them. Here's the windup—Paco rears back like he's about to flog one of the *Bounty* mutineers—here comes the lash and—the cigarette disappears.

I clap my hands to my mouth. Muffling the shriek of pain. A gasp from the crowd. Paco is ashen, he's done the unthinkable: damaged the on-camera talent. I take my hands from my mouth. Blood is oozing, covering my front teeth as I expose them—in a big shit-eating grin.

Now they all laugh. Realize they've been bamboozled. A blood squib, hidden in my mouth. Just like in the movies. And they're all over me, pounding my back, You wiseass sonuvagun, scaring the hell out of everyone. Well, you know me, anything for a gag.

I'm fooling them. They're accustomed to me as the incarnation of Jack Havoc. Handle with care. Liable to blow up in your face at any time. Now, on advice of counsel, I'm a pussycat. Within moments the story of how I clowned around with the bullwhip will be all over the studio. Proof of the emergence of a lower octane me. Roy the Good Boy.

Kenny Lomax, my stand-in and stunt double, is showing off for some of the cute little extras. He squishes a squib in his mouth and then as "blood" drips down his face, Kenny yells, "Paco, you owe me a kicker." Meaning the extra pay earned for doing a tough stunt.

Kenny is rewarded with a hoot from the crew. It's a running joke around here. Mostly I do my own stunts, but Kenny always claims he's owed money anyway. Last season I did a wrestle-and-tumble down a steep, rocky hillside and dislocated my shoulder. With a deadpan face, Kenny asked for the customary kicker—plus disability pay. My pain is his pain.

He's from the old neighborhood, Kenny. South Street loudmouth. We grew up together, then lost touch—until I got my TV show. That's when they all came out of the woodwork. I keep him around for laughs and to remind me where I'm from. His nickname is Killer. Killer Lomax. He lets everybody assume that he used to be a mobster. I let him do it. What the hell, we're all wearing masks, right? Actually the

correct spelling of the word is not "killer" but "killah"—
which is Yiddish for hernia. The one Kenny Lomax had when
he was eleven. We started calling him Killer as a put on. He's
been living off the reflected glory ever since.

He sidles up to me. We're dressed like twins in identical
clothes. The resemblance ends there. I'm fairly tall, he's not.
He's on the porkier side, and I sweat every pound. But he's a
bull. Kenny winks at me. I know what he wants before he asks.

"Hey, sport, you gonna be using your trailer?"

"Now?" I shrug. Making it tough on him. "No, I thought
maybe I'd work a little. How 'bout you?"

"Then it's okay I use the trailer." He waves reassuringly to
a little dirty blonde extra, waiting for him nearby, giggling.

"You leave a mess, I'll kill ya, Killer."

He smiles reassurance. "I always leave everything the way
I find it."

"The A.D. notices your playmate isn't in the street scene,
he's gonna fire her ass."

Kenny Lomax shrugs. "Well, that's the chance she takes."

We're back at work. A big part of my job is ignoring people. There's always a crew of dozens behind the camera, and
on a street shoot like today there are platoons of gawkers
and fans lurking behind the ropes. I have to pretend none of
them exist.

The scene we're doing is a walk-and-talk. Camera dollies
in front of me and Dave Viola, who's my comedy relief sidekick in the series. Kind of Gabby Hayes to my Hopalong
Cassidy. We're strolling down the street, babbling facts the
audience has to know, mixed in with the scat lines that com-
prise our relationship. I don't like the character much, and I
like Dave Viola even less. He's a graduate of the Borscht Belt
school of acting. When in doubt, mug furiously or cross your
eyes. We're supposed to be best friends in the series.

On the first take, Viola fakes a trip on the pavement and
makes one of his patented schmuck faces, thereby taking the
attention away from me and what I'm saying. The director

catches it, yells Cut! We do it again. This time Viola gives a Groucho-like leer at an attractive girl extra passing by. Before the director can cut the scene, I give Viola a snappy slap upside the head. But grin affectionately at him like it's part of the scene and go on with the dialogue. Viola rubs his head like a chastised kid and says his lines. We make it to the corner. Where a car zooms past and a hood with a gun leans out the window, firing at us. I yank Viola to the ground, saving my buddy's life for the umpteenth time. That's a print. Hey, we're not doing Shakespeare here.

"Roy make booboo on Davey," Viola coos at me. Clutching his head. Loud enough for the spectators behind the ropes to hear.

"It was a love tap," I say.

"Davey looooooooves Roy." Clutching his heart. So what the hell can I say?

"Roy loves Davey, too." I pat his head like he's an Airedale terrier. The spectators applaud. What they came to see.

We start to line up the next shot. Viola doing his getting-up-from-a-pratfall shtick while I draw my trusty Walther 9 mm automatic and fire after the fleeing car. It's just a rehearsal so I don't really pop any caps, I just yell "Bang! Bang!" The crowd behind the ropes loves it. Movie magic revealed.

"Second team!" the assistant director yells. Meaning it's time for the stand-ins to step in while the cameraman sets the new lighting. Kenny Lomax materializes on cue, his face flushed but his fly zipped. As he takes my place under the lights, he tells me my lawyer called.

I go to the phone in my trailer for privacy.

I'm not expecting a call from Nate Scanlon. He's been a whirling little dervish since Addie served me with the divorce papers six weeks ago. He and Jerry Giesler have been huddling and confabbing around the clock. Like negotiating the Korean War Peace Treaty. Mostly they've kept Addie and me on the sidelines, away from each other, which is fine with both of us. She's still living in the house on Kings Road above Sunset. I'm renting an Englishy cottage on Coldwater Canyon, just up from the Beverly Hills Hotel.

We did have to appear together in Beverly Hills court one morning to lock in her temporary alimony. Nate and Giesler worked it so we could be whizzed in and out through a back door. But somehow the four of us wound up in the same freight elevator heading up. The two lawyers chatting amiably, Addie and I standing in silence. She's lost some weight and looks pretty damn good, but it doesn't seem appropriate for me to tell her that. Suddenly she turns to me and says in this choked voice, "How could you?"

I know this is a ploy, but it works. Guilt flashes across my face. She's timed it beautifully: the elevator doors fly open and the press photographers, who've been tipped by someone—Nate and Giesler later accuse each other—fire away with their flash cameras. In the afternoon editions, I look like a murderer caught in the act and Addie looks like a wounded angel.

Fortunately, the judge doesn't allow photographers inside his courtroom. We sit there in our separate corners as if we're dress extras without any lines until the judge asks each of us the same question, "Do you understand and agree to what has been stipulated for the record here today?" We say our "I do's." Just like we once did for another judge. Guess it all ends the way it began.

I'm worried about public opinion. After all, what if the audience that's wallowing in all the innuendos being fed them by the press, decides they don't like Roy the Bad Boy anymore? Nate Scanlon thinks I'm an idiot to worry. "Errol Flynn was tried and freed on rape charges and he came away a bigger star than before," he lectures me. "Bob Mitchum gets nabbed puffing a reefer and does thirty days sweeping the floor at County Jail and the studio doubles his salary when he's released. Don't you get it? The audience loves guys like you—not in spite of, but *because* you're bad boys."

But I still worry. I know there's a line you mustn't cross. I'm just not that sure where it is.

When I climb into my trailer, I find that Lomax, the Lady Killer, has been true to his promise, more or less. The place is no sloppier than when I left it. Kenny calls it The Fuck-mobile, but recently he's gotten much more use out of it than I have. Not that I've been true blue during my marriage. I mean, I've succumbed to delicious temptation now and then. But only on a one-shot basis. No ongoing ring-a-ding-dings. I made that a rule. I've turned down a helluva lot more snatch than you'd imagine. But what am I going to do when I've got an insecure leading lady who's scared about the love scene we're filming tomorrow morning? Or, in the New York days, when the price of getting into an audition was screwing the casting agent? Okay, okay. I don't want to act like every extracurricular broad I ever banged was for my art. But give me credit for those that were.

What I'm saying is that basically I'm monogamous. Because it's the right thing to do. And because Addie seems to have a built-in pussy detector. She tags me more times than not. Recently I haven't been doing anything on the side. Maybe I'm growing up. Just my luck, my one slip and she's got a private eye with a spy camera on my case. Though how he tracked me, careful as I was, I still can't figure out.

I slouch on the couch in my trailer and dial Scanlon, Traxel, and Borison, Attorneys-at-Law. I say it's me and the switchboard chick puts me straight through.

"How do you feel?" Nate asks.

I say okay.

"Do you feel divorced? Because that's what you are."

He's major-league pleased with himself. Not only has he concluded the deal, but he also got the judge—after the last in-person press fiasco—to accept individual affidavits from Addie and me, saying we understand and accept blah-blah-blah. We don't have to go to court. We've been granted an interlocutory decree that'll be final in a few months. It's all over. We've managed to give her a package consisting of everything she could think of—she gets the house, full custody of the dog (yes, Fluffy is mentioned in the divorce agreement by name and attached photo), she keeps full title to her business—and that could be my revenge, if it keeps costing her what it's cost me. And, of course, she gets my

TV royalties. I pay her legal expenses, as well as my own. That one rankles. Like hiring the biggest bully in town and paying him top dollar to kick the crap out of you.

"I may be disbarred for being too efficient," Nate Scanlon says. "We lawyers, one of our favorite phrases is, 'Time is of the essence.' But we usually take as much of it as we can." He emits a deep contented sigh. "I've never rammed a divorce through this fast."

Is that a hint or what? I step up immediately.

"Thanks, Nate. Santa's gonna put something extra special in your stocking."

I hang up. Tickled that I'm now officially a pauper. Pending completion of the interlocutory wait. But it's a binding deal. Neither of us can change the terms. Nate's made that clear. So Addie may think she's fucked me over—but now I'm free to get on with my life.

As soon as Nate Scanlon can spring me from Burbank.

I reach for the open carton of Lucky Strikes on my dressing table, grab a loose cigarette, and scrounge around for my lighter. The gold-plated lighter I got for my twenty-seventh birthday. Inscribed, "Here's looking at you, kid. Love, Bogie and Betty." The lighter's not here. Killer Lomax, I bet. He loves that lighter like it's his own and it winds up in his pocket half the time. So he can torch my smokes for me during the day, he says. Sometimes it goes home with him overnight. That Killer, looking out for me even when he's asleep.

The A.D. raps on the door. "First team," he calls.

It's 7:30 when we quit. We came when it was dark and we're leaving when it's dark. Somebody once compared working on a TV series to fucking an eight hundred-pound gorilla. You decide when to start and the gorilla decides when to stop. Killer and I are in the backseat of the limo that'll take us back to the studio lot so we can pick up our own cars. As we pass through the opening in the ropes, the diehard fans are still there, Reva among them. Tiny Reva. First autograph I ever signed was for her. The radio days.

She was in junior high school then, must be eighteen, nineteen by now. Still looks like an adolescent elf. Her usual Prince Valiant haircut, dressed like a tomboy in dungarees, polo shirt, and sneakers. A small, earnest face that lights up when she sees me.

"Hey, wave to Reva," I tell Killer.

"You wave to her," he says. "*You're* the fuckin' light of her life." If only I knew then how prophetic his words were.

We're playing liar's poker, me and Killer, using the serial numbers on dollar bills for our bids. I've got two pair. But I claim I've got a full house—three sixes and two nines. He's chicken to call me, he folds. So he loses. He usually loses. I say it's because I can outbluff him using half my brain. He says it's because he has to suck up to the boss. He's a sore loser. Always was. I get a kick out of that.

"Got a light?" I put a Lucky between my lips. Killer slaps his pockets, finally comes up with a pack of matches from the commissary. "Where's my lighter?"

He holds the match steady for me. "You musta left it on the dressing table."

"It's not there, you little *goniff*. You've got it in your pocket right now, don't you?

"For how much?"

He's ready to bet. Because he's ready to win. I can read this guy, I really can. "Maybe your scuzzy little blonde friend cadged it while in the throes of passion. If she swiped it, Kenny—"

"She didn't swipe nothin'—I never took my eyes off her!" He fires up his own cigarette. Luckies too, of course. He smokes what I smoke. "It'll turn up in the morning, sport, you'll see."

Five nines, he says. I call him. He's really got 'em. For once he wins.

So now I'm driving home from Warners. Alone. Except for Jack Havoc. Sometimes it's hard to turn it off. I spend fourteen hours a day intensely trying to think, feel, and sound like him. Then I'm supposed to flip a switch and go back to being me. Can make you kind of schizzy sometimes. It's a problem I've been grappling with since I began acting.

During my radio days, I was known as "The Man of a Thousand Voices." Sometimes I'd play three, four different parts in the same show. I'd get so deeply into each characterization, I'd almost forget who I really am. The only thing I can compare it to is when I was a little kid and I went to the Barnum & Bailey circus. They had this tiny little car drive out and stop in the center ring. Then one by one, a dozen people climbed out of the tiny car—and the last guy out was a giant. I never could figure out how they did it. There wasn't a tunnel hole under the car. Anyway, when I became an actor, that's how I felt. Like all those people were stuffed inside of me.

Driving myself home from the studio helps to make the transition. But there's still room for confusion. I'm driving exactly the kind of car Jack Havoc does. And I must be on automatic pilot because I'm barreling over Laurel Canyon, which takes me down onto the Sunset Strip. His part of town. Going past all the glitzy nightspots. I hear Bill Conrad's narrator's voice booming inside my head. "He travels the night. Searching for danger. Ready to extend a helping hand to those who seek justice." Shit. It's like I'm living the opening titles of the series.

I turn on the T-Bird's radio. Miss Peggy Lee wailing away on "Hard-Hearted Hannah." I should feel elated. Addie signed off. Skinned me. Took me for all I've got. She thinks. Peggy Lee belts away, "there was Hannah throwing water on a drowning man." Music from the soundtrack of *Pete Kelly's Blues*. Jack Webb's flick. Another TV series guy out to make his mark in the movies. Gangway for Roy Darnell.

"I never knew what love could do, 'til I met you..." Miss Peggy doing the ballad now.

I switch it off.

Pull over to the curb.

Turn off the motor. The lights.

Hurting.

I'm divorced.

Failed at one of life's biggies.

Lost the person I thought was my best friend.

I look out the window. Surprised to see where I am. Kings Road. Parked in front of the house. Used to be our house. Now it's hers. Through the dining room window I catch a glimpse of Addie going down the hallway. She doesn't look my way. I watch until she disappears. I take a deep breath, try to swallow, but my throat is too constricted.

The thing about Jack Havoc is that, although he may be aching inside, he never cries.

I'm not Jack Havoc.

"What'll it be?" the bartender asks me.

"Martini." I've wandered into a dark, seedy dive on Santa Monica Boulevard. Just fits my mood. Couldn't face going home yet to an empty rented house.

"Any special kinda martini?"

"Can you make a 'West 76th Street'?"

"Hum a few bars for me."

"Bombay gin, splash of ruby port, lime juice, grenadine, and one teardrop."

It tickles him. "We're out of teardrops."

"I'll supply my own if you can handle the rest."

"Make it two," she says. That's when I first notice her. Two stools over. I nod at the bartender and move over one stool. Jeannie, she says her name is. She's a TWA stewardess with quite a few miles on her. But built like a brick shithouse.

"Y'know who y'look like? Whosis, the TV guy, y'know the one—"

"Jack Havoc," I tell her, "yeah, everybody says that, but I don't see it myself."

"No, y'really do, really." She giggles. "Bet you wish you had his money."

"Money won't buy you love."

"Sure it will, honey."

I tell her my name is Fred and I sell insurance for State Farm and how is she fixed for life? She laughs like I'm Noel Coward dropping double entendres. That's the last word I get in. She's a chatterbox. I gave up listening three rounds ago. I think I'm feeling no pain. But I'm wrong. When I look over at her, she's grinning and gabbing and popping her eyes for comic emphasis. And then the strangest thing happens. Suddenly I'm hearing Addie's voice coming out of her face. It's like one of those badly dubbed Italian movies. But it's Addie, loud and clear.

"I hate you, Roy, from the top of your head to your toenails!"

"If you're not happy, then just get the fuck out! But don't forget to leave me all the money!"

"Know what you are? You're a tacky little turd playing an even tackier asshole on TV—it makes me sick to have people see me with you!"

Selected samples from Addie's extended play album of Best Hits. All custom designed to land way under the belt. No blow too low. How much can a man take before he hits back? I look down at my hands, both fists clenched, white knuckles, itching to smash into her face, go ahead, *do it,* stop that vicious mouth, rearrange her smarmy face, and—I lurch off my stool so abruptly it topples over. I don't bother to pick it up, just toss some bucks on the bar and bail before I lose it.

"Hey, honey," I hear her call after me, "where y'runnin' to? I thought we're havin' fun."

Now I'm on the street, looking for my car. Close call. Few more seconds and I would've detonated. Done something I'd really regret. Too much booze. Really bombed. Might look like an easy mark for some guys out to roll a drunk. Okay. C'mon, you bastards, give it your best shot! Let's rock and roll. But the street's deserted. All the store windows dark. Here's the parking lot, only a few cars left, no attendant. My trusty T-Bird in back under the trees next to a pickup truck. Almost pitch black when I walk between the two vehicles. I'm almost at my driver's door when I step on something lumpy that goes rolling and makes a glassy clink.

I lose my balance and fall heavily against the side of my car.

A deep voice rumbles too close by. "Watch where you're goin', fucker!"

I see a bulky dark form go scurrying past me on all fours. Like a huge warthog. Going after the bottle that rolled away. "Come to baby," he says and then he rises up, triumphantly holding a jug of cheap wine. Big guy. Grinning like the Cheshire cat. Two of his upper front teeth missing, clothes greasy, grungy beard. A wino. Without much wine left in his bottle, but he uncaps and finishes it.

"Good to the last drop," he says.

"What the hell you doing down there?"

"Sorry if I spooked you. Just taking a snooze where it's quiet."

"Yeah, sure," I say. Starting to unlock my car door.

"Hey, mister, spare some change? Haven't eaten all day."

I dig in my pocket, give him all the coins I find there. He pockets them, but doesn't back off. Just smiles at me again, and he's close enough for me to get a good whiff of him. Wow. He smells like my dad did after he stumbled home from a toot. Ready to wail on little Roy.

And I know how it's going to end.

But we have to play out the hand.

"Look, pal," he confides, "when I asked for spare change, I didn't mean it had to be *just* change. A couple bucks, maybe a five spot'd be real nice."

"Sorry, gotta go now."

"Don't be sorry, pal. You can spare it. What kinda car is this?"

"Just a T-Bird."

"Looks expensive." He reaches out to touch the roof with his fingers.

"Don't do that," I smack his hand away. Lightly. "It spoils the finish." He stares at me. No smile. So I smile at him. "There's oil on our fingers, all of us, and it—"

"—spoils the finish. Wouldn't want to do that." Blocking me from opening the car door. Towering over me. "Ten bucks'd be just fine."

It's his turn to smile again. Like he's scaring me. Like he's got me where he wants me. Like I'm at his mercy. That's when I hit him. A short right into his face. He falls back against the pickup truck. Raises up the bottle and swings it at me. I step inside, gut punch him. He drops the bottle. I scoop it up and then it all comes erupting out of me like a lava flow. I clobber him with his own jug until it shatters, then I keep punching, like I'm working out on the heavy bag at the gym, then I'm kicking him when he's down, stomping on him, letting it all out, what Dad deserved and what Addie has coming to her and—and he's not moving. Breathing but unconscious. On the ground, blood all over, and I've got to get out of here.

I rev up the T-Bird. Take off. Jack Havoc soaring away into the night. After defeating the forces of evil. Avenging all insults and cruelties perpetrated on Roy Darnell.

But after I've driven a mile or so, I start to come down off my high. I stop at a gas station in Beverly Hills and call Killer Lomax on the pay phone. Tell him about this wino back in the parking lot. Tell him to get over there, if the guy's still unconscious drive him over to the nearest emergency room, drop him at the curb, but tuck five hundred bucks in his pocket so they'll take care of him.

"I'll clean it up," Killer assures me.

I can count on him.

I go home and sleep like a baby.

6

Reva

This is the tricky part, sneaking in under Mother's radar. Step number one, unlock the front door of the apartment. Step number two, slip off my shoes, tiptoe quickly in the darkness, across the living room and hope I don't trip over anything or make a sound that will attract her attention, because even though I can hear her snoring in the big bedroom, that doesn't mean Mother is asleep. Sometimes it's just a trap, and while I'm trying to reach my room, Mother will come out screaming like a banshee, "Reva-you-little-bitch-where-have-you-been-out-to-all-hours-with-your-trashy-loony-friends!" And sometimes she's swinging a stainless steel skillet and, lemme tell you, if the old gal dings you with that skillet, well, you really know it.

That's what it's like around here. She's still treating me as if I'm a seven-year-old, and you want to hear what *that* was like? I'll give you a couple of quickies, just so you'll get the flavor. I've always been what she calls "delicate," which means to her I never eat enough and do that just to spite her, of course. She would spoon the food into my face, real rough and angry, and *she* would cry if I didn't swallow. Once she called the police on me and when they came, and I'm hysterical at the sight of them clumping up the stairs, and she goes, "*You* tell Reva she's gotta eat!" Mother didn't understand why the cops were mad at her (instead of me). So when I was eight, I told her that I couldn't take it anymore and I'm running away from home, figuring I'll go hide out for a while around the corner at Pearl's candy store, she likes me. And Mother, she says, "Okay by me if you want to leave—but those shoes. I paid for them so they're mine." I took off my shoes and gave 'em to her and she opened the front door, but there was snow on the ground, so she won. Again.

What about my dad when all this stuff was going on? He'd either be out "trying to scrape together a living," as Mother used to call it, or he'd be slouched in his chair in the living room with the *Daily News* in his lap and *The Cisco Kid* on TV, snoring away, because he was always exhausted by the time he came home from work. He was this warm-hearted guy who came from Russia when he was a teenager and was so proud to have married an American girl, even though she was ashamed of his accent and the fact that he was just an electrician. Once when I committed some major transgression, Mother told Daddy to spank me. He asked if I was guilty. I shrugged and said, "I dood it," which was what Red Skelton said when he was the Mean Little Kid on TV. Daddy loved Red Skelton, and he started laughing and I got out of the spanking and Daddy would always say "I dood it" to me whenever I got in trouble. I sure miss him.

Mother says I was born a rabid movie fan, but actually she weaned me on weekly matinees at the Biltmore Theater on New Lots Avenue in Brooklyn, where we never missed the Bette Davis and Joan Crawford and Barbara Stanwyck tearjerkers. I asked her once why she cried at all the simpy kissy-kissy pictures, and she said, "Reva, I'm sorry you don't have those finer feelings, but maybe someday you'll understand." Of course, when I wept buckets after Bambi's father got shot by the hunters in the forest, she got frosted and hollered at me, "Stop being so damn silly, it's just a dumb cartoon."

Now I'm at the door to my room, snoring still coming nice and steady from her direction, and, final step, I ease the key into the padlock that guarantees me some privacy and you can imagine what a war it was to get her to agree to that one! But since I finished high school and started contributing to the household from my crappy little jobs, I insisted I was entitled to that much. There, the lock's open, I'm inside, sliding the dead bolt, safe again, at least until morning.

These days we live in an apartment house in Santa Monica that was built by Larry Parks, the guy who played Al Jolson in *The Jolson Story,* and he was a big star for a short while before he got blacklisted for being a communist or something. Anyway, he must not have been a very good communist, because he went into real estate and got rich constructing a bunch of apartment houses around L.A. Mother and I have the rear apartment on the first floor at this one and we get a big break on the rent because Mother is the resident manager. That means I get to schlep the garbage cans out to the curb once a week (I'm not too delicate for *that* chore), and Mother collects the rents for Larry Parks once a month. Imagine having a movie star—all right, an ex-movie star—for your landlord. I've never told him that I got his autograph years ago outside the Algonquin Hotel in New York when he and his wife, MGM musical star Betty Garrett, were in town for six hours en route to playing the London Palladium and that the Secret Six, me included, were the only collectors who got them. I mean, why complicate a business relationship?

Coming West a few years ago from New York was a good move for both of us. Mother's arthritis (the reason she drinks so much, she says, ha!) is much better in Southern California. It's better for me, too, living closer to the stars on a full-time basis, instead of being dependent on their occasional visits to the Big Apple. We're in a two-bedroom apartment, which is like Windsor Castle compared to what we had in Brooklyn. I wish my daddy could've lived to see it. But somehow my personal space hasn't changed much since I was a tiny kid. Still a closet-size room with one window facing a blank wall. Same Army cot with bargain basement headboard. The Nancy Drew decals I stuck on the redwood-stained bureau drawers—and got smacked for when they wouldn't come off—are still there. The undersized desk, where I did my grade-school homework and where I first wrote penny postcards to Hollywood for autographed pictures of the stars.

Under the window next to my bed there's a low bookcase made of wooden planks and cinder blocks, and my rows of autograph books are all lined up there. Plus several picture albums containing snapshots of various stars that I either took or bought from other collectors. The Romanoff's ashtray on my nightstand is comparatively new. I don't smoke, but I liberated the ashtray from a trash barrel behind the restaurant and I keep it overflowing with stubbed-out butts. Yeah, that's right. Cigarettes that once were in his mouth, then in his car ashtray, are now on my desk. Below what Mother calls the sacred altar.

Why does she have to make fun of everything? It's just a shelf with odds and ends on it. Memorabilia. Don'tcha love that word? It means that each object contains a memory, all related to Roy. Ticket stubs, *Broadway Playbills*, a scrapbook filled with clippings from newspapers and fan magazines, several scripts rescued from network and studio dumpsters, and a framed 8x10 glossy, autographed "To Reva, who was there for me from the beginning, with warmest affection, Roy Darnell."

It's a funny thing, the star a fan picks to be her top favorite. Sometimes it seems like opposites attracting: the overweight chick from Bensonhurst who thinks the sun rises and sets on super-skinny Audrey Hepburn. Or maybe it's a similarity that's the pull: the tongue-tied boy who picks bashful Gary Cooper as his favorite. I also know a prissy gal from Tarzana who's the head of the national Olivia de Havilland fan club. Those are not hard to figure out. But what do you say about this refugee kid in New York who does imitations in his native Bulgarian accent of his favorite, Jerry Lewis? All a mystery of personal tastes and quirks, I guess. Some of the collectors are kinda fickle, changing favorites from year to year. Always looking for a new face. But that's not me, of course.

For me, it's always been Roy. Sometimes I've tried to figure out why. Sure, he's a good actor, handsome and all.

And we have a history in common, like I feel we both started out together and he was sort of my discovery, though I can't ever say that to him. But from the beginning, just listening to him on the radio on *Let's Pretend,* there was this special connection. Like I could hear something, and then see something not everybody gets. I mean, even now when he's playing a tough guy (sort of elegant and all, but Jack Havoc does clobber Bad Guys in every episode), that's not the real Roy—inside of him, there's a gentle little boy who's been hurt, but he keeps plugging away. That's the essential Roy. I can see it in his eyes—in close-ups on the screen, or sometimes the way he smiles at me when I come up to him, particularly if it's somewhere he didn't expect me to find him.

In the beginning, Mother thought my collecting autographs was cute. But then one of the neighbors in Brooklyn told her it was strange, and she always worries what people think, so Mother's been ragging on me ever since. Running wild in the streets. That's what she calls it. And don't get her started on the subject of Roy. Did I mention that Mother became an astrology nut, really studied up on the stuff, worked out these involved mathematical charts where Cancer afflicts Aries and Mars is stepping on Venus with things ascending and descending all over the place. She got hold of Roy's sun sign and even his exact time of birth from an astrology magazine and she ran a comparative chart on me, and then she points at this mumbo-jumbo and says it's proof positive that Roy's very bad for me. On a permanent, long-term basis.

"He represents great peril, you must stay as far away from him as possible," she says, as if I don't get the idea that she's stacked the deck to make it come out the way she wants: quit collecting. I hate being manipulated.

Surrounding the framed glossy of Roy on my bookshelf is a series of smaller candid snapshots of me and Roy smiling together in front of various celebrated New York and Hollywood watering holes. In winter snows and sweltering heat waves. Rain and shine. Point being that us collectors, we're the way the Pony Express used to be, like the U.S. Post Office used to claim to be, like nothing could stop us.

Anyhow, that's how the Secret Six were back in New York.

I was the youngest member of the Group (that's what the Secret Six called ourselves), but I was used to that. I was always the youngest and smallest in any group I belonged to. The last to be chosen for any team, the last girl in my junior high school class who still hadn't gotten her period. You get the idea. But at least I was smart and proved my worth to the Secret Six by solving the problem of how to get into radio shows whenever we wanted to.

Back then there were a lot of star-studded radio shows emanating from New York that had audiences, *The Fred Allen Show, Cavalcade of America, Kraft Music Hall, The Kate Smith Show* and *Theater Guild of the Air,* not to mention the start of "live" TV shows like *Milton Berle's Texaco Star Theater.* You needed tickets to get in, of course, and the collectors used to canvass the line before the show and ask if anybody had extra tickets, but that was uncertain and a bother.

What I realized was that while the tickets were different colors from week to week, there weren't that many different colors, and by checking the trash barrels behind the studios we could find used discards and soon we all carried a rainbow of CBS and NBC tickets in our pockets. Whatever color they were looking for, we had. We'd get in line with everybody else and when they finally let in the crowd it was always a last minute rush so when you reached the usher at the door who was collecting the tickets, you'd just give him the right color ticket and he never had time or inclination to read it. You're probably thinking that's what got me into the Secret Six, but actually I came up with that innovation after I was already a member.

Want to hear about the way I got to join? It's kind of an interesting story. One Saturday afternoon on one of those sticky hot summer days, I'd been waiting with the hordes at the stage entrance to the Roxy Theater for Abbott &

Costello, who were appearing on stage in person. They never came out, but a flunky emerged to collect autograph books so the comedians could sign them inside. None of the Secret Six were there; you wouldn't catch them at a mob scene like that. But from eavesdropping on their conversations outside Sardi's and "21," I was already aware of their rule that you have to see 'em sign for it to count, and I also was scared to let my shiny new autograph book out of my hands because I might not get it back. So I didn't toss my book in with the others going inside and I walked off instead. It was almost time for the end of the matinee performance of *Streetcar* and I was only a few blocks away. The guy Roy Darnell was understudying had the flu, so Roy was going on and I could say hello when he came out.

It was still a little early as I got to the Ethel Barrymore Theater. When I stepped out of the baking sun into the shadowy shelter of the stage door alley, there was one other person there. A mulatto girl with frizzy blonde-streaked hair, wearing dungarees and a black blouse. She was four, five years older than me, and she was perched on an orange crate, leaning back against the wall near the stage door. She was smoking a cigarette and softly singing Teresa Brewer's hit song that you heard everywhere then: "Dum-dee-dum-dee-daddee-dum, all I want is loving you and music, music, music..." When she saw me, she stopped singing and offered me a cigarette. I told her I'd quit. "More like y'forgot t'start, right, missy?" She had a real nice smile. You had to smile back at her.

Her name was Tamar and she asked me what I was doing there. Told her I was an autograph collector and that tickled her some more. She wanted me to show her my book and when she saw I had John Garfield and Lena Horne, that really kayoed her. Not that she didn't see stars all the time herself. Tamar was the assistant wardrobe mistress on *Streetcar* and she was out here grabbing a smoke before going back in to collect the costumes after the performance.

"Just gotta keep track of 'em," she explained. "Hardly ever wash them clothes, them actors play some pretty gamy characters, know what I mean?"

I nodded like I did. But I didn't really know what *Street-car* was about until I saw the movie a few years later. I seized the opportunity to get the inside scoop and asked Tamar what Roy Darnell was like backstage. She thought about it. "Little sloppy, Roy. Tends to drop his costume on the dressing room floor, but I chastised him, in a nice gentle way, o'course, and he's a doll now."

That's when the idea came up. Tamar glanced at her watch. "Gotta go in pretty soon, but—hey, wanna come with me? See what it looks like backstage, watch the curtain calls from the wings?"

I couldn't believe it. "Sure," I said, "if I won't be in the way."

"Then let's go. But Doc, the snoopy ol' doorman, won't let you in here so we gotta go in the alley door on the other side of the theater."

We went around the front to the other alley, but before we went in there Tamar remembered that she'd promised to bring back a carton of cigarettes for Marlon Brando. "Got 'em upstairs." She pointed at her apartment, over there, in one of the rundown tenements a few doors down the street. "Just take a second, c'mon, hurry girl, we don't wanna miss the curtain call."

Tamar slapped her palm on the buzzer panel, pressing several of the buttons, and laughed. "Gets some of the neighbors pissed when I do this," she confided, "oughta use my key, but this way be faster." She got an answering buzz and shoved open the door. We went up to the second floor landing. From above, a voice asked who's there? "Jus' me, sorry t'bother ya," Tamar called back. A door slammed. Tamar put her index finger to her lips in a shushing gesture and then she sat down on the top step. She patted a spot beside her. I didn't know what we were doing, but I sat down. She looked deep into my eyes, like she was searching for something.

"Where y'live? What part a' the city?" she asked.

"Brooklyn. East New York–Brownsville."

"I hear you folks ain't been treatin' my people good out there. You been treatin' 'em like they a buncha niggers!"

"I—I—" I phumphed. Tamar slapped me across the mouth. Real hard, I tasted blood.

"Don' lie to me, you lil' Jew bitch! Lemme see that watch."

I heard myself talking. Trying to sound casual, as if what was happening was normal and okay, as I unbuckled the watchband. "It's not an expensive watch, just a—"

She slapped me again. I winced. Handed her the watch. She put it in her pocket and while she went through my purse and took the $3 she found there, she pointed at my hand. "Now the ring. Give it here!"

My daddy's ring. The one real present I ever got from him. There would be no more.

"Look, Tamar, don't get mad but that's kinda special, I mean I don't think it's worth much, but the sentimental value—"

I was spritzing blood at her as I babbled. Maybe that's why she punched me in the gut. My eyes filled with tears and I blinked to keep her in focus as I pulled at the ring. I really tried, but it wouldn't come off. "I haven't taken it off since my Dad gave it to me—"

A switchblade snapped open. Tamar pointed the tip of the blade at the ring. "Want me t'get it off for ya, honey?"

I tugged extra hard and got it off and dropped the ring into her waiting palm. She closed the switchblade and stood up. She told me that after she left I was to count to a hundred slowly before leaving the building. And if I yelled or came running after her sooner she would cut my eyes out.

"Y'believe me?"

I did.

She trotted off. I counted to myself, slowly, added an extra fifty after the hundred. Then I got up and went down the stairs, holding on to the banister because my legs were pretty shaky. It's not like I was scared, though, more like I was far away, watching myself, as if it was a movie. I was ultra-clear about every detail that was going on.

Open the front door. Peek outside. Make sure she's gone. She is. Step outside. Look all around. No Tamar. If that's her real name, probably not. A lie. Like all the rest. *Streetcar*'s over. Crowd coming out. Should I go to the cops? Where's the police station? There's a black limo, 8Z plates, the kind hired by the studios. Waiting near the stage door alley. There's some of the Secret Six. Pam O'Mara, the older gal who's like the den mother of the Group. Tillie Lust (her real last name, I found out later, is Lustig), a couple of the guys, the one they call Podolsky. Why're they here? Something special. I stand in the darkness. Be inconspicuous. Secret Six don't like me tagging after them. But I was here first.

Stage door opens. Pam O'Mara puts a flashbulb in her camera, it's Kirk Douglas and his wife, didn't even know he was in New York. Collectors converge. I duck under Podolsky's arm, shove my book in with the others, Tillie glares at me. Then her expression goes funny. Kirk Douglas and his wife get in the limo.

Here's Roy. Sure is cute. People asking him to sign their programs, without me starting it up. Guess he was real good today. Mr. and Mrs. Darnell. Roy and Addie. They were just married a few weeks ago. For richer for poorer, in sickness and in health. Secret Six all staring at me. Have to tell 'em I didn't follow 'em. Roy talking to me, "What happened, Reva?" Now he's looking funny. Pam and Tillie alongside me, "It's okay, Mr. Darnell. We'll take care of it."

They took me to the ladies room at Child's cafeteria on Broadway and cleaned me up. My face was swollen and bloody. There was more blood running down my legs. My first period, how's that for timing? Pam sent Podolsky and the one they call Charming Billy back to the theater to check on Tamar. That was before I started to puke. I thought I'd never stop. Tillie held my head. It was very embarrassing. I told them losing Daddy's ring was all I was upset about. Podolsky came back and knocked on the ladies room door and told us nobody named Tamar works at *Streetcar* and the assistant wardrobe mistress is a little old Polish lady.

When I was calm again, Pam O'Mara asked if I wanted them to take me to the police station. I said no, because then my mother'd find out. So how was I going to explain this mess? I'd tell mother that I fell down the subway steps in Brooklyn on my way home. "If she knows what really happened, she'll never let me come collecting again." They said they understood and they walked me to the subway and told me they hoped I'd feel better and they'd see me next week.

That was the big lesson I learned. Something good can come out of something bad. I'd lost Daddy's special ring. But after that I wasn't an outsider among the autograph hunters anymore. I was part of the Group.

March 16, 1951.

The day I became a woman.

The day I stopped being a crumb collector.

"Hey, good lookin'," I say with a wink at Roy's glossy framed image in the center of my bedroom shelf. I'm stretched out on my cot, looking up at the so-called altar, feeling pretty bad.

I picked up a copy of the early edition of tomorrow's *L.A. Times* and read it on the bus on the way home tonight. There's a story on the bottom of page one saying that Roy and Adrienne Darnell have been granted an interlocutory divorce decree that will become official in a few months.

Seeing Roy today shooting out on the location, even though I couldn't get close enough to talk to him or even that treacherous lout Killer Lomax, I knew there was something wrong. He must've known already and was taking it hard.

He tries to cover up his feelings a lot of the time, but I can usually read him. There are so many different Roys: the happy kid, the holy terror, the sad sack, the wild man, the dreamer, the screamer. I guess I've seen them all by now, on screen and off. He can change in a blink. Once, outside Toots Shor's in New York, after he was starring in *Jack Havoc*, he got into this violent hassle with the doorman for giving away his cab to someone else, and I don't know what came over me but I got in between them, to keep Roy, who was pretty looped, from getting into trouble. For a split second I thought for sure he was gonna punch me out, but then he focused and saw it was me, and all the rage vanished. He winked at me, then turned to the doorman and said, "You oughta thank Reva, she just saved you a busted schnoz." And he kissed me on my cheek. So much for Mother and her astrology predictions.

It's time for my evening ritual. I go into the closet and kneel, moving aside a stack of old magazines, and pry at a floorboard, pulling it out to reveal a sturdy wooden box. Even if Mother finds this hiding place, as she's found others in the past, I've got the only key to this padlock, too. I unlock the box, revealing the stack of precious journals that I've been confiding my innermost thoughts to since I was thirteen.

I look up at the shelf. Right in front of the big portrait of Roy, there's a black leather glove, hole ripped in the thumb, that he tossed away on Fifth Avenue in front of St. Patrick's Cathedral after slipping on the icy pavement and tearing it. It was a Sunday in March, there'd been a huge snow storm the night before, and the snowplows hadn't cleared Fifth Avenue yet so there were no cars or buses running, just people walking down the center of the street, like a winter wonderland. One guy actually whooshed by on a pair of skis.

I'd spotted Roy and Addie coming out of the church, don't know why I didn't go up to them and say hello, I guess maybe I thought it'd be sacrilegious or something, although the Group had successfully staked out Loretta Young and Irene Dunne together once at St. Paddy's Easter Mass, but they were superstars and quite rare in New York. Anyway, once I saw Roy slip on the ice, I thought it'd be embarrassing, so I just picked up the glove and followed them, Roy and Addie. I stayed on the sidewalk, and they were up ahead, in the snow-packed roadway, holding hands, talking and laughing, then they got into a thing of throwing snowballs at each other, Roy getting hit in the chest and pretending it was a fatal shot, hamming it up, making her laugh even harder, then he rushed her and rubbed a snowball in her face and then he kissed her. Nobody else was paying much attention to them. Roy wasn't famous yet, so I felt like this was a private movie and I was the entire audience and I loved the way they so clearly were in love with each other.

I'm sure of it.

I sit cross-legged on the floor and write my thoughts in the journal. They come out in a jumble:

> *I know I'm behaving bizarrely, is there such a word? Well, awfully strange anyway, like Mommy and Daddy are breaking up and what's to become of little me. It's only another Hollywood divorce, and I never got to know Addie that well, so it's probably foolish to be going on like this.*
>
> *But I feel bad for them.*
>
> *Especially Roy.*
>
> *And, yes, I do feel bad for me, too.*
>
> *See, I don't have high school football games and senior proms to look back on. I never took part in all that ordinary stuff, but now it feels like a chunk of my own personal history is being rewritten, retroactively. Memorabilia. Some of my most important memories are falling apart.*

I stop writing and look at the words I've put down. I don't know if they make any sense, but it's how I feel.

7

Roy

"A small expression of the agency's congratulations—or condolences," my agent says. He's brought two of Vendome's most expensive gift baskets, each overflowing with sweetmeats, cheeses, and a jeroboam of champagne. One basket gaily wrapped in red cellophane with flowing ribbons. The other somberly encased in black cellophane, the sort of thing you bring to a wake. "We didn't know if you were celebrating or mourning. So we covered both bases."

"I'm not sure either," I tell him.

"You know what they say. Into each life a little rain must fall. Well, Addie, let's face it, she was a deluge."

He never liked Addie. Can you tell?

As he leans over and sets the brimming baskets on the coffee table, I get a whiff of him. My agent smells good. He really does. It's not perfume or toilet water, whatever that is. He says it's cologne. Don't get him started, though, because he can do a half hour on the subject. He gave me a huge bottle of the stuff for Christmas, but I still haven't worked up the nerve to use it yet. He says just think of it as aftershave.

His name is Val Dalton and he's a moose. I'm big. He's bigger. Extra-large guy. He handles the two gift baskets like they're cupcakes. Sartorially, he's turned out as elegantly as a diplomat. Shirts and suits tailored in Hong Kong. Bench-cobbled British loafers with cute tassels.

Carefully sprayed pompadour. Don't get the idea he's a pansy or anything. Val used to play goalie in the pro hockey league in Canada.

He's originally from Kansas, family of dirt farmers. But he claims his great-great-great uncles were the Dalton Brothers, notorious bank robbers of the old west. "Makes me a birth member of the Ride Back Club," he likes to say. Translation: in the western movies when one of the guys gets left behind and the other cowpokes realize it. "We're the guys who'll ride back for him." Now *that's* a great background for an agent.

"I've got a question," I tell him. "It seems like half the country's getting divorces. How come they all manage to take it right in stride?"

"If that's the line someone lays on you, they're lying. Trust me, I'm an expert on this subject." Val is slightly older than I am, but he's been divorced twice and things have gotten noisy lately with his third marriage. "When it happens, even if you hate her guts, it still rattles you. Guys'll tell you you'll get over it in two months. Two years is more like it."

The quid pro quo seems out of whack. Addie and I were only married six years. Some shiny-nice ones, in the beginning. Quick. Cover the pain with a gag. "Don't I get any time off for—whaddayacallit?"

"Good behavior? Only if you qualify." My agent knows me too well.

We're sitting in my penthouse living room. Not mine, exactly. It's Jack Havoc's living room. A standing set on Stage 11. Posh perfection, with breakaway walls. The better to photograph you with. Panoramic view of the city. Look closer, just a backdrop. Running water in the bathroom for my bare-chested beefcake shaving scenes. But no toilet bowls, check it out, not anywhere in a Hollywood movie or TV show in those days.

Carpenters are banging nails, the electrical crew clattering lights into position for the next setup. Too noisy to talk here. So Val and I gather up my goodie baskets and step out of the penthouse into the semi-gloom, clutter, and confusion behind the camera, stepping nimbly over cables as we move toward my dressing room.

Stage 11 is the oldest one on the lot. Ghosts hide in the seventy foot high rafters and narrow catwalks. Sound-padding was added when Jolson began to shout for his *Mammy.* Cagney shoved a grapefruit into Mae Clarke's face right over there. The 3-D version of *The Phantom of the Rue Morgue* was shot here. Now my TV series is paying the rent.

We settle down in the dressing room. It's a roomy place, until someone Val's size comes inside. Then it starts feeling like a toy house. I pour some Chianti for us and then Val drops a bomb. The divorce isn't the only reason he came by.

"We've received an offer from Warners," he says.

"To do what?" I'm feeling guilty that I haven't told Val or anyone at the agency that Nate Scanlon is going to take a shot at breaking the Warners contract.

"They've got a theatrical feature they want you to do during the series hiatus."

"How about Marty's movie?" Martin Ritt, one of the best directors in Hollywood and an old pal from the New York "live" TV days, is about to make a waterfront movie with Sidney Poitier. He's been talking to me about co-starring.

"This would be instead. Warners will give you thirty-five thousand. Outside the TV deal. They know you're hurting for cash after the divorce settlement."

"The money's good," I admit.

"In return, they want you to extend your contract." Val fiddles with the foil on the red gift basket. "Agree to give them two extra years as Jack Havoc."

Deep breath. Let's hear it all. "What's the Warners movie?"

"A western. Aldo Ray plays Wyatt Earp. You're one of his younger brothers."

"How many younger brothers are there?"

"Three. You're the middle one. You don't get killed until the O.K. Corral."

"They're killin' me right now! C'mon, Val, this is horse pucky. Not even a 'B' movie, it's 'B' minus!"

"It's not what we were looking for, I know. But like you said, the money's good, and I'm sure we can get them to step up your Jack Havoc fees in a healthy way for the extra couple years. So you'll get to be a movie star a little later. What's the big hurry? Look at Bogie or Coop or Duke. You're going to have a long, long career, like them."

I'm not feeling guilty anymore. My agent is shilling for the studio.

"I'd rather do the picture with Poitier. Even if Warners grabs all of my loanout fee like they did the last time."

"The Poitier movie is no longer a possibility." Boom!

"Maybe you better spell this out for me, Val."

"Warners is exercising their right to pre-empt. You take the Earp picture and whistle all the way to the bank, or— they'll suspend you. Force you to sit out the hiatus, off salary. Until you go back to work on the series."

"They can do that?"

"According to the contract."

I look at Val Dalton. He's squirming. I know why.

He was there to welcome me when I first came to California. We'd never met, but he was easy to spot. Look for the tallest head on the station platform. In those days, flying was still a hassle, so actors being signed up by the New York talent scouts were shipped west by train. The Twentieth Century to Chicago, transfer to the Super Chief from Chicago to Pasadena.

That's how Val Dalton became a rising star at the agency.

Because all the senior guys there couldn't be bothered, schlepping all the way to Pasadena. For what? To meet some scruffy, scratching, mumbling kid who'd be taking the bus back to New York before anyone knew it. So they sent the big kid, Val, the agency gofer, to meet the trains. When some of us started to get somewhere in our careers, the only person at the agency we knew was Val Dalton.

But apart from business, the two of us have shared a lot of history. We've gotten drunk together in a Durango cathouse, won big and lost bigger at Santa Anita racetrack, risked our asses motorcycling through the Santa Monica mountains, told each other our dreams and fears. He's never lied to me. Before.

"So you think it's a good deal." I want to hear him say it.

"The agency recommends it."

"What do *you* say, Val?"

"I say—" here we go now, our relationship hangs on this "—let's tell Jack Warner to go screw himself! He just wants to exploit your name power from the series to bolster his crappy western. That helps him, not you. So they suspend you, so what? I know Addie cleaned you out. But if you need dough, I'll loan you whatever you need. Pay me back when you can."

"Thanks, man," I mumble like Marlon. I want to tell Val about what Nate Scanlon's doing. But I've promised not to. So guilt returns, bigger and better than before. While I'm so busy feeling sorry for myself, I again miss one of those moments that can shape your future. Life and death stuff, but who knows that at the time?

"The agency sent you over to sell me the deal," I say.

He shrugs.

"They gonna bust your balls when I pass?"

"Hey, I can always get myself another job," he says. I start to protest, but he laughs. "Don't sweat it, man. I'll just tell 'em you're a thick-headed, crazy actor. I know they'll buy that."

I walk him out of the dressing room. We start to shake hands. Instead we hug. A first. As he starts to go, I call after him. "Val, how come you don't like Addie?" I always pretended not to notice.

He stops, looks back at me. He's never tried to put it into words. The carpenters' hammering still going on in the background. "I know you think you were a lousy husband," he says slowly. "But Addie, as a wife—well, I felt like she was mostly rooting against you."

"It wasn't always that way."

"Glad to hear it. Call me. About anything. Anytime."

As Val goes off on his rounds, Killer Lomax comes rushing onto the sound stage. One glance tells me. I've sent him on a mission. He's hurrying back because he's come up empty-handed.

"Can't find that bitch anywhere," he says. "She's vanished."

Flashback time. Let me fill you in on some stuff you need to know.

It happened, of course, at Romanoff's. Just a few weeks ago. Killer and I were finishing dinner. The Bogarts were in New York. So we got Bogie's booth just below the bar. That's when I first noticed her. Perched on a stool. Waiting for someone. She disappeared from view when the bar got crowded. Now Killer had gone off on his merry way. Prince Mike and I were playing backgammon. He's good. I'm better. The crowd at the bar thinned. And she was still there.

"Who's that?" I asked him.

He turned his baleful face with the pouchy eyes toward the bar. "A brand-new face."

"Looks like a civilian," I said. Meaning not show biz. She was dressed in a simple black sheath, black pumps, string of pearls. Ladylike. Alabaster skin, no makeup except for a touch of lipstick. Did I mention gorgeous? Little younger than I am, but not too young. Long auburn hair, excellent legs. At first glance I thought I knew her from somewhere. No, really. Would I lie to you?

Kurt the maitre d' brought a problem to Prince Mike and the two of them went off to deal with it. What the hell. I got up and sauntered to the bar. She barely looked at me. Until I stopped beside her.

"He must be crazy," I said.

"Beg pardon?"

"Your boyfriend. Whoever he is. Standing you up like this."

She hesitated. Deciding whether to talk to me or not. Deciding yes. "It's a she. My old school chum. And this is definitely not like her. Unless she's changed." She looked around. "I haven't seen her in years. Maybe she's here and I don't recognize her."

"Then we can both look for her." I shielded my eyes like a sailor on watch. Stared off at the room. Buster Keaton in the Navy. She laughed. It was a nice laugh. And we were off and rolling.

She joined me in my booth. After all, you can keep an eye on the bar from there. She'd been trying to call her girlfriend on the pay phone. Left messages. So I had the waiter plug in a line at the booth. We played backgammon. I'm good. She was better.

Her name was Chris Patterson. She was from Alhambra, a blue-collar suburb just west of the city. Born and bred. Teaching music and art at her old high school. Never married. Bright. Funny. Just my kind of girl. Now I knew who she reminded me of—Addie. When I first met her.

"What happened here?" A Band-Aid. Flesh colored, wrapped around Chris's right index finger. I took her hand. Casually. To better examine the Band-Aid. Yeah, sure.

"Tennis blister. The P.E. teacher has the flu and I was filling in. Been a long time since I held a racquet. Do you play?"

"Used to. Maybe I should again." Still holding her hand.

"You could get hurt," she said. "I did."

"Gotta take a risk now and then."

She took her hand away. Looked flustered. Then tried her friend on the phone again. Visiting from Chicago, staying at the Beverly Hilton. This time her friend was there. Chitchat. Chris hung up. Embarrassed. "It's *tomorrow* night. We're supposed to meet here tomorrow night."

"Well, then we've got a lot of time to kill. Want to play some more backgammon?"

"I'm tired of backgammon," she said.

"I know some other games," I said.

We took my car. She was a stranger to Beverly Hills, so I drove around a little. Showing her some of the sights. Making sure I wasn't being followed. *Confidential* magazine was lurking everywhere lately. I didn't mention that to her. She wouldn't have understood.

See, I didn't tell you the best part. From the moment I began flirting with her it was clear that she had no idea who I was. Actors specialize in eye contact. I could see in her gaze that I was just a guy in a bar. Came out in conversation, she didn't watch TV, didn't even own a set. Hated all that noise and gossip. Just my kind of girl. When she'd asked what I did, I'd said just a hard-working insurance executive, how are you fixed for whole life? Don't know why I lied, guess I didn't want to let Jack Havoc spoil things.

I suggested a nightcap at the Hotel Bel-Air. Elegant. Swans gliding in the lagoon. Isolated. I could've taken her to my house. Addie was away in Santa Barbara at an antique dealer's convention. But Addie can smell things that hardly register on the Richter scale. We hadn't had that kind of earth-shaking battle in a while, and I wasn't looking for one. So as Chris and I were sipping cognac at a candlelit table in a dark corner of the Bel Air's near-deserted bar, I slipped my pal the bellhop a fiver. He brought back a key to one of the remote bungalows.

It was a magical time. No other way to put it. I hadn't been with a woman for a while. This was like a foreign film. Fireworks, the whole extravaganza. As if we were designed to give each other pleasure. But then, once we were past the initial lust, a tenderness emerged. We finally fell asleep, bodies intertwined. I could hardly tell where I ended and she began.

What I had no way of knowing, of course, was that it was all being recorded for posterity. Probably the boyish-looking private investigator who served me the divorce papers. A red-haired snake in the grass. Shooting pictures. Making something tacky and vile out of something sweet and beautiful. I don't think I can ever forgive Addie for that.

In the divorce papers Chris was referred to as a Jane Doe. Apparently they didn't know her name. I stayed away from all contact with her during the settlement negotiations. My career might be able to withstand—or even be enhanced, as Nate Scanlon insisted—by the glare of scandal, but Alhambra school teachers have been fired for less.

Now the divorce was done. I couldn't wait any longer. I wanted to tell her who I really am. Maybe she knows that already, from the newspapers. I wanted to apologize for unwittingly endangering her. Those are the reasons I gave myself. The truth is I just wanted to see her again.

So I sent Killer to locate her.

The Prince searching for Cinderella.

And the sonuvabitch brings back only excuses.

"Calm down, sport, calm down." I'm yelling at him in front of everybody on the sound stage. "Won't do any good racking my tuchis over the coals," Killer says, as he herds me back inside the dressing room. "I'm telling you—she's vanished."

He may not have been successful, but he insists he was thorough. No Chris Patterson teaching music and art or anything else at any high school in Alhambra. No one by that name ever graduated from there. The phone number she gave me doesn't work. Checked phone books for the entire vicinity. Nothing. Got a cop friend to run driver's licenses. The nearest Chris Patterson lives in Fresno and is a forty-two-year-old male plumber.

"Vanished," he repeats.

"Keep using that word and I'm gonna belt you, Kenny!"

"Okay. Try this. Maybe she never existed. Know what I mean? Wouldn't be the first broad who ever gave a guy a phony name and a wrong phone number."

I know he's right. She lied to me. Just like I lied to her. Makes us even on that score. I still want to find her. See her. But I'm frustrated, don't know what else to do. So I take it out on the Killer. Ream him for failing. "Teaches me a lesson," I yell at him, "sending a dumb schmuck like you to do a job."

"Fuck you, Roy! I don't have to take this shit!" He stomps out of the dressing room. Off the lot. Goodbye forever. Yeah, right. But it's not my finest hour. Even if being my whipping boy is part of his job description. Now he'll go off and pout until I persuade him back. I'll have to give him a consolation prize. Last time we hassled this bad, it took a Swiss wristwatch like mine. Speaking of which. The goddamn cigarette lighter. Still hasn't turned up. I feel better blaming him for that. Asshole!

I'm leaving the studio after work. One more day of shooting and we're done with this season's shows. If Nate Scanlon springs me, that could be it. I could be finished with Jack Havoc forever.

As I drive out the studio gate, a small figure darts forward and waves me down. Reva Hess, my best fan. I pull over to the side, roll down the window. She holds out a small bouquet of blue forget-me-nots. She looks like a tiny sparrow who's just fallen out of the nest. Tears welling in her eyes.

"What's the matter, Reva?"

"I'm so sorry," she says. Choked. "About the divorce."

What do you say? She bought the *Modern Screen* magazine version of our marriage. I take the flowers from her. "Maybe everything turns out for the best. Let's hope so."

"I'll pray that the two of you get together again, Mr. Darnell. You were the Perfect Couple. From the very beginning when you first got together. I remember."

Yeah. Sardi's. New York. Springtime. Golden day. I used to call it the best day of my life. Reva was there. I gaze at the kid's grief-stricken face and suddenly I'm very touched.

"You're very sweet. But, you know, sometimes things change."

"No, Mr. Darnell! Not when two people are meant for each other!" A tear slips down her cheek. Someone else is weeping for the end of this marriage besides me. I reach out my hand and brush the tear away.

"You're always there, Reva. Thanks. And why don't you call me Roy? Bet you do when you're talking about me with your friends."

She reddens with embarrassment. Awed by the offer. "Okay. *Roy.* Good night—and God bless you."

I'm caught in going-home traffic on the Strip. The forget-me-nots are on the seat beside me. Forgotten. I'm thinking of Chris. Nothing else. Just Chris. I'm still calling her by that name in my mind. I don't know what else to call her. Anymore than I know where to find her.

And suddenly there she is.

I'm on the block past Ciro's. Bored and irritable, I glance up at a billboard on the corner. Big as a movie screen. A glowingly healthy girl in a very form-fitting black one-piece swimsuit. Kneeling on the white sands of a tropical beach as she rubs Coppertone sun tan lotion on her arm. It's her. Whoever she is. Smiling seductively down at me. I smile back.

Now I know how to find her.

8

I'm running. Sunup was a few minutes ago. First light streams between the spires and towers of UCLA onto the oval track. A handful of us are doing laps. The Dawn Patrol. Mostly students, but outsiders permitted before classes begin. Couldn't sleep most of the night. Too much going on. So I'm out here, working my body, cleaning out the poisons. I'm here a couple or three times a week, alternating with the gym. I love to trot along and get lost in the crunching sound of my feet on the cinders.

Behind me I hear a sprinter coming up fast. Glance over my shoulder. It's my running buddy Burt Lancaster. He's the only other actor who uses the UCLA track. Matter of fact, he turned me on to it. We met at a party, and I was complaining there's nowhere to run on the west side.

I'm in pretty good shape, but Burt's much better. Look at him now. Backlit by the sun that highlights his long, tousled blond mane of hair. Bounding gracefully like a lion closing the distance on his prey. He overtakes me, we exchange a "Hey." He slows and we fall in step together. We're both long-distance runners. Sometimes we talk, sometimes we don't. Today's one of the talking days.

"How you handling it?"

"Doin' fine," I lie.

"Good man. I was divorced once, y'know. Just a kid. Took me weeks to get over it. Keep busy, that's the ticket."

"Hey, I work in TV. We're born busy."

He laughs. That big ha-ha laugh. Teeth gleaming. "Well, with any luck, you'll be out of TV soon. I'm waiting for you, kid."

In Hollywood, they call Gable the King. But that's an honorary title, left over from the pre-war years. At this point in time, Lancaster is the king. When TV siphoned off the movie audience, the major studios cut their overhead—and their own throats—by dropping all the contract people. "Hire 'em when you need 'em" became the slogan. But instead, the big stars went into business for themselves. Burt's been the most successful. His production company has made seven movies, all money-makers. *Marty,* the "sleeper" of the decade, won this year's Oscar, and he's just shot his circus epic, *Trapeze,* in Paris. A guaranteed hit if there ever was one.

His company bought the old William Morris Agency building on North Canon Drive in Bev Hills. He invited me over a couple weeks ago. Showing off. But why not? A lobby with a full-wall, two-story bird cage, filled with tiny rare finches and canaries. Original Rouault studies of circus acrobats on his office walls. The executive bathroom adjoining his office has gold-plated fixtures, he boasts. While pissing in the sink and laughing uproariously. Takes me down the halls, tells me who's where. Clifford Odets, Jerome Weidman, Paddy Chayefsky, A.B. Guthrie, Ernest Lehman, T.E.B. Clarke, Liam O'Brien, J.P. Miller, Terence Rattigan, Ben Hecht. They're all there, in their offices, typing scripts. He seems as proud of this array of top writers as he is of the birds in the cage in the lobby.

"Warm up a corner office for me," I say.

"We're gonna own this town," he promises. "Guys like you and me."

It's time to play *Meet the Press.* We're back at the courthouse, me and Nate Scanlon. Yeah, the same courthouse where we did the divorce dance. Now we're not ducking the reporters and photographers. We've summoned them. And they're all here.

First Nate has me walk with him down the corridor to visit a clerk and officially file the lawsuit. It's a kick, coming and going. The halls are jammed with felons and their lawyers and their loved ones and the witnesses against them, all milling around waiting for the courtrooms to open. Everybody recognizes me. I mean, heads spin. I'm gracious, friendly, shrug at the impossibility of signing autographs. You can see, I'd be here forever. Wish I could. A bruiser in a tank shirt with a paratrooper symbol and the words "Death From Above" tattooed on his bulging bicep suddenly blocks my way. Could be trouble, I think, looking for a bailiff. The bruiser smiles, two front teeth missing, but declares himself a fan. "Hey, Jack Havoc, why'n'tcha kick some butt and get me outta here?"

Outside the press has set up a Kodak Picture Point. Nate and I move into position. The courthouse framed behind us. Several microphones in front of us. The classic shot. Ready for the six o'clock news. I look around. Most of the media gathered are not familiar to me. They're the downtown guys who cover hard news rather than entertainment. But here and there a familiar face. Bob Thomas of AP. Vernon Scott of UPI. I greet the ones I know by name. And Nate Scanlon gets down to business.

"I have just filed a lawsuit on behalf of Mr. Roy Darnell against Warner Brothers studio asking that his contract be declared null and void because Warners has failed to live up to the terms of the agreement." He fills in the details, emphasizing the gratitude I feel for the people at Warners who helped create *Jack Havoc* and underscoring the count-less millions of dollars the show is generating for the studio and the network. That Nate, he can talk. I don't say a word. I'm there as a visual prop. Without me on camera, we might not merit the TV news shows.

It's a dangerous game we're playing. Jack Warner's repu-tation in labor relations is legendary. On the theory that "None of these bastards do any work worth a damn during the holidays anyway," Warner's occasional present to his employees was to close down the studio and knock everyone off salary before Christmas and then re-hire them after New Year's. And back in the post-war '40s, when the craft labor unions went on strike at his studio, Warner trucked in goons from the Long Beach docks to break heads on the picket line. Warners won the strike.

The press people start to throw questions at me. Nate fields them. "Will the show go off the air?" We have no way of knowing. "Is Warners going to counter-sue?" Ask them. "How much money have you been making?" Relatively little. "But how much?" A wisecracker from the rear shouts an answer for me. "Not as much as he's gonna make in the movies, right, Roy?" Everybody laughs. "C'mon, Roy, say something," another guy yells. I step to the microphones. "I want to thank all the fans around the world who have embraced *Jack Havoc* and hope they'll understand." Nate cuts it off there, expresses appreciation for their attention and cooperation and I wave to the cameras as he hustles me away.

"That went rather well," he says as we go for our cars in the parking lot.

"Just the way you said it would. Next time write me a bigger part."

"Strong, silent men. They're all the rage in the movies." He points northeast at the sky. "In about ten minutes, as soon as they start receiving inquiring phone calls from the press, there should be a mushroom cloud rising over Burbank."

Nate's so confident. So why am I worrying about unexpected fallout from our little atom bomb?

"Rafferty," he says. "R-A-F-F-E-R-T-Y." Proving definitively that Killer Lomax can spell. He's reveling in his moment, perching his glasses, which he rarely wears, on the end of his nose as he reads from a notebook. He's proud that he's brought back the bacon this time. The Killer takes a swallow of his vodka tonic and proceeds.

"First name, Kimberly. Calls herself Kim."

"Kim Rafferty." I try the name on for size. It fits.

We're celebrating the filing of the lawsuit. Killer was upset that something that big was in the works and he was kept out of the loop. I told him I would have told him if I could have. You know that, sport, we're brothers. But Nate gave me orders. Let him be pissed at Nate. That's what lawyers are for. We're sitting in one of the booths at the rear of Villa Capri, a schmaltzy Italian restaurant in Hollywood. Romanoff's is closed tonight for a private party, so we came here. It's one of Sinatra's hangouts. Used to be Jimmy Dean's, too. Poor Jimmy.

When we drove up, several autograph hounds were waiting to pounce. Including Reva. Guess she switched operations from Romanoff's for the night, too. The other fans were consoling me, What're you gonna do if you're not Jack Havoc anymore? And Reva, gossiping on the sidelines with Killer, jumped in. "He's so much more than just Jack Havoc." Good kid.

"Have a look," Killer says. Pushing an 8x10 glossy across the table to me. Actor's composite photo. Divided in quarters, featuring varied poses of Kim Rafferty. Grace Kelly ladylike, the way I met her. Plus Dale Evans cowgirl on a split-rail fence swinging a lariat. Swimsuit shot, as on the billboard. And a good straight-on close-up of her face. Just lipstick and a welcoming smile. I gaze at the composite while Killer rattles off details.

"Member of Screen Actors Guild, American Federation of Television and Radio Artists, and some model's association. Started out as a model for department store catalogs. Sears and Penney's, lingerie ads and shit like that. Been acting two years. Her agent's a nobody. Active mostly in commercials. She's been in a couple of cheapie feature flicks, one of them soft-core. Had a few lines on a *Lucy* episode. Nothing that amounts to anything yet..."

He's behaving like Sherlock Holmes, but once I saw her face on the billboard the rest was easy. I sent Killer to the ad agency, who shooed him along to the agent, and so on. With instructions not to tell any of them who was doing the asking. Say you're a casting agent, an ex-boyfriend, a process server or something.

"...she's not married, does come from Alhambra, dropped outta high school in her last year, owes three hundred dollars on a tired old jalopy, lives right here on Fountain Avenue, a *bachelorette* apartment, cute word, huh? Augments her income, which is to say pays the bills, by waiting tables at the Hamburger Hamlet on the Strip. She used to be shacked up with a trumpeter who plays at the Cocoanut Grove with Les Brown and his Band of Renown. Kicked him out 'cuz whenever he got loaded he'd belt her black and blue—"

I cut him off. "Did you keep my name out of this?"

Killer leans back. Takes off his glasses and sighs. "Roysie. What am I? Some kind of an idiot? I was the soul of discretion, like a fuckin' diplomat. You woulda been proud of me."

He's fishing for an atta-boy. I don't know why I won't give it to him.

"Is that everything?" I ask.

"What else you wanna know? Her shoe size, where she shops for groceries, what days of this month she's gonna be on the rag? Name it, I got it, sport, I—"

We're interrupted. By Dave Viola. My un-favorite costar. I've seen him drunk before. But never staggering. He looks like he's been to a wake. Maybe his own.

"'Scuse me, 'scuse me, hate t'interrupt, gentlemen, but—" swaying, holding a jumbo-size daiquiri "—just wanted to toast your very good health!" Downs a gulp that could daze an ox. Wipes his mouth with the back of his hand, grins his loopy grin, and before anyone can stop him, launches into one of his endless supply of Vegas lounge gags.

"Guy goes on a cruise to the Caribbean. Missin' Wendy, the girl he left behind, so-o-o much. Reaches Nassau, gets plastered in a bar, lurches into the john. Starts to take a leak. Notices this humongous black dude standin' at the next urinal. Glances down and sees the word Wendy tattooed on the guy's dong. Helluva coincidence, but—hey, he says, my girl's named Wendy, too! The Dude looks at him, laughs, points at his cock and says, 'Hey, Mon, what that say is Welcome to Nassau and Have A Nice Day.'"

Killer laughs. Toilet humor gets him every time. I've heard the joke before. "So is there a point to any of this?" I ask Viola.

"A point...tha's a good point...glad y'asked. The point is...I never been to Nassau, Roy, so that makes you the biggest prick I've ever seen!"

Killer tenses beside me. I'm relaxed. Who cares what this asshole says about anything? "You're outta line, Davey," Killer warns.

"Me? I'm outta fuckin' line? I'm not the one who's puttin' ninety-seven good people on the fuckin' bread line! You know I'm right, Killer, c'mon, admit it." He swivels back to me. "What're you doin' to us, man? If you take a hike, they'll cancel the show. Don't you know that? Don't you care?"

He starts to fling his drink in my face. But Killer is up and at him. Didn't think he could move that fast. Deflects the glass so it splashes all over Viola instead. Gets a hammerlock on him. Viola whimpers. "Didn't mean it, no offense, Roy, c'mon, babe, but don't do it, please, don't pull the plug on *Jack Havoc*. The rest of us got nowhere to go if the show dies."

"The people with talent will be okay," I say.

Viola stares at me until Killer shepherds him away. It's not hard. All the fight has gone out of him. I reach for the pack of Luckies on the table, pluck a cigarette, stick it between my lips. My hand is steady. Where are the damn matches? Someone reaches out with a light. It's Killer.

"Attaboy, " I say, "you just earned yourself a big fat raise. Effective now."

He smiles. "Then let me take a chance and mention an unhappy thought."

"Fire away."

"You been wondering how Addie's private eye wound up peeping in your window at the Hotel Bel-Air cottage with his camera that night. Suppose the peeper knew where to look because Miss Kim Rafferty told him."

My first instinct, definitely a Jack Havoc impulse, is to fracture him. When in doubt, kill the messenger. But it's a suspicion that's been lurking in the back of my mind, too. A possibility I've been ducking and rejecting because I don't want to believe it.

Now there's a way to check it out.

The elephant is shifting from foot to foot. Each time, it seems as if the pavement in the KTLA-TV parking lot in Hollywood may split open. Some of the tots in the sunny outdoor bleachers are tossing peanuts. The elephant ignores the peanuts. Maybe the smog from the freeway just below the parking lot is getting to the poor pachyderm. I'm feeling a bit queasy myself.

Because from where I'm sitting I can see her. But she doesn't see me.

Kim Rafferty is standing near the elephant with a guy who must be the elephant wrangler. He's wearing a turban and Nehru jacket like Punjab in the *Orphan Annie* comic strip. She's wearing a swimsuit, tighter than the one on the billboard, covered in silver spangles like a bareback rider in the circus. The elephant is naked except for a small two-seater basket strapped on his back and a banner across his belly proclaiming: TRAPEZE—Variety Boys Club Benefit.

A local TV audience participation show is in progress. I'm part of the audience. Up in the top row of the bleachers. In a loose windbreaker, oversize Italian sunglasses and a tweed Irish hat. So far nobody's recognized me. Now Kim is on camera, plugging the opening of Burt Lancaster's circus movie.

That's the latest item making me crazy. Does Burt have something to do with my getting snared by the private eye? Was she working for him then, too? Is Burt colluding somehow with Addie? Does that make any sense? I'm totally confused. Not to mention pissed off. Got to look at the likelihood I was betrayed by Kim. So am I here to confront and accuse? Or to give her a chance to explain—better yet, deny. Go ahead, bitch, convince me. And no more lies! Do I want to clobber her or kiss her? See? Queasy.

With the emcee's unctuous help, Kim is awarding a few seats to the gala premiere of *Trapeze*. Plus an extra-special prize. An elephant ride, right here, today! She reaches in the fish bowl, reads off the name of the lucky kid, who jumps up and races forward.

The wrangler signals with a steel-tipped pointy stick and the elephant kneels down. Kim climbs into the small basket on the elephant's back. The wrangler hands the kid up to her. They get set. Then the wrangler gestures. With a traffic-stopping trumpeting cry, the elephant rises to full height. The kid is thrilled and waves to Mommy and Daddy. Kim waves to the camera from way-y-y up there. The elephant, on cue from the wrangler, does a once-around the stage area. Despite her ear-to-ear smile, I can see Kim is scared shitless. The crowd applauds. The show goes to commercial. Quickly, the wrangler gets them both down and off the elephant.

She disappears around a corner of the building. I scale down the rear of the bleachers, drop to the ground, follow her path behind the building. She's still there. All by herself. Puking her guts out. I hand her my handkerchief. She takes it without seeing who's giving it to her. Then she does.

"Hi, Roy." Sees through my disguise. A wan smile.

"Hi, Kim." Not Chris. This is Kim. Whoever the hell she is. But you can't yell at somebody who's heaving. She looks awful. I take back the hanky, dip it in a bucket of water. Probably the elephant's. Gently, I cool her brow. She's ashen.

"Scared of elephants, huh?"

"Nah. Scared of heights."

"Then why'd you take this job?"

She looks at me as if I'm a dunce. "For the money."

"Wondered if I'd ever see you again," she says.

We're in a window booth at Denny's on Sunset, across from the TV station. She's just stepped out of the rest room wearing her street clothes. Tan slacks, white hunter's blouse with epaulets on the shoulders and shotgun shell loops on the breast pockets. She has her lipstick stuck in one of the loops.

"You look like you're about to lead a safari."

"Ungawa!" she says. "Onward into darkest Hollywood!"

Forced smiles. Awkward. The waitress brings our order. Coffee and a bear claw for the lady, iced tea for the gent. She doesn't touch her food. I start playing with my ice cubes. Neither of us seem to have a way to really start talking to each other.

"Last time we were together," she offers, "we were calling each other Bob and Chris."

"Yeah. I liked them. Too bad they never existed."

More silence. Then. "How'd you find me?"

"Doesn't matter." *Clink* go the ice cubes. Then I make eye contact. Trying to peer into her soul. If she has one. "Look, I just want to ask you one question and I'm gone."

"The answer is yes. I set you up. And I'm sorry I did."

So we just look at each other for a moment. Then I say, "For the money."

She doesn't break eye contact. Give her that.

"Well, I hope you got paid well. Because you did a great job. If you ever need a recommendation, as an actress or as a hooker—"

I'm getting up. She grabs my wrist. Strong grip.

"I'm not a hooker!"

I shake her hand loose. Feel like busting her face. "Could've fooled me. Remember what we did together, all night, in our little love nest—while your photographer pal played Watch the Birdie?"

"That was my choice. I didn't have to."

"How's that again?"

"I was supposed to get you to pick me up—which wasn't that hard—and phone in where we shacked up. After that, all I had to do is get the two of us naked long enough for the photos. Sleeping together was just…well, it was my spur-of-the-moment idea."

"Because it made for better pictures? Might earn you a bonus?"

"Because I liked you. I've never screwed anyone for money."

"You don't do what you did to guys you like."

"That's what I'm ashamed of."

She lets go of my wrist. I consider. Finally sit again. Can't hurt to listen.

"When they hired me to do it, I told myself it's just another acting gig. And I was kind of desperate; I'd just been hit with a big car repair bill. So I figured, why not? Play the school marm from Alhambra. But I didn't count on you turning out to be a nice guy. I—apologize. I'm very, very sorry."

I believe her. I know, I know. That's what I said when she acted like she didn't know who I was when we met in Romanoff's. But unless she's the greatest actress since Garbo, she's telling me straight this time. I mean, what's in it for her to con me now?

Okay, let's put it to the test. I ask her for the rest of what she knows and she tells me.

She got the elephant riding job through an ad agency; no, she's never met Burt. And she was hired for the Romanoff's caper by the red-haired snooper. A number of candidates were interviewed. All in search of the girl most likely to entice me. Kim wasn't told what the "role" was until after she'd been selected. When they'd been prepping a while, the snooper mentioned that he'd had me under surveillance for weeks but nothing had happened. They were under pressure to get things moving. So now they were going to make it happen.

"And how did that freckle-faced fucker know what kind of woman I like?" Polish head-slap time. "Addie told him, right?"

"Your wife rehearsed me. Trained me. Sort of like Eliza Doolittle in *My Fair Lady*. She told me what to say and how to say it. How to dress. What you like and what you don't like." No wonder she reminded me of Addie when we first got together. "She said I caught on fast. 'Kim,' she'd say, 'you're absolutely perfect. You are going to be the girl of his dreams.'"

How do I feel hearing all this? In a crazy way it lets me off the hook for all the lousy things I've done to damage my marriage. This really takes the fuckin' cake. Compared to Addie, I was just a kid getting his hand caught in the cookie jar. Succumbing to hot-blooded temptations now and then. What she did, though, is really cold. Premeditated. Viciously calculating. She conspired and manipulated and used our most intimate secrets to betray me. And for what? Money.

Hearing Kim tell it is sort of like sitting in a sauna. Every sentence she utters, my temperature leaps up a notch. Soon I'm way past steaming. When Kim tells me the stuff about Addie designing her as the girl of my dreams—by that time, I am molten. I want to scald Addie. I want to shake her until her fillings fly out. I want to put my fingers around her throat and squeeze and squeeze. I want to kill her. But I don't have to. That's why I have a lawyer.

9

Reva

I woke up this morning thinking of Greta Garbo. No wonder, because that's who I fell asleep to last night on *The Late Show*, watching on the small black-and-white TV set on the shelf in my room. Mother was out on the town with a bunch of "the girls" from the bank, somebody's birthday, an excuse for them all to get bombed at Trader Vic's. So I bolted my door and watched *Ninotchka*. That's about the only Garbo movie they ever show on TV.

People who remember her think she's become a recluse, but that's not true. Garbo moved to New York when she retired from the screen, so we'd see her all the time, the Secret Six, we'd spot her window shopping on Madison Avenue or coming out of the Museum of Modern Art, but when you asked her for an autograph, she'd never ever sign, she'd just walk right by you like she didn't even hear and grab a cab and be gone. But we'd keep trying, only now there's a whole new generation of collectors who don't even know enough to wish they could get Garbo.

It makes me sick. Well, maybe not that specifically, but something does—sick to my stomach. I barely manage to unbolt my door and hotfoot it to the bathroom. Thank god Mother's not in there. She's left for work already, so I can heave to my heart's content. What did I have to eat last night? Oh yeah, after Podolsky and I saw this double feature at the Nu-Art Theater of *A Place In The Sun* and an old 30s version of the same story, Dreiser's *An American Tragedy,* which was nowhere near as good, then we went for pizza on Pico Boulevard and Podolsky insisted on adding anchovies, so here I am, upchucking to beat the band. Try thinking of something else, think of Monty and Liz, the movie's still good as the first time I saw it in New York, and that, of course, reminds me of Billy...

Charming Billy—his last name is Elgort—wore a sailor suit when he came collecting, but he wasn't in the U.S. Navy. He belonged to a Sea Scout unit where he lived in Sheepshead Bay near Coney Island. Charming Billy looked old for his age, which is actually the same as me; we were both sixteen going on seventeen back during the icy-windy winter I'm talking about, and unless you know better, his uniform looked real. Some of the big stars who wouldn't sign for the rest of us were patriotic enough to make exceptions for our boys in the service. That's how he got Jean Arthur and Charlie Chaplin and Ingrid Bergman, although even the uniform didn't work on Garbo. Maybe if she thought he was in the Swedish Navy. And the Bergman thing backfired on him. Someone, I suspect Podolsky, told Ingrid that Charming Billy wasn't really in the Navy. So the next time she saw him, Ingrid demanded that he tear her signature out of his autograph book and give it back to her. You win some, you lose some.

This frosty early December evening, Charming Billy and I are waiting together on a super-star mission. We're huddled in the darkened doorway of the closed flower shop a few yards up from the entrance to the Sherry Netherland Hotel on Fifth Avenue at 59th Street, where Cary Grant is staying. We're freezing so we're hugging, actually we're grinding our crotches against each other and it's kind of the first real sexual experience I've had. We're doing lines from *A Place In The Sun* to pass the time. It's the scene where Montgomery Clift meets Elizabeth Taylor and we're getting each other pretty hot.

"Hello," I say. Cheek burrowed into the shoulder of his pea coat.

"Hello," he says. Bump. Grind.

"Why're you all alone? Being exclusive? Feeling blue?"

"I'm just fooling around. Maybe you'd like to play?"

Podolsky snickers. I forgot to mention he's jammed in the doorway with us. Reading the *New York Post* by the light from the street lamp. Pretending to ignore us. We ignore him.

"You're Angela Vickers," Charming Billy, who kind of looks like Robert Wagner, says in his best hesitant-sensitive Monty Clift voice. We all love Monty Clift; we know where he lives, in an apartment on East 54th Street near Lexington with his acting coach, Mira Rostova. "I read about you in the papers."

"Yeah, Liz baby," Podolsky growls, "I read you've got the biggest tits in Hollywood."

Charming Billy snickers. Because I haven't got anywhere near what Liz has got. But I grind my pelvis against his to get him to concentrate. He's got a boner. I can feel it.

"What else do you do?" I ask him.

"The usual things," Monty says.

"You look unusual," Liz says. Definitely a boner.

"First time anybody ever said that," he says.

"Because you always look like a fuckin' fairy in that sailor suit," Podolsky says. His face still buried in the newspaper. "Hah! Sidney Skolsky's column says Tab Hunter sleeps in the nude."

"With his dog Butch," Charming Billy adds. He laughs and breaks apart from me. He pumps his arms. The wind is blowing unobstructed at us across from Central Park. "God, I feel like an Eskimo. C'mon, Cary, time to descend from your luxurious penthouse. A deal's a deal."

We've cut a deal with Cary Grant. At least we think we have. Les Noonan, a feisty little teenage dynamo from Union City, New Jersey, who resembles his favorite, Jimmy Cagney, handled the negotiations on our behalf. Cary Grant has been in town for almost a week; we've all seen him around town a bunch of times and he hasn't signed for anyone yet.

Les prides himself on being the best in the Secret Six at breaking down a star's resistance. Once he chased Lana Turner's limo on foot up Park Avenue from the Waldorf Astoria on 50th Street, knocking on her window every time the limo stopped for a red light. At 72nd Street she surrendered and rolled the window down and signed his book. "When I touched the aluminum frame around the limo window to take back my book," Les loves to recall, "sparks flew. Tsst! Static electricity, I guess. But it was like a magic sign, celebrating the occasion." Poor Lana, she never stood a chance.

Les has taken it upon himself to break the Cary Grant impasse. I'm sure it wasn't designed that way, but the Sherry Netherland Hotel is a bastion against collecting. Only one revolving door into the lobby and the front desk faces the only elevator bank (with a uniformed Starter on duty) so there's no sneaking in side doors and going up back elevators out of sight of the front desk like at the Plaza, the Waldorf, the Ritz Carlton, the St. Regis, or the Essex House. Not at the Sherry Netherland.

So Les Noonan took the bull by the horns. He just phoned and asked for Cary Grant and, lo and behold, Cary Grant himself answered. Les identified himself as an autograph collector, "one of the little monsters who've been trailing you around town, Mr. Grant." That got him a chuckle so Les rolled on: "This situation is very uncomfortable for all of us, Mr. Grant. We don't enjoy intruding on your privacy and we certainly don't want to hound you, but we're really the best at what we do, and we've gotta get your autograph, so what're we going to do?"

Cary Grant said, "Why do I suspect that you have a solution in mind?"

Les confessed he did. "Suppose we leave our autograph books at the front desk in your hotel tonight. When you come down, you sign 'em all and get it over with. That doesn't draw a crowd like it would anywhere you start giving autographs in public, and then we all go our happy ways."

Cary Grant laughed. That bubbly Cary Grant laugh, Les reported to the rest of us. "Charming," he said. And we had a deal.

I know what you're thinking. This violates the basic precept of the Secret Six, that you have to see the star sign your book for it to count. But Les has devised an answer to that, too. While we're freezing in the doorway outside, Les is inside the busy travel agency on the corner, hidden in one of the phone booths that has a view through a door with a glass window into the lobby of the Sherry. When Cary Grant emerges from the elevator, he'll see him and signal us. In fact, that's what's happening right now.

Les comes running like Paul Revere spreading the word. "He's in the lobby, he's in the lobby," he yells to us, frozen like icicles in our doorway. He spreads the word to Pam O'Mara, Tillie Lust, tall-skinny Freddie Tripp, and the others hiding in alcoves and risking hypothermia farther up the street.

We can't gather in front of the hotel entrance and just look in through the revolving door because of the particularly nasty doorman. So we all rush across Fifth Avenue, dodging traffic, to our pre-scouted vantage point: behind the statue of General Sherman on horseback on the west side of Fifth Avenue. Directly facing the entrance to the Sherry. And inside, at the front desk, in unmistakable profile, is Cary Grant at the front desk. Pen in hand.

"He's signing my book," Tillie says.

"Bullshit, that's my book!" Podolsky say.

"Doesn't matter," adjudicates Pam O'Mara. "He's signing. It's our books. We can see it. It counts!"

"Fuckin' A," Les Noonan shouts. Everybody starts pounding Les on the back, jumping up and down, Charming Billy whirls and kisses me. It's my first kiss, next to the statue of General Sherman and across from where Cary Grant is signing my autograph book, and Charming Billy is copping a feel and we're all so gleeful and when Cary Grant comes out of the hotel we all yell his name and he smiles and blows us a kiss across Fifth Avenue before he climbs into his waiting limo and drives off.

Les trots across the avenue against the lights and retrieves our autograph books from the hotel desk. He dodges a honking bus as he brings the books back to us and everybody's gloating, "Look, he wrote our names, and good luck!" so I'm the only one who glances back over at the entrance to the Sherry and sees Roy Darnell coming out. He went in about an hour ago with a gorgeous blonde who's the Debutante of the Year, according to *LIFE*. Roy's alone now, but his hair is wet and slicked back like he just took a shower, and he gets into a cab and takes off.

Now it's New Year's Eve, only a few weeks after the Cary Grant triumph at the Sherry Netherland. There's snow on the ground and a party in progress at Pam O'Mara's apartment. She's recently moved into one of the walkups a few doors away from the "21" Club on 52nd Street. We're all envious of her. Pam can wait outside for the hard-drinking stars like Bob Mitchum, Franchot Tone, and Brod Crawford to close the bar at "21" and still be home in two minutes.

Tonight is special. Everyone's at the party, maybe sixteen, eighteen of us, jammed into Pam's tiny apartment, including Tillie Lust, lanky Freddie Tripp, Podolsky of course, Charming Billy (in civilian clothes), boisterous Les Noonan, cadaverously-thin Alabama-bred Abe Franks, Arleigh, our communications central. There's the twins who are actually cousins: Jimmy Quick (a fast-talker) and Johnny Click (with a flash-camera, even tonight); Rose Kaplan, our "mole" who works at UA; and Marco Ortiz, the self-styled "Latin From Manhattan" (Hell's Kitchen, actually) who speaks good Spanish plus passable Yiddish and Italian that makes him invaluable when chasing international stars. Although we're bound by our common infatuation with the stars, until now the Secret Six has been all business. We've spent hundreds of hours together in various combinations, lurking in strategic doorways and outside sundry posh spots, but tonight's our first purely social event.

It's funny to see us all gathered in one place. Everyone feels kind of awkward. Without stars to keep an eye out for, we have to look at each other and, to be honest, as a group we're kind of on the geeky side. Pam has music going on the hi-fi. Jane Froman (her favorite) singing "Blue Moon" and "With A Song In My Heart." Frankie Laine (Les's favorite) singing "Two Loves Have I" and "Jealousy." It's easier to dance to Jane Froman than Frankie Laine, but hardly anyone is dancing. It's like a junior high school dance. Boys on one side of the room, girls on the other. There's punch (without punch) and hard stuff for those that want it, plus cold cuts, but no one's eating yet (except Podolsky). Pam O'Mara suggests we divide into teams for a game of charades and it's a great ice-breaker. We're acting out famous movie lines like "Here's looking at you, kid" and "Smile when you call me that." Podolsky shines on "You can't send a kid like this up in a crate like that."

Charming Billy has been drinking Cuba Libres and pours me a stiff one. We sip, then slip away together on a business call. There's a young actress appearing tonight on *Philco Playhouse,* which is being telecast only a few blocks away at NBC in Radio City. Word is she's leaving for Hollywood to make a movie at Fox with Richard Basehart, and neither Charming Billy nor I have her. Who knows, she may turn out to be something. We stroll through the night streets, crunching snow underfoot, holding hands like boyfriend-girlfriend. It's the first time we've been alone together (without Podolsky, even) since the doorway at the Sherry Netherland. As we approach the RCA Building, we stop to admire the huge lighted Christmas tree and watch the skaters on the ice rink below. We're leaning over, cheek to cheek. The cold air nipping at our faces. He turns his face and lightly kisses me on the lips.

"What's that for?"

"New Year's Eve."

"It's not midnight."

"Why wait 'til the last minute?"

We skip, I mean it, *skip* down the street to the entrance to NBC and just as we get there the actress we're looking for comes out with her co-star on the show, who happens to be, you guessed it, Roy Darnell. He's been doing a lot of "live" TV. They both have traces of grease paint behind their ears and their heads are real close together and they're laughing as we approach them.

"Here's my girl Reva," Roy says. "Why aren't you out at a party?"

"I am, I mean, we are, Billy and me—few blocks from here," I stammer. "We just came by to see you guys."

Roy introduces us to the pretty but bland blonde with him, just like we're all friends who've casually run into each other on the street. I've persuaded Charming Billy to finally get Roy's autograph. He's been resisting, insisting Roy's never going to be anything, but just to spite me he has Roy sign his crumb book. We're not crumb collectors anymore, but we reserve our slick-pages autograph books for the proven performers and carry little spiral pads for the who-can-tells. Sort of like the farm system in baseball. The starlet-heading-for-Hollywood doesn't look like anything special. So we both get her in our crumb books. Her name is Grace Kelly. A couple of years from now she'll be the biggest female star in the world. And I'll have her. In my crumb book. Go know. That's what makes collecting so great. It's like being a prospector, panning for gold.

As they're walking off, Roy turns back and yells to me, "Reva, you be sure to have a happy new year!"

"Sure will," I yell back to him. "Same to you."

When Charming Billy and I get back, the party is swinging. Marco has the fruit bowl perched on his head as he hip-wiggles and lip syncs to a Carmen Miranda record. Lots of laughter and chatter, and as it gets toward midnight Freddie Tripp, who's a coffee-skinned Negro, slips on a Billie Holiday record he brought. The lights are lower. Some of the collectors are dancing together and it's a hoot. Mostly at arm's distance, but Podolsky is coming on outrageously to Tillie, who unfortunately has been stricken by an uncontrollable case of the giggles. Charming Billy and I are among those slow-dancing, Billie Holiday is singing "For All We Know."

Charming Billy leans me back in a big dip, so far back we fall into the closet. We're both cackling and he pulls the closet door shut and he's on top of me and I can't believe what's happening but as he's French kissing me he's got one hand under my skirt tugging at my panties while his other hand whips it out. Is this how I'm going to lose my virginity? Pinned on top of a bunch of snow-soggy overcoats? I'm trying to protest about the lack of romance, not to mention the potential embarrassment if someone opens the door, but then as Billy presses his boner against my inner thigh I feel it dissolve, I mean it just melts away, and I hear Billy whimper like a stricken creature and then he begins to softly cry.

"It's all right," I tell him, not knowing if it is or not. But I hug him because he obviously needs hugging and I whisper in his ear, "What's wrong, Billy?"

He gasps for breath and stops crying. "Remember when we were in the doorway at the Sherry? And you were pretending I was Monty Clift?" I tell him I remember. "Well, I was pretending the same thing—that you were Monty Clift." That's how I found out that Charming Billy was queer and, I guess, it was when he found out for sure, too.

So he zipped up and I pulled up my knickers and as inconspicuously as we could we came out of the closet, although Tillie spotted us and grinned and made the shame-shame gesture with her fingers. Pam O'Mara had her tiny black-and-white TV set on and they were showing the crowds in Times Square and doing the countdown, and at midnight Billy and I kissed, but it was like brother and sister. Everyone in the room kissed everyone that way, mostly on the cheek, because it was the start of a New Year. Out with the old.

When I think back on that night, this is the worst part. The word that went through my mind. Queer. What a harsh, ugly way to describe anyone. I looked it up in the dictionary once and the first definition was "Strange from a conventional point of view; singular or odd." That doesn't sound too bad. I mean, "strange" is a little off-putting, but it could mean "interesting" or even "mysterious." And "singular" is pretty good. "Odd," well, I can live with that. In fact, I've learned that I have to. Using the dictionary definition, I suppose all us collectors were queer. I'm not talking sexually, just emotionally, the kind of people who didn't fit in. Maybe that's been the real common bond, not just the movie stars. No matter how weird we were, we accepted each other's weirdness.

After what happened in the clothes closet I was afraid that I'd never see Charming Billy again, that he'd feel he could never face me. But he continued to come around and we still would talk about everything else as we waited outside Sardi's or wherever. We were still friends. But he never wore his sailor suit anymore when he came collecting.

Okay, okay, I know you're thinking, Nice going, Reva, you sailed right past that uncomfortable stuff about Roy. Him coming out of the Sherry Netherland with a wet head, or him strolling off into the night with Grace Kelly. I kept that sort of thing under my hat, never called attention to it, not even to my best pals in the Secret Six. Why? I guess because it played into my favorite fantasy which was that I knew that something terrible was going to happen to Roy and I'd imagine that I was the only one in the world who could keep him safe.

Of course, nothing got in the newspapers back then when Roy was fooling around because he was just another barely known actor, but I have to admit what he was probably doing. Cheating. His marriage to Addie wasn't all a fairytale romance. I mean, I don't know what, if anything, Addie was up to at the time, maybe they had some kind of understanding, but two wrongs don't make a right. And...well, maybe this sounds like making excuses for him, but it occurs to me that Addie *must* have known Roy was occasionally stepping out on her. He wasn't being all that careful—the Sherry Netherland, for god's sake—so while you can blame him, it also brings up a big question—after all this time, what made her file for divorce now?

I try to stop thinking about all these things I'll never really know the answers to because it just makes my stomach feel upset again.

10

Roy

"The fuckers framed me, Nate. They tried for weeks, maybe months to catch me cheating. But I was walking the straight and narrow. Had nothing going on the side. They got tired of waiting. So they hired a ringer, manufactured a situation. Not only to create grounds for a divorce, but also to ensure that they'd be able to murder me financially—with the royalties. Isn't that entrapment and fraud and—you tell *me* what?"

I should have been a lawyer. But Nate is the judge here.

He's ensconced in his jumbo-size desk chair. Fingers laced over his paunch. Buddha-like. I'm waiting for him to rub his hands gleefully and tell me how we're going annihilate Addie. Pulverize her with the legal system.

"You've got nothing," Nate pronounces. "Even if you can prove they set out the bait, you didn't have to bite. So you're back where you started. The divorce agreement already is entered with the court, final decree pending, and it's—"

"Wait, wait, wait. Why can't we jump in now? Call the attention of the judge to all of Addie's manipulative crap, I bet we can improve the settlement terms! At least split the royalties."

"It's a done deal, Roy."

"But it's a phony, put-up job!" Why isn't he as outraged as I am? "It's not fair—"

I stop. He's chortling. "*Fair?* Look, laddie, it's a game. You played around, got away with it more times than you can remember. This time you got caught. You lose. Think of it as a poker game. She won the pot—okay, so she *bought* the pot. But it's hers anyway. So just calm down."

I realize the tendons in my neck are standing at attention.

"Look at it this way," Nate says. "In a way, she did you a huge favor. If she'd waited until later to play her little game, she would've been eligible to share in the giant jackpot. Your movie deal."

That's a good point. I didn't think of that. Maybe because of the ache in my gut since Kim told me how Addie ambushed me.

"You've got to stay focused, laddie. We've got much bigger fish to fry. Has anyone from Warner Brothers attempted to contact you? Since we filed our lawsuit?"

"No, nobody. Wait. Except—" I snicker, "—my answering service said Jack Warner phoned. Figured it was one of my wiseass pals."

"So you didn't return the call."

"Just told you, it's a practical joke. The Colonel has never called me directly." Jack Warner had been handed a colonel's commission during World War II and assigned to duty at the Brown Derby. But he still liked to be addressed by his rank. "Why would he phone me now?"

"To go around me. And try to negotiate directly with you. To get you to say something that will undercut our position. Which is total surrender from them—and complete freedom for you. Under no circumstances are you to have any conversations with anyone from Warners. Understood?"

"Yessir!" It's my Major against their Colonel. I'm betting on Nate.

Despite Nate's instructions, I can't let go of the thing with Addie.

Maybe it's the mountain of bullshit that I've ignored over the years. Certainly I don't need a Scanlon chortle to realize it's childish to measure matters on a standard of "That's not fair." But it galls me anyway. I've been hit below the belt.

Been hit and can't hit back. So familiar. Just like all those times in our marriage. She can slap me or kick me or try to claw me. But I've got to be a gentleman and just carefully fend her off. Have I ever been tempted to haul off and belt her one? Oh yeah. What always stopped me? I'm not my father! And a part of me knew that if I ever hit her, even once, I might not be able to stop.

Besides, in a way I figured it was my payback. No, I'm not a masochist. But I read something profound on the wall of a men's room once. Amid all those messages about, "For A Good Time Call Mitzi," someone had scrawled, "Guilt is the price you pay for doing the things you want to do." That definitely sounds like me.

Actually, Addie wasn't physical that often. Words were her favorite weapon. She got to play offense, I was always on the defense. Not quiet little jabs. Her specialty was huge vicious verbal wallops. Right off the bat. Faced with opposition or criticism of any sort, even the tiniest, she'd immediately escalate to atomic weapons. Nothing in between. Didn't have to be about me ogling another broad. Could be anything. *You don't like the color of my new shoes? Then fuck you, go take a hike! Go to Mexico and get a divorce!* These were the choices: Heads, I win, tails, I win. Life with Addie.

Now it's gagging me. Can't swallow it, can't spit it out.

I drive past the store on Rodeo Drive. Catch a glimpse of her inside, kissing up to a wealthy blue-nosed, blue-haired customer. I can go in, make a scene. Embarrass her. Get tossed out again. Be fun. But wouldn't make it better. There's only one thing that would make it better. Don't even think it! Not even to savor the idea as a hypothetical. Except sometimes it seeps into my consciousness. Briefly, before I banish the thought. What if...? What if there was no Addie...I mean, what would Jack Havoc do?

Forget it! he'd probably say. *Water under the bridge.*

Can't forget it. Keep trying. But I can't.

Listen to good advice, man, Jack'd say. *Scanlon says we got bigger fish to fry.*

Yeah, but why should she be allowed to flim-flam the court?

So what are you gonna do—sit down and cry? Tried that already!

But she's fucking me over big time and I have to smile while she gets away with it!

Uh-huh. Smart money says that's exactly what you gotta do, Roy.

Bet you could figure a way to have it both ways, couldn't you, Jack? Couldn't you?

A truck's air horn blasts in my ear. I jump. Look around. I'm on the Strip. Light's green. I'm blocking traffic. So I move forward. Notice the Hamburger Hamlet across the street.

I'm not hungry. But I might find a friendly face there.

"Did you come for the onion rings—or me?" Kim Rafferty asks.

"Well, they make awfully good onion rings, but—what time do you get off work?"

"Would you believe—" glance at the clock, 7:45 "—in fifteen minutes?"

"I think I can wait that long."

"Roy, I'm meeting a friend for a movie. At the Academy."

"Oh. Special friend?"

"My drama coach. I'd invite you along, but she can only get two of us in on her card."

"Hey, I've got an Academy card, too." But haven't gone to the screenings for years now.

"They're playing a pair of old Hitchcock pictures. What do you say?"

I'd've said yes even if it was a Troy Donohue festival. I sip an iced tea. She goes about her business. Winding up her shift. She's a pro. No wasted motion. Tuned in to who needs what. Friendly smile, but she keeps moving. This is the original Hamlet. The place is decorated in dark wood with low-key lighting like an English tavern. Framed old *Playbills* and photos on the walls of the great ones playing Hamlet:

Barrymore, Gielgud, Olivier. A thriving joint. Started by an actor named Harry Lewis, who played baby-faced gangsters for a while. Guess this is one way for an actor to make sure he knows where his next meal is coming from.

Kim's closing out her register now, taking off her apron, going into the back. I'm not sure why I'm here. Breaking my standing rule about one night only. Assuming I get lucky. She emerges from the back room looking fresh and eager. I offer my arm. She takes it.

"This almost feels like a date," she says.

We take my T-Bird for the short ride over.

The Academy of Motion Picture Arts and Sciences, yeah, the Oscar people, own a private theater to screen new and old movies for their members. You'd expect a palace, but it's an inconspicuous neighborhood theater with no marquee located on a quiet block on Melrose in West Hollywood. Carl's Market is on the corner, there's an Italian joint down the street. Most of the neighborhood is residential, small one-family houses. The theater parking lot is full, but I luck into a space on the street around the corner on Doheny. Kim and I walk together toward the entrance. We're holding hands. It's kind of nice.

The ritual in front of the theater before show time hasn't changed. Much milling around on the sidewalk. Meet and greet. See and be seen. Maybe even pick up a tip on a potential job. The editors and cameramen and other technicians usually go right inside, but the actors work the pavement. They all know each other from years of performing together. Or waiting together anxiously in outer offices to compete against each other at cattle-call auditions.

When I first came to town, a friend brought me here. It was such a kick seeing those faces I had known all my life but never met. The actors who play the bellhops and the bank clerks, the doormen and the taxi drivers, the gum-chewing telephone operators and the sexy stenographers, the flatfoot cops and the bent-nose crooks. That's who turns out for the screenings. The character actors. The bit players. A star may make twenty or thirty movies during a career. These people have been in maybe three hundred pictures, usually for just a scene or two. Outside the trade, hardly anyone knows their names. Some are regulars with certain directors, comprising a virtual stock company for the likes of John Ford, Frank Capra, William Wellman, or Preston Sturges in the old days. Most just scramble for a living.

I look around the crowd and spot some supporting players. They're the ones who play parts that have names, rather than just "Fireman #2." And there's also a smattering of used-to-be or almost-were stars. Dressed in California casual. Quite a number of ascots and Gucci scarves to cover turkey necks. Lots of laughing. It's a weekly family reunion.

Kim introduces me to her elderly acting coach, who looks and sounds like Maria Ouspenskaya. "Vee study toget'er in Muscow," she tells me, "Maria and I. Everyone t'ought vee are sisters." I feel stares on the back of my neck. Several actors who've been on my show ease over to say hello. It doesn't feel like the old days now. I'm not one of them, I'm one of those who can hire them. The hunger is palpable. *Remember me?* Hoping this glancing social contact may turn into work. *Remember me!* Even if it's just for a day's work. I recall why I stopped coming to these screenings.

The autograph collectors lurk on the fringes and case the crowd. Delighting those they ask to sign their albums or pose for a picture. Making them the envy of the others. I see Reva standing at the curb, watching me. On a whim, I gesture her over. Introduce her to Kim and her acting coach.

"You're so pretty," Reva blurts to Kim, who blushes.

"She's an actress," I tell Reva.

"Oh, then can I have your autograph?"

Kim shrugs. Starts to sign.

"Could you write, 'To Reva,' with something nice, like 'best wishes'?"

Kim writes what she's told. Self-conscious. Because other actors are nudging each other and asking who she is. Kim thanks Reva, who asks if she can snap a picture of Kim with me. Kim waits for my response. Which is to put my arm around her waist and smile for the camera. *Flash!* More people stare curiously at us. Reva hopes we'll enjoy the movies. She disappears into the crowd.

"What a sweet girl."

"She's *my* fan, find your own." Kim laughs. So I go on. "Reva shines my halo, remembers my birthday, empties my ashtrays—" Kim's eyebrows go up. "Really. If I toss a gum wrapper on the sidewalk or leave butts in my car's ashtray, she scoops 'em up and takes 'em home."

"Doesn't sound very sanitary."

"Hygiene versus Passion? No contest."

The marquee lights are flashing. We go inside and find seats on the right side, fairly close. There's a ten-foot figure of Oscar up front next to the exit sign. "I went to a masquerade party," I whisper in Kim's ear, "and Burt Lancaster came as Oscar—with his head shaved, wearing only a jockstrap, and spray-painted from head to toe with gold paint."

She thinks I'm just making it up. The lights dim. Hitchcock time. *The Lady Vanishes* and *The Thirty-Nine Steps*. The master's lifelong theme already in place: an ordinary man placed in extraordinary circumstances. He must rise to the challenge or perish. Eventually, Hitchcock went so far down that road that his heroes became homicidal maniacs. From *Foreign Correspondent* to *Strangers on a Train*. Message there perhaps. The flip side of courage is madness? Where's the line of separation? Is Jack Havoc a hero just because he does what he does in the name of right and justice? Or do audiences love him simply because he can get away with it?

When the movies are over, we follow the crowd into the lobby and then out to the sidewalk again. A lot of standing around and discussing what we've just seen. Those that have worked with Hitchcock calling him Hitch. Much agreement: "They don't make 'em like that anymore." Yawn. I nudge Kim and raise my eyebrows. She nods, says goodnight to her coach, who is in deep conversation with *landsmen* Michael Chekhov and Leonid Kinsky. We stop at Carl's Market, pick up coffee, half-and-half, a quart of mocha ice cream. A half hour later we're at her place and in each other's arms. While the ice cream melts.

"Know what we are?" I light a Lucky.

"Hmmm?" She's lying beside me. Half dozing.

"A Meet Cute. That's us. It's how Boy Meets Girl. In the movies."

She props herself up on an elbow. "For instance."

"Department store. Claudette Colbert is at a counter. Telling a salesclerk she wants to buy a pair of pajamas—tops only. On the other side of the counter is Gary Cooper, who also wants to buy a pair of pajamas—bottoms only. That's how they meet."

"Cute. But we're cuter." She nuzzles my neck. "Tell me something about you that I don't know."

I take a drag on my Lucky and blow a smoke ring at the ceiling. "What can I tell you? You know everything. You took 'Roy Darnell 101' and passed with honors."

See, it's a weird situation. Although we're virtually strangers, she's been thoroughly briefed on me. Not to mention the backgrounding on Kim that Killer did for me. So we both know too much and too little. We're feeling our way. Being in bed in her cozy apartment after having made spectacular love makes it easier.

"What makes this a *bachelorette* apartment?" I ask.

"It's got a hot plate and a bidet. And don't change the subject."

"You go first. Who are you really?"

So she tells me. I listen, don't interrupt.

Mother died in childbirth. Father unknown. Senile grandmother in Glendale facility her only relative. Foster child. Lived in six different homes in eighteen years. From Eagle Rock to Alhambra. Molested at age eight by landlord. No one believed her. Raped at fourteen by foster father. Foster mother blamed her. Favorite writer: Charles Dickens. "Made me feel better to find out some people had it worse." Swiped candy bars from the supermarket and sold them door-to-door. Made money playing clown at kid parties. Drum majorette. Amateur magician. "Good with my hands—guess you know that, though." New York Yankees fan. "They never whine." On her own at fifteen. Usherette at Pasadena Playhouse. Got to understudy featured role in *Junior Miss*. Went on twice. Arrested for stealing cosmetics from Thrifty Drugstore. Suspended sentence. Bicycle rider, ice skater, good dancer. "Strong legs." Loves being whistled at. Terrified of being crippled. Can't swim. Breaks out if she eats strawberries. Loves chopped liver. Used to be a waitress at Canter's Deli on Fairfax. "They make the best chopped liver." Thinks the Marx Brothers were funnier than Martin and Lewis. Lived at the Studio Club. Had Marilyn Monroe's old room. Thinks Elvis is better than Sinatra. Hates trumpet players. Loves acting. Scared she's not very good.

"And that's the story of my life—so far. Your turn now."

"Well, of course, most of what you know about me is high-grade bullshit. Concocted by the studio with the helpful collusion of the media. It's called the Star Making Machine."

"Okay, then tell me a good lie."

"Good lie, huh? Let's see." Another Lucky drag. Another smoke ring. "Okay. Got one for you. Quote. Roy Darnell, better known as two-fisted Jack Havoc, was a juvenile gang warrior on the streets of Philadelphia—"

She finishes the rest, "—until Roy was arrested and reformed by a sympathetic police sergeant. Unquote. That's in a lot of the news clips. Not true?"

"I was never a gang kid. And I never got arrested. See, after my dad died, his ex-bookmaking partner hired me to hang around his candy store, sweep up, work the counter—and if the cops raided him, my job was to chew and swallow the betting slips. One day this Philly plainclothes detective comes in, he's huddling with my boss. Suddenly, my boss yells, 'Now, Roy, *now!*' So I start gobbling up the slips. The detective knocks the slips out of my hand—and laughs himself silly. I didn't know it was a gag 'til then. 'I'm gonna arrest you, y'little punk,' he cackles, 'for eating evidence.' But he was only trying to scare me."

"That's a good above-the-belt story," she says.

"What's that's supposed to mean?"

"Above-the-belt—where it doesn't hurt. Got any below-the-belt stories? Something you never told anyone else."

I think for a minute. Can I trust her? I decide to risk it. I tell her about my wonderful home life as a kid, how Daddy'd come home shit-faced mean drunk and start beating on my mother, really letting loose like he's Joe Louis punching for dollars, and when I would jump in to help her, even though I was just a little kid, he'd turn on me—"and the funny part was then she'd always join in on *his* side, my mother, just glad to get him off *her* case, I guess, so then they'd both be whacking me, the parents that flay together stay together, and…and it always ended the same way." I stop talking. Rub my eyes with my fingers. Rub hard. But I can still see how it was.

"How?" Kim asks. Softly. Like the dentist does when he knows he's hit the nerve. "How would it end?"

"In the empty lot. Out behind the house. The refrigerator." The words lurch out of me. Still burning. Even after all these years. "This old refrigerator. Dumped. Abandoned. Dad would lock me inside. Punishment. Leave me there. I'd be so scared. Nobody to protect me. That's when I first heard the voice."

"The voice of who?"

"He didn't have a name. He wasn't real. I mean, he was real to me. My friend. My only friend. I could hear him. Inside the refrigerator. Inside me. 'Sit very still,' he'd say. 'Try not to breathe hard, you'll use up the air too fast. Nice and still. Don't worry, Dad'll come back and let you out. Or maybe Mom.' We'd be alone in there. My guardian angel and me. Sometimes, by…by the time one of them finally came and opened the door, there was hardly any air left, I'd be…gasping, but…"

I stop talking again. Take a deep, deep breath. "That's a story I never told before."

She's looking at me. Like she wants to cry.

I kiss her gently. We cling to each other as if there's a hurricane roaring outside the window. But we're temporarily safe from the storm.

11

Roy

It's fight night at the Olympic Auditorium in downtown L.A. Another Hollywood tradition. George Raft and Bugsy Siegel used to have ringside seats. Now Killer and I do. We haven't been here in a while, but it's part of my new high profile. Stay in the public eye while suing the studio. Killer arranges with some of his pals to have the tuxedoed announcer introduce me before the fights start as one of the celebrities in the house. I'm called right after Art Aragon. "Ladies and gentlemen, from Hollywood, weighing one hundred seventy pounds, Jack Havoc in person—Mr. Roy Darnell." I clamber up into the ring, feint a punch or two with Aragon, and then clasp my hands and raise them triumphantly over my head. Good round of applause.

The crowd is boisterous tonight. A pair of bantamweights, an Inglewood Negro vs. a Boyle Heights Mexican, are mixing it up in the ring for the opening bout. Killer and I are pounding beers and screaming at the fighters. The Mexican takes it by a TKO. A popular decision. It's their turn now in the winner's spotlight, the Mexicans. Just like the Jews and the Italians and the Negroes had theirs. The hungriest guys on the block are always the ones to bet on.

The beer is starting to work, so I head for the men's room. Not too crowded, and the P.A. system announces the start of the main event, which empties the john even more. I step up to drain my lily, as the stuntmen say. I'm pissing up a storm when I become aware of the guy at work in the adjoining urinal. Balding with strands of dyed black hair plastered across his scalp, a pencil mustache, wearing a garish sports jacket and a glazed smile. It's Jack L. Warner himself. He glances over at me.

"Hey, how'sitgoin', kid?" he slurs. Half-lit as usual after dark.

"Goin' fine, Colonel." Should've remembered he likes the fights.

"Guess this is where you been hidin' out. In the crapper. Left messages everywhere else." He glares over at me. Causing his aim to wander. Enough for a few drops of piss to hit the toe of his spit-polished shoe. He notices and shakes his leg. Vigorously.

"Jack be nimble," I say. My fucking sense of humor.

Zipping up, Warner suddenly grins wolfishly.

"Jack be quick," he says. Fists up, he starts to spar with me. Now he clinches, lightly pounding my kidneys. "Had enough, had enough, had enough?" He pushes free, dances on his toes and beams his toothsome Douglas Fairbanks smile at me. Sounds of applause and bell ringing in the distance. "You're all right, Jack," he says. Hears himself, laughs. "Get it? I'm all right, Jack. You're all right, Jack."

He loves the fact that he and Jack Havoc have the same first name.

Especially once the show was a hit.

"Y'hear the one about the rabbi, the priest, and the minister, they get on a plane, and—" Warner is famous throughout Hollywood as an enthusiastic but semi-coherent storyteller "—wait, better one, hear about Johnnie? I gave him all his big breaks, Mr. John Fucking Oscar Winner Huston, favor to his old man I let the kid write some scripts, who knew if he could even write, then I made him a director, let him shoot that depressing piece of shit, *Treasure of the Sierra Madre,* didn't think I'd ever get my money out of that one, Bogart walking around looking like an unwashed armpit. Where am I?"

Standing at the washstand. Rearranging his meager strands of hair. I'm rinsing my hands a couple of basins away. We're alone in the rest room now. The Colonel watches my reflection in the mirror. He rambles on.

"Oh, yeah, John. True story, y'know how he is about the ponies, lost a fortune last year alone at Del Mar. But he gets this hot tip, so he phones what'shername, Evelyn—" Huston's wife, Evelyn Keyes "—and he says, 'Honey, I can't get away from the set, but go upstairs to the bedroom closet, top shelf, little metal box in back, twenty grand in cash. Take it all and drive to Al the bookie, bet everything on this horse to win. Gotta hurry, baby, it's important.' Evelyn gets the money off the shelf, but she can't stand to see John lose more money on a horse race, so she puts the cash back up in the closet. True story, no joke. She listens to the race on the radio and, God help her, John's horse comes in first by a nose. John comes sailing home, in the door, Evelyn's waiting, looks like the vampires got her, all white and scared, 'John, I gotta tell you, I didn't place the bet.' He doesn't blink, just says, 'What's for dinner, honey?' She can't believe it. Whips up dinner, John's telling her about the terrific practical joke he played on the cameraman. Never a word about the horse race. They sit down to eat, and she can't hold it in. 'John, the reason I didn't place the bet is—' And he leans over and belts her. Knocks her right out of her chair. 'You never should've tried to explain.'"

He laughs, pounds my shoulder with his hand. Maybe he isn't that drunk.

"Great story, huh? Let's you and me be like that. Ducking my calls. Made you a fuckin' star. Tryin' to break contract. Thanks I get. But, hey—" he holds up his hand, palm out "—hey, forget it. *Don't try to explain!* Just tell me— bottom line. What do you want?"

"Colonel, all I want is—out."

"I know, I know, court papers, all that bullshit, wanna be a movie star, right? Okay, listen, we cancelled the Wyatt Earp picture. Hal Wallis, that momser, he's doing one with Burt and Kirk. So—how 'bout this? You're Machine Gun Kelly! Get to slaughter half the world. We're all set to shoot. How's that sound?"

"Like another 'B' picture."

"'B'-*plus*," he flares. "I don't make 'B' pictures. Look, gotta start somewhere, that indie picture you did last year, a bomb, so you do this one, let me make a few bucks, gangster pictures can't miss, Cagney, Bogart, Garfield, then next year, after you finish all the TV episodes for which I'm gonna give you a little salary sweetener right now, but next year I'll have an 'A' picture waitin' for you. Better'n *Casablanca*. Whaddayasay?"

This, of course, is precisely the conversation Nate Scanlon didn't want me to have. I shrug. "You'll have to discuss that with Nate or Val Dalton."

"Fuck them, I'm discussing with you, man-to-man."

Deep breath. Okay. "I want out."

Jekyll into Hyde. His face goes crimson. Vein pulsing in his temple. Suppose he keels over. Do mouth-to-mouth resuscitation on Jack Warner? Hey. Look. He's trying for a smile. Still beet-red, but flashing the full set of choppers.

"Be careful what you wish for, kiddo. You might wind up crying."

He punches me lightly on the arm and struts off. I can hear the crowd yelling in the arena. Jack Havoc wouldn't have let it drop there. Ending on that turd threatening me. He'd have had the last line.

Don't sweat it, Colonel, I'll be laughing all the way to the bank and waving an Oscar in each hand.

Yeah, right. That's what I should've said.

As I wend my way back to my seat the contender is battering the champ. Maybe there's going to be a new champion. Killer looks up as I slip in beside him.

"Where the hell y'been? Almost missed the main event."

"Uh-uh. The main event was just fought in the men's room."

"Who won?"

"Judges haven't decided yet."

After the fights, I go straight home and put in a call to Nate. To both his office and home numbers. Ring-ring-ring.

And then the answering service. Same service covers both places. I say it's urgent. The operator says she's very sorry, Mr. Darnell, but Mr. Scanlon can't be reached. He's on the road, driving back from Tahoe.

I have a hard time falling asleep. Then I oversleep. Wake up frazzled. Phone's ringing. "Yeah?" It's Nate. I launch into a recitation of my run-in with the Colonel. "I don't know what he's going to try next, but I bet it's going to be something real cute."

"Did you threaten him with bodily harm?"

"No! Who said—"

"I just got off the phone. Bautzer called me." Greg Bautzer is the powerhouse lawyer defending Warners in the lawsuit. "They've folded."

"What?"

"Thrown in the towel. Warners is giving you your release. We don't have to go to court. We don't have to do anything except celebrate. Didn't I tell you I'd get you out?" Not a chortle. A full-bodied bellowing laugh of triumph.

I'm stunned. The war is over? Just like that? One shot across their bow and it's time for dancing in the streets?

"Bautzer asked me to relay a personal message to you from Jack Warner. I jotted it down. 'Lots of luck, Jack Havoc. There's always a home for you here at Warners.' Kind of nice and generous of him, don't you think?"

I'm not so sure. I am delighted, but uneasy. I can't bring myself to interrupt Nate Scanlon's enthusiasm, but surrender wasn't what I saw in Jack Warner's eyes when he walked off last night.

In just a few days, Jack Warner and the status of my career will be the least of my worries. All I know tonight is that I feel the start of one of my migraines. Haven't had one of those in months. Hoped they were a thing of the past. But I dig a darvon out of the back of the medicine chest, wash it down with some tequila.

12

Reva

My least-favorite scene in my most-favorite movie, which is, of course, *A Place In The Sun,* is when Shelley Winters goes to see this sleazy doctor because Monty Clift has knocked her up, and Monty stays slouched out in the car smoking while Shelley goes in alone to see if the doctor will perform an abortion. She doesn't say that right out loud, because the censors won't let her, and besides she's ashamed that she's not married, but the doctor and the audience understand what she's asking for. The doctor turns her down. "I can't help you," he says. He says it twice.

The reason I particularly dislike the scene is because it makes me sorry for Shelley Winters and I don't want to feel sorry for her, because Monty and Liz Taylor are clearly meant for each other and Shelley's out to ruin everything, which she ultimately does, but she has to die in order to do it. In her own way, of course, Shelley loved him, too, but a lot of good that did Monty.

So that's what's running through my mind as I'm sitting here in the waiting room of this medical office on Wilshire near Fairfax. My mother works as a teller in a bank just a few blocks away. She'd flip if she knew where I am and why.

I'm late.

First time. I've never been late. I'm like clockwork.

I never even made the connection with the puking. Until I accused Podolsky of wrecking me with his passion for anchovies, and he listened and said, "Sounds like morning sickness."

I've been terrified ever since, because I think maybe he's right.

"There's a ninety-eight-year-old woman in Tibet who just gave birth to triplets," Podolsky says. He's sitting beside me in the waiting room reading a copy of *National Geographic* he found here. I don't know this doctor I'm about to see; his name is Irving Berman, and Podolsky knows him from when he had the flu and someone at work recommended Dr. Berman. Podolsky says he's a nice man. We'll see.

The inner door opens and the nurse comes out. She leads me into an examination room. "The doctor will be right with you." She has the information sheet I've just filled out and she clips it into a folder and hangs the folder on the outside of the door. She closes the door as she leaves. I don't know where to sit. There's an exam table covered with white paper and a chair next to the counter with the sink. I decide to lean against the exam table. There's a knock on the door, and here's the doctor. He's a smallish guy with salt-and-pepper curly hair and a shaggy mustache, he looks sort of like Sam Levene, the character actor. Dr. Berman is carrying the folder, he tosses it on the counter and leans against the counter, real informal. We're eye to eye.

"So you're a friend of Barry's," he says.

For a second I forget that's Podolsky's first name, then I nod, in fact, I bob my head. I want Dr. Berman to like me. I want him to help me. I don't even know for sure if I need help, or what kind, but I'm grinning like a goof.

"You nervous?" he asks.

I nod.

"What do you think's wrong?"

"I think maybe—I'm pregnant."

"It's going around," he says. "And Barry's your young man?"

I laugh. It's more like a sputter. I'm sorry right away. "Don't tell him I laughed," I say, "he's my real good friend. But he's not, I mean, we didn't…"

Dr. Berman shrugs. "Okay. We don't have to go into that now."

"Well, I just want to be careful, because there's someone very well-known who's involved, and I definitely don't want to cause him any, you know, unnecessary embarrassment."

"Let's concentrate on you," he says.

He begins the examination, very gently, and I find myself stretched out on the table, looking up at the ceiling, remembering how I got here.

There are some things that are glamorous in the movies but very disappointing in real life. The Hollywood Bowl isn't one of them. I first saw the place from a front row seat in the Biltmore Theater in Brooklyn, staring up at Frank Sinatra and Gene Kelly on the screen doing scenes at the Bowl with pianist Jose Iturbi in *Anchors Aweigh.* Now, on a balmy summer night in the summer of 1955, I'm really here and it's as good as a movie even though Podolsky and I are in the cheap seats way up close to heaven.

I've only recently arrived in L.A. Mother and I made the move right after my father died in the Naval Hospital on Staten Island. Podolsky came out to the Coast several months ago but already looks like a native with a Cary Grant tan, sunglasses worn day and night, indoors and outdoors, and loose-fitting, untucked Hawaiian shirts under which his autograph book can be easily concealed and quickly drawn when he sees stars.

Tonight is Tchaikovsky Night at the Bowl. The big event at the end of the evening is the *1812 Overture* culminating in cannon explosions and dazzling fireworks. But the program begins with Roy Darnell, formerly radio's Man of a Thousand Voices, now TV's Jack Havoc, narrating *Peter and the Wolf,* so you know why I schlepped Podolsky here.

It's a special occasion: today is Roy's birthday. I haven't seen Roy since I got to L.A., we've been too busy finding an apartment, a job for Mother, a couple of part-time jobs for me and although I've made contact with the local collector community via Podolsky, who has his own job at Wallich's Music City at Sunset and Vine, I haven't been out yet to Warner Brothers Studio in Burbank where they shoot *Jack Havoc*.

The Bowl is filled to capacity and I don't know exactly how I'm going to get to Roy to give him his gift—before we left New York, I bought him a necktie at Sulka's that I once saw him admiring in the window—but collectors are nothing if not resourceful.

"We'll improvise," I tell Podolsky.

"And if all else fails—you can always give me the necktie."

Up here in the bleachers, the music lovers are munching on hot dogs and popcorn and sipping sodas from the vending stands. Way down close, separated from the stage by an illuminated water-filled lagoon, there are rows of cozy, upholstered box seats. The elegant folk there are eating box dinners (what else) of cold chicken and Caesar salad accompanied by white wine (the menus are posted near the Bowl entrance).

"That's where they'll be," I tell Podolsky. "I bet Addie's there right now."

The house lights dim and the lights on the stage grow brighter as the orchestra takes its place and the conductor, Carmen Dragon, is applauded as he comes to the podium. "Ladies and gentleman," a voice on the P.A. system announces, "Mr. Roy Darnell."

Roy walks out of the wings and steps behind a small lectern at the side of the stage. From the heights where Podolsky and I are sitting, he looks about five inches tall, but I can recognize his distinctive walk.

The music begins and Roy's voice—voices, really—delights the audience in the enormous outdoor amphitheater. He's Peter and the wolf and the Cossacks and all the forest creatures. It reminds me of the good old days at *Let's Pretend*. When the various instruments finally come together for the big finish, there's a wave of appreciative applause and then the house lights brighten again for intermission.

"Let's go," I say to Podolsky, and we're off. The crowd's looking for refreshments and rest rooms. We're looking for stars. There are ushers at the lower level to guard the box seats from intruders, but there are so many bodies moving around in a confined area that it's easy to slip past them. We stroll along nonchalantly, scanning the box seats, and Podolsky spots Gregory Peck and his wife chatting with Claudette Colbert and her husband. After that I catch sight of Addie and a couple of other chic people standing outside a front tier box. Then I see Roy coming toward us in the center aisle, shaking hands and accepting congratulations. I'm so excited that I shriek, "Roy!" and start rushing toward him. I get pretty close before a powerful hand grabs my arm and yanks me to a halt. I stare up at this guy I've never seen before. He's got bulgy eyes and a mean mouth and he looks like Elisha Cook Jr. from the neck up and Charles Atlas from the neck down. He's squeezing my arm so hard my eyes are tearing.

"Hey, Killer, don't kill her!" Roy calls to the guy. "She's a friend."

The guy eases his grip. But I'm already ignoring him as Roy reaches me and kisses me, yes, kisses me on the cheek. "Reva, where'd you come from? You're supposed to be in New York."

"Yeah, well, I moved out here," I say.

"Permanently?"

I nod.

"In order to be near me, I bet," he says. "Kenny, this is Reva, my first and foremost fan. This is Killer Lomax."

We shake hands. It's like putting my hand in a bear's paw, but this time the bear is gentle. "Pleased to meet you, Killer."

Then I wish Roy happy birthday and give him the gift box and he unwraps it right there and he likes the tie, says it's just his taste, and I say, "I know," and he says, "You know everything about me." The thing is he looks the same as before but he also looks different. What's different is that there's an aura emanating from him. Maybe it has to do with gaining success and recognition, but since then I've noticed it in a number of other cases. Take Charlie Bronson, who was a lowly paid character actor bopping around town unnoticed for years, but then he went to Europe and became a star, and after he returned to Hollywood I saw him one day on an escalator going up at Bullock's department store in Westwood and just by looking at his back, before you could even see his face, you knew it was Somebody. A Star. Well, that's what's happened to Roy since I saw him last.

Two little boys have come running up to Roy to get him to autograph their programs. Pretty soon there are some young girls swarming around him, too, squealing and holding out their programs. The days when I had to ask Roy to sign in order to attract attention to him are clearly over. "I love *Jack Havoc*," one of the girls is gushing. Killer Lomax is standing beside me, carefully watching the fans surrounding Roy.

"Sorry if I scared you," he says. "But you shouldn't oughta run at people like that."

"You're Roy's bodyguard?"

"Me?" He doesn't look threatening when he smiles. "Nah, I'm just his pal. We go way back. And look at him now..."

In New York, the Secret Six made it a policy to cultivate good relations with the support troops who surround the stars. The studio publicists, the limo drivers, the doormen and parking valets at the best hotels, theaters and restaurants—they all could provide much-needed info. I brought that idea to California with me. So, of course, I make it a particular point now to schmooze whenever possible with Killer Lomax, the new gateway to Roy's activities.

At first it's just basic meat-and-potatoes stuff. "Howyadoin'? When's Roy coming out?" But as we see each other more and more over the months at various spots where we both have to hang out and wait for Roy it gets to be more sociable. I'm fascinated by what Killer can tell me about Roy as a boy. How they used to swipe Baby Ruth bars from the candy store. "I'd stand chickee—" that meant being the lookout "—but Roy always took the risk snatchin' the merchandise. If we got nabbed, he'd usually sweet talk us out of it. If he couldn't, we'd run like hell. He was fast on his feet even then, Roy."

I like to listen to him talk. His Philly accent is a lot like my own New York accent, even though he says some words funny, such as "gaz" (instead of "gas") and "attee-tude" (instead of "attitude"). He enjoys sounding like a gangster. Maybe because in a minor way he is one.

"Call me Kenny," he sometimes says, but I prefer "Killer." It seems much more exciting and a guarantee that despite the increasing crowds that mob Roy during public appearances, Killer will keep Roy safe. Killer also functions as Roy's stand-in, which is puzzling because he doesn't look at all like him. But Podolsky, who has become very knowledgeable about movie-making techniques, explains that away. "All they need is a body, a hulk, to stand there while the lights are being set."

Killer is also Roy's stuntman, drinking partner, and social arranger. "He wrangles for Roy," Podolsky says one day while we're noshing on corned beef sandwiches at Canter's Deli on Fairfax. There are horse wranglers, dog wranglers, camel wranglers, whatever type of specialty wrangler is required on the set. "Killer Lomax," Podolsky insists, "is Roy Darnell's chippie wrangler. He rounds 'em up, moves 'em in, and moves 'em out. Gee-haw!"

I'm pissed at Podolsky for saying that, but I know it's true. Since I've been in Hollywood, I've become aware that Roy is still being unfaithful to Addie. I've seen a threesome go into Chasen's—Roy plus Killer, who's wearing a gorgeous starlet on his arm. But later on, when they come back out to the parking lot, it's Killer's job to get the car while a tipsy Roy smooches the starlet in the shadows.

When I delicately broach the subject with Killer, he's bluntly honest. "It's that bitch Addie. If she was more of a wife to him, Roy'd be home shackin' up with her instead of doin' the town with me."

"Well, I hope Roy and Addie work out whatever it is before Hedda or Louella pick up on it."

"Shhh! It's our secret to keep, sis."

That's what he calls me, "sis." Like little sister. I'm proud he trusts me.

Then an even more pressing problem develops. Roy is drinking too much, and he's a belligerent drunk. Fist fights with photographers have made him a front page figure. Roy the Bad Boy. "When he gets a snootful, he thinks he's really Jack Havoc," Killer confides to me. "Lately that's my number one chore, keeping him out of trouble."

"How do you do that?"

"Well, I've tried talkin' 'til I'm blue in the face, but when he's blitzed he don't hear nothin'. So now I got a new technique. Bull by the horns, y'know?"

"No, whaddaya mean?"

"I tried it last night, outside Mocambo's. We walk out at one ayem into an ambush. A photographer's baiting Roy, calling him a motherfuckin' fairy, tryin' to get him to swing, while his buddy is ready and waitin' to get the fight pictures. And start the lawsuit. So...I just took Roy away from it all."

"But—how?"

"Just grabbed him from behind, wrapped my arms around him like a straitjacket, lifted him off the ground, and carried him into the car, kicking and screaming. He cussed me out last night, but he thanked me in the morning."

"You ever get there too late?"

He frowns, then shrugs, like there's something he doesn't want to mention. "Now and then. So I just jump in and— tidy up after him. Best I can."

The more I talk to Killer, the nicer he seems. He's had a hard life, growing up on the wrong side of the tracks. "Sis, it's a wonder I'm not in jail," he says to me one chilly evening when I've snuck onto the Warners back lot to watch the night shooting for an episode of *Jack Havoc*.

We're supposed to be in Paris, but actually we're on the cobblestoned European street, dressed up with French signs. It's a block away from the New York street and around the corner from the Western street. From where we're standing among the cables and cameras, our teeth chattering as the Burbank mist settles in over Paris, we can see Roy and Anne Francis, his co-star for this episode, come out of the French bistro and walk up the street. Anne Francis is playing the daughter of a CIA agent who's been murdered and she's trying to find out whodunit. Jack Havoc is helping her. They flirt a little and chat about the case a lot as they stroll along and at the corner there's an old woman selling flowers, and as she offers one to Anne Francis, a shot is fired from the rooftop across the street that's intended for Anne Francis but it gets the old lady instead and Jack Havoc pulls out his gun and goes into action. He shoots the gunman off the roof and the gunman, who's a stuntman, falls down into the gutter.

That's the scene. I know, I know, we've all seen it a million times, but the director is trying to make it interesting by doing it all in one long uninterrupted dolly shot. The problem is that every time they try it, something goes wrong in the middle or tantalizingly close to the end. This time the old woman is killed on cue, but she bumps into Jack Havoc in her death fall and he misfires at the wall. The eager stuntman hears the shot and jumps off the roof anyway. It's a mess. "One more time," the director yells through his bullhorn.

"They're gonna be doin' this shot all night," Killer whispers to me. "C'mon, let's get some coffee. I'm turnin' into a friggin' icicle."

He leads me to the catering truck, where we get steaming coffee and then up onto the prop truck, where the propman pours double shots of cognac into our coffee to really warm it up. No one challenges me because I'm with Killer. From the tailgate of the truck we watch them blow another take.

"Let's go inside Roy's trailer for a couple minutes, warm up a little."

I've never been inside Roy's trailer before. It's strictly a guy's place, a table set up with cards and poker chips, dirty dishes in the sink, some of Roy's street clothes tossed around, a couple of small comfortable club chairs, a couch that's got bedroom pillows on it at one end under a goose-neck lamp; I guess that's where Roy stretches out and studies his lines. There's a framed poster of Roy as Jack Havoc hanging on the wall facing the couch.

Killer laughs as he watches me taking it all in. "You look like you just stepped into a cathedral." He gestures at the couch. "Siddown, sis."

I do. I can breathe Roy's scent in here. It's very musky and intimate. Killer is at the cabinet over the refrigerator getting a new carton of Lucky Strikes. He pops out a fresh pack, tears it open, offers me one. I shake my head.

"Don't smoke? Good. Don't start. It's a filthy habit." He picks up a gold lighter from the poker table and lights his cigarette. Then he shows me the inscription on the lighter, "Here's looking at you, kid. Love, Bogie and Betty."

"This is the house that Bogart built," Killer says. "Bogie opened all the doors for Roy."

"But Roy was ready," I say.

"Ready, willing, and able," Killer agrees. He slips Roy's lighter into his pocket. He notices that I noticed. "Hey. What's mine is his and vice versa. We're brothers. Besides, I have to be ready—for when he needs a light." He plops down on the couch next to me, leans back. "Know what the secret of success in Hollywood is?"

"Having a lot of talent—and a good agent?"

He laughs. "Not bad. Those things are important, but the real secret is not givin' a shit. If you let 'em know you do, that's when they screw you. They can smell the fear when you really want something. They want you scared. 'Cuz then they got ya." He points at the poster on the wall. "That's how Roy was when he came to town—didn't give a shit. Strong. Now I think they're startin' to get to him."

"Can you help him?"

"Any way I can, sis. He's the one and only. I know you, of all people, can dig that."

"Of course." I'm flattered. It's like I'm part of the inner circle.

"We've got that in common. Among other things."

His face is close to mine and he kisses me, not in a very brotherly fashion. His face is bristly and he smells of cigarettes and booze, and he pushes me down flat onto the couch and before I know it he's on top of me and we're clinching and he's telling me what a terrific person I am and he's got his pants off and so do I and so on and so forth until we're naked, except he still has his shoes and socks on and he's telling me "C'mon, baby, give it to me," and we're doing it, really doing it, his face buried in my hair and I'm looking up at the poster of Roy on the wall, so maybe I'm doing what Charming Billy did that time, only it's not Monty Clift I'm imagining I'm with, but it doesn't take all that long, either. I feel a little pain because it's my first time, and you're supposed to, I guess, and then he grunts and there's stickiness in my crotch that I'm not sure if it's blood or semen or both. Then he's climbing off me and tells me, "The can is down there," and I go to this tiny bathroom and clean myself up and now I guess I'm really a woman, but I really don't feel that much different.

And that was it. Truly wham-bam-thank-you-ma'am. But without the thank-you-ma'am part. The end of my five-minute love affair.

But maybe not quite the end.

"What did you think of him?" Podolsky asks as we wait in the empty corridor for the elevator.

"The doctor? You were right, he's very nice."

"So what'd he say?"

"He said I'm healthy, and maybe I'm pregnant, in which case he'd be glad to provide prenatal care, but that's it, 'cuz abortions are illegal in California, and I should try not to worry because we won't know for sure until the results of the rabbit test come back."

Podolsky gazes at me through his Jimmy Dean horn-rimmed glasses. He looks worried enough for both of us. Then the elevator dings and the door opens and we get in.

13

It's a balmy night on the edge of Beverly Hills and the klieg lights set up on the sidewalk in front of the Fox Wilshire Theater pierce the cobalt sky. It's the world premiere of *Trapeze*. There are bleachers set up for the fans. They cheer like crazy when Kim and I get out of the limo. I catch a glimpse of Reva in the front row. She's chanting my name, "ROY-ROY-ROY-Y-Y-Y!" and now the other kids pick it up. I give them a Pepsodent smile and a royal wave, blow a kiss to Reva. It's the first public appearance I'm making since Warners let me out.

"So, listen, Roy boychik," George Jessel, the emcee on the interview platform, brays into the microphone, "So you quit your job in TV. Think you could put in a good word for me?" Lapsing into heavy-duty Yiddish accent: "*Jake* Havoc— vouldn't be so bad."

I laugh. Ha-ha. "I'll tell 'em you're interested."

"Jack Warner can make it up to me for giving away my part in *The Jazz Singer* to Jolson. And who might this lovely young lady be?"

"She's too old for you, Georgie." He's been married countless times to younger and younger girls. "This is Kim Rafferty. A new actress you'll be hearing a lot about."

"Listen, Kimmy, if your talent as a thespian matches your radiant beauty, I predict a fabulous career. And if this guy gives you trouble, let me know. God love ya, Roy. Roy Darnell, everyone!"

We step down to make way for Burt Lancaster, his costar Tony Curtis, and Tony's wife Janet Leigh. Burt gives me a rib-cracking hug and whispers in my ear. Grins and pinches my cheek. Then leaps up onto the interview platform and makes the fans shriek. He looks like a Greek god making a personal appearance.

"What'd you think of all that?" I ask Kim as we proceed up the red carpet leading into the theater.

"Those fabbbbulous things George Jessel was saying about me? I thought maybe I'd died and gone to heaven and didn't know it." Jessel is best known lately for delivering heartfelt eulogies at celebrity funerals. "What did Big Burt whisper to you?"

"Thanked me for coming tonight. He said, 'Feels like you're part of the family already.'"

After the movie, there's a two-ring circus, I mean, an actual circus, set up in the parking lot. Ed Sullivan is there to tape the festivities and interview the stars. Burt and Tony do handstands for Sullivan. I schlep Kim along when I do my spot, which involves Kim's friendly elephant. After that the limo whisks us to a sound stage at a small studio in Hollywood, where a private party is in progress. Only four, five hundred guests. Still in the French circus motif. Jugglers and mimes and tumblers circulating in the crowd.

There's a lavish buffet—Kim asks why the chicken legs are so stringy and I have to tell her they're frog legs. She won't eat them once she knows. Dom Perignon champagne flows. Burt introduces me to his director, Sir Carol Reed, one of my favorites. The kind of director I dream of working for. Studio executives are treating me like I'm hot shit. And I'm delighted that Kim is there to see it all. Remember how I mentioned Cinderella when I sent Killer in search of Kim? Well, tonight is like Cinderella's Ball. But I'm playing two parts—Prince Charming and also the Fairy Godmother who makes it all happen for her.

Midnight comes a little early at this ball.

"Look who's here," Kim says.

I look where she's indicating. Rosalind Russell is talking with Jack and Mary Benny. Oh God. Behind them, near the bar, I see what Kim saw.

Addie.

She's here. At the party. Squired, as they say in the gossip columns, by Guy Saddler, her art director chum. First time I've seen her since divorce court. I nudge Burt. "Did you invite her?"

"She's Guy's guest. He worked with me at Universal when I started out." The alligator grin. "I could throw her out—or *you* could."

"Hey. Let 'em eat cake. What do I care?"

Now Addie has spotted us, too. She mutters to Guy, who glances over. Then she holds her champagne goblet up in my direction. I hoist mine in return. Like the Red Baron saluting a worthy opponent. We're both out of bullets, so we may as well be polite. Kim has turned her back so Addie, her ex-employer, won't see her face.

"Great party," Kim says. "Can we go now?"

I tell her we can't. Not for a while. This is my world, not Addie's. I belong here. She doesn't. I'm not going to let her chase me out before I'm goddamn ready to go. Which I'd like to do right now, of course, but I won't give her the satisfaction.

A minuet for four ensues. Two couples elaborately ignoring each other. Keeping lots of people between us. I'm constantly aware of her exact location. She's keeping track of where I am. We try not to get caught looking at each other. But Addie is circling and circling. Craning her neck. Trying to get a clear view of the girl I'm with. Kim does everything she can to prevent being recognized. "She'll kill me if she knows it's me." Kim holds her goblet in front of her face, dabs at her mouth with her linen napkin, casually pirouettes to constantly keep her back to Addie. Who's getting desperate. Starts to come closer. Guy restrains her. Shaking his head. She turns to hassle with him. While they're at it, Kim and I slip away from the party.

And burst out in laughter as soon as we step outside.

Clutching at each other, we howl. Uncontrollably. Staggering in the direction of the limo. "Did you see her?" I crane my neck in exaggerated imitation. Doing Addie as a spastic bird. Making Kim beg me to stop, she'll wet her pants if I don't. Which both of us find even funnier. It's been a long time since I laughed like this.

A shadow stirs just ahead of us.

Kim pauses. Startled. Are we snookered? Yes. But not by Addie.

Reva steps out. My tiny fan. "Hi, was it a good party?"

We both laugh again. Relief. "Great party, great," I gasp to Reva.

"We—we thought you were the wicked witch." Kim still laughing. Wiping the tears away from her eyes. "Reva, how'd you manage to get inside the studio?"

"Professional secret," Reva says with a wink. Perky as one of Santa's elves. Walking along with us. "Is Killer Lomax here tonight, too?"

"I gave him the night off."

She shrugs. "Can I take a picture of you two?"

"Already got one," I tease. "From the last time."

"But not all dressed up like this." She backpedals out in front of us. "Only take a second. Just keep walking toward me."

We do. She snaps. Camera flashes. And we hear:

"It *is* you—you treacherous twat!" The dulcet tones of my almost-ex-wife. She's bearing down on us like a battleship. Guy Saddler's trying to catch up to her. He grabs her sleeve, she shakes him off. Confronts Kim, pointing an accusatory finger. "I'm going to sue your filthy little ass off!"

I intercede. Protective. "For going to a party with me?"

"Let me tell you a thing or two about your little playmate here, she's—"

I cut Addie off. "You don't have to tell me anything."

Addie looks glazed for an instant. Stares at me, then at

Kim, then she's got it. Lewd, nasty smile. "So *that's* how it is." Targeting Kim again: "I paid you to *fuck* him—not to *date* him!"

Kim shrugs. "That was then. This is now. I'm on my own time."

"Aha! This explains everything! A plot against me. The two of you! In cahoots! Conspiracy to defraud!"

"What the hell are you talking about?"

"Think I'm a fool? So clever. You sneaky sonuvabitch!" Ranting. Wild eyed. "Tricking me into filing suit for divorce so you could screw me out of a fortune!"

"Huh?" I turn to Saddler. "Better get her out of here, Guy."

"Admit it, admit it!" Addie yells.

"Sweetie, you already got all the fortune I have."

"But not what you're *going* to have! You knew you were about to break your TV contract. Now there's no limit to how much you'll make—and that money should've been mine!"

She's getting too close to the truth. I go on the attack. "Yeah, that's what I did! I *forced* you to file for divorce, I *tricked* you into faking evidence against me, *twisted* your arm to take my royalties and everything else in sight—remember how much that dress you're wearing cost me at Coco Fuckin' Chanel's salon in Paris? And those diamond earrings, ten thousand, right there. Made you keep those! I sure am sneaky."

"You're not going to get away with it! Neither of you! I'll see you both in jail."

"Addie, you take any of this garbage to court and the judge will have you fitted for a straitjacket. You already made your deal. Now you gotta live with it. We both do."

She stops ranting. Stares at me. Knows I'm right. Hates that it's so.

"I hope," she says in a hushed voice, "that you never have a moment of happiness." She's putting a curse on me. It hurts. I won't tell you it doesn't. Kim takes hold of my hand. Squeezes.

"Addie," she says, "why don't you get on your broomstick and go take a flying leap?"

Interceding for *me*. Protective.

Kim holds up our hands, fingers interlaced. "Finders keepers," she says to Addie, "losers weepers."

"Tramp," Addie says to her. Pivots on her heel, stalks away. Guy Saddler trailing.

I hear a small voice behind me. "How could she say those awful things to you?"

It's Reva. Forgot she was there. She looks shaken. Like a child caught in the middle of a vicious fight between her parents. I know that feeling. "I bet she never loved you," Reva says.

I don't want to think that's true.

Kim and I go back to her place, and suddenly I'm incredibly hot for her. I can't get her clothes off fast enough or into her bed soon enough and we make stupendous, passionate, endless love.

You believe that?

It's what I wanted to happen. But when we got into bed, nothing happened. Endless love never started. A first for me. Limp dick doesn't begin to describe it. I'm embarrassed. Shocked. Disappointed. Confused. Angry.

"That bitch! Still messing up my life."

"Shhhh!" Kim whispers. She's rubbing my back.

"Old faithful never failed me before, I swear." Make a joke of it. If I can.

"It's okay. You're upset. Perfectly normal reaction."

I ask her to suck me. She does. Doesn't help. I try conjuring up my wildest fantasies as inspiration. Nothing helps. Story of the big head and the little head. The big one is hot to trot. But the little one is out to lunch.

"We'll try later, sweetheart," she murmurs. Spooning with me. Holding my shriveled penis gently in her hand. That's how we fall asleep. My last thought before I nod off is that this is a really good person.

When I wake up in the morning, she's gone. There's a note. "Roy, see ya later, gotta go to work. Love, Kim." It's a lovely morning.

As I drive up to my rented faux English cottage, my next-door neighbor is tinkering with his power mower on the lawn of his miniature Mexican hacienda. It's United Nations row on this street.

"Hi, Phil," I yell from the driveway and keep moving. Phil is a talker. He sells insurance, so I guess that's a good thing. For him.

"Hey, you just missed your friend," he calls over. That stops me. Brings me closer.

"Was it Killer?" He's tried to interest Killer in a term insurance policy.

"No, a big fella. He was ringing the bell, knocking, then I saw him kinda prowling around, peeking in back. So I asked him what he wanted. Said he was looking for you. So I said you were out. And he says—"

See what I mean? Saying "Good morning" to Phil can trigger a filibuster.

"Did you get his name?"

"Yeah, but I can't remember it. Think he left a message stuck to your front door. He—"

"Thanks, Phil." I'm moving for the front door. But he's got to finish what he's saying.

"He said he's your agent."

Now I have to put this in context for you.

There's an old Hollywood joke about the writer who comes home to find his house has burned down. Helpful neighbor—not unlike our Phil—tells him that's not all. This motorcycle gang pulled up, right after your agent stopped by. They robbed the place, raped your wife, killed your dog, and set fire to your house on their way out. The writer listens to all that. Stunned, he says, "My agent came to my house?"

Obviously it's different depending on your level of success. I'm sure John Wayne's agents stop by his house all the time. Probably wash and detail his car while they're there. Since *Jack Havoc* I've had agents over for dinner. But for me it's still a bit unusual. Particularly unannounced. I find Val Dalton's business card wedged in the molding on my front door. He's over at the Beverly Hills Hotel coffee shop having breakfast. If I get back soon enough, why don't I join him?

The Beverly Hills Hotel is a great big pink landmark on Sunset Boulevard. When it was built, back at the time the first movie pioneers came west, it was an elegant watering hole in the middle of a green wilderness. Nothing else around, except orange and date groves. Since then the city of Beverly Hills has grown up. And several of the busiest streets converge at Sunset, making it seem like all roads lead to the sedately garish old hotel. The Polo Lounge, a lovely, airy garden room, is the place for power breakfasts at the Beverly Hills Hotel. But the regulars eat at the windowless coffee shop downstairs near the barber shop. That's where I find Val Dalton, his tall frame scrunched onto a counter stool. Devouring eggs Benedict and reading *Daily Variety.*

He sees me and pats the empty stool next to him. I sit down. The grizzled waitress comes right over. "Hey, lover," she says, "what am I gonna watch if you're not gonna be on TV no more?"

"There's always *Gunsmoke.*"

"Nah, I got tired of waiting for Marshal Dillon to jump Miss Kitty. Want the usual?"

Meaning black coffee, an order of Canadian bacon and dry toast. Val and I play tennis at Sam Goldwyn's court nearby once or twice a week and eat here. I nod, she pours my coffee and goes off. I inhale deeply.

"Mmm, something smells different."

"New cologne," he says. "Real butch."

I pick up Val's trade paper. "Anything in here about me?"

"Army Archerd's column says you were cavorting at the *Trapeze* opening with a mystery lady."

"Kim Rafferty. New friend. You'll meet her. You might even want to represent her."

"We're not taking on any new clients at the moment. Matter of fact—" he takes a sip of his coffee "—that's what I stopped by to talk to you about."

"Yeah, yeah, first tell me—how close are we to wrapping up the Hecht-Lancaster deal?" Val makes a so-so gesture. "What's the snag, is it—"

"There you go, darlin'." The waitress plops down my order. "You gotta eat more than that if you're gonna be the next Rock Hudson."

"What're we going to do with the old one?"

She laughs. Goes off. I start dabbing butter on the toast.

"Look, Burt was all over me last night, he said I'm going to be the next Tony Curtis. Hey, the next Rock, next Tony, throw in a little next Marlon. I could be an all-star cast, all by myself."

Val laughs. That's what your agent is supposed to do. But he's my friend, too. I detect a tension in him. "There are still some major deal points open," he says. Playing with the sugar cubes.

"But Burt really wants it to go through. That's our ace. Right?" Val nods. "And Nate says the bullpen is full up, right?" As of last week two other majors and one indie and a TV network are interested in doing business with me.

"We've been coordinating activities closely with Nate—and that's part of the problem."

"I didn't know there was a problem."

"Couple of 'em, actually." Deep breath. "The agency is in process of reviewing our talent roster. There are some clients for whom we may not be the best choice—as far as servicing goes. Depending on their current career goals."

I can't believe what he's saying. "Are you guys firing me? Dropping me from your goddamn roster? Just when I'm verging on a really important movie deal?"

"I'm supposed to recite that gobbledygook double-talk and cut you loose. But between us? Straight talk? It's Nate."

"Look, I know he's a thorny asshole. But look what he did for me. He—"

"Roy, the agency is salivating over the commissions they figure you're about to generate. Hate to lose a penny of 'em. But they're scared shitless."

"Of what? Being too successful?"

"Of Jack Warner. He's blaming the whole lawsuit thing on us. He says we put Nate up to it. So as long as you're a client, he won't deal with our agency—"

"Sonuvabitch! I knew he was up to something! C'mon, Val! Don't let your guys panic. This is just a power play. To punish me. Get you to dump me. You're playing right into the Colonel's hands. He'll fart and holler and two weeks from now he'll forget all about it."

"They're betting he won't."

"Screw him! I'm gonna have Nate sue the studio for—"

"The agency will deny what I just said."

His cologne scent is curdling with the smell of flop sweat. I feel bad for Val. Don't kill the messenger. Time to regroup.

"Okay, the hell with the agency. I can go down the street and pick up ten agents before lunch. But come with me, man. We've talked about it before. Use me as a calling card to make a new deal for yourself some other place—or, better yet, don't be my agent, be my partner, we'll make movies together." Like Hecht and Lancaster.

I'm expecting his lights to go on. They don't.

"Guess I'm making an assumption here. Where do we stand in all this, Val? You and me."

"I agree with you, Roy. It's cowardly of the agency to roll over this way." He looks me right in the eye. I'll give him that. "But I'm staying with them. Want to know why?"

"Dying to."

"Not for the agency's reasons. For my own. You had Nate engineer this whole caper without giving me even a hint."

"That was the way Nate wanted it! He insisted! He'll be the first to tell you—"

"No, Roy, *you* should have been the first to tell me. I think you ought to be represented by someone you totally trust. And it's clear that's not me."

Man's got a point. I see it now. I'd protest if I could. But I can't. I'm just filled with regret. And dread.

"Then I'm losing you, huh?"

He shrugs. There's pain in his eyes. "You did already."

14

Roy

"Golly gee! The big fella is just a big crybaby."

That's Nate Scanlon's considered opinion on Val Dalton's objections.

We're in Ah Fong's, one of Beverly Hills' best Chinese restaurants. Owned by Benson Fong, a Chinese actor who made enough money for the down payment by playing Japanese villains during WWII. Nate is delicately devouring an order of minced pigeon in lettuce cups.

"Val is acting like a spoiled child who's sore about being snubbed. That's not businesslike," Nate says. "There was no choice. If we'd told Val about the end run we were planning, somehow it might have leaked, gotten back to Warners prematurely and spoiled this opportunity."

I guess I did the right thing.

But I'm scared. I feel homeless, rejected, misunderstood and, most of all, guilty. Is this what playing in the big leagues is like? The Warner Bros. poison seems to have spread all over the agency scene. I've been discreetly putting out the word that I'm available. Not even a nibble. I sense that everyone who's anyone is scared to come near me. It's simple arithmetic to them: the gain of new commissions on one client (me) isn't worth the potential loss of many Warner commissions on all their other clients (bigger bucks).

So at a crucial juncture in my career, I'm left without an agent.

Nate pooh-poohs the problem. Says he's taking care of business on my behalf. Doing everything an agent would for me. So just relax. "Once we set up your movie deal," Nate says, "they'll come running."

I tell him that relaxing is easier said than done. He says try the Peking duck.

The duck is delicious, but I come away from lunch with a case of indigestion that stays with me for the rest of the week. I live for the daily phone calls from Nate and hang on every morsel of optimism in his voice. What's making me particularly nervous is that the deal with Hecht-Lancaster seems to be fading away. Nate doesn't say that out loud. "We're still talking with them," he says, "but it's a very complex structural arrangement."

"I don't know what's so complex if both sides want to make it happen."

Despite the assurances that the deal with Burt is alive and well, I worry. Because more and more Nate's telling me about the status of offers from the other companies. I don't want to hear about them. I want the Lancaster deal to go through. It's got to go through.

I tell Nate that. Again and again. He says there's no argument, he also wants the Lancaster deal to go through.

Then on Thursday, he calls to tell me he thinks Paramount may make a firm offer tomorrow. And oh, by the way, the Lancaster negotiations have turned icy. No return to his last calls. I tell him to phone Burt directly. He says I don't understand. That's not how it's done.

I want to scream at him, but that wouldn't be businesslike.

The vein on the left side of my forehead starts to throb. Announcing the start of a doozy of a migraine. I spend the rest of the day at home cozying up to hot and cold compresses and gobbling painkillers. Trying to suppress this feeling I have that I'm the only passenger in a toboggan sled that's starting down this steep icy mountain with no one in the driver's seat.

The parking lot next to the UCLA track is almost empty

when I pull in. Just a few student bicycles in the rack and one other car. Burt Lancaster's forest-green Jaguar. I park next to it and look out across the oval. Burt's already out there running laps. It's five minutes to sunup.

I do my stretches then move out onto the track. Be casual. Don't look anxious. He spots me. Tosses a mock salute. Good sign. Just be cool. A pair of jocks out for a jog. That's what I'm here for. A workout. Nothing else.

Yeah, sure.

He's moving at a steady pace. Doesn't look that fast. Until you try to catch up to him. Long legs pumping. Smooth form. Jim Thorpe, in the flesh. Okay. Put on a little steam and I come up alongside him.

"Pick 'em up, Roy boy, pick 'em up and put 'em down!"

Is it my imagination or is he stepping up the speed?

"Got to stay in shape, Roy boy, the body is your temple. Your synagogue! You take care of your bod, and your bod will take care of you. Kid like you, when I was your age, I could lift that entire building!"

He's pointing at Royce Hall. I have no reason to doubt what he's saying.

"I'll start out with duplexes and work my way up," I say.

He laughs. Just like in the movies. A boisterous bark. All teeth and a yard wide. He loves being topped. Proof that you're not afraid of him.

"Want to talk a little business?" he asks. I nod. "Then step into my office," he says. Gesturing at the track. "You're getting fucked, boy. Plain and simple."

Suddenly my sneakers seem stuck in cement. I have to force myself to keep up with him. Dreading what he's going to say, but desperate to hear every word.

"Jack Warner's dropped the dime on you, kid. Bunch of dimes. Called all his fellow moguls. Convinced them to make an example of you as a matter of principle. Those cocksuckers who can't even *spell* the word *principle*. He's tellin' 'em all that if one TV actor can jump the reservation, others'll try. Contracts will be meaningless. Blah-blah-blah. God help you, you've become a cause, kid."

"But you—you run your own operation. You're an independent. UA doesn't tell you who to hire. You make all your own decisions. You told me that."

"True. All true. However. You've caught me at an awkward moment in time. Big secret. My partner, little Harold, and I are in negotiations with MGM. Not for a slate of pictures. To go over to Culver City and run the whole damn studio. What the hell we need it for, I don't know. But when they want to elect you king, you shouldn't say no."

"Kings aren't elected," I say.

He laughs. Not such a big one. "Smart kid, that's what I like about you. Street kid. Why I wanted you with us. But—there's a board of directors we'll have to answer to at MGM. And our lawyers say it'll look bad if we're trying to hire someone who walks away from contracts."

"That's not how it was, Burt, they—"

"Hey, I'm convinced, boy. On your side. But there's nothing I can do now. After we get over to MGM, once the dust settles, we'll do something together then."

"Yeah, well—sure. If I'm still available. Just wanted to give you first crack. Got a bunch of other irons in the fire."

"Hope they're still there after Colonel Warner works his way through his phone book."

I'm sweating. Not from the run. "What do I do, Burt? What would you do?"

"Go back to New York. Use your clout as a TV star to get a Broadway play. Make it a hit play, if you can. Wait the fuckers out."

"Hide in the atom bomb shelter until they sound the all clear? And by the time I get back out here, everybody's forgotten who I am. *This* is my moment! It may never come again!"

He looks over at me. "I'm sorry, kid. Really. If you need any money to tide you over…"

"Thanks, Burt—but I was looking for a hand up, not a handout."

"Good man. Next time," he says. "I'll make it up to you next time."

The phone is ringing when I get back to my place from UCLA. It's Merle Heifetz. Remember him? The Jewish leprechaun from Warners' publicity department. The one who invented Roy the Bad Boy. He's at the Hotel Bel-Air and has to see me. Like now. I tell him sure, buzz right over. My press agent is coming to my house.

I grab a quick shower and I'm in my terrycloth robe, toweling my hair, when Heifetz arrives. My pal. The only suit at Warners I trust. It's not nine-thirty yet, but he looks like he needs a drink. I offer him one. He takes a stiff Scotch. I'm sipping black coffee. And he lays it out for me.

He was just doing a breakfast interview at the Bel Air dining room with Dave Kaufman of *Variety* and Jack Warner's vice president for Research and Planning, some guy I never heard of. The angle of the story they were pitching to Kaufman was this exciting new scientific approach the studio is now taking to predict the popularity and potential of projects.

"What's that mean, Merle? A crystal ball from the prop department?"

"It's something the ad guys on Madison Avenue came up with. They do questionnaires and surveys and graphs and shit to figure out why we brush our teeth or how we pick the cars we buy. Only now they're applying the same techniques to movies and TV. It's called Motivational Research."

Frankly, I'm a little bored. What's got Heifetz so rattled?

"Roy, I didn't know where it was going until we're with Kaufman this morning. This asshole vice president whips out a sheaf of papers—and suddenly he's using the *Jack Havoc* show to illustrate how his system works. And he proves, scientifically he says, that the success of the show is not Roy Darnell in the leading role."

I laugh. "Then what the hell is it?"

"According to his graphs, it's Dave Viola and his comedy riffs, that's why the show's been a hit." I'm not laughing now. "And he says that's why, based on this research, Warners and the network are going to renew the show—starring Dave Viola and a replacement for you. New character, Jack Havoc's brother. Their charts and statistics, divided into age groups and income groups and whatever the fuck, indicate that you've been kind of holding the show back. A negative factor, he called you."

Heifetz knocks back the rest of his Scotch. A big belt. I think I'm going to join him.

"Honest to God, Roy, I didn't even have a hint beforehand. I called you as soon as we finished the interview." He shakes his head. "The bastards are out to incinerate you."

"When will this be in the paper? Tomorrow?"

Heifetz nods. "Kaufman thought it was a real good story."

Then we both have stiff doubles. It's not my days that are numbered. It's my hours. This time tomorrow morning I will officially be a dead man in Hollywood.

"I'll bushwhack 'em for you, Roy—if you just tell me who to whack."

Killer is dead serious. I think he's starting to believe his own legend. But don't read this wrong. When Killer volunteers to do a job on someone, he's mouthing off and not really talking about homicide. Clipping a drunk in a bar on my behalf is more his speed. But back when we were kids, when I wasn't a gang kid, he tried to be. Matter of fact, he was one of those fuckers who chased me home after school every day. He was too runty to do much harm barehanded, but he'd clop you with a brick if he could. Funny world, huh? Now Killer's batting on my team. But kneecapping a guy with a tire iron on a dark night is about as far as he might go.

It's a thoughtful offer.

Thing is I don't know exactly who to aim him at.

Jack Warner obviously heads the short list of candidates. But Nate Scanlon warned me not to talk to him under any circumstances. Maybe when I saw the Colonel in the crapper I should have just run. Maybe he wouldn't be taking it so personally. How about Val Dalton for dereliction of duty? Or the honchos at his agency for fleeing the field of battle? I definitely could focus my wrath on this research turd, Warner's flunky, who made his mumbo-jumbo numbers dance to the Colonel's tune. For that matter, I could send Killer after Dave Kaufman, who's about to sink my canoe by printing all that bullshit in *Variety*. Nah, I always liked Dave. I've been ducking his calls all day. I want to phone him back and give him an earful. But Nate forbids me to do that. Says it's better for the possible lawsuit that may eventuate if I have no prior knowledge of the libel about to be perpetrated.

Christ.

If lawyers spoke simple English, what a lovely world it would be.

Killer and I have been here all day in my living room. Command post. Chewing over what Burt and Heifetz told me. Manning the phones. Which consists mostly of talking to Nate long distance. He's in Washington, D.C., at a board meeting for some veteran's group. When I first tracked him down there and filled him in, Nate started with the same old reassurances. It's no big deal. Who believes what they read in the trades anyway? We've still got a hopper full of offers. Just sit tight. Ride it out. Blah-blah. But *then* he starts talking about a fuckin' lawsuit. I figure it this way: you can't collect damages unless you've been damaged. So get braced. I'm about to get my head kicked in. How's that for simple English?

See, perception is the ball game in Hollywood. Never mind how things really are, how do they appear to be? Back in the '30s a trade paper guy wrote an article calling Katharine Hepburn, Marlene Dietrich, and Joan Crawford "box office poison." The guy probably had nothing else to write about that day and had to fill up space. But the next day the whole town was gossiping, and those three talented ladies had to fight their way back into the business. Took 'em years.

Perception.

So here we sprawl and pace and smoke and curse in my rented living room. Me and my childhood pal Kenny the Killer. Plus a limitless supply of Scotch. Handfuls of darvon. If my fuckin' head doesn't stop throbbing I may have to go to UCLA Emergency for a shot. Four lines on my phone. But nobody to talk to. Except long distance Nate. And Kim, but she's at work and can't talk long. Bogie's in some tiny town in Italy making a picture. And I'm on the skids. Nate says I'm being dramatic. Maybe I ought to send Killer looking for Nate. For underestimating the enemy (or overestimating his own smarts). But then I'd have to find another lawyer. Hey. Maybe the asshole who deserves to be blamed for this whole mess is—me. Yeah. That's what I'll do. Give Killer a direct order to kneecap me. That doesn't sound like fun. Easier to just blame it all on Bogie's bogey man. The treacherous tailor. *Pincus fuctus.*

So I sit tight. Very tight. Bad day. Good Scotch. I pass out watching Jackie Gleason on *The Honeymooners.* Shaking his fist. "To the moon, Alice, to the moon!"

By the end of the week, Nate is back from D.C., and all my other offers have evaporated.

15

Reva

I'm not ashamed to tell you, I'm getting desperate.

Killer has been ducking me ever since our roll in the hay. I asked him why on the night I ran into him and Roy outside the Villa Capri, but we only had a moment to talk while Roy was signing autographs for some of the other collectors, and Killer denied ducking me. "I've just been busy, sis." Sure, I'd seen what kind of busy when I spotted him on the street location escorting that slutty blonde extra into Roy's empty trailer. That was before I started puking and before I went to see Dr. Berman, who still hasn't gotten the lab report back yet because of some kind of screwup at the lab.

This morning Mother pounded on my bedroom door and woke me up with a jolt. "I've got very important news for you, Reva."

"Okay. Tell me." Hoping the morning sickness doesn't hit while she's delivering her bulletin.

"I just checked your chart and your Moon is in Scorpio and there's a trine with Aries so these next few weeks are a very delicate time for you. There could be a catastrophe in your life."

That's my mother the astrologer for you. Always there after the fact. The day after President Roosevelt died she ran a chart that established unquestionably that the day he died was gonna be a real bad day for him.

Podolsky has driven me up to Will Rogers's old house in the Pacific Palisades. We're parked in the crowded row of spaces facing the polo field. Will Rogers was a big movie star in the '30s, but he began life as an Oklahoma cowboy. He started the polo game in front of his house, and the tradition has continued long after his death. Some of the riders are just rich playboys, but there's a hard core of celebrities who Podolsky assures me show up every week.

Frequently including Roy—and if he's here, I'm hoping Killer Lomax will be with him.

I spot Roy down on the grassy field with the other players. They're riding Arabian stallions and wearing jodhpurs and white crash helmets. There's Tyrone Power and Cesar Romero and Darryl Zanuck, the mogul who runs Twentieth Century Fox. They're all galloping around the field, wildly swinging mallets, and I wonder how Roy learned how to ride so well. I guess from acting in that crappy cowboy picture he made down in Durango last year.

"There he is," Podolsky says.

I think he's spotting another celeb. But he's spotted Killer.

Down the line of expensive cars where spectators are hanging out, watching the game. Killer's loitering against a Silver Cloud Rolls, talking to Reginald Gardiner, the British character actor who specializes in playing witty upper-class drunks. They've both got beer bottles in their hands.

"Okay," I say, with a deep breath, "here I go."

Podolsky wishes me luck and I walk along the ridge in front of the parked cars. No one pays any attention to me, and Killer has his back to me so he doesn't notice my approach. I'm not sure exactly what I want to say. I hope Killer hasn't told Roy about him and me. Probably not, because I haven't sensed any change in Roy's attitude toward me up until now.

When I get fairly close, I stop and wait. Killer glances my way. He gives me a small smile and a small wave and is about to go back to his chat session, but Reginald Gardiner has swiveled away from him to hit on a buxom brunette perched on the hood of the next car, so this is my chance.

"What're you doin' here?" Killer says, surprised but not suspicious.

"Oh, just in the neighborhood, thought I'd stop by."

He really grins. "You are somethin'—you oughta be in the C.I.A. Bet you could find out where Hitler's hiding."

"Only if he signs autographs."

He laughs, wraps his arm around my shoulders and gives me a hug, then gestures at the game. Roy is thundering down the field and swings his mallet, gives the ball a devastating crack. "Scores again! Our boy's showin' 'em how." Then shakes his head. "But look at that! Fuckin' Zanuck won't give Roy the time of day."

"Why not? They're on the same team."

"A long story, sis." He keeps looking off at the field, but his arm is still around my shoulders.

"I've been wanting to talk to you, Kenny." It's the first time I've called him Kenny.

"Yeah? About what?"

So I tell him. When I get to the part about missing my period, I really have his attention. He lets me continue without interruption through the snafu at the lab and how it's not official yet, but how scared I am. There's real sympathy on his face. When I stop talking, he touches my cheek gently with his hand.

"Gee, that's rough, sis. Your very first time out, and bingo!" He shakes his head ruefully. "So...looks like we gotta do something about this."

I nod eagerly, my eyes brimming with tears. He said "we."

"Important thing is to keep it very quiet," he says. "Not only for your sake and mine, but for Roy, too. *Confidential* or some other rag gets hold of this, it'll get all twisted around so that Roy's to blame, that'll be the headline, and we don't want that."

I shake my head, I definitely don't want that, it's the reason I didn't want to tell even the doctor any names.

"But you're cool, right, so there's nothin' to worry about. If you gotta go down to Tijuana and take care of it, I'll pay for the expenses," then his eyes narrow. "You're sure it was me, huh? You haven't seen any other action since then, have you? Those guys you hang out with?"

"No, absolutely not. Kenny, I don't want to make any trouble, but—if my mother finds out, she'll kill me, she'll definitely throw me out of the house. And if I just disappear for a few days, you don't know her, she'll call the police—"

"No cops! I said I'd pay the freight, you gotta handle the details. That's fair."

"But I—I don't know who to go to, or where, or—"

"Jeezus! Ask your goddamn girl friends, they'll know." He's getting irritated and I don't want him to. "Look, I gotta go take care of some stuff for Roy—he's got exceptionally heavy things happening right now, I can't even begin to tell you, so we don't want to add anything to his load."

I tell him I understand completely. I thank him for the help he's offering. I want to tell him I'm still scared, but I don't. He's going off now. I don't want him to go feeling I'm a burden. I want to do something to show him I'm grateful. I want him to like me.

"Kenny," I call to him, he stops. "Here—" I hold out my hand to him, he's curious enough to come back. I open my palm and he sees the cigarette lighter inscribed, "Here's looking at you, kid. Love, Bogie and Betty."

He takes it from me and stares at it.

"Where'd you get this?"

"I—found it." Can't bring myself to say, "I dood it."

"Where?" he demands.

"On the ground. That day when you guys were on location, remember, and—"

"I sure as hell remember! You were lurkin' around all day. What were ya, pissed 'cuz I took that other little twat in the dressing room instead of you?" He holds the lighter up in front of my nose. "You snuck in and fuckin' stole it, didn't ya?"

I'm shaking my head, not in denial but disbelief that he's guessed the whole thing. I wanted to punish Killer that day. But I only wound up hurting Roy.

"Don't lie to me! Y'got any idea the kinda heat I been takin' over this fuckin' thing since it's been gone?"

"I didn't mean to…" But, of course, I did. "I wanted to give it back."

But not right away, of course. After I took it home, the lighter became the centerpiece of the Roy display in my bedroom. I loved it so much, it didn't occur to me how much Roy was missing it, until there was an item in Army Archerd's column in *Variety* the other day about how Roy's favorite keepsake had disappeared. I knew then I had to return it and this seemed to be the ideal occasion.

Just shows how wrong you can be.

Killer's sausage-like fingers close around the lighter, forming a fist. "Thanks for nothin', bitch," he says. "Now do me a big favor and stay the hell away from me. Permanently."

16

Roy

I'm still a star for at least a little while longer before the word spreads everywhere that I was shitcanned by Jack L. Warner. The studio arranged a personal appearance prior to the start of our hostilities. My name has already been announced in the newspaper ads. Can't disappoint my fans while I still have them. And it's for a good cause. The I Am an American Day Celebration on the Fourth of July.

Red, white, and blue bunting bedecks the streetlight poles along Hollywood Boulevard from Vine Street to LaBrea. Streamers draped overhead. Crowds line the curbs on both sides of the wide avenue. Kids wave little flags. Food vendors and pickpockets work the crowds. Local TV cameras cover local TV anchors excitedly reading off the descriptive details. Cars and floats, interspersed with high school marching bands and the vets from the American Legion Post. The only thing different from the ordinary small-town parade is that a flock of TV and movie stars are participating.

The assembly point for the parade is in the parking lot behind the Pantages Theater. I'm using my own car. Top's down on the T-Bird so Kim and I can sit up on the back and greet the folks. Killer is going to drive us. An efficient-looking gal with a clipboard checks us in. Gives us our position and hangs white identifying signs on the doors of the car with big black lettering that says:

ROY DARNELL ("Jack Havoc")
KIM RAFFERTY
KENNY "KILLER" LOMAX

Kim is thrilled and hugs me. "Equal billing with the star—doesn't get any better than that." She kisses me. I've told her most of what's happening. She doesn't believe it's all going to disappear like *Brigadoon*. Killer gestures me off to one side. He looks all churned up.

"How'd my name get on there?" he asks.

"I called Heifetz. One last perk."

He looks over at the sign. "Never saw my name big like that before." He punches me lightly in the shoulder. Like Tracy used to do to Gable, before winking and calling him Y'Big Lug. "Thanks, Roy," Killer says.

We roll out onto the boulevard and slowly move west. A lot of start-and-stop. Waves and smiles for the fans. Screams and whistles from the fans. Our car is behind Tab Hunter and Natalie Wood and in front of Robert Wagner and Debra Paget.

"Look, there's your little friend," Kim says.

It's Reva. She darts out from the curb, runs to our car. "Hi, Roy! Hi, Kim!" A cop yells for her to get back. But she kneels, calls for us to "Hold it!" and snaps a photo before racing away from the sternly approaching cop.

"Dumbass broad," Killer mutters.

Bill Welch, a local TV newsman, strolls up to us carrying a hand microphone. A cameraman with a shoulder rig is grinding away. "Roy Darnell," he greets us, "TV's Jack Havoc. What's this I hear about you leaving the show?"

"Moving on, Bill. Everything changes."

"To bigger and better things."

"You bet."

"Got any special thoughts for us on this special day?"

"Just that it's the proudest thing any of us can say—I am an American."

"Amen. Great seeing you, Roy." He turns away. Facing his camera. "I see Jeff Chandler, ladies and gentlemen, Big Chief Cochise himself." He walks off. We creep forward.

Stop again. The horsemen of the Leo Carillo Riding Club are strutting their stuff. Old Leo, the Cisco Kid's sidekick, dressed all in black, cues his snow-white mount to rise up, pawing the air with its two front legs. Leo doffs his black sombrero with the silver spangles. It's a surefire applause getter.

As we inch forward, I can see Uncle Sam up ahead. He's on foot, engaging the people at the curb. "I want you!" he's yelling. "I want you!" Pointing a finger. Like in the famous Army enlistment poster. He's quite tall, wearing a blue and white striped frock coat, a red vest, white top hat with tri-color bunting. "I want you!" he shouts at a toddler. Scaring her into hysterics. Uncle Sam pats the toddler, tips his top hat and pivots away. Toward our car. I'm surprised to recognize, despite the white paste-on eyebrows and white goatee, that it's Dave Viola. He grins maliciously and straight-arm points at me:

"I *don't* want you!" he shouts.

I laugh as if he's said something funny. "How'd you get so tall, Uncle? Wearing Dave Viola's elevator shoes?"

"No, my boy, I just got bigger. All at once. Got so-o-o big they gave me my own TV series. Haven't you heard?"

"Yeah, congratulations, Davey." What the hell, he didn't do anything.

"You, on the other hand, got smaller. Teenchy-tinyyyyy! Couldn't happen to a snottier guy."

"Hey, do me a favor, Uncle, go back to scaring the kids." I turn my back on him to wave at the crowd on the other side of the street. But Viola high-steps around the rear of the car like he's in the March of the Tin Soldiers—and he's in my face again. He tosses a snappy salute. Points his finger again. Loudly proclaims:

"Roy Darnell, folks! Noooooooobody wants youuuuuuu!"

"What's wrong with that man?" Kim is whispering to me. "Is he stoned?"

"I'll take care of this, boss," Killer says. He leaves the motor running and hops out of the T-Bird. Uncle Sam is mark-time marching in place, elbows swinging. Repeating

"Nobody wants you, Roy Darnell, nobody wants you!" Killer ambles up to him and pauses. Viola looks at him, grinning like a jack-o-lantern. "C'mon, Davey boy, don't make a fuss in front of all the nice people."

"Yes sir, no sir! Yes sir, no sir! Three bags full! Just listen to your Uncle Sam!"

Killer grabs his arm and starts him away from my car. Viola goes with him, then breaks loose and runs back over to me. Sticks his tongue out—and gives me a big juicy Bronx cheer. The kids in the crowd snicker and shout, some of the grownups clap.

"Get him out of here, Killer!" I shout.

Killer's got Viola again, but Viola won't go. "Nyah, nyah, it's my series now, all mine! You're out! You're gone! Always treating me like a dumb hick! You stink! I'm the star now and the whole world knows it!"

"You gotta can this garbage, Davey," Killer orders.

"Or else what? *What?*" Then just like in the comic strips, the light bulb goes on. Viola's giving birth to an idea. "Want me to go? Huh?"

Killer nods.

"Y'really want me to go? Then go with me!"

"Whaddayatalkinabout?"

Viola nods at a motorcycle and sidecar parked near the curb. Painted red, white, and blue, of course. "Go with me," he repeats to Killer. "I don't want him—but I want *you.* I'm the top banana now. Come work for me. Right now. I'll pay you twice what he does." Killer looks at him. "Okay, pay you *three* times as much but the offer ends in the next ten seconds. Ten-nine-eight—"

Killer looks over at me. Sonuvabitch is tempted! "—seven-six-five—" What the hell. The Titanic's going down. Every man for himself. "—four-three—" Our eyes are locked. Me and Killer. Killer and me. My boon companion. My steadfast friend. I nod to him, giving him my blessing. "—two-one-zerooooh!" Hoping he won't go. "So what's the big decision, Killer-willer-diller? Him or me?"

"You," Killer says hoarsely. "I'm with you."

"Well then, let's go!" Uncle Sam links arms with Killer and marches him off to the motorcycle. Viola climbs into the sidecar. Killer gets on the cycle, kicks the motor over and drives off. With never a look back at me.

"What's going on here?" Kim asks.

"Guess you're driving."

I manufacture my best smile as the parade moves on.

I'm crying in my beer. Not literally, but you know what I mean. And I'm knocking back accompanying shots of the hard stuff. Boilermakers. Perfect drink to drown your sorrows in. Popping darvons like they're salted peanuts. Fuckin' head throbbing like a jackhammer. "They always know," I pound the flat of my hand on the mahogany bar. "The rats, they always know when to desert the ship!"

"Shhhh!" Kim has her finger to her lips. Pretty lips. Ruby red. "You're disturbing the other people," she whispers.

"What other people?" Louder yet. "Crummy place is empty. Used to be a hot spot. Where the elite meet to eat. And get schnockered. Where'd all the goddamn people go? Huh? *Where?*" I'm talking to the bartender now. But he's not talking to me. Just sighs and rolls his eyes and goes off to polish some glasses that don't need polishing.

Actually there are some people in the place. Not many, but some. A booth here, a table there, a smoochy couple down the bar. Hey, there are no small audiences, just small actors. I pick up the salt shaker and pretend it's a hand mike. Walk among the peasants. Mr. Show Biz.

"We're coming to you from the Cock 'n' Bull, a pseudo-British pub, near the end of the Sunset Strip. A heartbeat away from Beverly Hills, where—" I burst into song "—every heart beats true for the red, white, and blue." Came here from the parade. Don't ask me how many boilermakers ago that was.

"Keep it down, buddy," my friend the wandering bartender calls.

"Shhhh!" I say to him. If looks could kill, I'd certainly be badly bruised. I'm down near the smoochers and the girl unlocks lips long enough to glance up at me and then stare.

"Aren't you—Roy Darnell, the actor?"

"No, madam," I reply courteously, "my name is Captain Spaulding—" erupting into song again "—the African explorer, did someone call me schnorer, hello, hello, hello!" Doing my best Groucho crouch-lope in front of the smoochers. Tapping the ash off my imaginary cigar. She looks scared. He looks angry. Off his barstool, drawing back a fist, I'm still loping, moving target is hard to hit, but he's going to try. Where's Killer when you need him?

"Stop it!" Kim yells in my face. She's interceded between me and the ham-fisted smoocher. "You're behaving just like that lunatic at the parade!"

Dave Viola. She's right. I am. Don't want to do that. I bow and apologize to the smoochers. Kim and I go back to our drinks. "Thought you liked the Marx Brothers," I say.

"Only Harpo. He never talks."

Okay. I can take a hint. So I hop back on my barstool and polish off another round. Can I go fifteen rounds? For the championship. For the crown. Uneasy lies the head that wears a crown. Yesterday you're the prince of Hollywood, tomorrow you're a bum. From harboring Oscar ambitions to filing for unemployment insurance. In one mighty leap. I feel Kim's hand on my shoulder. Patting. Rubbing. Consoling. Yeah. That's good. Oh, so good.

"Ever been to New York?" I ask her.

She shakes her head. "Heard of it, though."

I smile. But the mirror behind the bar registers it as a grimace. "New York, New York, a really wonderful town."

"The Bronx is up, but the Battery's down," she teases. Borrowing Comden and Green's lyric.

"Yeah, that's right. Sure you never been there?" Give her a real smile. Man in the mirror confirms it. "I had this terrific apartment on 52nd Street, top floor front, four-story brownstone walkup. Leon & Eddie's and the '21' Club were our neighbors. But the thing that made it great was that it was over one of the jazz clubs—"

"Isn't that the street where they all are, the jazz places?"

"Uh-huh. That's it. In bed at night, with the window open, the music would drift up. We'd be there in the darkness—"

"You and who else?"

"—and real late sometimes there'd be this woman's voice. Smoky and full of hurt. Didn't sound like anyone else you'd ever heard. Six notes and you knew you were listening to greatness."

"Who was it?"

"Billie Holiday. She'd been in jail on a drug thing. For a year and a day. When she got out they revoked her cabaret license. Cops won't let her sing in any New York nightclub—"

"For how long?"

"Forever. So she'd sneak in downstairs, just before closing, because she *has* to sing. Just has to. Even if it's against the law. If she can't do that, it's like she's dead."

"That's—so sad." Kim's eyes misting. For Lady Day.

"Hey. Maybe I can do the same thing. Sneak into the studio late at night and make movies by myself. When nobody's watching. What do you think?"

Kim's eyes misting. For me. "Who else was with you, in bed, listening…"

The bartender delivers another boilermaker. I must have signaled for it. "Addie. My never-lovin' almost ex-wife."

"Did you love her? Back then?"

"What, are you taking a survey? Gonna report back to Addie, see if the info is good for bonus points?"

I'm hoisting the shot glass to my mouth. She slaps at my hand. Probably aiming for my face and missed. Splash. Waste of good whiskey. "Okay, okay, I'm sorry, stupid thing to say."

"Very stupid." She blots up the booze with her napkin. Cleaning up my mess. Oh God. This is a good one. A keeper.

"Hey. Want to go to New York with me sometime?" I ask. "Sure."

"How about right now? Let's go."

She looks at me. A long one. Then. "I've got a better idea. You have any Billie Holiday records at home?"

"All of 'em."

"Then let's go there and get naked and climb into bed and leave the lights off and listen to her sing in the darkness."

"And who knows, I might get lucky—"

"Never know."

I don't need a pity fuck. "Don't you want to call your camera crew so they can meet us there?"

She flinches. Stares at me. Can't believe what she heard. A rap in the mouth. I wait for anger. Tears? All I get is an infinitely weary shake of her head. "See you around sometime," she says.

Before I can stumble off the barstool and plead with her to stay, she's gone.

Botched that pretty good, didn't ya, kid?

I recognize the voice. It's inside my head. Jack Havoc. Must be more drunk than I think I am.

"Well, I do what I can," I mutter. "She's better off without me anyway." Meant it as self-sacrificing, but it comes out as self-pity.

Yeah, but she didn't know that. He laughs.

Other boozers conjure up jolly little green men, I've got a snotty alter ego putting me down.

"Know something? You're not funny."

Neither are you, pal. This your new hobby—burning bridges?

"None left to burn, Jack, haven't you noticed?"

"Hey, mister." Raspy voice. Not inside my head. Look up. The bartender. Standing right in front of me. Like he's gazing at a loony. "Who you talkin' to?"

"Just trying to remember the words to an old song. 'Smoke Blows Up Your Ass.' Ever hear it?"

Face reddens. Pushes the tab on the bar toward me. "Time for you to settle up and scoot on home."

I smile. "Want to show me how to scoot?"

Watch it, Jack Havoc's voice says inside me, *he's got a sawed-off bat under the bar.*

Check it out. I notice the bartender's left hand is on the counter, but his right is out of sight. Below the bar. Could be holding a billy. I toss some bills on the bar. "This ought to cover it. Had a great time, can't wait to come back."

The bartender sullenly counts the bills. Watches me go. He turns to ring it up. I catch a glimpse under the bar. Where he's been standing. See the sawed-off bat.

"I owe you one," I say.

And then some, Jack Havoc says.

We're in the car. Jack and me. My imaginary pal is playing navigator. I'm driving. Never gonna drink again.

"Hey, I'm goin' the wrong way," I say.

Goin' the right way, he reassures me.

"Not for where I live now, buster, I—" and I get it as I see it: the turn up into Kings Road. I make a left without signaling, cut off an MG who blasts his horn after me. I give him the finger.

Making friends wherever you go, Jack says.

"Up yours." Steering like I'm handling a sixteen-wheeler. Around the steep curves. Climbing higher and higher. "If you're so smart, why am I coming up here? And don't tell me force of habit."

The criminal always returns to the scene of the crime. He laughs and lights a Gauloises.

"Don't be blowing that frog smoke in my face," I warn him.

What're you gonna do when you get there?

"Oh, you know. Knock on the door. Say, 'Trick or treat.'"

Now that's funny. Save that one for me on the show.

"We don't have a show anymore. Don't you read the trades?"

There's the house up ahead. Other side of the street. All lit up. Flag flying on the pole on the lawn. Ten, twelve cars in the driveway, some out front. I park across the street. Turn off my motor and lights.

And she didn't even invite you to the party, he says.

"Just shut the fuck up—or get out of my car!"

Your car? Sponsor gave it to Jack Havoc. That's me.

I'm not paying attention to him. I'm staring across at the picture window in the living room. Happy couples celebrating the Fourth. Some boy-girl, some boy-boy. The high society folk gathered at the piss elegant watering hole I'm still paying for but can't even piss in anymore. There's Addie, flitting and flirting, gesticulating with a can-you-fuckin'-believe-it foot-long cigarette holder. Auntie Mame on the rampage.

I get out of the car and walk around the side of the house toward the back. Where the view is. Why we bought the house. Good-sized lawn and small pool. Overlooking the lights of the city. They go on and on. It's like being in an airliner swooping in for a landing. "Welcome to Los Angeles, ladies and gentlemen, please keep your seat belts fastened." There are a couple of giggling partygoers sitting barefoot on the edge of the pool, dangling their feet in the water. I stay in the shadows so they don't see me. I hear a popping sound and the night sky bursts into Technicolor. Fireworks from the park down near Melrose. Followed by another overlapping display. Whistling sound, exploding rainbow. Attracting Addie and Guy Saddler and the rest of her hoity-toity guests. Hurrying outside. Holding their highballs, oohing and aahing at the fireworks. Politely clapping for the ones they particularly like. As if it's all being staged for their private pleasure.

The queen and her court.

He's followed me out here. Jack Havoc.

A round of applause if you please her, he says, *otherwise—off with your head.*

"Yeah. Thinks she owns the world," I mutter. Or am I just thinking it.

She owns your world, babe. He laughs.

Another whistler. Screeching. Soaring up and up. Like a V-2 bomb over London. Detonating higher than the others. Dazzling white light, like a strobe, catching everyone in arrested motion. Addie standing so near the rim of the lawn. Straight drop. Hundreds of feet down into the canyon. White light fades. Into something cold and dark.

There's an easy way out of all this for you, Jack Havoc whispers. *But you don't want to think about that, do you?*

I don't answer him.

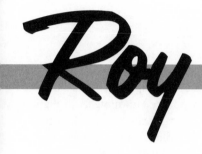

17

Nate Scanlon stomps around his office like God's angry man. Trampling heathens and infidels underfoot with his imaginary infantry boots. "Warners thinks they're fooling with snotnose kids? We'll fix 'em! You're going to own Burbank."

It's a comedown. Burt Lancaster said we were going to own the whole town. What Nate has in mind is another lawsuit against Warners.

"For restraint of trade. Sure, they'll fight it—but we'll win, if we have to take it all the way to the Supreme Court."

By which time, of course, my career will be long gone. I'll be as well remembered by then as Sonny Tufts.

Nate is brimming over with righteous indignation— maybe magnified by guilt at having marched me into the Okefenokee swamp. He's giving vent to his rage. Me? I'm cool, man. Projecting serenity, with a dash of nonchalance. All to conceal my feelings of absolute panic. I am going down the tubes, nevermore to be heard from. And my lawyer is going to file a brief.

Nate stops pounding the carpet and turns on me. "Oh, yeah," he glares. "It is my duty to inform you that I have received an offer for your services." Daring me to ask.

"An offer?" I repeat. Heart goes pit-a-pat. Hope dies slowly.

"From Warners," he says. "Don't get too excited. You're not going to like this."

Okay. I steel myself. "Let's hear."

"The Colonel called. Personally. He wants you to film one more appearance as Jack Havoc. In which your replacement is introduced—and you are killed. Your replacement vows to avenge you."

"To be continued next week," I say. "For the sake of argument—what's he want to pay?"

"They want you to work for guest star rate."

"That isn't *half* of what I was making under the old deal!"

"That's what I said. The Colonel said, quote, 'That contract unfortunately is no longer in force,' unquote. And then he cackled as if he had a feather up his ass." Nate kicks the coffee table. It's as sturdy as Nate's old Army foot locker and can take it. "He called it an opportunity to provide an orderly transition. He said you ought to do it for your loyal fans."

"Yeah, well, according to his research geniuses I don't have any loyal fans, so you can tell Jack L. Warner to—"

"Don't get your shorts in a bunch. I already turned 'em down."

Nate plops down on the chair opposite mine. We gloom together in silence. Then. "There's always a home for me at Warners," I recall. "Isn't that what the man said? When he let me out of the contract?"

"Yeah, but he didn't mention that if you came back you'd have to sleep in the outhouse."

More gloom. Then I ask the question that's been buzzing in my head.

"How about we go back to the divorce judge? Explain that circumstances have *drastically* changed."

"See if we can renegotiate? Hold on to the royalties?"

I nod. He's way ahead of me. Already shaking his head.

"Not a chance, my boy. It's a done deal. Anyway, I'd have a hard time pleading poverty with your face on the current cover of *Look* magazine."

"Not alone, a group shot. Along with Jack Webb and Dick Boone and Jim Garner. That story was done months ago, it just happens to be appearing now and—"

"—and the judge has never had his face on anything except his driver's license. So he might think it's a big deal.

I'm telling you, Roy, he'll have the bailiff toss us both out of the courtroom."

So I asked my question. That's my answer. And my head starts to ache again. I feel myself being pushed in a direction I'm afraid to even contemplate. Step by terrible step. Closer and closer. But wait, maybe—

"Suppose Addie was willing, if she'd be agreeable, could we go back then?"

Nate looks as if it's a trick question. "Sure, if she's cooperative, we can do anything, but—are we talking about the same Addie?"

"I—I just thought I might ask her. Explain the spot I'm in."

"That's a negotiation I'll leave to you," Nate says. Not holding his breath.

It does seem like a tall order.

After that horrible scene in the parking lot after the *Trapeze* premiere, when Addie attacked Kim and accused me of cheating her out of my next fortune. *After* I told Addie in no uncertain terms that she's cut *her* deal and nothing can change it. Yeah, *after* she made her wish that I never have a moment of happiness.

So—how can I go back to her now?

Asking for a goodwill gesture, a voluntary rewrite of the divorce judgment that gives me back a chunk of the assets I've already signed away to her?

Well, to tell the truth, I'm not quite sure how to go about that either.

I drive into Beverly Hills, park in the lot around the corner from Adrienne's Emporium. Walk up to the front of the store. Peek in, yeah, she's there. Talking to the sedate sales biddie. No one else around. Been a long time since Addie's shop showed a profit, so she might not be in a particularly giving mood. But who knows? Nothing ventured.

All I have to do is bounce in there, flash my *Photoplay* smile, do a bit of the old soft-shoe, charm the pants off her. I used to be able to do that with one testicle tied behind my back. Take her for a nostalgic spin down Memory Lane, and ease into it—You'll never guess why I dropped by.

She'll guess.

Flowers. Definitely. Gotta find a world-class bouquet.

I hurry to the florist on Beverly Drive. Closed. Death in the family. Hey, I'm not doing that well myself. But McDaniel's supermarket is only a couple of blocks away on North Canon Drive. They sell flowers. I hotfoot it over, start looking at the bouquets. Roses? Six, eight dozen roses? Nah, too on-the-nose. Violets—surrounded by lacy baby's breath? Too high school prom. Nice big cactus plant? Too close to the truth. Armful of lilies of the valley? She hates the Valley. Sunflowers? Colors are right, but still too middle of the road.

Need something tasteful, understated in an overstated sort of way. Something that plugs into the old happy days. Yes! I see them. Calla lilies. That'll do the trick. Tall, regal, an echo: "The calla lilies are in bloom, such a lovely flower…" Addie's favorite actress. Katharine Hepburn. She said the lines in *Stage Door*—or was it *Morning Glory*? One of 'em for sure. We saw both flicks as a double feature at the Thalia on the West Side before we were married. On the way home, I bought her three calla lilies from a sidewalk vendor. Addie held them in her arms and imitated the Great Kate: "The calla lilies are in bloom…"

"My, my. Talking to ourselves now, are we?" Sardonic voice. Right behind me.

I turn. Not Jack Havoc, can't be, I'm sober now. Worse. It's Guy Saddler. Dressed in white, from his patent leather loafers to his French sailor pants and chambray work shirt—with a Gucci tri-color scarf knotted around his neck, matching the Gucci necktie he's wearing as a belt.

"Hey, Guy—you look like you mugged Fred Astaire in the parking lot and stole his wardrobe."

"Fred copies me," he says evenly. He's at the fruit and vegetable counter, meticulously filling a bag with perfect gleaming red apples. "Going to the funeral?" Nods at the lilies.

"Who's dead?"

"Well, reliable rumor has it that you are. Addie and I were

giggling about that just this morning. Roy Darnell, D.O.A. in Tinseltown."

"Don't believe everything you hear," I say. Dropping the calla lilies back in the rack. That game's over. Starting to leave.

"You know, dear boy, it's really rather ironic," he calls after me. Should have kept going, so much might've been different if I did. But curiosity prevails. I stop. Listen.

"Addie was so angry at you when it looked like you were going to be a mammoth movie star and she felt you'd tricked her out of her fair share—"

"Blah-blah. We've been there already, Guy."

"—but now the slipper is on the other foot, isn't it?"

He examines the shiny apple in his hand, turning it this way and that, like the serpent in the Garden of Eden. Offering knowledge. If you bite.

"Meaning what?"

"Well, I'm probably telling tales out of school, but it's such a delicious twist, especially after what you tried to pull. I told her it was a hoot. Tit for tat. Because, of course, she'd done the very same thing to you."

With waspish delight, he spells it out for me. Addie's store. Not a money pit, but a money maker. She's been hiding assets like crazy. Phony write-offs, stashing the cash and the bailout checks I've been giving her in a numbered Swiss bank. He ought to know. He's her silent partner. Blabbing now, of course. Can't resist. Just can't. Best for last: Guy has used his contacts to arrange a national affiliation. Lots and lots of Adrienne's Emporiums will be sprouting all across the land. As soon as the divorce decree is final.

"That's the cream of the jest, you see. She's going to be a very wealthy woman—even without a penny of what she's getting from you in the divorce." He winks at me. "Just thought you'd like to know."

I'm on top of the world. Looking down. Don't like what I see. Not a bit.

I fled McDaniel's market. Guy Saddler's snicker pursuing me. Had to get away from him. From everyone. Fast. So here I am. A place where I've never been, never even thought of going to.

The bell tower on top of Beverly Hills City Hall.

Walked, almost ran, blindly down the street. Too many people. Ducked into the post office on Santa Monica Boulevard. More people. Stopped at the water fountain. Just long enough to wash down the last of my darvons. Pushed a few doors. A staircase I hadn't noticed before. Up, up, up. Leading here. Where I'm alone. With my frantic jumble of thoughts. If the pain in my head doesn't stop I'm going to have it chopped off. Ha! Why bother? Got other people who'll do that for me.

On a clear day you can see the ocean. It's not a clear day. So I have a terrific view of the smog hanging over the chic shopping streets of Beverly Hills. Little toy cars darting this way and that. Tiny antlike people scurrying about. All going somewhere.

Not me.

I'm going nowhere.

All washed up.

Not only has Addie skinned me in the settlement, but she robbed me before and after. Raped me financially. I know better than to try and prove it. Guy Saddler wouldn't tell me all that if Addie hasn't made the trail untraceable. I should be entitled to at least part of what her business is worth—or about to be worth. But she's maneuvered it so I get goose egg. *Gournisht. Nada.*

Unless...

The unthinkable thought.

It's starting to seep out.

Of course, I'd been happy when the divorce moved along so briskly. Didn't know Addie had her own agenda going. While I was doing it to her, she was doing it to me. I'm beyond anger. Filled with hate. Boiling with outrage. That cunt! She lied, stole, absolutely ambushed me. And her punishment is she wins it all.

But the wild thing is that there's a new sensation rising within me. I feel relief. Release. Almost thankful. Because she's given me the excuse I craved. Done something that tips me over the top. Supplied my justification to think the unthinkable. Which goes like this:

Addie doesn't win until the divorce judgment is finalized.

In two weeks I am a pauper. Probably permanently.

Providing she's still alive.

There. I said it out loud.

Until then we are still married in the eyes of the courts of California. And a surviving spouse owns the entire joint estate. If anything happens to Addie before then, I'll not only retain my TV royalties—I'll probably even own a controlling chunk of the store. Which is a local gold mine about to go national. Even if she's changed her will, which she probably hasn't bothered to do yet, as co-owner the worst I'd hold on to is half. Of everything. Without begging.

Sounds fair to me. Either way.

Of course, just wishing won't make it so.

I look over the small city below. Hodge-podge of rooftops. Sun glittering off the gold dome of the Beverly Theater, like the top of the mosque in *Gunga Din*. "We've got to save the regiment—before it's too late." Let's just imagine. Adrienne's Emporium is about there. Two blocks over, one block up. Suppose I just stroll in at lunchtime. Find the bitch alone and—and—

That's where I get hung up. Because the simple fact is— I don't know how to do this.

Not in real life.

But I do, says the voice inside my head.

It's Jack. He's back.

No, I've been here all along. Just waiting for you to wake up to what has to be done. His voice is soothing. *I'll show you how.*

"You don't know anything. You're just a fucking figment of my imagination."

Hey. I was there with you. When the technical advisers on the show taught us.

"Who remembers all that stuff?"

I remember. Listening to those guys was an education. He's materializing now, I swear he is, I can see his body language as he rattles 'em off. *They showed us how to kill with a gun, a garrote, a stiletto. How to eviscerate, asphyxiate, defenestrate, defoliate. Doing 'em in by drowning, burning, poisoning, bludgeoning, disemboweling, freezing, frying, am I forgetting anything?*

"It's enough."

Lucky we were working on an action show.

"What about getting caught?"

You won't. He puts his arm around my shoulders. Protective. *Don't be scared, Roy. I'll be with you.*

I listen. He makes it sound easy. My headache starts to fade.

18

Reva

This is the first time I've ever shown my entire autograph collection to anyone all at once, and I must say that Gunther Weybright is a very attentive audience. He flips through page after page, book after book, even the crumb books which, of course, do contain some real nuggets, and he seems quite impressed. "You have been a most industrious person," he says.

Podolsky gives me a surreptitious but encouraging nudge.

We're in Mr. Weybright's store on La Cienega Boulevard. He buys and sells rare books, first editions, and autographs. Neither Podolsky nor I have ever met him before, but we've both noticed his store in the past. The Coronet Theater that plays old movies is just down the street. Once Podolsky and I went to see some Charlie Chaplin shorts there, and right before the show was supposed to begin the manager came to the front and scanned the spectators, and I guess none of us looked like cops because he ran a rare bootleg print of *Modern Times* instead.

Across the street we once got Elsa Lanchester, who was the Bride of Frankenstein and also Mrs. Charles Laughton in real life, when she was arriving to do her one-woman show for children in a tiny stage theater up the street. She signed for us, then realized she'd left her stage door key at home so she had to crawl in a window. We helped her get inside the theater, and I know I'm rambling on here but I'm scared Mr. Weybright will say No, because I really need money desperately now that Killer won't help me, but I'm also scared Mr. Weybright will say Yes, because that will mean the end of my collection.

It's probably a good time to clear up some misconceptions about autograph collectors. The kind we are, anyway. There are people who approach it as a business, they get autographs and try to sell them. We all look down on them. To us it's a hobby, pure and simple. The notion that we get multiple signatures and trade them with each other also isn't true. You know, three Susan Haywards for one Bette Davis. Horse pucky. There has to be a reason if you get a repeat signature, like for instance, if there was a misspelling the first time and it came out "Gay Cooper" instead of "Gary." Some of the autographs never improved, like Marlene Dietrich, who always wrote "M-line-D-line." No other defined letters.

Jimmy Stewart would write "James" only on request, otherwise he was "Jimmy." James Cagney would always sign "JCagney," no matter what, but as I look around the walls in Mr. Weybright's store I see a framed letter hanging behind his desk signed "GWashington," so maybe collectors have always had these problems. Sometimes we got a new autograph when the actor graduated from crumb book to good book. The only other repeats permitted were on 8x10 glossies or the candid photos we shot ourselves. I'm not saying everyone obeyed these rules, but if you were part of the Secret Six, that's how it worked.

The point I'm making is that inasmuch as I don't have any repeats, if I sell my collection that's it. Either I quit or I suddenly need everybody and I know it's too late to start over again, so all I'll have is my memories. The only tangible reminders of those hundreds and hundreds of occasions that are so precious to me will be gone.

But what choice do I have?

Mr. Weybright looks like my high school biology teacher. A musty man in a beige misbuttoned-down-the-front sweater, over a white shirt and red bow tie, he purses his lips as he turns the pages, occasionally remarking about a particular signature. "Babe Ruth," he says, "genuine Americana, and President Eisenhower—"

"That was from before he was president."

He nods. "Pola Negri, is she still alive?"

"I'm not sure," I tell him, but when he leafs on I confirm that John Garfield is dead and he seems pleased. Finally he closes the last book and pats it with his liver-spotted hand.

"So what do you think?" I ask him.

"Generally speaking, not exactly my field. I specialize in historical figures. I have several Andrew Jackson letters, a playbill signed by John Wilkes Booth, proclamations personally autographed by Woodrow Wilson and Franklin Roosevelt, that sort of thing. Of course, I deal in some entertainment personages, such as Harry Houdini and Sarah Bernhardt. This would be a first for me."

"How much?" Podolsky asks, because I'm afraid to.

"I could offer—" Mr. Weybright purses his lips "—a hundred and seventy dollars."

He can see my disappointment. I'd hoped he'd say something in the thousands, that's how much they're worth to me, but that's not how it is.

"You see, essentially it's only the deceased figures who have value, and the historical figures, and there aren't that many of those in your collection. But I'm willing to gamble, and wait, some of the entertainers may…" he gropes for a word, "…they may *mature* profitably. All right, let's round it out, I'll say, two hundred dollars."

For everything. That's all it's worth to him. Podolsky and I have calculated costs and with round trip bus fare and the cost of an abortion in Tijuana, according to a gal he asked at his job in Music City, plus what I have in savings, that might just barely be enough.

"Of course, someone else might be able to make you a better offer. Perhaps one of those book stores that specialize in the entertainment field."

Podolsky and I have tried them already. First Podolsky tried to talk me out of selling my collection. "You'll regret it for the rest of your life," like I don't know that already, so I had to insist, particularly since I still haven't heard anything definitive from Dr. Berman, except the lab screwed up so much that I had to go in and take another rabbit test and now I'm still waiting for the results, but I'm sure they're really just double checking and it's going to be bad news and I have to deal with this problem, because I can't take care of a child and Mother wouldn't and I couldn't even ask her.

So Podolsky drove me to several Hollywood Boulevard stores to get my collection appraised and they all were totally disinterested, wouldn't even take the time to go through my stuff. This is the one and only shot. Mr. Weybright's offer. I better grab it. It's the only chance I have, there's really no other way. I have to do it. I open my mouth to accept, but what comes out is, "I'm sorry, I can't do it."

"I understand," Mr. Weybright says, "as one collector to another."

I look at Podolsky, his horn-rimmed glasses are half-fogged because of the tension, he wipes them clear on his sleeve and helps me stack my autograph books back in the carton we brought them in. We carry them out to the trunk of his car.

"Let's stop at Walgreen's," he says. "I need to take an aspirin, my head's killing me."

He's not the only one.

So we go to Walgreen's, where my problem is solved, for only a nickel.

I use the pay phone to call Dr. Berman's office and the nurse puts me through and the doctor says he's got good news, the report just came back, and it's negative. I am not pregnant, but apparently I am severely anemic, and combined with emotional stress, that's probably why my period is off. He can give me a shot to boost my iron count and there also are dietary steps I can take to improve my condition.

After I hang up the phone I just stand there and Podolsky notices, I guess I'm smiling, but funny. "What'd he say?" he asks me.

"Dr. Berman told me to go eat a chopped liver sandwich and everything will be okay."

Roy

Addie is a creature of habit. Friday nights, after closing, she is alone in the store. Updating her inventory, working on her accounts. Licking her wounds (she used to lament), or calculating her wins (now I know) for the previous week. Hard, lonely work, poor thing. Juggling those heavy books, hiding all those pesky assets. Performing a feat of reverse alchemy. Making a silk purse look like a sow's ear.

Her only interruption comes at six o'clock when the delivery boy from Linny's deli, two blocks away, brings her dinner. Always the same: an Eddie Cantor sandwich. That's a lean corned beef and liverwurst combo on rye. Pickle, mustard, and raw onion on the side. And a Dr. Pepper. It's the only off-diet meal she permits herself all week.

The delivery kid knocks on the back door. She comes out of the office, unlocks the door, takes the food bag from him and signs for it. Gives him a two dollar tip in cash. He leaves. She goes back to her labors. Scarfing her high-cholesterol repast while gloating over her covert success. Kind of like Bogie in *Treasure of the Sierra Madre,* sifting gold dust with greedy fingers.

I'm parked down the street. I see the deli kid come and go.

Now she's alone. Benjy the guard and the sales biddies all long gone.

I walk around to the alley and up to the back door. It's covered with sheet metal for security. Afterward, I'll pry at the metal to make it look like a forced entry. But for now I've got a key. I turn the key. Open the door to my future.

Step inside. Turn into the storeroom. Dark. Bit of light splashing in from the hallway. Dimly illuminating the shelves. Stuffed to overflowing with bolts of fabric, lamps, shades, cornices, framed decor artwork, metal ornaments, brocaded toss pillows, candleholders, paperweights, fireplace andirons. Shipping clerk's packaging table. Neat and empty. Except for the usual tools. Scissors, staple gun, bills of lading impaled on a pointy spike, coils of twine, several sharp knives.

Fat City. Choice of weapons.

I stand in the semi-darkness and wait. After she finishes eating, Addie always dumps the garbage back here. Doesn't want the deli's garlic smells stinking up her office overnight. So ladylike. I hear her heels clicking now. Coming down the corridor. Manicured hand reaches in to grope at the wall switch. She enters as the light goes on. And sees me. Leaning against the wall. Boyish grin. Hands stuffed deep in my pants pockets. Mr. Casual.

"Hi there," I say. Like we're running into each other at a church social.

"What the fuck are you doing here?" Pissed. Not scared. Not yet.

"I need a special gift. For a new divorcee." Cute, huh? "Thought I'd give you the business."

"You're shopping—after closing, in my stockroom? In the dark? How'd you get in?"

"Usual way. Through the door."

"You still have a key?" I shrug. "Give it to me! Right now, you asshole—or I'm calling the alarm service."

"Hey, you want it—you got it."

I take my hand out of my pocket. Key in my open palm. She snatches the key. Triumphant. In charge. Doesn't even notice. Then she does.

"Why are you wearing gloves?'

"As Little Red Riding Hood said to the Big Bad Wolf in grandma's bed." I wigwag my gloved hands in her face. Now she's got it. Fear jolts her nervous system. She tries to cover. Terror in her eyes, but her voice is steady. I'll give her that.

"Well, let's go out front, Roy, see what we can find for your friend—" She lunges for the alarm service key pad on the wall. They don't call it the panic button for nothing. Gets Beverly Hills cops here within two minutes. But I'm ready for her. Leap forward. Between her and the panic button. Intercept. Catch her hand. She makes her other hand into a claw and tries to rake my face, but I grab that wrist, too. We're locked together. Hands upraised, we're frozen.

"Want to tango? Always takes two." I yank her across the narrow room, like Fred and Ginger gliding to the RKO orchestra, and slam her back against the shelves. I let go of her and bow politely. "Thank you for the dance." She's staring at me, wild-eyed.

"What do you want?" she asks. Kind of imploring.

"Nothing much, sweetie. Just for you to die."

And that's when I hit her. With a pewter candlestick from the shelf. The first blow bashes in the side of her face and she goes over backwards. Down to the floor. I sit astride her and keep hitting her and hitting her until her face is a ketchupy mush and—

"Oh, God, no, I just can't do it!" I scream.

The crash of the waves obliterates my cry.

I'm barefoot on the moonlit beach at Zuma Beach. Almost dawn. An insomniac trudging the deserted sands all night. While trying on imaginary scenarios for size.

I'm all by myself. Except for Jack Havoc.

Calm down, he says. *Why can't you do it?*

"Because—because I'll get caught."

No you won't. How?

"All that blood, it'll splash on me! What's the point of wearing gloves if I go back out on the street looking like a slaughterhouse butcher?"

So don't get bloody. Beating her to a pulp, that was your idea. Not that it's a problem. I mean, you'd be wearing black clothes, so it wouldn't show. But if it worries you, clop her on the back of the head, not much blood in the scalp, or choke her to death, that'd be fun—

"I keep telling you, I am not going through with this!"

Still haven't given me a good reason why not.

"Who're you that I have to give you reasons?"

Don't have one, do you? Fucker's laughing at me.

"An alibi! I'll be the first one the cops'll go after. Nearest and dearest."

So you'll have an alibi—we'll cover that base, I skipped over it 'cuz you said it was the deed itself you were scared about—

"I'm scared about the whole damn thing! Situation's bad enough the way it is, I don't want to go to prison for the rest of my life—or the fuckin' gas chamber!"

Bubela, babela, you're gonna walk away from this smelling like a rose. It's like taking a lesson at Arthur Murray's. You'll be a rich man, Roy, if you can just follow these few simple steps.

"Oh yeah? Easy for you to say. Tell me my alibi. C'mon, wisenheimer. Lemme hear. What's my alibi?"

Okay, and then you'll cool out and we can get this show on the road?

"First tell me the perfect alibi."

Let's see. You couldn't have been in the store because you were somewhere else…

"Yeah, riiiight. Like where? Having cocktails with the Pope?"

Good example. A person who'll swear they were with you. How about Kim?

"I can't even get her to return phone calls."

Your ex-pal Killer would've been a likely candidate.

"All of Killer's alibis belong to Dave Viola now."

So the trick is to have you seen somewhere by a lot of people and then you slip away, do your stuff, and get back in time so no one knows you were gone.

"Sure, that sounds real easy." Maybe sarcasm will get him off my back.

Don't shoot me down, Roy. Spitball with me. What if…if you were in a private steam room, or…a photo darkroom—

"Hey, got it," snapping my fingers. "Suppose I was locked

in a bank vault, like Houdini. Better yet, maybe in jail, a nice jail with an inconspicuous revolving back door."

You don't want to find an answer.

"No, you just don't have one."

It's not so difficult. Art gallery opening. Eat some hors d'oeuvres, lose yourself in the crowd, sneak out, sneak back in. What's the matter with that?

"Too damn risky. Don't you see that? It could fall apart in so many ways, I can't even begin to count 'em—"

Hey, man, just tryin' to help you out here.

"Don't help me! Leave me alone!"

Look, if it makes it easier for you—pretend it's a show. You've done these scenes before. Remember playing the lead in Dial M for Murder *in summer stock? You were great.*

"But I got caught! The perfect crime and they still nabbed me."

That was their idea of a happy ending. We'll write our own. You bump her off, empty the cash register and her purse, grab her watch, the diamond earrings, anything else that's loose and valuable. Burglar got surprised in the act and killed her. It'll work.

"They'll be able to trace her stuff—"

You'll drop it all off the pier into the ocean.

"Get out of my head! I don't want to talk about this or think about it or—"

Hey, man, I'm not in charge of what you think. He lights a Gauloises. Blows smoke in my face. *So let me get this straight. You're just gonna sit back and get reamed by that treacherous bitch, gang-banged by the whole damn scheming-dreaming town, castrated by Jack L. Warner and—*

I cover my ears, scrunch my eyes tightly shut, and make a loud humming-droning sound. "Uhhhhhhhhhhhhhhhhhhhhhh!"

And the waves crash.

When I open my eyes, he's gone.

I realize I'm changing.

When I first arrived in L.A., I'd be driving along on a sunny day and the smog would get to me. My eyes would water and sting so bad that I'd have to pull over to the curb and blink and blot until my vision cleared. Now, that doesn't happen anymore. I know it's not because the smog has vanished. Bob Hope wouldn't still be making jokes about it. And they wouldn't still be announcing on TV which days the school kids should avoid unnecessary exertion. It's me. I've changed. I've built up a tolerance for what used to throw me. Maybe I've mutated. For better or for worse.

Want to hear something funny? Now I've changed my brand of cigarettes. Dropped Luckies, after all these years. Started smoking Gauloises. Don't say it, I know, that's Jack Havoc's brand. Okay, could be it's a case of life imitating art. Or is that overstating the case for a lousy TV series? But Jack Havoc blowing that French smoke in my face stirred a desire. I know it was just imaginary smoke, but actors are trained in sense memory, so the smell I conjured up was vivid to me. Enough so that today, when I was out of butts, I bought a carton of Gauloises.

So that's what I'm doing. Hiding out in my rented house, smoking Jack Havoc's cigarettes, torching 'em up with my gold lighter from the Bogarts, that fucker Killer "found" it in the lining of his jacket. Bet he wouldn't've given it back if he knew he was gonna get a better offer so soon. I'm drinking large quantities of Stoli on the rocks (yeah, Jack Havoc's favorite beverage), and trying to figure what my next move should be. Short of murder.

As mad as I get at Jack Havoc, I have to admit that I envy that confident voice of his. He's got guts and smarts and a nothing-can-stop-me determination. It must be great to be so certain of everything. But I'm not Jack Havoc.

And while I sit here unshaved and unbathed and unnerved, I'm amazed at how much I miss Kim. Amazed and depressed. Because I've left messages for days with her answering service and Kim hasn't called me back. She might be my last, best chance. If I haven't blown it with her forever. Hey, anyone's entitled to get blitzed and make an asshole out of himself once. Right? Well, I'm convinced. But how do I get her back?

I look at the calendar. I look at my watch. Does Lancelot sit around lamenting about losing Guinevere? Or does he shave and shower and get on his horse and go do something about it?

Miracle of miracles, although it's Sunday night, there's a big fat parking space waiting for me on Sunset just a few doors down from the Hamburger Hamlet. It's crowded inside the restaurant, and unfed customers clog the entrance waiting for tables. I shoulder forward, hear people whispering my name to each other behind me. Enjoy it while I can. I look for Kim, but she's not on the floor. Behind the counter I see the owner, ex-actor Harry Lewis. He's dressed in a blue blazer with gold buttons and an old school tie, but he's slinging plates from the kitchen with the best of his staff. He's like a ballet dancer. Showing 'em how it's done. Harry spots me and waves me over. We know each other from some boozy evenings at Bogie's house in Holmby Hills. Harry played Edward G. Robinson's gunsel in *Key Largo* and got to smack Betty Bacall, for which he paid dearly in the last reel.

"Hey, stud," he says, "if you're looking for her, you just missed her. Or are you here for the chili?" He slips out from the counter and we chat in an alcove near the rest rooms. There's a drunk on the pay phone behind us pleading with a bookie for credit.

"Thought I might take her to the movies," I say. Harry seems to think everything's hunky dory. Maybe it is.

"That's where Kim went. The Academy's running the old *A Star Is Born*. She said she was in a mood for a good cry. Heard anything from Bogie?"

"Still working in Europe. I tried phoning him today in Rome but he had a couple days off. He and Betty went to Paris." So I won't be able to cry on his shoulder until he calls back.

"They'll always have Paris," Harry says. Quoting *Casablanca*.

"Here's lookin' at you, kid," I counter. Like a pair of

Freemasons exchanging the secret sign. "Standing room only in here," I say.

"Uh-huh. Business is great. We're opening two more places before the end of the year. After that, who knows?"

"Tomorrow the world."

"Yeah. I'm making more money than if I'd managed to stay alive at Warners for the full seven year deal, pay increases and all. And it's steady. People don't have to go to the movies, but they have to eat." I laugh. It's a joke he must use a lot. "Incidentally, congratulations on getting loose from the Colonel. Invite me to the premiere of your first big movie. Maybe you'll even let us cater the party."

"You're on, Harry." Tap his shoulder. Exchange grins. Good guy. Maybe he'll give me a job as a waiter. People have to eat.

It's my lucky night. Another juicy parking space opening up on Doheny across from Carl's Market. I tool the T-Bird up to the curb and hop out. There are Academy members across the street streaming toward the theater located around the corner. Kim's not one of them. I start walking briskly toward the crosswalk when I hear a familiar female voice call my name.

I turn expectantly. And see that it's little Reva. My first fan. Maybe she'll turn out to be my last fan. "Hey, Reeve, how are you?"

"Fine and dandy." She falls in step with me. "Goin' to the show by yourself?"

"Hope not. Kim's supposed to be here."

"She's so nice."

"Yeah, she sure is. What're you eating?" She's popping something into her mouth from a small box in her hand.

"Jujubes. Want some?"

"Haven't had one of those in years." She shakes several colorful candies into my palm. Taking candy from a kid. I start to chew, realize I haven't eaten anything else all day.

"What's playing tonight?" she asks.

"What? Oh. *A Star Is Born,* not the Judy Garland musical. The old one—"

"With Janet Gaynor and Fredric March. The original version. I loved it."

"That was before your time, you're just a kid." Enjoying the gummy candies. "Where'd you get to see it?"

"The Museum of Modern Art in New York. Saw all the old classics there. Garbo's movies. They're the best."

"You've got good taste. A serious student of the cinema."

"A lot of the collectors are." Collectors. That's what she calls her fellow autograph hounds. "She lives in New York now, Garbo, did y'know that? So all the collectors back there have seen her. Lots of times. But she never signs autographs. Not ever. Nobody gets Garbo. That's like Mount Everest. The unattainable."

Here we are walking and talking like two old friends. Which, in a weird way, I guess we are. But it's the first time we've had anything resembling a real conversation. "You miss New York?" I ask her.

"Not the weather. How about you?"

"Well, matter of fact, I'm probably going back there for a while. Do a play."

"You are? Well, then I better start saving my pennies so I can get back there and see you again on Broadway."

We're approaching the milling crowd in front of the Academy theater. So I start scanning the faces, looking for Kim. Almost forgetting Reva is at my side.

"Know what my favorite line is in *A Star Is Born*?" she asks.

I turn back to her. Certain she's going to recite the famous tag line, "This is Mrs. Norman Maine." But she surprises me.

"In the beginning of the picture, someone tells Janet Gaynor that the odds of becoming a movie star are one in a million. And she says, 'But what if I'm the one?' Like you. I always knew you were gonna make it."

Looks like you were wrong, sweetheart, I think. But at the same time I'm touched. "Thanks, Reva, that's very sweet." I pat her cheek. She beams a smile and her face reddens.

"Hope I wasn't out of line saying that," she mumbles.

"Just what I needed to hear." Then, gazing past her, I catch a glimpse of hair that looks like Kim's. "Good talking to you," I toss over my shoulder as I take off. But it's a false alarm. Not Kim. I prowl the population in front of the theater. No sign of Kim.

On the fringes of the crowd I can see Reva and the pack of collectors also patrolling. They're looking for stars and I'm looking for salvation. I'm buttonholed by two old friends from New York, both veterans of the "live" TV wars. Ralph Bellamy used to be *Man Against Crime* and Bill Gargan used to be *Martin Kane*. I guested on both their shows in my scrambling New York days. Reva and her cohorts spot a photo op and move in on us to flash their cameras. Caption: Three used-to-be TV stars. Talking about the good old days. I've gotta get away. I spot Kim's acting coach, the Maria Ouspenskaya lookalike, chatting with an elderly English couple. I elbow over to them.

"Hi, 'scuse me, good evening. Where's Kim?"

"Not veeth you? Must be here sahmplace. Maybe vent inside."

Maybe she did. I go inside. To the far right section of seats where we sat the last time. No Kim. House lights are flashing, show's about to start. Aisles crowd as the sidewalk set makes their entrance. Usual waving and blowing of kisses. I stand beside a couple of aisle seats and keep scanning the faces. Not as large a turnout tonight as for the Hitchcock double. Maybe Kim's in the ladies room. Lights dimming. I take the aisle seat, not near anyone else. If she comes in now we can whisper unheard.

What am I going to say? Start with I'm sorry. Don't give up on me. I'm teetering on the edge. I need you.

But she doesn't appear.

The RKO logo comes on screen. The globe with the transmitter perched on top. Sparking out a telegraph message to the world. And suddenly I know it's impossible for me to sit through this movie. Of all movies. Story of an actor on the skids. Who suicides in the ocean for a third act curtain. Mourned only by the woman he loved and lost.

Who's just starting the biggest and best part of her life. Without him.

I know that story. I am that story. Gotta get out.

I do it inconspicuously. Crouch in the darkness and slip through the nearby blackout curtain. Small alcove. Exit door. Push it open. Slip out into the alley behind Carl's Market. Fast. Close the metal door behind me. Get into my T-Bird. Where to now?

Go see Addie.

Stop dramatizing so much. Forget that crazy stuff about bumping her off. Just stop by. Pick up a cold bottle of champagne on the way. Maybe we can have a civilized chat. Like grownups. I'll explain my situation. Calmly. Honestly. Tell her I'd appreciate it if she could help me out. The royalties. If she says no, she says no. Worth a try. Sure, she doesn't love me anymore, but must be something left. Even if it's only pity. I'll take that. Settle for whatever I can get now. Then I remember. I've got an edge. Something going for me.

Today's our anniversary.

Roy

There aren't any other cars parked on the street up on Kings Road. The house looks as dark as the others near it. Guess she's not home. But I've come this far. I walk up to the front door. Reach for the doorknob. Force of habit. Catch myself. You can't just walk in here anymore. I ring the bell. Wait. Nothing. I'm about to leave when the entryway light above my head goes on. Through the carved wood door I hear Addie's muffled voice: "Yes?"

"It's me, Ade." I smile, knowing she's peering through the peephole.

The door swings open. She looks like hell. No makeup, eyes red and nose swollen as if she's got a cold. Or been crying. Hair yanked back into a ponytail held by a rubber band. Clad in a baggy-tufty baby blue sweater with a hole in one elbow and grass-stained dungarees. Her gardening outfit. Barefoot. Perfectly pedicured carmine toe nails. Wearing the diamond earrings but not her wedding ring. When she sees what I've got, her eyes widen.

"Happy anniversary." I show her the bottle of champagne. Offer her the flowers.

"Calla lilies," she says. Then going into Hepburn's lockjaw Yankee twang. "Such a lovely flowahhhh." She hugs the flowers to her chest. "I just noticed the calendar. Didn't think it was still in your memory bank."

"Some things you never forget. Luncheon at Sardi's." It

gives me a heart pang to say it. "Boy Meets Girl..."

"...and They Hate Each Other On Sight," she says.

"And here's the switcheroo—they *didn't* live happily ever after."

She laughs, points at the bottle of Perrier-Jouet. "Hey, if that champagne's cold, you can come in. We'll hoist a toast to the ghosts of yesteryear."

"Thought you'd never ask." I give her my little boy smile. I'm in the door.

Now I better explain. Today isn't the anniversary of the day that we were married. It's the anniversary of the day that we first met. She was still working as a trade paper reporter. I was still shagging radio roles and plugging a way-off-Broadway production of *Hamlet* about to open in a church up in Yorkville. I was playing Laertes. We desperately needed some publicity. So I'd phoned her office, pretended to be the CBS publicity guy for *Let's Pretend,* pitched her an interview with this brilliant new actor—"The Man of a Thousand Voices."

Me, of course.

We met at Sardi's. She tagged me right away. Knew the man who'd phoned her wasn't the CBS flack. She said my voice wasn't much like his.

"Okay," I said, "then you better call me 'The Man of 999 Voices.'" She laughed.

We went to bed that night.

My place.

Billie Holiday's tremolo voice wafting in through the window from the jazz club below, singing "I Wished On The Moon."

A million years ago.

Now Addie's leading the way into the den. Where the bar is in our—oops, *her*—house. I hear a man's voice coming from there. Whiny-sarcastic. Guy Saddler? Turns out to be Oscar Levant. Doing his talk show on TV. It's on a local L.A. station and it's a sensation. The piano virtuoso turned psychotic-hypochondriac. The show's done "live" and people tune in to see if this is the week he's going to flip out on camera and be carted off in a straitjacket.

"Know what Oscar said just before you rang the bell?" she asks. "That he's not allowed to watch Dinah Shore's TV show because he has diabetes."

We both laugh. Levant always tickled us. Something in common. A taste for nasty-funny. This is starting off nicely. She's at the sink behind the bar, pouring water in a tall vase for the flowers. I'm grappling with the cork on the champagne bottle, wondering how to gracefully get the conversation around to the subject of money. My money.

"Strip the tinsel off Hollywood," Oscar is telling his studio audience, "and you'll find the *real* tinsel underneath."

"Amen," I intone. "Guess you heard I ran into Guy at the supermarket. We had quite a chat—" The cork fires off like a rifle shot. Addie jumps with fright. Almost drops the vase.

"Silly. I don't know why I still do that."

"Always takes you by surprise." I pour champagne into the tapered flutes we bought in Majorca. "So we're drinking to…"

"…our first love cottage."

"My fourth floor walkup…"

"…shared by half the cockroaches in mid-Manhattan. Funny the things you miss."

She clinks glasses with me. We sip. Was she crying about that before I came? Nostalgia for the old days? This may be easier than I'd hoped.

Addie flops down on the deerskin couch that cost me a fortune. Coquettishly tucks her bare feet beneath her. Gestures for me to sit near her—but not too near. On the club chair that used to be my TV-watching spot. I put the champagne bottle on the bulky glass coffee table, so we both can get at it. That's the ticket. Good wine and lots of it. She tends to get girlish after the first couple of drinks.

"I could never have a mistress," Oscar Levant is saying, "because I couldn't bear to tell the story of my life all over again…"

Thanks a whole lot, Oscar, you had to remind her?

"And how's your new little friend?"

"Who? Oh, Kim. Fine, I suppose. I don't know. That's over."

Addie smiles. Like Gale Sondergaard as the Spider Woman. "Well, easy come, easy go. And the lady definitely was easy—right?"

I shrug. Let it go. Finish off my champagne, reach for the bottle. Start to pour myself more. She holds out her glass, too. Glad to oblige. I fill hers again. To the brim.

"I'm moving back to New York," I say. "Blowin' this burg." Giving it a gangster reading.

She smiles. "Roy, maybe it's a good thing you're not going to play Jack Havoc anymore. Honestly, I think you were getting confused sometimes as to who's who." She sips the wine. "Guy didn't mention you were leaving."

"Just decided. Things aren't working out for me here."

"Guy told me." She looks concerned.

"So I wanted to talk to you about—"

She interrupts. "Guy has a vile mouth sometimes."

"Tell me about it. He said the two of you were tap dancing while you made up an invitation list for my funeral. Unquote."

"Lying old queen! I'd never take joy from your troubles."

I'm tempted to remind her about the curse she placed on my brow. But things are going so well. "Guy mentioned the great stuff coming up with the store—or should I say, stores. He said you're going national and—"

She reaches out and covers my hand with hers. "Roy, I know we've exchanged some pretty harsh words lately, but I've been thinking. We were together a long time…"

I squeeze her hand. "A lot of good times," I agree. "That's why I knew, if we could sit down and discuss things, calmly and fairly…"

"Yes, fairly, like…like old best friends…" She squeezes my hand back.

I can't believe it. I'm in like Flynn.

"And I know," she says, "that despite everything that's happened, because of all we've meant to each other, and because you were there every step of the way and you saw how terribly hard I've worked, so I know that you'd never do anything to harm me."

What the hell's she talking about? I'm not here to hurt her, I'm here to beg for crumbs. Crumbs she'll never even miss. Royalties that *I* worked hard for. She mistakes my confusion for hesitation.

"Promise me, Roy, promise you won't do anything…foolish."

"Like what?"

She drains her champagne glass. Nervous smile. "Oh, I don't know. Guy is such a gabby old twit. Gossip he might have babbled to you about off-shore bank accounts—he's always making up stories and then believes them himself." She pours herself some more champagne.

It comes to me in a flash. Why she's been crying, why she's being so unexpectedly nice. And who's really conning who around here.

"You're worried that I might drop a nickel on you. With the IRS or someone."

Her latest glass of champagne is at her lips. But she quivers as if I've physically shaken her. Wine spills down her chin and onto her chest. She stares at me.

"That could spoil your whole day, couldn't it, Addie? Not to mention scaring away your big investors."

"I knew that's why you came here tonight! To shake me down. You cocksucker!"

She hurls her glass at my face. I block it with my hands. The glass careens off me and smashes into the mirror behind the bar. I stare at it in amazement; she's really out of control tonight, busting up her own property. I look back just in time to see her coming at me. The champagne bottle raised high, she's swinging it at my head like a battle club. I manage to duck under the bottle and butt my head into her belly. Ooof! Wind's knocked out of her. It's like a shtick out of an old Fredric March–Carole Lombard comedy. Girl tries to clobber Boy, but Girl never manages to lay a glove on Boy. I feel a giggle bubbling up inside me. Until I see her stumble and fall headlong onto the coffee table. It collapses like a movie prop. A jumble of shattered glass. She's on her face. Not moving a muscle. Then I see the pool of blood seeping out beneath her.

I know she's dead. Even before I kneel and turn her over. Her eyes are still wide open. Unblinking and unseeing. I look deep into them and see my life ending with hers. There's a stiletto-like shard of glass sticking out of her chest.

"And they say that Shakespeare stole his plays from Christopher Marlowe," Oscar Levant is prattling, "and then murdered Marlowe when he complained. That's my idea of a true artist."

I reach out to feel for the pulse beneath her chin. The way the tech advisor taught me for the show. No pulse.

Careful now, Jack Havoc says. *Watch what you touch, got to think about fingerprints.*

"Where'd you come from?"

Been with you all along. I didn't say anything 'cuz you were doing great all by yourself.

"You make it sound like I came here to…"

Didn't you?

"It was an accident. You saw it!"

Hey, you know what Freud says. There are no accidents.

"But it was! I didn't have the slightest idea in my mind of—"

Okay, okay, if you say so, then I believe you. Sly smile. *But you're gonna have a helluva time convincing anyone else. Roy the Bad Boy, whose hobby is punching out people.*

"Maybe I ought to call an ambulance. They still might be able to revive her—" I reach for the phone. But it's as if an invisible hand grabs my wrist. Stopping me.

You don't want to do that, pal. If Lady Luck dealt you the winning cards, just say thank you and cash in all the chips.

"You mean, just walk away?"

Like you were never here tonight. Who's to know?

"Yeah." I'm wiping my prints off the champagne bottle. "I'll wash up my glass, put it away. They find her, everybody'll assume she drank too much and fell down. Got jabbed by the broken glass, bled out, did it all by herself. That way they won't even be looking for anyone else."

Won't fly, amigo.

"Why the fuck not?"

Because of that. He points at the mirror behind the bar, where the champagne glass she hurled hit. The mirror is shattered. *Better stick with the original plan. A burglary that went sour.*

"Yeah, but—what about the alibi?"

C'mon, kid, you already got that base covered. You were at the movies. Now hurry up.

I trash the den a little to make it clear there was a scuffle. Don't have to worry too much about wiping off fingerprints. I used to live here. I get a screwdriver from a kitchen drawer, go into the backyard, close the door, and pry it open. Put the screwdriver back. Race into the bedroom, grab a pillow-case. Yank open bureau drawers, mess up the contents, dump the baubles and bangles from her jewel box into the pillowcase. Mostly junk jewelry. She generally keeps the good stuff in the bank vault. I see a relic of the past. My first gift to her. A gold-plated locket. Inscribed "For Addie, Love Forever. From Roy." With a three-for-a-dollar photo of us inside. Junk jewelry. I toss it in with the rest, heft the pillow case. Ready to go. Starting for the front door.

Jack Havoc calls me back.

Forgetting something, aren't you, boychik?

I can't think what. Look around. Frantically. Checking my watch. Gotta get back to the theater. "Don't play guessing games with me, Jack. If you know, tell me!"

The earrings, he says. *No self-respecting burglar is gonna leave them behind.*

He's right. I rush back into the den. As I take the earrings her eyes are still staring up at me. "What big eyes you have," I whisper.

I don't have much time. *A Star Is Born* probably runs just under two hours. Most of the big pictures of that era did. No time to detour to the Santa Monica pier to dump the contents of the pillowcase into the ocean and still get back to the Academy before the end of the movie. Just sling that crap on the floor of the T-Bird's back seat. Get rid of it later.

And burn rubber now. Of course, I catch every goddamn red light along the way. When I reach Melrose and Doheny, my parking space on the street is long gone. I spend the next ten minutes circling the area, not finding another space. I'm tempted to go into the Carl's Market lot. But it's so well lit I'm afraid someone will spot me getting out of the car. It's imperative that no one is able to say that I wasn't inside the theater for the entire show. I explode with frustration.

Pounding on the wheel won't help, Jack Havoc says.

"Who asked you?"

Don't panic. Go around once more. C'mon. I feel lucky.

"Sure, sure, that's what you said before, but it didn't—" There it is. My space. About to happen. A Nash Rambler just pulling out. On Doheny. Down the block from where I parked earlier. Next to a leafy tree. Providing good, deep shadows.

See pal, gotta have faith.

I zoom into the parking spot. Hop out of the T-Bird. Got to get there before the show's over. I walk rapidly, forcing myself not to run. Don't want to draw attention. Skulk up an alley onto Melrose, cross the street. I've already figured my best vantage point: in the dark doorway of the veterinarian's office facing the theater. I get in position. Take a deep breath. Theater parking lot is still full, so the show must still be on. Then I panic. I left the car unlocked, with a back seat full of incriminating evidence. Got to go back!

Right then the front doors of the theater open. Happy Academy members and their guests come streaming out. Overflowing the sidewalk, bodies moving in every direction. Can't go back to the car, hell, stuff's on the floor, who's going to notice anyway. I stroll across to the front of the theater. Blowing my nose in my handkerchief to conceal my face, until I'm on the curb. Then I look around at the crowd. Standing tall. See and be seen. Looking for a friendly face. There's one. The ideal one.

William Wellman, the director of *A Star Is Born.* Ramrod straight as the Lafayette Escadrille fighter pilot he was during World War I. He's surrounded by back slappers. Accepting congratulations for a movie he made a generation ago. I elbow my way through to him. We've played doubles together at the Beverly Hills Tennis Club and beat all comers.

"Wild Bill," I yell, "you've done it again!" Using the classic sneak preview critique.

"There he is—the best netman in town!"

We hug, we kibbitz. Swirl of well-wishers around us. Autograph collectors moving in to snap photos. Great! Proof positive that I'm here. I catch a glimpse of Reva among them. I wink at her, she smiles back. I invite Wellman for a drink and we stroll to Dan Tana's bar a block away. My alibi's getting better and better. We hoist a few. I tell Wellman a little about my travails with Jack Warner. He's sympathetic.

"Been there myself," he says. That's why *A Star Is Born* was so important to him. "Salary I collected for writing and directing, that was my Fuck You Money." He defines that as "sufficient funds so that the assholes can't make you do anything you don't want to do. Gotta have that, Roy," he counsels.

Maybe I do. Now.

When I get back to my T-Bird, it's almost midnight. But I'm pretty sure that Addie won't be found before tomorrow morning. At the earliest. I yank the car door open, look in back, and—okay, the pillowcase is still there. But some of the contents are strewn onto the floor. Probably jostled loose in transit. I climb into the car, slam the door and turn around. Start to scoop the loose items back into the pillowcase. When I notice something on the floor among the pieces of jewelry.

A bright green jujube.

The kind of candy I haven't eaten in years.

Until tonight.

When Reva offered me some of hers.

The Safeway market on Beverly Drive at Olympic is closed for the night. Parking lot deserted. I drive around to the loading area and stop, can't be seen here from the street. Turn off the motor. Try to control my mounting sense of fear. I bring the pillowcase up front. Spill the stuff onto the passenger's seat. Stir it around. Don't know what I'm looking for. But in a moment, an idea occurs to me. A terrifying idea. I poke among Addie's trinkets and find one of her diamond earrings. Poke some more...more and more frantically...but...

The other one's not here, Jack Havoc says.

"Yes it is!" I tell him. Showing it to him triumphantly.

Okay, he says grudgingly, *but, hey, where's the locket?*

Heart pounding. I grope through the trinkets again. But I can see he's right. The locket's gone. "For Addie, Love Forever. From Roy."

She took it. Like when she's swiped butts from your car's ashtray.

"But she's never taken anything valuable."

Didn't tonight either. Just a cheap little locket.

I don't say anything. Resisting what he wants me to say. But he won't let it go.

Reva found the locket here in the car. She saw the rest of the jewelry.

He waits. I still don't say anything.

She knows you moved the car. Knows you went away and came back. So she can destroy your alibi. He's examining the jujube. *And with the locket to back her up, they'd believe her.*

"Yes." Have to admit that much.

She can put you in the gas chamber, Roy. Don't let her do that.

"I'll—I'll take care of it!"

How?

"I'll get the locket back."

That's only half the job. He reads my mind. *You don't have any choice.*

"I know," I say. Poor Reva.

part two

"I have a little shadow
That goes in and out with me,
And what can be the use of it
Is more than I can see."

—Robert Louis Stevenson

21

Reva

Almost all the lights are dark inside the other apartments in our building as I climb the steps to the second-floor landing. The neighbors are mostly blue-collar folks who turn in early, but I see a light flickering behind the closed blinds in our living room. Gotta be the TV set, so that means Mother is inside waiting for me, but the question is whether she's awake or asleep in front of the tube.

I hope for the best and carefully unlock the front door and slip quietly into the quasi-gloom. Mother is on the sofa, stretched out facing the TV, her head propped up on a pillow, snoring softly. She's wearing her ancient green robe and her feet are bare. Her hands are clasped in the prayer position and tucked under her cheek. She looks defenseless and benign, almost like a little girl.

A black and white Abbott and Costello comedy is on TV and it's the middle of the movie so I know Mother has been in dreamland a while, because she hates Abbott and Costello and would have turned it off if she was up when it started. It's a picture I like, the one set in the Arabian desert, and the part I like best is when pudgy little Costello is locked up in a jail cell with this huge hairy guy, who starts out super-friendly because he's been alone in jail so long he's starved for companionship. Costello asks him why he's in here, and the guy tells his story, real pleasantly, but whenever he comes to the word "Constantinople," the hairy guy flips out and goes after Costello. "Slowly I turned, step by step, I knew what I had to do..." and he grabs Costello and shakes him and chokes him until Costello calms him down, and the guy goes on with his story, and Costello tries at all costs to avoid the word "Constantinople," but, of course, it keeps coming up, "Slowly I turned, step by step..."

Guess in a way that's the story of me and my Mother. Only I've never figured out what the trigger word is. I mean, it could be anything or nothing. But like Costello with the "Constantinople" guy, I know what I have to do: put Mother to bed. If I just leave her snoozing out here all night, she'll wake up with a crick in her neck and that'll be my fault. Thing is when I move her, she may be a purring pussy-cat or a clawing cougar, it could go either way.

"Mother?" I lean down and whisper. There's a sweet per-fume emanating from her that I recognize as the smell of gin. I notice the empty Bombay bottle on the carpet beside the sofa. Gently, I shake her shoulder. Her eyes flutter open, she sees me and she smiles, "Hi, honey." It's going to be a good night.

"Time to go to bed," I say. I swing her feet down, sit her up. She grasps my arm and, with a little effort from both of us, she's standing.

"Gotta go t'bed," she mumbles.

"I'll help you," I say.

I put my arm around her shoulder and guide her, because her eyes aren't really open and she's none too steady on her feet, but we make it into her bedroom. I settle her down, cover her up, tuck her in. She smiles, still without opening her eyes, gives me this cute little wave, and murmurs, "G'night."

I stand looking down at her, because it's one of the nicest moments we've had in a long time, even if she slept through it.

Without warning, my eyes get all misty. Not for Mother, but for me.

I'm remembering when I was the one who got tucked in at night, by my Daddy when I was a little girl. No matter how late he came home from work at the Brooklyn Navy

Yard or how tired he was, he'd come tell me a bedtime story.
It was always about the funny adventures of Psoop Psoop,
this klutzy but plucky kid in Russia. He made the stories up.
Maybe Daddy never got very far in school before he ran
away to America, but he had a wonderful imagination. I
suddenly miss him so much it aches like it used to.

Then I go to my door, unfasten the padlock, go in and
bolt the door, and I'm secure. The rows of autograph books
are back in their proper places on the shelves. I'm glad that
the breakup between Roy and Killer Lomax that I saw at the
July 4 parade seems permanent. That lout hasn't been
around since, and judging by our conversation on the way to
the Academy tonight, Killer didn't say anything to damage
me in Roy's eyes. I'm worried about Roy, the way he looked.
But what with the divorce and quitting the TV show, and
now he may be leaving town, I guess he's under a lot of
strain. Aren't we all, though?

I get my journal out of its safe place under the floorboard
in the closet and then I sit cross-legged in front of my collection of Roy stuff. There's a gap in the centerpiece, where
the torn glove from St. Paddy's used to be and then the cigarette lighter from the Bogarts took its place. It looked great
alongside the Romanoff's ashtray filled with Roy's butts.
Only I had to give the lighter back. I should have realized
Roy would miss it, even though Killer made out like it was
his. Now I've got a suitable replacement for that center spot.
The locket. I take it out of my purse and carefully position
it on the shelf so that the faces of Roy and Addie shine down
upon the room.

Then I stare at the locket. I can remember when Addie
started wearing it. In fact, I admired it one February afternoon at the *Streetcar* stage door and she gave Roy such a fabulous look and squeezed his hand and told me, "It's my
Valentine's Day present," and it's obvious what's happened
now, with the divorce going on and all, she's cleaning house
and dumping on him all those trinkets and bits of costume
jewelry that once meant so much. I mean, how do you give
back that locket? It's like pitching away a part of yourself.

Roy's probably been carrying that stuff around in the back seat of his car for God knows how long, not knowing what to do with it. I'd thought of taking the glitzy pair of earrings, but they might be worth something, not like the tarnished locket that I'll keep here on the shelf to preserve the echo of the good days. A perfect piece of memorabilia.

With pen in hand, my current journal open in my lap, I continue looking up at the locket on the shelf, studying the smiling faces. Roy and Addie—the girl who laughed when the other collectors called him a "Nobody."

"She never was right for you, was she, Roy?" Like the Fisherman and his Wife, you gave her a palace and it still wasn't enough. Maybe this new girl, Kim, she might be the one to really make you happy.

These are good thoughts, and I better get 'em down on paper before I forget, starting with our accidental encounter tonight. I start to write about when I ran into Roy on the street near the Academy where he first parked his car before the movie and he sees me and he says, "Hey, Reeve, whatcha eatin'?" and I say, "Jujubes, you want one?"

22

I know something's wrong. Even though I'm still half asleep. Eyes closed. Just swimming up to consciousness. Even then I know. But for an instant I can't remember exactly what it is. Just that it's bad. Real bad. Then it all comes crashing back.

Addie's dead and Reva can unravel my slim shot at an alibi.

She knows I left the screening at the Academy and came back. With Addie's jewelry in my back seat of my car. She's got that fuckin' locket, so she's got proof positive.

What I do today will determine the rest of my life.

But the thing is…I don't know what to do.

There's this pounding in my head. Won't stop. Then I realize it's not my head, it's the front door. Someone's knocking. Loud. Banging. Calling my name.

I stagger out of bed, glance at the clock. 10:16. Slept away half the morning. Whoa! The whirlies! Hung over from the bottle of brandy I killed all by my lonesome last night. In an effort to turn off the projection machine running inside my brain. Kept playing a continuous loop of the night's events. Until I passed out. Stop that fucking banging! Grab a robe, run my fingers through my hair, barefoot to the front door.

"Yeah, yeah, okay, I'm coming."

I swing open the front door and there are two strangers on my doorstep. Mutt and Jeff. Big guy and little guy. Not so little, really. My size. Thin as a whippet, funny smirk on his face. Sharp dresser. Wearing a Sy Devore navy blue blazer and gunmetal gray slacks. I almost bought that same blazer from Sy a few weeks ago. The big guy, he's older, with a Gable mustache and bad skin, and he's dressed in a baggy seersucker suit that's probably off the rack at Penney's. He's the one who says he's sorry to make so much noise but your bell's busted I guess, and he flashes the badge and does the honors.

"Mr. Darnell, my name's Tigner and this is my partner, Sergeant. Marshak. We're detectives with the sheriff's office."

Dum-de-dum-dum! It's life imitating Jack Webb. The opening scene from any episode of *Dragnet.* I want to snicker at the corny intro. But the voice inside me sounds the warning.

Shape up, dummy, this isn't Dragnet—*it's* Candid Camera *and these two dipshits are monitoring every blink you make.*

Thanks, Jack, I needed that.

I rub my eyes. Stare at them blearily, don't have to fake that. "Look, if it's about all those parking tickets, I told my accountant to pay 'em and—"

"The check is in the mail," the little guy, Marshak, says. With a wink to go with the smirk.

"We're here about something else," Tigner says. "Mind if we come in?"

I don't mind. Invite 'em in. Give 'em cups of coffee. Curtain going up. I'm ready for my close-up, Mr. DeMille. They're pretending they're here on some kind of routine thing, no rush to tell me exactly what. I'm acting like I don't have a care in the world. Thinking what a good thing it is that I detoured to the Santa Monica pier last night before bedtime and dropped all of Addie's jewelry in the bay. Everybody's nonchalantly studying everybody for subtext, as we actors call it. Difference between me and the cops, of course, is that when it comes to bullshitting, I'm a pro, I do it for a living. But then, of course, they're pros, too, adept at using their shit detectors. Interesting situation.

Wanna see the garden? Just a lap pool. Great little house. No, I'm just renting. Yeah, I live here alone, just got divorced. Terrific location for getting back and forth to the studio in Burbank, a straight shot over Coldwater and hang a right and—hey, what're you guys doin' around here anyway? You're County cops and this is Beverly Hills.

And Tigner tells me. He does the heavy lifting for the team, conversation-wise. There's been an incident on Kings Road, at the house you used to live in. A break-in. I'm afraid we have very bad news. Mrs. Darnell was injured.

Injured? Not dead? Okay, Tigner, good feint. "How bad? What hospital is she in—"

"Actually we just came from the house," Tigner says. "The medical examiner pronounced her. She's dead." How big should I play it? Drop my coffee cup? *Nah, too much,* Jack Havoc says inside me. I settle for just staring at Tigner. Focusing on his walrus mustache. While I absently tilt my cup, so coffee spills on the patio, as if I'm unaware of it.

Tigner takes the cup from my hand. "Maybe you better sit down."

He eases me into a chaise and I give my best impression of a man going into shock. A good actor can change colors like a chameleon. Red for embarrassment, gray for despair. This calls for green for I-may-toss-my-cookies. Marshak brings me a sip of cognac. "Tell me what happened," I say.

Tigner does his *Joe Friday* routine. Just the facts. Happened last night. Little after nine. Yeah, we're pretty certain about the time. Have to ask, sir, where were you about then? I tell him I was at the movies. Only a couple miles away, if I'd only known. Afterward? Had a few belts with an old buddy at Tana's on Santa Monica. Why, you don't think I—? He assures me. Just routine.

What he says is polite and comforting, lots of "sirs" and "Mr. Darnells," but it all comes out vaguely challenging. Subtext. He's been jotting now and then in a spiral notebook. Makes you feel that if he doesn't jot, it's not important. Yeah, sure.

Tigner and Marshak step away to confer. I make out I'm not watching them. Finish the pony of cognac. *You done good, buddy boy,* Jack Havoc whispers. Then Tigner comes back over. "Can we ask you for a big favor, if you're feeling up to it?"

I shrug. Man in pain. "Whatever I can do."

"Could you come back over to Kings Road with us now? We're not sure precisely what was taken. Maybe you can help us make out a list of the stolen items."

It's the last place in the world I want to go. "Yeah, sure, be glad to help."

We're speeding, yes, absolutely rocketing down Sunset Boulevard, heading for the Strip. Marshak is at the wheel of my T-Bird. He volunteered. "Better if you don't drive so soon after a shock like this." Tigner has gone ahead in their unmarked Chevy. I figure this way Marshak gets to ask me more questions. But he doesn't seem interested in anything but the performance of my car. "Always wanted to take a spin in Jack Havoc's chariot," he says.

Apparently cops don't have to stop for red lights or stop signs. Marshak gives even the busiest intersections a mere glance and punches through. Just like Jack Havoc in a high speed chase. But the other cars on the road are being driven by civilians, not stunt men. It doesn't seem to bother him.

"We've met before, y'know," Marshak says.

"Where?"

"On the set. Over at the Van Nuys courthouse. Coupla months ago. I was in uniform, herding traffic for your production company. Off-duty cop picking up some extra shekels. We knocked back a few midnight brewskis in the prop truck, me and you, and talked about how I could become a TV writer."

I remember him. "Arzy." Funny, sarcastic, smart. "You had a beard then."

"Just off an undercover assignment. Shaved it as soon as we got the convictions."

"But Tigner said your name is Marshak."

"R.Z. Marshak. Richard Zachary. Everybody runs the initials together. Arzy. I'm half of Hollywood's best-known robbery-homicide team. See, Tigner's first name is Harry. So all the wisenheimers at our station call us—"

"Arzy and Harry," I laugh. "The Nelson Family. Most normal people in the western world."

"Well, the similarity doesn't go that far."

"So what's with your partner? He talks to me like he thinks I snatched the Lindbergh baby."

"That's just a game we play."

"Oh, yeah. Good cop, bad cop. And he's the bad cop."

Arzy glances over at me. The smirk. "Got it backward, Roy. I'm the really badass cop. Listen, I took to heart what you told me. Organized some of my best police stories, maybe one of 'em is right for *Jack Havoc.*"

"I'm not gonna do that show anymore, Arzy."

"But you'll do something else. Might fit that. We ought to get together and let me pitch you a few ideas sometime."

"Right, we will, but—right now—"

"Hey, of course, not now, it's awful what happened to your ex-old lady, but we know who did it."

He's making the turn up onto Kings Road. I hold my breath.

"I mean, we don't know his name and house number—but there's a cat burglar who's been hitting rich houses up in the hills. Done six in the last two months. Same M.O. as this one. Always show-business folks. Forced entry. Scoops up all the best goodies and vanishes into the night."

We round the corner and there's the house. Various county vehicles parked, including Tigner's Chevy. An ambulance is in the driveway. The white-coated attendants have flipped open the rear door of their ambulance, and sit on the tailgate smoking and waiting. Talking with a uniform cop. They look over at us as Arzy screeches to a halt at the curb.

"So you think this break-in guy is the sonuvabitch who—"

"Gotta be. He hasn't been violent before, but I guess your Addie got unlucky and came home while he was at work."

We get out of the T-Bird and walk toward the front entrance. In my head, Jack Havoc chuckles and whispers, *A fuckin' neighborhood cat burglar. Could you die? I mean, are we the two luckiest guys alive or what?*

Arzy lets me go in first and I'm about to turn left and head for the den. But I catch myself. More information than I'm supposed to have. So I wait for him. Hint of a smirk from him. And he goes right, leads the way into the bedroom. The tossed drawers and scattered contents still strewn on the floor. There's a forensic guy dusting for prints. A police photographer snapping away. Tigner is standing in the middle of the room watching everyone work. He nods at me. Takes out his spiral notebook. Points at the empty jewel case on the floor.

"What would've been in there?"

"Mostly costume stuff. She kept the real goodies in a safe deposit box at the bank, unless she was wearing 'em someplace special."

Arzy wanders out. Tigner asks me to recall any specific items that might have been swiped. I furrow my brow. Make out like I'm pulling it piece by piece from distant memory. Actually, I'm just reciting what I saw last night as I dumped the contents into the pillowcase. He jots. Of course, I make no mention of the locket. Why be that helpful? I tell him that's all I can think of…but then I snap my fingers. Hey, the earrings! Her favorite earrings. Diamonds, worth ten grand. Did she have 'em on?

Tigner makes a last jot and closes his notebook. Well, she was wearing earrings, we could see the indentations on her lobes, in fact, there's a couple scratch marks where the guy yanked them off. C'mon, I'll show you. He guides me into the den. The fingerprint dusters have been here already. Arzy is perched on a bar stool, near the phone, waiting for us. Addie's body is still there. On the floor. Covered with a sheet. There's a tent-like peak in the center and I know that's where the glass shard is protruding from her chest. But I don't know that, right? I don't have to fake my horror at what I'm seeing. The sunlight shining in from the backyard makes it even worse. Like the morning after a wild party. Before the maid comes in to clean up the mess. But not this time. This mess is forever. Tigner kneels and lifts a corner of the sheet. Just enough to reveal one side of Addie's face. He points at the ear lobe. There's a scratch and a few dots of blood.

"He thinks the earrings were diamonds," Tigner says. Dropping the sheet back in place.

"Can we get a full description?" Arzy asks me.

"Insurance," I mumble. "It was listed. The broker's got an appraisal and photos on file." I tell him the name of the insurance broker. "Who found her?"

"Cleaning woman," Tigner says. "Came in early, had her own key. Shrieked loud enough to scare the neighbors. They thought the Russians were landing."

"Poor Milly, she's been with us a long time."

"Oh. Your pal Bill Wellman says to give you his best," Arzy says. "Thoughts and prayers are with you. Wants you to give him a call when you can."

"You talked to Bill? Already?"

"We're quick and we're thorough, Roy. Didn't want to leave a biggie dangling. Wellman confirms your alibi. I'm sure a lot of other people will, too. Famous face in the crowd like yours. So it's official you were at the Academy Theater watching Wellman's old movie when Addie got it. Now we can move on."

"How come you're so certain exactly when—when she died? I thought the medical examiners can only give you an educated guess."

"We can nail this one to the minute," Tigner says.

"Clockwork," Arzy says. He lifts a plastic evidence bag off the bar. Shows it to me. Addie's wristwatch is in the bag. The crystal is smashed. Time stopped at 9:43. I'm stunned. I don't even remember seeing the watch on her wrist last night. I'm not sure if this is good for me or not.

"It's an expensive watch, why didn't he take it?" I don't mean to say that out loud, but I do.

Arzy is tickled. "Jack Havoc on the job. Putting the clues together for us. Did I tell you this guy's sharp, Harry?" Then back at me. "Her hand was twisted underneath her body, so he probably didn't notice the watch." He pushes off from the bar stool. "Want to see how the fucker got in?"

Marshak goes to the patio door. Indicates the gouge marks I made last night. Behind us the ambulance guys have wheeled in a gurney and they heft Addie, sheet and all, onto it. I'm torn between looking at that and what Arzy's showing me. "He usually uses a crowbar. This is one of his neater jobs. Normally rips the shit out of the molding. If there's an alarm gonna go off, he wants to know about it right away."

"What about silent alarms?" The gurney wheels are squeaking as they wheel her away.

"Most folks who invest in security systems don't want silent alarms—they want all the noise they can buy." The smirk. "One thing's for sure—these robberies are selling a helluva lot of alarm systems in the neighborhood. You see Armed Response signs sprouting on all the lawns."

"Maybe you ought to look in that direction—some alarm salesmen drumming up new business."

"We're already on that one. But keep those Jack Havoc suggestions coming." He gestures around the den. "Anything else you notice that's gone?" I study the room, shake my head. He suggests we check out the other rooms, although they don't seem to have been disturbed. I do what he asks but don't have anything to add to the list.

"That's it then, I guess." Arzy is leading the way back to the front door. "Know what movie your pal Wellman made that really knocked me out? *Battleground.* 'Sound off, one-two, sound off, three-four...' Slogging through the fuckin' snow. Battle of the Bulge. Thought I was living a rerun couple winters later, when I was in Korea with the Marines, freezin' our ever-lovin' noogies off."

He opens the front door and I see a mobile TV van parked at the curb. A reporter and camera team are shooting the loading of Addie's body into the ambulance. The TV reporter spots me and instantly refocuses his camera crew.

I've seen him on the channel five news but never met him
before.

"Roy," he sticks his microphone in my face, "are you
under arrest?"

Before I can tell this asshole to go fuck himself, Arzy
intercedes. "Mr. Darnell is here at the request of the sheriff's office to aid us in our investigation. At the moment we
are pursuing several leads but do not have an official suspect
yet. But we believe the murder took place during the commission of a house robbery."

The TV news reporter asks Arzy to identify himself and
he does. Then the reporter shifts back to me. No more Mike
Wallace belligerence. Now he's Mr. Sympathy. "This must
have come as a terrible shock to you, Mr. Darnell. How long
were you and Adrienne Ballard married?"

"Six years. She was a wonderful woman. There'll never be
another person like her." All true. Depending on how and
when you read it. But the TV snooper can't let it rest.

"Even though the two of you were getting divorced?"

"Things change—but I still thought of her as my best
friend." Little white lies. What the hell.

"I think that's enough for now, guys." Arzy takes my arm.
Walks me away from the electronic grave-robbers, who
switch focus back to the ambulance. Getting the tag shot of
it pulling out into the street.

"Thanks, Arzy." We're back at my T-Bird.

"No sweat." He leans against the T-Bird door. Preventing
me from getting inside. "Know something? When I see the
break-in marks, all gouged out like that, sometimes I think,
Maybe this turkey's sending us down the wrong trail. Maybe
he doesn't get in with a crowbar—maybe he uses a key. And
the rest is just frosting. Oh, I almost forgot."

He takes a set of keys out of his pocket. My keys. From
when he was driving us here. He tosses them to me. Gives
me his Mr. Innocent smile.

"Hey. Do you still have keys to this house, Roy?"

What am I going to say? I open my palm, point at the key
ring. "Just this one. Gave all the others back when I left."

The smirk. "Might as well throw that one away. Doesn't work. I tried it while you and Harry were doing the inventory. She had the locks changed a couple weeks ago. We found the locksmith's bill in her papers. Guess she didn't trust you anymore, Roy."

"Look, Arzy, you're gonna hear a lot of stuff. I mean, it's no secret that Addie had officially resigned from my fan club."

"Yeah, I figured. Lots of photos all over the place, but none of you."

I shrug. Give him my best Jimmy Stewart. "When you're gone, you're gone."

It's the right thing to say. He claps me on the shoulder. My buddy.

"Hey, we've all been there, pal. Go ask my ex for her opinion of me." He opens the driver's door for me. "Take it slow. I'll be in touch."

I get behind the wheel and pull out. In the rear view mirror, I can still see him. Standing in the middle of the street. Watching me go.

"What's he looking at me for?" I say.

Jack Havoc doesn't answer. He just laughs.

"Think that's funny?"

He's not looking at you, narcissist. It's the car. He likes my car.

"Then what's all that cat-and-mouse shit? About the keys and photos and all."

It's his job. Check out every angle. Just like in the movies.

"Then you don't think he thinks I—"

What I think is you've gotta watch what you say.

"Like what?"

Like that crap about Addie not being a member of your fan club. Want to give him any more hints where to go looking?

"That didn't mean anything. It was just a cute way of letting him know that Addie was pissed at me. He's gonna find that out anyway."

C'mon, Roy. Fan club. Just 'cuz it's in your mind, it doesn't have to be comin' out of your mouth.

He's right, of course. All I can think of is Reva. What she's heard. What she's making of all this. Where I can find her.

Now you're talkin', kid, Jack Havoc says.

When I walk into Romanoff's, it's a show stopper. Instantly half the lunch crowd spots me and whispers to the other half. The noise level noticeably decreases. Now I've got several hundred of Hollywood's elite all pretending they're not gawking at me. Gossip in filmland moves faster than a speeding bullet. So everyone in the room knows about Addie's death. But suddenly these diners have ring-side seats at the best show in town. The first public appearance of Roy, the widower.

I'm dressed appropriately. Wearing an MCA black suit, white shirt, dark tie. Mourning clothes. Went home after Kings Road. Called my lawyer. Nate Scanlon said he wanted to see me immediately. But he thought it was important that, as he put it, "We show the flag." I let him talk me into it, when all the while Romanoff's was where I desperately want to be anyway. Reva's happy hunting ground.

The frozen moment as I stand here in the entrance to the dining room seems to call for the MGM orchestra to begin playing a Rachmaninoff dirge. Prince Mike himself comes forward. Looking more lachrymose than ever. He puts a hand on each of my shoulders. "My dear fellow," he says, "what can one say at a time like this?" He hugs me to him. I hug him back. Feels like a cue for the audience to burst into tears and applause. But instead, chewing and chattering resumes as Prince Mike leads me to the second booth on the left. Bogie's booth. Bogie's still in Europe. Nate Scanlon is already there. Waiting for me. He half-rises, gives me a serious handshake. "Sit down, laddie, I'll buy you a drink."

I nurse a glass of white wine and ignore a plate of scrambled eggs while Nate and I discuss current events. I tell him what happened with Arzy and Harry. He says it sounds like I handled the situation very well. Not to worry about any of the questions pointed my way. The police must be thorough in a high-profile case like this. But clearly it's a burglar who ran amok. Of course, my reputation for temper tantrums is a factor to be considered. But given my very conspicuous presence elsewhere at the time of Addie's death, that can become a plus factor. Perception is everything in a situation like this. Sympathy can accrue to a man of action, frustrated by the inability to act. "They'll feel for you."

It's already happening. Our conversation is interrupted a number of times by people stopping by the table. Expressing condolences. Hang in there, man! Our thoughts and prayers are with you! They'll catch that guy!

Out of respect for Addie, what Nate and I don't talk much about is money. Just a few quick, discreet mentions. Our combined estates will very likely be entirely mine, he says. "But there's plenty of time to explore those matters, Roy. We mustn't seem precipitous."

Someone else approaches the booth and I look up. It's Guy Saddler. Tears welling. Looks like he's lost his last friend in the world. He probably has. I feel an unexpected jolt of compassion for the old queen. He just stands there. So I get up and, to my own surprise, I hug him. He does not hug back. Instead, he hisses in my ear. "You cocksucker. I don't know how you did it, but you killed her!"

My arms fall away from him. Nate is the only one close enough to have heard what he said. And he's out of the booth now, draping his arm around Guy's shoulder, smiling, as he murmurs in a soft voice: "Mr. Saddler, if you ever repeat what you just said publicly, we will sue you for malicious slander and take every penny you have in the world." He squeezes the nape of Guy's neck and gently sends him on his way.

I slump back down in the booth. Nate moves in beside me. "He's just overwrought," he says. "I think I calmed him down."

When it comes time to leave, Prince Mike stops by again and rips up our check. Lunch was on him. "I wish I could do more," he says. "I'm so glad you came here today, Roy. My place is always your place." And, of course, all the gossip columns will mention I was at Romanoff's. So everybody wins.

Now I'm anxious because this is what I'm really here for. We go out onto Rodeo Drive and there are the autograph collectors. My plan is to play it casual with Reva. Then drive away, circle back, keep an eye out—see which way she goes and make my move. "Just have a chat," I think.

Yeah, sure, Jack Havoc scoffs.

The collectors are all mobbed around Audie Murphy, who's just driven up. He's the little baby-faced farm boy who was America's most decorated hero in World War II. Starting with the Congressional Medal of Honor. He's since come to Hollywood as the star of Western "B" pictures. I don't know him well, but we've chatted at parties. He's a Jack Havoc fan. Tell you the truth, he makes me nervous. Here's a guy who personally annihilated a regiment of Nazi soldiers. For real. He sees me now and his face transforms into a storm cloud. He breaks away from the fans. Grabs me off to one side. Nate moves with us. To protect me, if needed, I guess. I may need the help.

"Sonuvabitch," Audie says, "goldang it t'hell." He punches my biceps. It hurts. "Heard the news. M'heart went out t'ya, pardner. Then I got this great idea, wanted t'find you soon as I could, tell y'the idea." He moves closer. Conspiratorial. Nate closes in. Audie looks askance at Nate. It's scary.

"He's okay, he's my lawyer," I say.

Audie eases off. "Well, then, counselor, you might wanta cover your ears 'bout now." He's got hold of my arm. Like a band of steel. "When the cops nab the guy who wasted Addie, whaddayasay we put up bail for him, get his ass out of the cage—and then we blow him away! You and me, Roy! Don't fuck around with the courts. Just ice him! BLAAAM! Adios, amigo." He gives me his choirboy smile. Huck Finn gone apeshit.

Nate chortles. "Now here's a man after my own heart."

I tell Audie it's a good idea and I'll give it serious thought. The collectors are snapping pictures of Audie and me. I recognize a number of their faces. From all these years. There's that guy, goes back to New York, the kid with the spiky crewcut. Funny name. Podolsky! What's his first name. Oh yeah. "Can you write, To Barry, with something nice like best wishes..."

"Hey, Barry," I say, "where's our best girl? Where's Reva?"

"Dunno, Mr. Darnell, she was supposed to be here. I'll tell her you were askin' for her."

"Yeah, do that, please." I want to ask Podolsky how he's going to get in touch with Reva? Does he have a phone number? An address? But I don't need Jack Havoc to tell me that's going too far. Too conspicuous. Particularly if something happens to Reva later on.

The valets have brought up my T-Bird and Nate's Lincoln Continental. We go for the cars. Podolsky calls after me. "We're all very sorry about what happened, Mr. Darnell."

I make a sad-brave face and give him a little wave of gratitude. For all the good that does me. But you never know who's watching. I slip the valet a fiver and get in the car. Put it in gear. Roll away. With absolutely no idea where I'm going. Always knew where to find Reva before. No problem. Just look over my shoulder. Always right there. Whether I like it or not. Except now, when I need to find her. If she was going to miss a session shadowing the stars, why couldn't it have been last night? Then she wouldn't have that locket in her pocket that can shatter my alibi. Proof beyond a reasonable doubt that I was up at the house on Kings Road last night.

"Where the fuck are you, Reva?" I want to shriek.

Jack Havoc reads my mind. *Maybe she went to the cops.*

23

Reva

Hollywood is a state of mind. How's that for a deep thought? Geographically it doesn't exist, at least not the way I imagined it did when I was still back in Brooklyn. The word used to conjure up a vision of a movieland village, all the studios in a bunch, surrounded by the palatial residences the stars lived in. Of course, the map of L.A. has a section called Hollywood. But I discovered that hardly any of the stars live there and most of the studios are somewhere else. MGM is in Culver City, Warners and Disney are in Burbank, Twentieth Century Fox is in Westwood, Universal is in a patch of the San Fernando Valley. The stars live all over the place.

When I first came to California, I took five buses out to the far reaches of the valley and walked two miles up a hill to Clark Gable's ranch. All the other collectors said he'd set the dogs on me, but instead he offered me lemonade and signed my book with a neat dedication: "To Reva, You have the determination the pioneer women had…" and he drove me in his pickup truck back to the bus stop in Encino. My point is, if Clark Gable lives in Encino, then that's definitely part of Hollywood, too. Despite what the map says.

But if there is a center to Hollywood, I guess it's Grauman's Chinese Theater. It's located on Hollywood Boulevard, and everybody who comes to town visits the forecourt of the theater, where all the handprints and footprints and autographs of the top stars are preserved in cement. That's where I am now. Don't ask me why, because I'm not exactly sure.

All I know is Mother got me up this morning, yelling through the door. "Reva, wake up, they're talking on the television about Roy Darnell."

"What're they saying?"

"I don't know. He got robbed or attacked or something." By the time I reach the kitchen, the newscaster is on to a possible strike at the Goodyear tire plant in Downey, so I go back into my room and turn on the radio, and while I'm getting dressed I listen and it's awful. A daily report being made in this real pleasant voice of all the shitty things going on in the world. After a while, they come around to Roy Darnell. That's when I hear about the burglary at his old house and how Addie is dead. It knocks me for a loop.

Most of all I'm flooded with relief that Roy's still alive and well. Then comes a wave of shock as I think, oh God, he might have been up visiting Addie at the time the mad dog burglar struck. Roy would surely have been killed defending her. Or maybe the killer was really after Roy and Addie just had the bad luck to get in his way. Or…am I impressing you? Because I'm totally knocking myself out. With my resourcefulness! With my inventiveness! With my ability to elaborately ignore the absolutely obvious! Isn't it incredible? I could probably sit here on the edge of my bed and think of twelve more possibilities. All but one.

Jimmy Durante once did a show on Broadway called *Jumbo,* and he's stealing Jumbo, who's an elephant, and somebody yells at him, "Where you goin' with that elephant?" And Durante, who's standing in Jumbo's shadow, gives this innocent shrug and says, "What elephant?" So that's me. Trying to ignore the idea looming over me big as an elephant because I simply just do not want it to be true. That Roy murdered Addie and stole her jewelry to make it look like a burglary and didn't have time to dump it because he had to race back to the Academy to create an alibi.

I'm shaking.

"What the hell's the matter with you?" Mother is standing in the doorway, dressed in her bank teller's clothes, ready to roll off to the B of A.

"I dunno," I say.

"Don't you catch a cold, Reva." She advances on me. "Take some vitamin C. Wear a sweater. You start up with one of your famous summer colds, you're gonna get a smack!" She looks like she wants to give me one now just to be on the safe side.

I promise that I'll never get sick again and she's reassured enough to take our scuffed '52 Nash Rambler and drive off to work. I'm supposed to meet the kids in Beverly Hills at Romanoff's to cruise the lunch crowd. But when I'm standing at the bus stop on the corner of Bundy and Santa Monica Boulevard and the bus into Hollywood pulls up, I get on. I'm not ready to go talk to people yet. Not even the collectors.

So here I am at Grauman's Chinese standing in Judy Garland's footprints. They're very dainty and tiny, and my feet fit perfectly. Only it's not like *Cinderella,* and simply because I can fill her shoes doesn't make me a movie queen. All around me, tourists are doing the same thing. First ogling the autographs. I see how impressed they are that they're at the spot where all the big stars once actually were. The men try Gary Cooper's shoeprints on for size. The women see how they compare to Ginger Rogers. They all ooh and aah over the novelty items pressed in the cement: Betty Grable's legs, John Barrymore's profile, Al Jolson's knees (from kneeling and singing "Mammy"). But, of course, no Greta Garbo, no legendary gunboat-size feet, no autograph; not even theater showman Sid Grauman got Garbo.

I pause at Humphrey Bogart's footprints. "Sid," Bogie had etched in stone to Showman Grauman, "May You Never Die Till I Kill You." What a weird thing to write. Bogie must've been drunk and trying to live up to his tough guy image: "Drop the gun, Louie!" But still weird, even as a joke.

Bogie. Roy's pal, Roy's booster, Roy's role model. Maybe Roy's gone his teacher one better. Bogie gets into real life fights in saloons (so does Roy) and Bogie kills enemies in his make-believe life (and Roy...?). I turn my back on Bogie. There's a blue-uniformed policeman leaning against his parked black-and-white cruiser, flirting with a pair of cute tourists in tight pedal-pushers, and I'm walking toward them.

I could do it.

I should do it.

It's too big a secret for me to carry around all by myself.

I'm still just a kid.

So why not do it?

I could say, Excuse me, officer, can I talk to you for a minute? He'll look a bit annoyed, because I'm distracting him from coming on to the teenagers, but I'd say, It's very important, it has to do with a murder. That'd get his attention. Maybe I shouldn't say murder, a killing is better. Or— a death. I'm approaching them now, only a couple more steps, the cop senses there's something up with me, probably because I'm staring so hard at him, he's laughing with the teeny-boppers but he's looking me over. Go ahead, do it, unburden, it's what a decent, law-abiding citizen ought to do. Roy may have a perfectly simple explanation for everything; this will give him the chance to clear himself, and then it won't be on my conscience, one way or the other, so do it.

"Hi, Officer," I say.

He gives me a half-salute, three-fingers up to the visor of his cap. Like a Boy Scout. I keep walking. Toward him. Past him. Down the boulevard.

Larry Edmunds Bookshop is on the boulevard, just a couple, three blocks east of Grauman's Chinese. The Egyptian Theater is on the same side of the street, with its huge DeMille-style statues out front. Musso & Frank's Restaurant, where all the old-time writers like Dashiell Hammett and F. Scott Fitzgerald used to hang out, is across the street. But it's Larry Edmunds Bookshop that's mecca for all the devout collectors and fans. If you want lobby posters, back copies of *Modern Screen* or *Silver Screen*, books about the movies or the stars, or 8x10 glossies, including portrait shots and production photos, then Larry Edmunds is the primo place. That's why I tried them first about buying my autograph books, but no go. It's a place with crammed shelves, cramped pathways between them; watch it, bobby-soxers from nearby Hollywood High are sitting on the creaky old wooden floors, lost in a reverie while they leaf through the wonderland of glamour and glitter.

It reminds me a little of a seedy old bookstore in New York on Sixth Avenue near 42nd Street, where Tillie Lust, the sexpot of the Secret Six, first showed me the ropes. We didn't do anything decorative with our crumb books, but for our real autograph books we'd find tiny head shots of the stars and paste them on the pages where they'd signed. Some head shots were easy to get hold of, because the actors were currently popular, but then there were others who were harder to locate and that's where the Sixth Avenue Bookshop came in handy. The back issues of the magazines were a treasure trove. Of course, we never paid for anything, Tillie would chat up the store manager, her shoulders back, flaunting the nubile knockers beneath her fluffy pink angora sweater (with matching beret), while I sliced out the photos I needed with a razor-sharp Exacto knife that I bought after I joined the Secret Six.

Now I'm hunkering down on the splintery floor in the back of Larry Edmunds store on Hollywood Boulevard, riffling through the bins of 8x10s for any new production photos that may have come in. I'm in luck, there're several from *Jack Havoc*. It demonstrates the show is a hit, because they don't stock much stuff from TV shows. I study the pictures, marveling at what a good actor Roy is, you can see it even in still photos—when he's playing Jack Havoc there's a whole other look to him. Devil-may-care, still good-humored, but often with a wild glint in his eye that I find irresistible. You never know what Jack Havoc might do, and I guess that's what the audience likes, too. He might break the law, at least bend it pretty far out of shape, but always for a good reason and to help someone in need.

I can't decide which of the stills I want to buy; actually I want them all, so I think about that for a while, and it keeps me from thinking about Roy's real life situation. Then I come to a decision and I get up and stroll nonchalantly up the cluttered aisle, stepping over a scruffy Brando T-shirted lookalike, hunkered down in the Acting Scenes For Auditions section. I pause up front to examine a new picture biography of Lana Turner, and then I wander out of the store onto Hollywood Boulevard. I start back toward the bus stop that brought me here, but I hardly go a step before a foot comes down on top of my foot, and I look up and see one of the Larry Edmunds clerks, a witch named Hazel (really), who always gives everybody a hard time over nothing.

"Hi, Hazel," I say. "You're standing on me."

She's just bug-eyed and gloaty, like Judith Anderson in *Rebecca* when she burned down the House of Manderley. I realize I'm clamped in place. And I also realize I'm in trouble when Hazel pats my back and pulls up the shirttails of my blouse and yanks out the *Jack Havoc* stills I have tucked back there.

"Gotcha, you little thieving brat," Hazel says. "Shoplifting snot!"

"I was gonna pay for those," I begin and I stop because it sounds lame even to me. Hazel is really tromping on my toes. I'll have to leave this foot behind if I want to take off and I sure as hell want to. That's when the car pulls up to the red zone in front of the store. It's a police car, and the cop who gets out is the same one who was flirting with the girls at the Chinese Theater.

I guess we were destined to talk after all.

24

Roy

So here we are. Just a couple of guys. Lolling about the living room of my faux chateau on Coldwater Canyon. Maundering about murder. I'm sipping vodka straight. Straight from the bottle since I broke the seal. He's creating a First Stage Smog Alert with his friggin' frog cigarettes. We're wrestling with the latest wrinkle in the situation.

It seems I can't recall her name.

Yeah, yeah, I know, it's Reva. But Reva *what?* I'm stumped. Stymied. I mean, how do you go about tracking down somebody without knowing their last name? Kessler? Chrysler? Foster. Fenster. Koster. Lester. Chisholm. Massey. Russert.

Rumpelstiltskin is my name.

"Not funny, Jack."

Then why am I laughing?

"Because you're an asshole."

And you're a clown. He does Butterfly McQueen: *Mercy me, Miz Scarlett. Ah just can't seem to remember that lil' ol' name. Imagine that. And me, an actor, who gets paid for rememberin' pages and pages of dialogue, entire plays, but this one word has just done gone with the wind.*

"So I'm blocked. It happens, you know."

Oh, I know. Don't shuck a shucker, Roy Boy.

"I think the expression is, Don't kid a kidder."

You're hoping it'll all go away. By itself. So you can weasel out of your responsibilities.

"I'm trying, Jack! Maybe you don't think so—"

I think you'd rather sit here and slaughter that bottle of vodka and then nod off, and while you're asleep maybe the Good Fairy will wave her magic wand and all your troubles will disappear.

"Fuck you."

Truth hurts, don't it? He thinks that's funny, too.

Finally, to shut him up and prove that I do want to do something, we set out in the T-Bird. I take the vodka bottle along for company.

Think like an autograph hound, he advises me. As if I need the advice. *Where would she go on a night like this?*

We whiz past Romanoff's. Check out both the Bev Hills and Vine Street Brown Derbies. Stage doors at NBC and CBS. Sidle along the Strip. Ruth Olay is opening at the Crescendo. That's a good bet. A singers' singer. She draws a stellar crowd. Including a cluster of familiar-looking fans. Rushing at Jack Webb and Julie London on arrival. Fred MacMurray and June Haver. There's Podolsky. But no Reva. We roll by the Hamburger Hamlet. I phoned Kim this afternoon. No answer. Left a message with her service, "Tell her I'm okay." No call back yet. Can't think about that now. Got bigger problems.

By now the vodka is all gone. I run a red light at Doheny and Sunset. Get stopped by a motorbike cop. He recognizes me. Volunteers that he doesn't like my show. At least Jack Havoc has the good sense to just sit there and keep his mouth shut. While I give my best performance of a shitfaced drunk acting stone sober. The cop still wants me to walk the line heel-to-toe and touch my nose with my eyes closed. But while we're discussing it, his radio squawks. An armed robbery call. He takes off. Warning me to call it a night. Even Jack Havoc agrees with that.

So I navigate home and fall into bed. Sleep the sleep of the totally bombed. The Good Fairy does not appear in my dreams. I have nightmares. Reva is in one of them. I run into her in a dark alley. She's wearing the gold chain with the locket. The tell-tale locket that can be Exhibit A against me.

We're talking. Friendly and nice. Only thing is, she's got a spike of glass jutting out of her chest. Just like Addie. It's bleeding. Not gushing. More of a seeping stigmata. I'm too polite to mention it. She doesn't seem to notice. Or care. I'm hoping she'll just keel over. And die. Just like Addie.

I'm not alone when I wake up in the morning. There's a row of vultures. Perched at the foot of my bed. Looking over at me. Licking their chops. But not quite ready to pounce. I know they're just garbage inside my head, like Jack Havoc, but they're still scary as hell. I shake my head, it makes me dizzy, but then the vultures are gone. Who says vodka gives you a smoother hangover? But at least it's not a migraine.

Getting dressed is a slow motion ordeal. Triphammers in my head. Hands aquiver. Fortunately my choice of wardrobe doesn't require any deep thinking. Put on my best black suit. Not navy blue—gotta be black. Like Bogie's joke. The Tailor and the Nuns. *Pincus fuctus.* Black necktie, white shirt, black socks, black lace-up shoes. Somber. Respectful. I'm reknotting my tie for the fifth time when the long black limo pulls into the driveway. Glance at the clock. They're early. Nate Scanlon and his wife Laraine are picking me up. We're going to Addie's funeral together.

There's a knock on the door. Without waiting, Nate steams in. Alone. "I told Laraine to wait in the car." He's carrying a thin, rolled-up magazine in his hand. Waggles it aloft like Joe McCarthy waving his supposed list of 168 communists in the State Department. "Do you know a publication called *The Town Tattler?*"

"Grady Braxton's loony leaflet? I've seen it. Why? Is my name in there?"

"Have you ever met Mr. Braxton?"

"Never set eyes on him. But I know about him. Everybody does."

"Tell me what you know."

So I tell him. Grady Braxton used to be a Hollywood flack, part of the militant corps of suppress agents at MGM.

Braxton got fired for coming on too strong to a young starlet. Offered to swap publicity for sex. "I'll get you in all the columns, if I can get my column in you." She tape recorded the offer and played it for L.B. Mayer. No one else would hire him after that. So now Braxton has gone renegade, starting up *The Town Tattler*. "All The News Nobody Else Will Print." A revenge sheet. Circulation is in the scant hundreds; nobody'll admit to buying it. But it turns up on most of the sets around town. Teamsters and propmen off in corners, reading and snickering. No ads. Braxton can't get any. Just wall-to-wall rant.

"Nobody believes anything that dingaling writes," I say.

"How fortunate for us," Nate says dryly.

He hands me the skinny trumped-up trade paper. I unfurl it. I'm looking for the item that's got Nate so steamed. I don't have to look far. There's a picture of me in the center of the front page. An oldie but a goodie. Roy the brawler, snarling drunkenly at a nasty photographer. Surrounded by a headline story:

ROY THE BAD BOY LOSES HIS 'BEST FRIEND'
By Grady Braxton

Did you catch the moment on the tube, kiddies? It was so moving. Roy-the-Bad-Boy Darnell, being interviewed outside the Hollywood Hills house where his almost-ex-wife, fashion maven Adrienne Ballard had just been found murdered. How do you feel about that, Roy?

"She was my best friend."

Gulp. Golly.

Guess Roy's a better actor than we thought.

Here's the inside *Tattler* scoop on how things were between Roy the Destroyer and his "best friend."

Roy and Addie were involved in a knock down, drag out divorce that had left him without the proverbial pot. Particularly after he got dumped from his junky *Jack Havoc* TV show (don't believe that stuff about how he jumped, Roy got *pushed* by someone with the initials Colonel JLW).

Reason Addie got the whole kit and kaboodle was that she had the goods on Roy, a notorious boudoir bandit. And we are talking about red-hot, through-the-transom photos of Roy making acrobatic whoopee with a luscious hooker (*Confidential* magazine, please note). That's spelled (porno)graphic.

Wait. It gets better.

Since he was caught with his britches down, romantic Roy Boy has gone public and continues to date the hooker—or did all of you folks at the *Trapeze* premiere think he was with a Park Avenue debutante?

And did you hear about the catcalling set-to in the preem party parking lot between Addie and Roy over said hooker?

Just to reassure you that it's still our same ol' Roy, he of the Terrible Temper, he greeted the subpoena server who presented him with divorce papers in front of Romanoff's with a wildly off-target roundhouse punch. Then he caused such a ruckus at Adrienne's salon that the security guard had to bum rush macho man Roy out onto the Rodeo Drive pavement. Which prompted Addie to change the locks at the salon—as well as at the house.

Maybe she was *your* best friend, Roy. But you sure as hell weren't *her* best friend.

The cops insist that Quick-Fisted Roy isn't a suspect in Addie's slaying. That he's got a rock-solid alibi. But could he have had a little help from his friends?

Just asking.

I look up from *The Tattler*. "Guy Saddler," I say.

"I assumed as much."

"So now we sue Saddler into oblivion, like you told him we would?"

"Difficult. In fact, impossible. The article makes no mention of Mr. Saddler. If we try to question the writer, he'll undoubtedly stand on his First Amendment rights as a journalist and gallantly refuse to name his source—I get the sense that this Mr. Braxton would love to be a public martyr."

"And if a judge clapped him in jail for contempt, Braxton could save on his rent." I like that idea. "How about we sue Braxton instead?"

"I've checked and his resources are nonexistent. He publishes this weekly opus out of a tiny apartment on North Fuller Avenue in West Hollywood. His pulldown Murphy bed is his desk and his office. Besides, if we sue him—he might win."

"Come again?"

"The truth is an absolute defense. That's a principle of law. And basically, apart from the cheap shots and snide innuendoes—"

"That I hired hitmen to go after Addie!"

"Braxton only speculated on that point. But the essential facts of the story are correct, aren't they?"

Suddenly I'm in the witness box and my lawyer is prosecuting.

"Basically...yes."

"Including the reference to your socializing with the woman who was paid by Addie to entrap you."

"He didn't say that, he—"

"Of course, he didn't! Mr. Saddler conveniently omitted that fact. Not as a courtesy to you. To keep Addie looking like an angelic victim. But have you been dating that woman?"

I feel my face getting red. "Well, sorta, yes..."

Nate shakes his head. I've disappointed him. "Why on earth would you do that?"

I shrug again. Big on shrugs today. "Man-woman stuff," I mumble. "Hard to explain. But I'm not seeing her anymore," I quickly add.

Okay, I know I'm taking credit here for something I'm not entitled to. Kim dropped me. But I'm getting scared. I lost a good agent because I cut him out of the loop. Am I about to lose a terrific lawyer for the same reason?

"Guess I should've told you...are you pissed, Nate?"

"A lawyer assumes that his client will withhold a certain amount of information. For whatever reason. But we always find out...sooner or later."

I've been chastised. I pluck my forelock and mutter abject apologies. And I'm granted forgiveness. I'm not being dumped. Good, because I need Nate as my ally. But, oh, Nate, if you had any idea what I'm holding back from you. Kim's just the tip of the iceberg. I hold up the copy of *The Tattler.*

"Then what do we do about this?"

"Let's hope that your first reaction was correct—that apart from salacious amusement, no one believes anything Braxton writes."

Turns out I'm totally wrong about that.

Al Jolson is waiting to greet us. Up on a raised podium. A bronze figure. Looks like the ol' minstrel man himself, dipped in chocolate syrup, crouched on one knee, arms outspread. Can't you just hear him bellowing his trademark promise? "You ain't heard nothin' yet." Strange claim for a cemetery. But here we are. At Jolson's final resting place.

Our limo swings left into the driveway off the Culver City street, just east of Sepulveda. It looks like we're entering an elegant golf course. The lot is full and cars are parked clear out to the front curb. Maybe they've overbooked and the funeral services before us ran long. I'm getting pissed, because when I contacted the mortuary yesterday, they assured me they'd handle everything. Then as we drive closer, I see a sign spiked in the ground reading "Darnell Services" with an arrow pointing toward the crowd surrounding the chapel. More people on foot along the private road, hurrying not to miss the event. I recognize several of their faces. There's a festive lawn party feeling in the air.

"Who are they all?" Nate's wife asks.

We were expecting a few dozen mourners. Addie's friends and some of her clients. Some of my friends. I'd forgotten about the media. And the fans and tourists.

"The time and location of the services were in the *Times* this morning," Nate says.

Our limo winds slowly through the bodies clogging the roadway, leading up to the front of the chapel. Faces peer in at us through the windows. They recognize me. Excited reactions. Just like a world premiere. And I'm the star of this show. When the limo stops, the driver comes around and tries to open the door. It's not easy. The gawkers are jammed in tight. Suddenly, the chapel doors open and a rescue party appears. A flying wedge of five Warner press agents, led by Merle Heifetz, my Jewish leprechaun, reaches us. They surround us and get us through the crowd. I catch sight of several of the familiar autograph hounds. But no Reva. I try to look suitably somber. It won't do to wave and smile at the fans on this solemn occasion.

"Does Jack Warner know where you are this morning?" I ask Heifetz.

"What me and my boys do on our own time is our own business," he says. Then he leans close and murmurs in my ear. "You'll find the temperature's a lot cooler inside the chapel. Everybody's read or heard about the story in *The Tattler.*"

If he hadn't told me, I would have guessed. Judging just by the body language as I make my way down the center aisle with Nate and his wife. Behind us, the studio flacks are guarding the front doors. Admitting only the A-list mourners. The chapel is packed. Standing room only. But somehow as I move toward the front pew, a wide path opens up. Then closes behind me. There are nods, occasional glancing instants of eye contact. But basically I'm a leper. No one comes forward to hug me. Or even touch me. Until we're almost at the front row. David Niven emerges from the crowd. Claps me on both shoulders. "Chin up," he says. Niven lost a wife a few years ago in a tragic accident. He knows what it feels like.

And what do I feel like?

Whipsawed. To the throng outside, I'm the tragic hero. To the guests inside, I'm the villain of the piece. A pariah. They may not believe Braxton's snively dig that I had Addie killed. But they're certainly ready to hold me accountable in some way for her death. At the very least for making her desperately unhappy. In Hollywood, placing blame is a favorite indoor sport.

Once we're seated, the organ music subsides. The robed rabbi enters from a side door. He goes to the lectern. Next to the closed coffin. He's a smallish man with a prematurely gray, wavy pompadour and a mellifluous voice that could have made him a fortune in radio. He soothes. He consoles. He laments. His words are amplified by the microphone in the lectern, carried by speakers to the overflow crowd outside. Before we know it, he's guiding us all through the shadow of the valley of death. The only thing he doesn't do is give any real sense of who Addie was or what she was like. Not his fault. He never knew her.

We bow our heads for a moment of prayer. Then he introduces me.

It comes as something of a shock. I have to talk to these people now. I walk toward the lectern. Behind me I can hear the gossipy buzz. The rabbi shakes my hand, offers deepest sympathy. Then I'm alone. Looking out at those faces. I've dined and laughed and drank and worked with so many of them. Why do they look so skeptical? So hostile. I never did anything to them (well, maybe I cuckolded a few husbands in the crowd, but still…). One crappy story in a tawdry scandal sheet and they think they know the real me. They think they know the real Addie. But they don't. I spot Arzy Marshak leaning against a pillar way to the back. What's a cop doing here? This isn't a Mafia funeral.

So I'm up here. Facing them all. I've got to give a eulogy now. And I haven't prepared. Guess I thought I'd just get up and wing it. Say some pleasant things and the sympathy of the mourners would carry me through. But now I'm confronting the kind of crowd that used to gather around the guillotine in Robespierre's Paris for a morning of family fun. I can't look at them. My gaze goes over to the casket. Addie's in there. In that shiny, gilt-handled, plush-lined box. My Addie. I can hear people coughing in the audience. Whispering. Fuck 'em. I keep staring at the casket. Uptown word for coffin. Sanitized.

"I'm a liar," I finally mumble. The microphone amplifies my words. "A liar. Guess all actors are. That's how I met Addie." Looking at the coffin. "I lied to you..." Now I have to look away. I stare out over the crowd. Past them. Forget them. Remember her. Remember how it was. In the beginning. When it was good.

"I was a hungry young actor. Very hungry. Working on a kid's show for CBS Radio. And playing Laertes in a makeshift production of *Hamlet*. Doing Shakespeare in a church with a leaky roof. We needed publicity. So I phoned this woman who worked for one of the New York trade papers. Pretended I was a CBS publicist and pitched her on interviewing The Man of a Thousand Voices—that was me. She swallowed my lie and we made an appointment to meet at Sardi's for the interview." I can remember what the weather was like that day. How the air tasted.

"Before she got there, I slipped the maitre d' five bucks to give us a good table and pretend I was a big shot. I didn't know what Adrienne Ballard looked like so I stood at the bar and approached every likely looking Rosalind Russell *His Girl Friday*-type woman who walked in. But she turned out to be this Columbia University law school student, moonlighting as a reporter. In harlequin glasses and a pullover sweater and saddle shoes. Long chestnut hair, tucked behind her ears. Hair kept getting loose. She'd shake her head then, like a frisky colt."

Remember? Remember how you felt.

"I guess I fell in love with her even before we ordered drinks—and she told me she knew I'd lied. Knew the real CBS publicist I'd pretended to be. 'Then why'd you agree to meet me?' I asked her. She smiled and said, 'Curious, I guess. Don't lie to me anymore, okay?' I promised I wouldn't. It wasn't a promise I kept."

I pause. Swallow. Keep focused, kid. Keep looking at the back wall. Gazing way into the past. "She was very independent. First time we went to see a movie, I bought the tickets and she ran ahead inside the theater to pay for the popcorn and drinks. So we negotiated some terms that night. She didn't want me opening car doors for her, that seemed old-fashioned. But when she was all dressed up and wearing heels, then it was okay to open her car doors. I agreed. I had to. I was completely captivated by her."

What else do you remember? Come on. The good stuff. Getting caught in a summer downpour in Central Park, dancing through the puddles like Gene Kelly and Debbie Reynolds. Yeah. Tell 'em that. And how she made me absolutely crazy when she was cramming for the New York bar exam and how proud I was that she passed on her first try—and how when I told her I had a job in L.A. she said, without even a blink of hesitation, "Okay, then we're moving out there." After all her hard work, dropping it all for me...

I tell 'em that.

"Addie got a job in business affairs out here at Columbia, negotiating contracts. Did a good job, but she got fired—by Harry Cohn himself. He grabbed her ass, which is something he didn't do to the male negotiators. She stomped a four-inch stiletto heel down on his big toe. And she was out on the pavement on Gower Street before King Cohn stopped yelling. She came home and told me, 'Guess I'm not supposed to be in show business after all.' That's when she opened the boutique. And it became her life."

I come back to the here and now. The chapel. The crowd. I don't know what they're thinking. But they're listening.

"There was an article today in a rag that claims to be a trade paper. Lot of lies in there. I ought to know. Takes one to know one." I think about that for a second. "But the worst lie was that the writer questioned something I'd said on TV. Which is that Addie was my best friend. So let me tell you about one of the bad times we had—back when we were still living in New York. She was struggling through her last year of law school and my career suddenly dried up. I mean, Gobi Desert dry. I couldn't get a day's work anywhere. Sometimes it happens. I've learned that since, everything just stops for a while. But back then I thought it was the end of my world. I was in deep depression. Grim. Ready to quit show biz and take a job selling men's suits at Macy's. Or just jump in the East River. I couldn't decide which.

"Addie didn't waste time trying to pep me up. She said, 'C'mon, we're going out to dinner at the Deli.' I said 'I'm not hungry.' She said, 'Well, I am—and besides, I've called ahead and Sollie's making this special appetizer just for me.' So we went. And when we got there she had them bring out this special thing and the waiters made a ceremony about it because it was an Academy Award, a golden Oscar, on a platter, and the inscription was 'With love to Roy Darnell, the Best Actor in the World, from Your Addie.' Turns out the gold covering was just tin foil and Oscar was made of pumpernickel underneath—" I hear a few laughs "—and we ate him with chopped liver and he was delicious, and if that's as close as I ever come to winning a real Oscar, that's fine, because the pumpernickel Oscar gave me back the courage to keep on trying." I swallow again. "So don't anybody tell me that Addie wasn't my best friend."

I walk away from the lectern. As I pass some of Addie's friends in the first row, I'm amazed to see that they're smiling empathetic smiles. A couple of them have tears running down their cheeks.

And I realize I do, too.

I'm not an un-person any more. Standing out under a tree. Casket being lowered. "Ashes to ashes, dust to dust." Only the triple-A mourners out here with us at the grave site. The rest are roped off down below, watching from a distance. As the ceremony ends, I'm patted, touched, embraced, kissed. I hug and kiss back. Then I move with Nate and Laraine Scanlon to our waiting limo. Climb into the back. Slump into my seat. Exhausted. Nate looks at me approvingly.

"You pulled that one out of the fire, laddie."

We're rolling, heading for the street. Mourners lining the driveway, strolling slowly toward their cars. As we go by them, many wave. I wave back. That's when I see her. Reva.

In the crowd, several people in front of her. She sees me, too. Eye contact. A sad smile. She raises her hand, I think she's going to wave—but instead she points at her neck. And I see the locket. She's wearing the locket. My gift to Addie. Reva did swipe it! The lynchpin of my survival is hanging around her neck.

Then she's gone from view. I want to yell at the driver to stop the limo. I want to jump out and run back and grab her and snatch the locket, without that locket it's just my word against hers, and—and—I do nothing. I can't. Not without making a spectacle of myself. Calling attention to what I must conceal. So I sit there. Paralyzed. And then, as we drive farther and farther away, I smile at the irony. You'd think that the shock of seeing her like that would at least jog my memory loose. But I still can't remember her last name.

In Hollywood, the choice you make about who's going to cater those very special at-home events is viewed as quite important. You could go with Chasen's, featuring their legendary chili. Or with the Brown Derby, creators of the original Cobb salad. I had Romanoff's do Addie's wake. She would have approved. Prince Mike's buckwheat blinis with sour cream and caviar, washed down with White Russians, were her favorites. So how's that for blending sentiment and snootiness?

The point is that the food is plentiful. The booze is flowing. And everybody at my house is getting ripped. Including the host. I wasn't sure how many mourners would come back here for the wake. Turns out quite a few. My friends, her friends, our friends. Just goes to prove what the man said: you can fool some of the people some of the time. Maybe even enough of 'em *all* of the time?

Only if you do something, Jack Havoc says.

I keep ducking him, losing him in the crowd, but I know he's there. What's he want from me? I can't walk out on my own party.

It's not a rowdy party. Nobody getting pushed into the lap pool. But it gets to be kind of a warm occasion. A celebration of Addie. Her waspish tongue. I start the ball rolling. "Once we were dining at this piss-elegant Mexican restaurant down on Olvera Street," I recall, "and these loud mariachi players came over, and the leader asks, 'What would you like us to play, señora?' Addie points to the far side of the restaurant and says, 'Over there.'" Soon lots of people are adding their own Addie-isms. Some nasty, some bawdy, all funny. The lady did have her moments. If you were into take-'em-off-at-the-knees sarcasm.

I slip into the bedroom, lock the door and try phoning Kim again. Haven't had a call back and the service says, "Yes, she did pick up your message." I leave another message, "Please call." Then I try the Hamlet. She's not on duty. In fact, the cashier says, she's taken some time off. "I think she's got an aunt in Idaho." I hang up. There's no aunt in Idaho. She took off. Guess she knows about Addie. Probably heard about the article in *The Tattler.* Can't blame her for hiding from me. Wish I could talk to her.

At last the crowd is thinning. Going home time. It's dark outside, caterers loading their gear. I stand in the doorway and bid farewell to the last of my guests. Well, almost. When I come back inside, there's still one left. Slouching in the leather club chair he always slouched in. Belting my best single-malt Scotch like he always did. The prodigal returned. And damned if I'm not pleased to see him. We hardly got to say more than hello when he arrived. So I pour myself another drink and sprawl on the couch opposite him. "Glad you came, Kenny," I say.

Killer Lomax lifts his glass with my booze in salute. "Thought you might need some old friends around at a time like this."

We clink glasses and sip. The Corsican Brothers. Reunited. For a few minutes anyway. "So you said you flew in from Vegas? You win or lose?"

"Won at blackjack. Lost it all back plus interest at the craps table."

"The dice never loved you. Even when we were kids."

"Except that one time, remember, in the front hallway of

Marty Ganzer's house? I made six straight passes, cleaned everybody out—"

"—and then the cops busted up the game and confiscated all the money as evidence—"

"Hell, they put *my* dough in *their* pockets! Story of my fuckin' life!"

And we're laughing together. Like we're still punks in South Philly.

"Anything else goin' on in Vegas?" I ask him. Not really giving a shit.

"Viola did a standup for two nights at El Rancho. Filling in for Joe E. Lewis, he's got the flu."

"Bet our Davey was a million laughs. How's it goin' with you and him?"

Killer makes a *comme-si-comme-ca* gesture. "He likes bobbysoxers, as close to jailbait as you can come. Still acts like an idiot on his own time. Can't hold his liquor."

"Not like us," I say. Taking another pull on my drink.

Killer snaps his fingers. "Ran into somebody you know in Vegas. Actually, he came all the way there 'specially to see me. Hollywood cop workin' on Addie's case—"

"—Arzy? Arzy Marshak? Skinny guy, built like a sprinter."

"Nah, big asshole with a Joe Stalin mustache, bad skin."

"Harry T," I say. "Tigner."

"Yeah, that's him. He checked out what I said, that I was sitting in the audience at the El Rancho laughing at Davey's bullshit when Addie got cashed out, blah-blah. Sorry to bother me and he took off."

"He thought I might've had you knock off Addie?"

"Hey. Figures they'd come knocking on my door." He takes another hit of Scotch. "Lucky we both have alibis."

"They told me they're lookin' for a serial burglar!"

"Coverin' all the bases, sport. You know how cops are."

My head's spinning. Trying to digest this information. Probably just what Killer says. Routine. Being thorough. Like they said.

"All those funny stories everybody was tellin' about Addie," Killer says. "I had one, too, didn't mention it, though. 'Cuz it wasn't really that funny. Couple months ago, Addie came on to me. 'Help me get the goods on Roy. I'll make it worth your while…he doesn't ever have to know it was you.' Got the feeling that the sky was the limit—she was offering anything from a blow job to a Swiss bank account." He finishes the Scotch, looks reflectively at the empty glass. "I pretended she was just kidding. But she wasn't. Maybe she even wanted me to rig the frame they got you on later."

"Why didn't you mention this to me at the time?"

"You were still talkin' about patchin' things up with Addie back then."

"You tell Tigner about this?" I'm sorry as soon as the words are out of my mouth. I can see the reaction on Killer's face. His lip curls.

"Nah, see, there were only two people present at that conversation, me and Addie, and inasmuch as she's gone—well, you remember the South Philly code, don't you, sport? You don't rat on people," he smacks down his empty glass. "Even on people you don't like."

He rises. I get up, too. Grab his arm. Don't want to end it like this.

"Hey, Kenny, I'm sorry—I didn't mean to suggest that you'd ever—"

He shakes my hand off his arm. Glares at me. I've never seen him this angry before. "You asked how it's going with Viola? Lemme tell you—compared to you and me, it's like being a nursemaid. But he's a decent guy. Basically, you always treated me like a shithook. So that's what I was. Now I'm startin' clean. And it feels good. I can help him. I'm tired of trying to help you, Roy. We're done."

He's going for the door. I trot along with him. Trying to make nice. Not knowing how to turn this one around. "Well, if you ever need anything from me, my door's always open to you, Kenny—"

I hear a hiss in my ear.

Ask him, Jack Havoc says. *Don't let him get away without asking him.*

We're in the driveway now. Killer climbs into his car. I'm standing beside the open window. "Thanks again for comin'—"

Ask him!

"Hey, you see Reva at the funeral? You know, little Reva, what'shername again—?"

He looks up at me. Sorta funny. Could he know why I'm asking? C'mon. Getting paranoid. "I'm not your fuckin' Rolodex. Jesus. You're her whole life—and you can't even remember her name? Fuck you, Roy. I don't know you anymore."

And he drives off.

Really finessed that one, didn't you? Jack Havoc says.

He's being snide, of course. That's when this thought hits me. There's no point in trying to explain it to him. Or Killer Lomax either. It hardly makes sense to me. I mean, I know it's only just delaying the inevitable. But it suddenly occurs to me that forgetting Reva's last name may be the nicest thing I've ever done for anybody.

25

Reva

The blue-uniformed cop who drove me from Larry Edmunds Bookstore to the police station on Cole Avenue in Hollywood has me sit beside a desk in the big squad room downstairs while he two-finger types a name-address-phone number report. Then he turns me over to Detective Vallenzuega, the juvenile officer, whose cluttered cubbyhole is one flight upstairs. Detective Vallenzuega points at a bench and tells me to wait there, while he takes phone calls that have nothing to do with me. That gives me time to think about whether or not I'll tell about Roy. It's like picking the petals off an imaginary daisy. Do tell, don't tell, do, don't, do, don't. There's lots of time to torture a decision, because it's a long wait, but, hey, that's one thing I learned how to do as a collector. Wait. Try to think of something else, anything else....

We once waited for hours on a freezing winter morning down at the Hudson River pier where an Italian liner, the *Andrea Doria,* was docking. Anna Magnani was on board. She was the star of *Open City,* a great foreign film about Rome in World War II, that Roberto Rossellini directed, but what she was most famous for in America at that moment was that she and Roberto Rossellini were a hot item before Rossellini dumped Magnani for Ingrid Bergman, whom he knocked up while she was still married to this Swedish dentist. That was the scandal of the century, at least up until then. So it's a Sunday in March, and the wind blowing off the river is frigid enough to turn the liquid on your eyeballs into ice, but we're the Secret Six, so we hang in there.

It was the day I really became a coffee drinker. Before that I didn't like the taste, but the weather was so cold and I put so much sugar in each cardboard cup that it kept me warm and tasted good and I was hooked. We hadn't found out Magnani was coming in on the *Andrea Doria* until it was too late to go down to the customs house and get passes letting us onto the pier, so we were reduced to covering her arrival the hard way. We were staked out in an area only partially protected from the elements, near the car ramp where every vehicle that exited the pier had to stop, roll down the window and turn in their pass. That gave us a chance to peek inside the limos. We took turns standing out in the cold, while the others shuddered nearby.

Tillie Lust, bundled like an Eskimo in an imitation fur coat with hood and still looking like a teenage sexpot, was stamping her feet and telling me about the lost love of her life. "His name's Chuck, he's an Italian guy used to live in the South Bronx, and he's the star of the football team at Taft High, tall, dark and handsome."

"Hubba-hubba," I say, to keep warm and keep her talking. It's like I'm picking up pointers from a prom queen. "So what broke you up?"

"There were too many cultural differences."

"Because he's Italian and you're Jewish?"

"No, because he only cares about sports and never goes to the movies."

Abe Franks, a farm boy who hails from deepest Alabama, who came up north to finish high school under the GI Bill and never went home, asks what we're talking about.

"About Anna Magnani, of course," Tillie says. "Did you hear what she did to Ingrid Bergman?"

Abe, who's as sweet-natured as he is gullible, bites. "No, whut?"

"Magnani went to the airport in Rome when Bergman flew back to have Rossellini's baby, and when Bergman came down the airplane ramp, Magnani threw meatballs at her."

"Man, tha's one tough lady," he drawls. "Did Ingrid get hurt?"

We start laughing and Abe knows he's been had, so he laughs, too. "Ah knew you was just kiddin'."

Finally we spot a star, at least a semi-star. It's Lionel Stander, the gravel-voiced character actor who was so mean to Fredric March in *A Star Is Born.* He is sitting in the back seat of this 8Z limo with his young wife, and he's got a big mop of hair and is wearing his topcoat draped over his shoulders, so he looks like Dracula, but we're glad to see him because he's a rare autograph, since he's been making movies in Europe for a few years.

"Welcome home, Mr. Stander," Pam O'Mara says, as we offer our books in through the car window. "What's your next project?"

"Starting Tuesday I'm gonna play a starring role in front of the House Un-American Activities Committee," he rasps pleasantly. We read about his testimony later in the week, how he got the HUAC chairman to turn off the TV cameras and lights, "because I only perform on TV for entertainment or philanthropic organizations, which I don't think this is." The Committee confronted him with the evidence against him, mostly based on some other character actor's testimony that Lionel Stander tried to persuade him to join the Communist Party because it was a good way to meet girls. Stander was blacklisted for a bunch of years after that.

So we're still on the lookout for Anna Magnani, but most of the passengers seem to have disembarked. Now the conversation has shifted to the day's headlines. Billy Daniels, the debonair nightclub and TV singer, Mr. Old Black Magic himself, has had his face slashed in a lover's quarrel.

"They had to take umpteen stitches," Pam reports. "They say his face is gonna be okay, though."

There's a long pause after that; none of us know what to say. It's too serious to make jokes about. We all like Billy Daniels, he's always nice to the collectors.

"Love," Tillie finally says. "Guess y'gotta watch out for love sometimes, it can kill you."

"Just tell me straight—what the hell do you find so fascinating about this punk Roy Darnell?"

Detective Phil Vallenzuega, that's what it says on the name plate on his battered desk, is ruddy-faced and built like a barroom bouncer, barrel chest merging into beer belly. His horrendous houndstooth sports jacket is draped over the back of his desk chair.

The waiting is over.

After nearly two hours.

Too much time to consider too many possibilities. Maybe they're going to give me the third degree, force me to tell everything I know, make me betray Roy. They have their ways. One thing's for sure, it's getting late, after five o'clock now. They can't put you in the gas chamber for swiping movie stills, but I'm wondering if I'm going to be sleeping in a cell overnight. Then I heard Detective Vallenzuega mention my name on the phone. Followed by two grunts and an uh-huh. He hung up and gestured me to the chair in front of his desk.

"Ho-kay, Reva," he says.

His voice is kind of too small for the size man he is. Not pipsqueaky, just surprising, when you expect an Ezio Pinza basso to emerge from that huge chest.

"Has anyone ever said that you look like Wallace Beery when he played Pancho Villa?" I figure let's get started on the right foot, but Detective Vallenzuega won't play. He just shakes his head.

"You're the first. How old are you, Reva? Fifteen, sixteen?"

"Nineteen."

He frowns and looks at the report the cop gave him. "Nineteen. Then why'd they send you up here? You don't look nineteen."

"Maybe that's why." I add, helpfully, "Mary Pickford was still playing teenagers when she was in her thirties."

He puts down the report. "I gotta send you downstairs. In the eyes of the law you are no longer a minor—"

"Hey, did you see Ginger Rogers in *The Major and the Minor*? She fooled Ray Milland and everybody into thinking she was a kid."

"I don't go to the movies much. They rot your mind."

"Do I really have to go downstairs? And sit at someone else's desk for two more hours?"

He thinks it over, then shrugs. "Ho-kay, we can do it here." He indicates the phone, the last call he got. "We've verified that you do not have a prior arrest record. But you've made an auspicious debut. Shoplifting. The bookstore people say the photographs you took are worth in excess of $150, which makes it grand theft, a felony offense—"

"Horse pucky!" I snort. "They're selling those stills for a buck apiece—"

He cuts me off. "So, let's suppose it's just a misdemeanor. Misdemeanor theft could still mean thirty days in jail and a $500 fine."

I start to cry. Because I feel like crying and because it seems like it might be a good tactic. It isn't. He doesn't blink, just wearily pulls a half-empty box of tissues out of his drawer and shoves it at me. I blow my nose and stop crying.

"Look, girly, we know what you been up to. You got tagged this time, but how about those fifteen, twenty other times you thought you got away with it?"

"I never did this before in my whole life," I protest, knowing that he's just playing the percentages, trying to bluff me. "Honest, Detective Vallenzuega!"

He looks at me speculatively, looks at the report on me again and shakes his head. "I don't get it. What's so special about this Roy Darnell that you're ready to go to jail over him?"

That stops me, because for a second I think he knows. Then I realize he doesn't, unless I tell him. So here we are at the crossroads again.

"This Darnell is bad news, any way you slice it. He's always taking a poke at photographers, brawling in saloons and on the streets, cussed out the cops who tried to break up a fracas last month in front of Ciro's. Don't you read the papers? His wife just got bumped. What kinda person is that to look up to?"

I could tell him. Really tell him. The shoplifting charge would vanish.

"Roy Darnell's a good actor," I say lamely in my defense.

"So's Lassie, but we're talking about you." He leans back and his swivel chair squeaks under the shifting load. "Know what happens when you get a police record? It follows you around. Forever. You have to declare it when they ask you on job applications, so you won't be able to get work at a decent place. That's what's gonna happen. Is that worth it to you?"

I respond on cue, with vigor. "I'll never do it again. I swear."

He sighs. "I'm not scaring you, am I? See, you're too old. This works best on kids." He shakes his head. "Reva, Reva—you're a smart cookie. So let me level with you. With a clean record and your Corliss Archer looks, plus squirting a few tears, well, the worst that's likely to happen—if the D.A.'s office is even willing to spin their wheels and go to court—is a suspended sentence or probation and maybe a light fine. Probably just a stern warning from the judge. 'Behave yourself in the future, young lady.'"

"I will. I really will."

Vallenzuega is studying my face. His brow furrowed. And this next part jolts me because it doesn't seem to go with the regular spiel. It's like he senses something. "Reva," he says slowly, "Why do I get the feeling you want to tell me something?"

Because I do.

You'd be a hero, I'd be famous for a day, we'd both be on the news.

Because I don't.

All I have to do is keep my mouth shut, give Roy the benefit of the doubt. So I change the subject. Fast.

"What's that funny button on the lapel of your jacket?" I ask. "Are you a Shriner or an Odd Fellow or something?"

He glances at the jacket hanging over the back of his chair. "Just a thing the company gave me. So I wear it."

"What's it mean?"

"Got nothin' to do with what we're talking about, so—"

"I have to answer all your questions, but I ask you just one—"

"Ho-kay. I was working in Hollenbeck Division couple years ago and my bank is in Pasadena. It was payday and I wanted to make a deposit so I took a quick spin over on my lunch hour in a company car. I go in the bank and when I'm next in line I notice that the guy in front of me at the window is sticking up the place. So I grab him and we're wrestling around for his gun, rolling on the floor and all, struggling away, and I finally subdue him and call for backup and that was it."

"The lapel," I say.

"Oh yeah. So it got in the newspaper and then someone put it in for consideration for the Medal of Valor. See, but there was a problem, because I was using an LAPD car and I was over the city line in Pasadena. So they couldn't decide whether to bring me up on charges for misusing department property—or give me the medal."

"But then they decided," I say. "So that thingy means you won the Medal?"

"Uh-huh. For being in the wrong place at the right time."

"Or maybe it's the other way around." I start to laugh. "Just like me." I'm talking about more than Larry Edmunds Bookshop, but he doesn't know that.

He laughs too, and it's the first time I've ever shared a laugh with a cop.

"Ho-kay, now we're back to you. What am I gonna do with you?"

"Look, can't we just chalk it up to experience?" I say. "I really learned my lesson, I mean, it was just a stupid whim, I took the still photos because I didn't think anyone else'd want 'em as much as I did and—"

There's a knock on the door, so I don't have to keep rattling away. "Come in," Detective Vallenzuega calls. The door opens and it's my mother. I'd sooner see a prison matron standing there.

"I'm Reva's mom," she says, coming forward like an angel of mercy, squeezing my shoulder. She's wearing her pink business suit that combined with her upswept champagne blonde dye job makes her look like a cone of cotton candy. Her working duds. That means she didn't get to change clothes after work, probably walked in the door from the bank when they got her on the phone. She's been plowing through rush hour traffic to get here, and she hates traffic. Normally we would be seeing Vesuvius in eruption under such circumstances, but she's as pleasant and caring as Eleanor Roosevelt.

"How's my little girl?" she says to me. "You all right?"

"I'm fine, Mother." I can't believe this.

"Whatever's happened, I blame myself," she confesses to Vallenzuega. Wide-eyed. Pleading for mercy. "Reva's a good girl, but she associates with people who are beneath her, and it's my fault for letting the bad element rub off on her."

I know those lines, but from where? Suddenly I've got it. Mother's doing Joan Crawford in *Mildred Pierce*. Life imitating art. Could you die? But to non-movie fan Vallenzuega, it's a premiere.

"If there's some way you people can find it in your hearts to forgive her, I guarantee it'll never happen again. She's never been in trouble before. She's a good girl," she repeats.

Vallenzuega has been watching her. Not blinking, mouth half-open, not wanting to miss a second. Maybe he doesn't go to the movies but he can spot a performance when he sees one. Now he nods, as if he's been persuaded by her impassioned plea. "I believe you, ma'am. Reva and I have been having a good talk and I think the best thing for everybody is if I release her—into your care."

Mother smiles gratefully and dabs at her eyes with the matching pink hankie she has tucked up her sleeve. I glare at Vallenzuega, who gives me a covert wink.

"Watch out for all those movies," he says to me.

"I know," I say, "they'll rot my mind."

We go down the stairs together, Mother and I, hand-in-hand, am I dreaming? Vallenzuega at the top of the staircase, waving goodbye, wishing me luck. "Don't let me see you back here, kid."

"I'm not a kid," I call back to him.

As soon as we're out of the building and around the corner, heading for our car, Mother stops and turns on me. No more Eleanor Roosevelt. Lizzie Borden's back in town. "You little cunt, do you know I could lose my job at the bank because of you and your crazy shit?"

She slaps me very hard across the face. I can feel each of her fingers outlined on my cheek, but I don't cry. I never cry in front of her.

"Stealing stupid photos of Roy Darnell—didn't I warn you, again and again, that he's bad news for you? It's in your chart, Reva, and the stars don't lie!" I'm not sure if she's talking movies or astrology.

Mother navigates like a Destruction Derby driver through the rush hour traffic back to our apartment with hardly another word, which is fine with me. If she thinks she's punishing me with her silence, well, do it some more.

We clump up the stairs. Home sweet home, "Want something to eat?" I shake my head, I haven't eaten all day, but suddenly I'm too exhausted to even think of food. I go into my room and leave the lights off and just fall into bed. I sleep straight through to the morning and still wake up tired, not knowing what to do, but then I read the obituary page of the *L.A. Times,* and at least I know where I have to go.

Now I'm at Addie's funeral. I wasn't successful in getting close enough when Roy arrived in his limo for him to see me. The jam of photographers and curiosity-seekers were in the way. The service has begun inside the chapel, and we can already hear the minister's platitudes floating out over the P.A. system. Killer Lomax arrives, shouldering his way through toward the entrance. We're maybe fifty, sixty feet apart, with people jammed between us, but somehow our eyes meet—and he looks away fast. Then he's at the closed door where they aren't letting anyone else in, except it opens a crack and Merle Heifetz, the studio flack, recognizes Killer and lets him in, even though Killer doesn't work for Roy anymore. For auld lang syne, I guess.

At the sight of Killer, I feel bad all over again. I don't know exactly what I've done to deserve the feeling, except let the guy jump my bones, for which he can't even bear to look at me. Well, screw him!

But then all thoughts of Killer Lomax are banished as Roy begins to speak. Through the glass front of the chapel I can see him way inside, though he's as indistinct as he was on the night he was on stage at the Hollywood Bowl. But I can hear the terrible pain in his voice, and his choked remembrances of the good times with Addie make me want to cry. Suddenly I'm certain that I've done the right thing. His voice has always been the clearest indicator of what's going on inside of him. I could always read it. And listening to him—it's like an oral lie detector test—I know beyond a doubt that whatever tangled events might have happened last Sunday night, Roy didn't kill Addie. I'm so relieved.

The chapel ceremony is finished, and I'm part of the crowd watching the burial from the road. It's over now, I can see Roy in the distance, moving to his limo. I push closer to the edge of the road and I'm in luck, because just as the limo passes me I see that Roy has spotted me and I give him a sad smile to let him know that my heart is with him and I touch the locket around my neck. I'm so glad I decided to wear it this morning.

None of the other collectors are interested in going over, but I persuade Podolsky to drive me to Roy's house, where the wake is being held. We stand around outside for a while, but then Podolsky has to take off to go to work at Music City. Guests are leaving now, but I keep waiting. Maybe if they all go, I can just walk up to the front door and knock and tell Roy that everything's okay. I feel like Jack Havoc, looking out for someone in trouble, and I'm the only one who can help him. Now it's getting dark and the next-to-last car drives off, but I recognize the only car that's left. It belongs to Killer Lomax, and those two can drink away the whole night together, and besides I have to go to work. So I walk up to Sunset Boulevard and wait for the Santa Monica bus.

26

Arzy & Harry

The gambler's shuttle from Las Vegas swoops down like a bat out of the night sky onto the runway at Burbank Airport. Arzy Marshak watches as the prop plane taxis to a stop in front of arrival gate number three. He spots his partner, Harry Tigner, among the first passengers clambering down the metal staircase. Actually, it's Harry's horse-blanket sports coat that stands out in the darkness. Arzy has tried to steer Harry toward a classier wardrobe, but some things Harry just can't hear.

"How was your funeral?" Harry asks him. He's carrying a briefcase and an overnighter.

"Celeb City. The great and the not-so-great."

"And how'd our boy do?"

"Showstopper. He made 'em laugh, he made 'em cry, he made 'em wet their pants. Roy's a star, what can I tell you?"

The unmarked cop car is parked in the red at the curb outside Burbank's main terminal. Windshield visor turned down to reveal the police decal that fends off parking tickets.

"We got to make a stop," Arzy says as he gets behind the wheel.

Harry settles beside him, looks at him questioningly. Arzy shrugs.

"You're not the only one who works nights."

"So how was Vegas?" Arzy is racing up over Laurel Canyon toward Hollywood.

"Wanna hear? Last night went to see Sinatra at the Sands, nobody can get in, but remember Rick Caulk, used to work Robbery-Homicide in Hollenbeck? He's in charge of security now at the Sands, so we have a primo booth on the main floor. Sinatra comes out, starts singing, you can see right away he's in a crappy mood, does six bars of 'The Lady Is A Tramp,' cuts off the band with an afongoo gesture, starts 'I've Got The World On A String,' lasts three bars on that one, I figure we're about to see the world's shortest night-club appearance."

"Over and out?"

"Looks like. But then somethin' happens. Sinatra looks out into the audience and who does he glom but his kid, Frank Jr., who's there with a bunch of his schoolmates. It's a surprise to Ol' Blue Eyes. He comes to the front of the stage, talks to the kid with all of us listenin'. 'Hey, Junior, y'do your homework? Okay, then you can stay up late with the grownups.' And now he's happy, and I'm tellin you, Arzy, it's like whatchacallit, Dr. Jekyll and Mr. Hyde. Sinatra proceeds to do a fantastic show, sings his heart out."

"So that's how Vegas was?"

"Did I say that's the end of the story? Afterward, Caulk and me, we go into the lounge, it's Jam City, but for us they got a table. Table with a view of the throne. The booth where Sinatra and his party are holding forth. They've wheeled a piano up next to the booth and Sammy Cahn, you know, the songwriter, 'Three Coins In The Fountain' and all that, Sammy Cahn is sittin' at the piano, playing a medley of the hits he wrote for Sinatra, while there's a Meat Parade goin' on. Every good-lookin' broad in the whole town is finding an excuse to strut back and forth past Sinatra's booth in hopes of catchin' his eye or his fly, but Sinatra, he don't even seem to notice."

"Because his kid's there."

"Nah, the kid's gone off with his friends. It's just like the king or the emperor—he's fuckin' jaded, Frank, I mean, if you've had Ava Gardner, maybe everything else is chopped liver. So you get bored. So what he does, 'cuz he's bored, is he gives a little wave of his hand and they wheel away the piano with Sammy Cahn still on it, they're goin' so fast he can't even get off it."

"You're kidding."

"No shit, I saw it. I mean, Cahn got off eventually and came back..."

Arzy laughs. He gets a kick out of Harry. "So the point you're making is?"

"These so-called stars of yours—they think they're so fuckin' entitled, they think they can get away with anything."

"Hey, you wouldn't be talking that way if Sinatra'd given you some of his sloppy seconds."

Harry laughs. Arzy is the only man he allows to poke fun at him. "Maybe not."

"So that's how Vegas was?"

Harry shrugs. "Roy's pal Lomax panned out, I pushed at it real hard, but he was definitely there while Addie was getting bumped here."

"Figured we couldn't get that lucky, a guy nicknamed Killer turns out to be the killer."

"Maybe Roy's got other friends. Anything new around here?"

"I stopped by the Santa Monica courthouse. Picked up a transcript of the divorce stuff. It's like that guy in the sleaze sheet wrote, she got everything—but she expired just before it went into effect. So all bets are off. Roy keeps everything."

"We definitely call that motive."

"Or lucky coincidence. For him. Let's see what we got here."

Arzy has turned right onto the Sunset Strip and almost immediately gone right again, up a narrow road leading past the quaint old Château Marmont Hotel to a residential street overlooking the lights of the city. There are several police vehicles already parked in and around the driveway of an expensive cantilevered house.

The front door is open and the two detectives walk in. Another plainclothesman, Joe Leary, is talking to the affluent couple who own the house. The husband is wearing a tux, his wife a designer dress and important jewelry. They're both ashen beneath their tennis court tans.

"We just feel so violated," the husband says. His wife, hands quivering, nods emphatically. Noticing Marshak and Tigner, Leary excuses himself and saunters over to them. "Harry, thought you were in Vegas."

"Just got back."

"Not bad. I once got to go to Cucamonga on the company's dime."

"What's the score here?" Arzy asks Leary.

"The usual. Couple went to dinner, he's a record producer, there's some kinda awards dinner at the Ambassador, and when they came home they discovered our pal the Hollywood Hills crash-and-basher had paid them a visit. They're providing us a list of what's gone. He's at the point of remembering Nikon cameras and other goodies they probably never had but the insurance'll pay off on."

"How'd the perp get in?" Harry asks.

"How's he always get in? This time he jimmied the kitchen door. Go see."

As they walk to the kitchen, Arzy raises a meaningful eyebrow at Harry. "The *usual*. Like Addie's house and the half dozen knockovers before that."

"Maybe so."

"Which would indicate that the cat burglar is our guy—and could be we're just spinning our wheels with Roy."

"Could be."

The techs are crawling all over the place, examining, photographing, sampling, but Arzy and Harry go to watch Gil

Andrus, the ancient, irritable fingerprint specialist, working meticulously at the kitchen door.

"Pickin' up anything good?" Harry says.

"Nah, he never leaves prints."

"That's what you said about Leopold and Loeb," Arzy says.

"I'm not *that* fuckin' old, kiddo."

Harry peers at the gouge marks on the door frame.

"Usual pry tool, looks like," Andrus says. "He's gonna wear that sucker out."

Harry turns to Arzy. Their eyes meet, they both get the same idea at the same time. It's often like that with partners.

"Andrus, can I borrow that measuring thing of yours?"

"My *what?*" He glares at Harry. "I got a lot of measuring devices."

"You know, the one with the two points."

"You mean the calipers."

"Yeah, right."

Andrus digs in his black equipment bag and brings out a device similar to a draftsman's compass. "Now what're you gonna do with it?"

Harry measures the widths of the gouge marks on the frame and Arzy jots the measurements in his pad. "Mind if we hold onto the calipers for a while, get 'em back to you tomorrow?"

"Be my guest," Andrus says. "But you lose 'em, you gotta buy me another pair."

The house on Kings Road is dark and deserted and there's police tape across the front door. Arzy and Harry rip it loose, unlock the door and go in. They move through the house, switch on the lights in the den where Addie died and continue over to the sliding door leading to the patio. They open it and step out onto the patio, close the door and gaze at the signs of forced entry. Harry takes out the calipers and measures each of the gouge marks. Arzy jots down the measurements, and when he's done they compare the results with the numbers just taken at the other house.

"*Not* the usual," Harry says.

"These are narrower," Arzy agrees. "Two different tools."

"I'm betting this place is the exception. And all the others match."

"Wanna go past the office and check the file?" Arzy asks.

"Yeah, but first—let's give a sniff around here."

They check the drawers in the bar and find nothing, but in the kitchen they hit pay dirt. Opening a cabinet drawer, they find some tools—a hammer, pliers, a screwdriver, and a small wrench. Harry picks up the screwdriver with his handkerchief and they go back to the patio door. The screwdriver fits exactly into the gouge marks. They look even closer and notice a slight flaw on the blade of the screwdriver. It matches a slight flaw on each of the gouges. They go back into the kitchen and carefully empty the drawer where they found the screwdriver. There is a tiny metal shaving on the bottom of the drawer that seems to match the sliding door in the den. They bag it as possible evidence.

Harry stirs the third heaping spoonful of sugar into his coffee cup. He's a die-hard sugar freak. "So what've we got?"

"Just barely enough to make the D.A.'s office snicker at us."

"How about you? Enough to make you change your vote on Roy?"

"I'm teetering pretty good," Arzy says.

They're occupying a booth in the coffee shop section at Schwab's Drugstore on Sunset Boulevard at Crescent Heights. It's a place made famous by gossip columnist and hypochondriac Sidney Skolsky, who maintains a desk and a medicine chest in the rear of the store. Out-of-work Hollywoodites sip coffee and swap lies all day long at Schwab's and, on occasion, Marlon Brando stops by for a lotion to dispose of crabs, or Marilyn Monroe drops in to reload on mascara and cry on Skolsky's shoulder about her love life. Local cops eat and drink here for free.

"Does the screwdriver make it an inside job?" Harry speculates.

"Feels more like a coverup. After the fact. Make a murder look like a burglary."

"So the killer just hitchhiked on the fact that a cat burglar is working the neighborhood."

"If the killer was even aware of that. That coulda been a piece of luck."

"So Addie opened the door and let the killer in."

"See how easy it is—now all we have to figure out is who actually did the deed." Arzy sips his black coffee and ignores the cheese Danish on the table between them. "Let's divvy what we've got. What do you want?"

"Cherchez la femme," Harry mumbles through a mouthful of Danish. "I'll track the broad, the one who framed Roy and then dated him. Sounds like an interesting relationship."

"I'll go see if I can poke any holes in Roy's alibi."

27

I'm parked in a rental car under a shady elm tree on a sleepy street in Santa Monica. Slouched low, in for the long haul. Been here over an hour already. It's a street in transition. Some of the low-cost, pre-fab bungalows built just after the war are still left. Giving way to newer ten, twelve unit two-story apartment houses. The entrances to the apartments are all on the outside, like in a motel. I'm looking at the doorway to the apartment where Reva Hess lives.

Yeah. Reva *Hess!*

It came to me like a dream in the middle of the night. Actually, it was the TV set. Channel 11. I'd boozed my way to sleep on the living room couch with the tube still on. When I opened my eyes, there was a documentary. About Spandau Prison in Germany. Where the last of Hitler's inner circle monsters is doing life. Rudolf Hess.

Hess!

Yes!

Bingo!

Eat shit, Jack Havoc. I'm on the job.

The rest was easy. Grab the phone books. Make a list of every Hess. Not that many, really. Start phoning at seven o'clock. Wake 'em up? Too fuckin' bad. Is Reva there? Doing a prissy lady. Pays to be the Man of a Thousand Voices. No Reva there? Next. Until the woman in Santa Monica who answers yells, "Reva-a-a-ah, phone call."

And then I hear her voice.

My Reva.

I make up a bullshit story about how she's won second prize in the drawing, she doesn't ask what drawing, everyone's always entering drawings, and we're sending you two tickets to the premiere of *Around The World in 80 Days* at the Carthay Circle Theater, just want to verify your address.

And here I am. Made in the shade. Under the elm tree. Waiting for her to appear. Why the rental car? C'mon. She'd spot my Jack Havoc–mobile a mile away. I'm in disguise. Nothing bizarre. Just my biggest pair of sunglasses and a wide-billed L.A. Angels baseball cap. I've found if you dress down and don't put out celebrity vibes, nobody notices you. That's definitely how I want it today.

The mother came out a half hour ago. Dressed in a starchy blouse and a tacky suit for work in an office or a bank or something. I remember her face from years ago in New York. She used to accompany Reva in the beginning. The mother's gone fleshy since then, looks like booze weight. She drives off in a three-year-old Nash Rambler. I keep watching the door to the apartment.

You got a plan for when you see her? Jack Havoc wants to know.

Thought I'd shaken off the sonuvabitch. But he's here in the rental car.

"I'll improvise," I assure him. "Actors are good at that."

Do it right, kid. There are no retakes in real life.

"So sayeth the Old Philosopher from the Faraway Hills." I'm feeling terrific.

Now the door opens and the girl of my dreams appears. Reva. On the second floor landing. Locking the door behind her. Wearing white tennis shoes, beige slacks, a black V-neck T-shirt—and, bingo, there's the locket. Take 'em both out and I'm home free. No links between me and Addie's sad demise.

"We're gonna wrap this up in a hurry," I tell Jack.

He's just sitting there. Staring at her. Almost licking his chops.

She skips lightly down the stairs. I turn on the car motor. The street is deserted. When she reaches the sidewalk, I'll just glide up beside her. "Hey, Reeve, give you a lift?" It can be that easy. But, just before she reaches the sidewalk a door opens, ground floor front. Out pops a tow-headed schoolkid. Nine or ten. Backpack, lunchpail.

"Hi, Reva!"

"G'morning, Everett."

Strolling together now. Toward Santa Monica Boulevard. Okay. No rush. Let 'em get ahead. Then roll along behind them.

On the Boulevard, they both turn east. Past the market, shoppers going in and out. Reva buys herself and Everett donuts at the outdoor counter on the corner of Bundy. They both munch as the bus pulls up. She waves and gets on. Everett waves back and walks on.

I follow the bus. It's not hard. Just annoying. Creeping through traffic. I can let the bus get ahead on the non-stop streets. Just so I'm close enough to see if Reva hops off at the next stop. Or the next. But she's in for the long haul, too. Down Santa Monica Boulevard. Through Westwood.

Where the hell's she going? Jack's impatient.

"Think like an autograph collector," I tell him. "If she gets off at Beverly Glen, it's near Twentieth Century Fox."

She doesn't get off at Beverly Glen. Now we're in Beverly Hills.

"Maybe Rodeo Drive. Down the street from the Derby and Romanoff's."

You sound like a Hollywood tour bus driver.

She stays aboard. Moving into west L.A.

Got any other bright ideas?

"Bet she's going to the Goldwyn Studios, up ahead on Formosa."

Wait. But. *Lost your bet. You sure she's still on the bus?*

I don't answer. There's no talking to him when he's in a mood like this.

We're going past the film labs and the industrial film houses that make the movie trailers. Then, just when I'm feeling real nervous—maybe she did get off the bus without me noticing—she gets off at Vine Street. Crosses in front of the bus. Heading north. I'm stuck in the right hand lane. Traffic's locked beside me. So I have to go a block past Vine before I can get over and make a U-turn.

Take your time, Jack Havoc says. *Doesn't matter if she disappears on us again.*

"You wanna drive?" That shuts him up. That and the sight of Reva. Still on the west side of Vine Street. Strolling up toward Sunset.

Wouldn't you love to just reach out and grab her off the street?

"Too many people." He's getting crazy.

I'm just saying, wouldn't you love to?

Up ahead, Reva crosses Sunset. I catch the red light. She enters Wallich's Music City.

Okay, genius, what you gonna do now?

I'm not sure. Should I park the car and—what? Go inside? Risk being spotted by her? Better to stake out the place. How long can she be in there? Only one entrance to the store, right there on the corner. Before the red light changes, I spot her again. Just entering one of the sound-proof listening cubicles inside the record store. Facing out through the front window. There's a white-coated sales-man with her, carrying a small stack of LPs. I know him. Her pal Podolsky. They chat a moment, then he leaves her. She settles down. Starts enjoying the music.

That makes it simple. Just ace a little old lady out of a parking space. Commanding a view of Reva across the street in the window. Put coins in the meter. Slouch down. Watch and wait. She'll be out after a while.

Jack Havoc laughs.

"Okay, what?"

Role reversal, he says. *Usually she stands around and waits for you to come out of places. Now you know how it feels.*

"Couple of minor differences, of course."

Oh yeah. For instance, she knows everything about you. And you know next to nothing about her.

"Well, I guess today's the day I play catch up."

At noon they both leave Music City. Reva and Podolsky. They ride out of the employees' parking lot in a fading blue Hillman Minx convertible. Top down, Podolsky driving. I follow them, hoping he's going to drop her off somewhere. Preferably somewhere secluded. They only go a mile or so to the entrance off Melrose to the Paramount lot. A photo shoot in progress in front of the famous two-story wrought-iron gate. Like a senior class graduation picture. All the major stars working on the lot are there, linked arm in arm. Fred Astaire, Audrey Hepburn, Alan Ladd, Betty Hutton, Charlton Heston, Shirley MacLaine, Dean Martin, and Jerry Lewis. Photographer behind the 8x10 camera on a tripod cues the herd, they all smile and take a simultaneous step forward. Click!

Of course, there's a crowd watching. Mostly office workers and blue-collar guys on lunch break from the studio. Plus a number of autograph collectors. Reva and Podolsky have joined them. They move in now for signatures and snapshots before the stars retreat behind the studio walls.

Reva and Podolsky get back in the parked Hillman. With a couple of the other fans. Reva's now insulated by that many more. I tail them up Melrose to LaBrea. Another stop. I hang back and watch while the collectors nosh at Pink's Hot Dog Stand. Jammed with people. Will she ever be alone?

Back in the Hillman. Continuing up Melrose, past Robertson. They're parking again. Reva, Podolsky, and the others walking to the Academy Theater in the next block. Apparently there's an afternoon performance today. I find a parking space facing toward the theater. Moviegoers are arriving. I spot Ernie Borgnine, who recently copped the Oscar for *Marty,* as he's engulfed by the autograph hunters. Like a school of piranha swarming.

The Academy, Jack Havoc says, *scene of our past triumphs.*

"If you don't have anything to say, just shut up."

Just reminiscing. Your first real date with the lovely Kim.

"Don't start, Jack."

You figure they've got a cop camped on her doorstep? I mean, if they went after chumpy Killer Lomax.

I've been thinking of nothing else. "They don't know who she is. And she was probably on the train goin' to visit her aunt in Oregon or Arizona or wherever at the time."

Hey. Y'convinced me. Salty old Walter Brennan and Marjorie Main, Ma Kettle herself, are signing autographs across the street. Must be Old Fart's Day at the Academy.

As I look, I see Reva and Podolsky break away from the crowd and come back up the other side of the street. Toward the Hillman. We're on the move again.

The Hillman goes south down Doheny to Pico. Right turn, heading toward Beverly Hills. I stay several car lengths behind them. Enough traffic to keep me from being conspicuous. Left turn at Beverly Drive, going into the Beverwill area. A middle-class neighborhood. One cut-through street leading into Culver City. Fortunately, there are a few other cars taking the shortcut. But I have to widen the gap to keep from being spotted.

Gotta be MGM, Jack Havoc says. *What else is there in Culver City?*

Turns out he's no better at guessing Reva's itinerary than I am. The Hillman continues south to Washington Boulevard, but turns left—away from MGM. We're traveling along Car Row now. All the new car dealerships and maintenance shops.

"Maybe the Hillman needs a lube and oil change," I suggest.

Then why's he stopping in front of the Ford dealership?

That's what the Hillman is doing. In a parking space. But motor still running. Neither Podolsky or Reva making a move to get out. They're staring through the plate glass window into the car showroom. Discussing. Then Reva excitedly points at something or someone inside. Podolsky switches off the engine. Reva's taking out her pen as they enter the showroom.

I swing around and park on the other side of the boulevard. Through the plate glass window I can see Reva and Podolsky approaching one of the car salesmen. He says something in greeting. Probably the classic line, "Hey, folks, can I sell you a car today?" But Reva says something to him. The salesman shrugs. Grins. Looks a tad embarrassed. Then Reva and Podolsky offer him their autograph books and he begins to sign them.

Tom Drake, Jack Havoc says. In amazement.

"You're kidding." I'm amazed, too.

Sure enough. It's him. Tom Drake. One of MGM's young male stars during World War II. The guy who caught the trolley when Judy Garland sang "The Trolley Song" in *Meet Me In St. Louis,* the star of *The Green Years* and *Words and Music.* While the A-team was away in the service, guys like Tom Drake, Van Johnson, Dana Andrews, and Lon McCallister were headliners.

'Til the war ended and the heavy hitters came back home, Jack Havoc says. Reading my mind. *That's why you gotta get it while you can.*

"Wowee. There's a bulletin." But I'm still watching Tom Drake.

From kissing Judy Garland to hawking ragtops. In one quick fall.

"You don't know that! Maybe he owns the fuckin' car dealership! He was real hot."

So were you.

Now we're a mile-and-a-half down the road. At MGM. Flagship lot of Filmland. Boasting that they have "More Stars Than There Are In The Heavens." There's a small mortuary on the corner next to the huge alabaster white Thalberg Administration Building. Evidence of a stubborn grave-digger who refused to sell his land, so they had to build around him. The guard at the studio gate is named, unbelievably, Ken Hollywood. It's a slow afternoon, so he intermittently chats with Reva and Podolsky. Apparently they're old friends. Every once in a while business intrudes. Ken Hollywood has to automatically raise the gate for an incoming or outgoing vehicle. Or Reva and Podolsky have to approach Van Heflin, who's on foot, leaving the studio for the parking lot outside, or Jennifer Jones, who stops her Bentley at the barrier long enough to sign autographs. But star sightings are few and far between.

I'm parked a half block away, slouching low, as usual, yawning and trying to stay awake. There's a lot of dull, dead, downtime involved in collecting autographs. Beside me, Jack Havoc has nodded off. Now I nudge him. Reva and Podolsky are rolling again.

The Hillman wends its way north out of Culver City into Westwood.

Maybe they're goin' to Fox now. Hey, Mr. Zanuck, can Betty Grable come out and play?

But they go past Fox. Into Beverly Hills again. North on Linden Drive. Past the house where Bugsy Siegel was shotgunned to death. Onto Sunset Boulevard, east to the far side of the Beverly Hills Hotel. I'm pacing them all the way. Onto Coldwater Canyon and—now I'm starting to drive on automatic pilot, because—I can't believe it—they're turning into the driveway of my house.

I go beyond the entrance. Make a U-turn and glide slowly past the opening to my place. Podolsky is still in the car, reading the *Hollywood Reporter.* Reva is at my front door. Knocking. Knocking again.

Too bad there's nobody home, Jack Havoc says.

"But why's she even here? With that schmuck."

Someone's honking behind me so I have to continue on. Make another U-turn and come back. By this time I see Reva getting into the Hillman and Podolsky is starting to emerge from the driveway. I follow him back down to Sunset. He leads the way into Santa Monica.

Polite gent, Jack Havoc says, *driving his little girlfriend right to her doorstep.*

Wrong again. The Hillman doesn't turn on Bundy. Instead continues on along Montana Avenue. Mostly residential, but up ahead there's a run of stores and restaurants for about a dozen blocks. In the center of this activity, the Hillman pulls over into the red zone near a corner. Reva gets out. I hang back. She says a quick goodbye and Podolsky drives off. Reva is alone at the corner waiting for the red light. I swing into the center lane on Montana, signaling a left. She'll be playing into my hands when the light changes.

Look, if she walks down that side street, nobody's there, it's all shady-dark from the big trees—

Telling me what I know. Green light. Reva crosses. I make my turn. But she doesn't proceed down the side street. When she reaches the curb, she turns toward a neighborhood movie theater near the corner. The Aero. Playing Hitchcock's *The Man Who Knew Too Much* and Frank Sinatra as *Johnny Concho.* Reva waves familiarly at the woman in the ticket booth and walks inside. Without buying a ticket.

Double feature. She'll be in there for hours, Jack says. *Hey, perfect opportunity. You go inside, too. All that darkness. Probably hardly anyone in there this time of day. Murder in the Movie House. Try to kill her during the Hitchcock picture, cover up Reva's screams with Doris Day's.*

I'm staring at him. "Are you for real?"

Of course not. Just want to keep you on your toes. Make sure you're considering all the possibilities.

I'm about to tell him what he can do with his possibilities.

But here's Reva again.

Coming out of the Aero.

Standing at the door to the ticket booth.

The woman inside opens the door and they switch places. The woman taking her purse with her, walking off. Door's closed again. Changing of the guard complete. Reva is now in charge of selling tickets. To a little old couple lined up at the booth window.

Okay. She works here. Going on duty. Be here for hours. What are you gonna do?

"I don't know about you, but I'm hungry."

Jack Havoc is singing. He sounds a bit tipsy.

Oh, she's only a bird in a gilded caaaaage...

We grabbed a quick bite at Zucky's deli nearby on Fifth and Wilshire. Corned beef on rye. Two beers. That became three beers. First food I had today. The beer hit him hard. I'm not feeling much pain, either. At least I don't think I am. It's dark now. We're parked comfortably with a view of the marquee of the theater and Reva in the illuminated ticket booth. Occasionally when she moves or a car passes, the light bounces off the locket. That damn locket. Like Pandora's box. If the world gets one peek, I'll never be able to clamp the lid back on again.

I can just imagine the scene. "Where did you get this locket, Miss Hess?" Found it on the floor in the back seat of Roy Darnell's car. "Do you recognize the faces pictured inside the locket?" Sure, Roy and Addie Darnell. "Was the night you found the locket the same night his wife was killed?" Uh-huh. "See anything else there?" Oh, just a bunch of other jewelry stuff. "Would you look at this insurance company photo of a pair of diamond earrings." Yeah, I saw them there, too. "Your Honor, the Prosecution rests its case."

If you had a high-powered rifle, you could pick her off from right here. Baaaaang!

"I'd still need the locket. And anything else incriminating that she swiped."

Incriminating. He savors the word. *Sound like a goddamn lawyer. Incrimmmmminating evidence.*

"I'm just saying that what we're looking for is the proper time and place. And this isn't it. A brightly lit booth on a busy street."

Never here, always somewhere else. Not now. Definitely not in the movies. How 'bout in the ladies' room? What the fuck happened to improvisation?

"Hey, Jack, something scorching your ass today? I woke up happy and you've been ragging on me ever since. What's worrying you? Spit it out."

You, babe. You're worrying me.

"Why? You were after me to get us close to Reva. So now we're close. There she is."

Yeah, but when push comes to shove—is there really any shove in you? This isn't gonna be like tossing creampuff punches at flabby photographers.

"I'll handle it."

Just keep in mind. If you screw up, you won't be peddling Fords in Culver City—you'll be sniffing cyanide fumes in San Quentin. He leans back against the head rest. *How's that scene grab you, big fella?*

When we were at the deli, I made a couple phone calls. To the transit authority. And to the Aero Theater. So I know a few things now. The way I figure it is that when she gets off work she'll go home. There's no bus along Montana that'll get her there. But if she walks up to Wilshire, she can take the bus to Bundy, then transfer and get off at Santa Monica Boulevard. Back where she started this morning, just around the corner from her apartment. That's what she'll probably do. Because it's a little too far to walk all the way home. And it'll be late. Because the last showing of *Johnny Concho* goes on at ten.

I'll be able to pick my spot. Lot of dark secluded streets along that route.

Jack Havoc is dozing in the seat beside me. Or maybe he's pretending. You never can tell with him. I'm studying Reva. In her glass booth. Can't take my eyes off her. Like watching a goldfish in a bowl. Funny. She's been on the periphery of my vision for years now. But tonight is the first time I've ever really looked at her. Seen her. Not so pretty. But sort of attractive in a tomboy way. Small but pleasant. Smiles at every customer who steps up to her window. Sasses the ticket-taker who brings her out a Coke. Nice girl.

Hard to imagine she'll be dead so very soon.

Okay. Time to give that one a little attention. Killing someone. Committing murder. I've done it on stage. On screen. But this will be a premiere. No camera, hopefully no audience. But I'm hoping I can use the same muscles. It's just a scene. An acting moment. I'm trained in bringing up sense memories and adrenaline. Block out everything else. I've played Othello strangling Desdemona. Six nights a week and two matinees. But then you wash off the grease-paint and go home. Leaving any guilt behind.

It's the same!

Just do what you have to do. And go home.

That's the ticket.

I look at the dashboard clock. Almost ten o'clock.

She'll be off soon.

A Chevy parks across the street in front of the closed and darkened beauty salon. A man gets out and heads for the box office. Must be a die-hard Sinatra fan, catching only the last half of the double. But now the man walks out of the dark into the bright lights under the marquee. And I recognize him in an instant.

I jab Jack Havoc in the ribs. He's awake and alarmed.

We're both staring at Reva in her booth.

Talking through the glass. To Detective Sergeant Arzy Marshak.

"He mustn't see me. Not here," I say.

Go, GO! Jack Havoc says.

I turn on the motor and we gun away.

28

Arzy & Harry

"So did you happen to see Roy Darnell arrive at the theater last Sunday night? Before the screening began?"

It's the first question of the day Arzy Marshak asks. It won't be the last.

The morning sun beams idyllically down on the Brentwood estate where a Hollywood legend lives. It's the start of what will turn out to be a very long day. Arzy sips orange juice hand-squeezed from the trees in the spacious yard. He sits beneath a sun umbrella, beside a turquoise pool large enough to stage an Esther Williams water ballet. Opposite him, in the navy blue swim trunks with the U.S. Marine Corps logo, featuring no paunch, good muscle tone, also drinking orange juice, although his is laced with vodka, is Arzy's host—"Wild Bill" Wellman. White hair, trim white mustache, skin tanned brown. Steel blue inquiring eyes.

"First I noticed him was inside the Academy," Wellman says.

"Was he alone?"

"I'm not sure. I was on the other side of the theater. Heard a commotion in the far aisle. Looked over and saw Roy with a bunch of people swarming around him. It's like that when someone who's hot shows up at one of these screenings. Everybody likes to get near 'em, maybe some of the prosperity will rub off."

"So he might have been with someone—"

"Or he might've been alone. Wasn't anyone with him when he congratulated me in the lobby after the show. I mean, we went off together and got pie-eyed. Just the two of us." The blue eyes probe. "I told you all this on the phone the other day."

"Just trying to fill in a few details. How did Mr. Darnell seem to you—after the show?"

"Elated. Like he'd seen a good movie."

"A real goodie."

"Before your time, wasn't it?"

"I'm a fan. Seen most everything you've directed. From *Wings* to *The High and Mighty.*"

"Sounds like you're a flyer."

"Close. *Semper fi.* Airborne."

"Korea?"

"Yeah."

"How was it?"

"Just like *Battleground.*"

"Except for the happy ending," Wellman says. "We had one. You didn't."

"Hey—I'm here."

"Still do any jumping?"

"On the weekends sometimes. When I don't have anything else to do."

Wellman pours more juice in Arzy's glass. "Bet you could tell some stories."

"Matter of fact, that's what I want to do. Write stories for movies."

"War stories? Cop stories?"

"Got a bunch of both."

"How's the story you're working on now?"

The old bastard's fast. "Haven't got the ending worked out yet."

"Bet it's the one about the Hollywood star who gets his dick caught in the wringer and can't get it out."

"That's one way to go." Then, "So basically you saw Mr. Darnell at the start of the movie and after it ended."

"Yep. See, in between all the lights were out. You really think he did it?"

Arzy shrugs. "I'm just a bird dog. Keep my eyes open and go where it takes me. But you don't buy it?"

"Me? What do I know? You're the pro. Far as I'm concerned, Roy's a nice guy with a strong tennis backhand, who can hold his liquor. But if you think he killed his wife and went boozing with me afterwards like nothing happened, then—"

Wellman pauses. Arzy takes the bait. "Then what?"

"Then he's even a better actor than I thought he was."

Arzy nods and closes his notebook. He likes what he hears: in between, when the lights went out, Roy was on his own.

Harry Tigner is at the Crossroads of the World. It's an inconspicuous courtyard on Sunset near Highland. A dozen small offices surrounding a European-style kiosk. The tenants include an accountant, a barber, a dentist, an insurance broker, an escrow firm, and the office of Aaron Fisher, Private Investigations, which turns out to be an office slightly bigger than a phone booth, with autographed glossies on the wall of several contented clients. Harry doesn't recognize any of their faces. Maybe Arzy would.

Fisher himself is a chesty kid with big shoulders, wearing a blue V-neck sweater over a white button-down shirt. Dirty white sneakers. Looks scarcely old enough to buy beer legally. Slouched behind a desk small enough to have been swiped from his junior high school homeroom. He seems unperturbed that Harry has come knocking on his door this morning. Almost flattered.

"Figured someone'd be along after a while," he says. "But just for the record, how'd you find me?"

"Adrienne Ballard Darnell's checkbook," Harry says. "She wrote two checks payable to your office. For services rendered."

"Uh-huh."

That's all he says. The punk is going to make me fish for the details, Harry thinks. Here we go.

"Care to tell me what those services were?"

"Well, I don't know, there are fiduciary responsibilities in my business. Clients count on my discretion, you know, confidentiality."

"Your client's dead. You don't want to obstruct an ongoing police investigation."

Fisher grins. Makes him look like a Norman Rockwell character. Fuckin' red hair and freckles and all. Enjoying himself. "Of course not. Just want it made clear for the record that I'm behaving in an ethical—"

"Don't annoy me, transom-peeper. Or I'll step on you."

Fisher's smile fades. Color goes out of his face. Leaving the freckles in bold relief. Like an instant case of chicken pox.

"Just for the record, how'd you get to be a P.I.?"

Fisher shrugs. "Took some criminology courses at Santa Monica J.C. Got all As. Worked as a traffic cop in Pacoima for six months. Passed the civil exam for P.I. with flying colors. Hung out my shingle—and here I am."

"How'd you happen to connect with Mrs. Darnell?"

"She was looking for someone. Found me in the Yellow Pages. I got myself listed by my first name, double 'A' so I'm at the top of the page."

"Terrific. Tell me what you did to earn your fees."

"I did two jobs for the lady. Second one was to serve the divorce papers and a domestic court subpoena to Darnell. Got him outside Romanoff's when he was signing autographs. He took a swing at me. Missed, of course, sozzled sonuvabitch. Fell in the gutter." He snickers. Seems disappointed Harry doesn't join in.

"Tell me about time number one."

"That was the fun time. Miz Ballard, I mean Mrs. Darnell, wanted to test Mr. Darnell's fidelity."

"You set him up."

"Well, let's just say I put temptation in his path—and he ran after it like a horny little bunny."

"Who was the bait?"

"Just some girl. I hired her. Mrs. Darnell coached her. I told her what to do. Darnell did the rest."

"Where'd you find her?"

"In Scandia. She was at the bar. I bought her a drink, we chatted a little. She's studying acting, aren't they all? Okay, I said, y'busy tomorrow night, I got a part for you to play. One performance. Two hundred bucks. She said she'd want it in cash. I said it was a deal."

"Name."

"Chris Patterson. She said."

"She said."

"Yeah, I think it was a phony moniker."

Monniker. This sleazy pseudo–Sam Spade Jr. Providing dead-end leads.

"I need to know what she looked like."

"About five-four, long dark red hair and—"

"Don't tell me. Show me. Show me the pictures."

He hesitates. But only for a second. Then goes to the file cabinet, unlocks it, finds an envelope. Tosses it across the desk to Harry, who looks at the photos. Roy Darnell caught flagrantly in the act. Getting it on with a drop dead gorgeous gal. Some guys have it all and it's still not enough. A couple of the pictures show her face clearly.

"I'm gonna hold on to these," Harry says, rising.

"Be my guest." That shit-eating Norman Rockwell smile again. "I've got the negatives."

"Yeah. I bet you do. Don't do anything with them unless you check with me first."

Arzy Marshak is being given a lesson in how to properly cool a thousand bodies.

"I lower the thermostat to sixty-seven degrees," explains Reese Shelton, the manager of the Academy Theater. He lets Arzy see as he adjusts the dial on the wall near the front of the theater. "Normally, you'd think that's too cold for comfort. But you have to allow for the combined body temperatures of nearly a thousand people—that's how many seats we have. Add in all those 98.6s and it's perfect by the end of the first reel."

"Think you'll fill the place today? A weekday matinee?"

Shelton leans closer to Arzy. Confiding. "There are quite a few of our members who aren't working at any given time. Besides, it's a rare showing. A golden oldie called *Kentucky,* with Loretta Young, she's still very well-liked by our members. Walter Brennan won the Oscar for it."

"First time they gave an award for Best Supporting Actor."

"You're absolutely correct." Shelton looks at Arzy with new respect.

Arzy waits while Shelton locks the protective plastic cover on the thermostat—"So no one else can fool with it." Arzy idly looks up at the golden ten-foot-statue of Oscar looming over them. It reminds him of the giant robot in *The Day the Earth Stood Still.* Gort was his name. "Klatoo barada nikto." The instructions that activated the unstoppable robot. Just behind the statue, there's a curtain covering a doorway.

"What's through there?"

"A backstage exit door," Shelton says.

Shelton is a brisk, precise little man, wearing rimless glasses and a beige lightweight summer suit without a crease on it. He leads the way back up the side aisle. The first patrons are trickling in for the showing. "About where was Mr. Darnell sitting on Sunday night?" Arzy asks.

Shelton points at a row twelve back from the front. "Around there. On the aisle. I noticed him when I came down to adjust the air conditioning."

"Was he alone?"

"There were other people in the row. *A Star Is Born* is one of our most popular attractions. We had to turn away thirty or forty latecomers."

"Who was with him?"

"I'm not sure if anyone was. He might have been alone or not. I mean, I wasn't keeping tabs on him. Even if he is a star, as far as we're concerned he's just another Academy member. No special privileges."

"Like reserved seats."

"Exactly." They're moving into the narrow lobby now. There's a mousy attendant at the door. Checking Academy membership cards. Those are shown for admission. The forecourt outside and the sidewalk beyond are filled with socializing moviegoers. Arzy catches a glimpse of Walter Brennan, taller than you think, signing autographs near the curb.

"Wait," Shelton says. "I think there was a woman with him. Auburn hair, worn in a page boy. She comes here now and then. Or am I thinking about a couple of weeks ago? Mr. Darnell might've been with her at the Hitchcock double feature."

"Can you be sure?"

Shelton turns on him. In a huff. "Really, Sergeant, I'm not here to call the roll and keep track of who's sitting with whom. I've got a lot more responsibility than that."

"Maybe if you think about it for a moment—"

"You want to know that sort of gossip, go ask them!" He points out toward the curb. At the autograph hounds surrounding newly arrived Loretta Young.

Arzy goes outside to watch. Waits until the feeding frenzy around Loretta Young abates. Then the half dozen fans retreat from the front of the theater. Arzy moves in on them while they're delightedly gazing at their still-wet signatures.

"Hi, can I talk to you guys?" He shows them his badge.

A teenage boy sporting an Angels ball cap says, "We're not makin' any trouble. The manager says we can be here if we don't block the entrance."

Arzy explains that he's not here to roust them. Just to glean some info. "Were any of you here on Sunday night when *A Star Is Born* was playing?" They all were. So far, so good. "Did you see Roy Darnell?"

They all nod. Curious now.

"Did he come alone?"

"Nah," says the Angels fan, "he came with Reva."

The others laugh.

"Who's Reva?" Arzy says.

An anorexic teenage blonde with bad skin says, "Otis is just teasing you. Reva's one of us. She's a big Darnell fan. They weren't together, they just walked up together."

"Did Roy Darnell meet anyone here?"

"I think I saw him with that redhead," says Otis, the Angels fan.

"The one he went to the *Trapeze* preem with?" says another.

"Yeah, her."

"She wasn't here last Sunday."

"Sure she was," the skinny blonde says.

"That was weeks ago, Marcie. On Hitchcock night."

Arzy interrupts the round robin discussion. "Who we talking about?"

"This new broad Roy is dating," Otis says.

"What's her name?"

He shrugs. "Ask Reva. She got her."

"What do you mean, she *got* her?"

"Her autograph. She got her autograph."

"In her crumb book," says Marcie, the blonde. "She's nobody."

"But she wrote her name in Reva's book?"

"I think Reva snapped a picture of her, too, with Roy."

"Where's Reva? She here?"

"She was. You just missed her," Otis says. "She took off after she got Walter Brennan."

"Reva what?" Arzy flips open his notebook. "What's her last name?"

"Sure, that's the gal he was with. A real looker."

Harry Tigner is showing one of the photos he got from Sam Spade Jr. to Garry Foley, the KTLA-TV cameraman who covered the *Trapeze* premiere. Harry has folded the photo so that only the face of the woman with Roy Darnell is visible.

"You wouldn't happen to remember her name?"

"I was too busy grinding away with my camera—and staring down her cleavage. But Darnell probably introduced her to Georgie Jessel. They always introduce their dates, like we're all at a party."

"What happens to that footage?"

"We keep it on file for a while. Want me to look and see if I can find it?"

Harry says he sure would. And he waits. He's left word with police dispatch where he is, so Arzy can find him if he has to. Now he sits in the TV station's newsroom. Reading a copy of *Variety* to fill the time. It's like it's written in another language. People are "ankling to Gotham." An actor is "giving the perf of his career." The "web's o. and o.'s are etching record quarterly profs." Foley returns. With regrets.

"Sorry, I checked and you're a day late. They've recycled those tapes."

"What's recycled?"

"Reused. They don't keep much on permanent file. Makes you feel like you're creating sand castles that wash away with the tide."

Another dead end.

Harry gets in his unmarked cop car and drives west up Sunset. Maybe he'll check out the Hotel Bel-Air where the sting took place. Maybe someone there remembers something. But, quite fortunately, Harry catches a red light on the Strip just beyond Ciro's.

Arzy Marshak is camped out on the street across from the apartment house in Santa Monica. It's dark now, and he's been listening to a salute to Sinatra on his car radio. It's Ol' Blue Eyes' birthday. Arzy wonders if he'll still be sitting here on Frank's next birthday. But now there's action.

A Nash Rambler desperately in need of a wash drives into the carport of the apartment house. A pudgy woman in her forties, dressed in a rumpled lilac-colored suit, gets out and lumbers up the stairs to the second floor landing. Either tired or blitzed. Maybe both. She enters the only unlit apartment.

Arzy follows. Up to the apartment door. He knocks. Waits. There's stirring inside. "Who is it?" the woman's voice calls.

"Mrs. Hess? I'm Detective Marshak—"

The door is yanked open. The woman looking belligerent. Suit jacket off, holding a wet towel in her hand, a red salsa dribble on her white blouse. "It's about Reva, isn't it? What's she gone and done now?"

The voice is eighty-proof margarita. Goes with the salsa. Arzy reassures her, "No, no, Reva hasn't done anything wrong, I just want to talk to her. She might be able to help me on a detail in a routine investigation."

She invites him in. "That damn daughter of mine is out of control, I don't know what to do with her. They picked her up for shoplifting the other day in Hollywood. I had to beg to get 'em to let her go." Absently rubbing the wet towel at the stain on her blouse, making a widening wet blotch. "What can I do? I can't watch her every minute, I have to work, and if I stop off for a cocktail after work at El Coyote with the girls from the bank, well, then I come home and here you are on my doorstep."

Arzy hears El Coyote. Goes with the salsa and margaritas. "Why don't we both sit down, Mrs. Hess. You've had a hard day and I don't want to add to it."

There are four chairs at the dining room table. Two of them are cluttered with piles of newspapers. The other two chairs are about the only clear space in the living room, dining room, or kitchen. Swaying stacks of magazines and cardboard boxes clutter every available surface, even along the walls. All the kitchen counters are filled to overflowing with groceries, canned goods of every description piled two and three high, boxes and boxes of breakfast cereals, spaghetti, macaroni, crackers, cookies, condiments and spices, bottles of ketchup, soda, juices, and liquor. It looks like Mrs. Hess is about to go into competition with the A&P.

"Are you having the cabinets painted?" Arzy asks. Trying to make sense of it.

"No, the cabinets are full, too. I just hate to be running out to the supermarket every ten minutes for something or other. Would you like a drink?"

"Thanks, but I'm still on the clock. About Reva—"

"It's this craziness with the autographs. It was cute when she was a little girl in New York," she's pouring herself three fingers of Jack Daniels. "I thought it'd build up her self-esteem, but it's all she lives for."

"Hobbies can get pretty intense. Actually, that is what I wanted to ask her about. I understand she was at the Academy Theater the other night and saw Roy Darnell there—"

"Is that what this is about? That poor woman, killed in her own home. But what's Reva got to do with that?"

"Nothing that I know of. I just wanted to ask her to show me one of her autograph books, I think the kids call it a crumb book—"

"Those aren't kids, they're freaks, scum."

"Do you know where Reva keeps her autograph books?"

"In there, in her room." Mrs. Hess gestures with the tumbler of Jack Daniels at one of the two doors leading to the bedrooms. The one with the padlock on the doorjamb. "I'm not permitted in there, isn't that a disgrace? Her own mother. But you're a police officer, you can go in, I give you permission, so you don't need a search warrant, I'll give you a screwdriver or a crowbar and—"

Arzy doesn't want to get in the middle of this. Unless he has to. "Where's Reva now? Will she be home soon?"

"She's at work. She works late tonight."

"Does she carry the autograph books she's using now with her?"

"You bet she does. Doesn't go to the toilet without them. Might run into a star."

"Where does she work, Mrs. Hess?"

29

Reva

As soon as the last movie goes on at the Aero, I start tallying up the night's receipts, because usually no one else shows up. Occasionally there've been exceptions. Like the night we were running a James Cagney Festival and Elvis Presley and his posse of Memphis homeboys appeared five minutes after *Angels With Dirty Faces* went on. Farley, who tears the tickets, and Gloria, at the candy counter, not to mention Hal, the usher, all went crazy. I was cool, and, of course, I didn't ask Elvis for an autograph 'cuz I don't think it's right to mix business and pleasure, and besides I had Elvis already. But I did hang around to the end of the show after midnight, and let me tell you it was a kick to see the sleepy audience's surprise at seeing Elvis unexpectedly strut out into the lobby doing the famous Cagney hitching-his-pants-up-with-his-elbows shtick and shouting, "You dirty rat!"

Tonight's quiet and I'm halfway through filling out the tally sheet when I hear footsteps. I look up and there's this guy standing in front of my glass booth. Snappy dresser, hair slicked back, smile as toothy as Chester Morris.

"Reva?" he says.

"Yeah," I say. With no idea how he knows my name.

"I'm Sergeant Marshak." And he shows me an LAPD badge, just like the one they fill the screen with behind the credits for *Dragnet*. "I'd like to talk to you a little, okay?"

"I—I'm working," I say.

"Uh-huh. I understand. I'll step aside for the customers, all right?"

Somehow I know it's about Roy. I'm fingering the locket, better stop doing that. The cop keeps smiling at me. I'm scared.

"Nothing to be scared of," he says.

Like a mind reader. I better keep my mind blank.

Before he walked up, I'd been thinking about Tom Drake. Podolsky and me getting him today at the Ford car dealership felt like finishing off a piece of personal business. Three years ago, Tom Drake was passing through New York, just for one day, on his way to some MGM location in Maine, and he was staying at the Trianon Hotel on Park Avenue at 58th. Most of the group got him at lunch at "21" except for Podolsky and me and Freddie Tripp. So we three converge at the Trianon and Freddie makes the phone call from the pay phone in the Chock Full o' Nuts around the corner. Tom Drake himself answers and Freddie tells him we'd like his autograph and asks when's he coming out of the hotel. Tom Drake says, "It's such a cold day, why don't you guys just come upstairs now?"

So we're saying to each other, "What a nice guy, just like the guys he plays in the movies," and we walk into the lobby of the Trianon Hotel, which is one of those places we can't sneak into because the front desk is right next to the elevators. We've got the room number, so we're heading for the elevator, when the clerk at the desk calls out, "Excuse me, where're you going?"

"To Mr. Drake's room," I tell him. Loud and clear.

"Is he expecting you?" The clerk has seen us waiting outside on other occasions. This is a favorite lodging spot for MGM stars.

"Uh-huh. He told us to come up."

The clerk gestures us over to the desk and nods at the bellman to keep an eye on us while he checks the registry— "It's 1535," I tell him, helpfully—and he frowns at me, checks anyway, then dials 1535 and asks Tom Drake about us, and his tone tells you he *knows* we're lying, but then he listens and hangs up and he's not happy, but what can he do?

"Very well," he says, "you can go up."

We start for the elevator, but he calls after us.

"Except for you," he says. Pointing at tall, skinny, sweet-natured Freddie Tripp, who happens to be dressed better than Podolsky and me, because he's wearing a new blue top-coat. But he also happens to be a light-skinned Negro. I never think of him as anything but Freddie Tripp, but obviously the clerk sees only black.

"You'll have to use the freight elevator. The bell captain will show you where it is. You two others can go up on the main elevator."

We stand there frozen for a second. I mean, this isn't some movie like *Home Of The Brave* or *Pinky*, this is for real, this is racial prejudice happening right here. And to tell the truth I don't know what I'm supposed to do about it. But Freddie Tripp does.

"You guys go up," Freddie says to me and Podolsky. "I'll wait for you."

He turns and walks away from the bell captain. Into the revolving door. Out of the hotel.

"Isn't that rotten?" I whisper to Podolsky.

Podolsky nods. "Absolutely shitty. C'mon, let's get it over with."

He starts walking for the elevator bank. Ready to go up. I realize I'm not moving. He stops and looks back at me. Then he comes back close. Hisses in my ear.

"Reva, this doesn't have anything to do with us, c'mon before the clerk changes his mind. I mean, Tom Drake's here for only one day!"

"I know. So you go," I hear myself saying. "I'll wait outside with Freddie."

I walk out of the hotel. Freddie Tripp is standing on the sidewalk, stamping his feet against the cold. He glances at me.

"I didn't feel like going up," I say.

I stand near him. We don't say anything, and in a few seconds the revolving door turns. Podolsky comes out. Looking sheepish. "Screw Tom Drake," he says, "who needs him?"

We told the others in the group that Tom Drake checked out before we got there. We never told them how the clerk tried to make Freddie Tripp feel ashamed of being black, but all he accomplished was making me feel ashamed of being white like him.

Don't get me started on the subject of shame. It's a feeling every seasoned autograph collector is familiar with. Not comfortable. Just familiar. When you first start collecting, when you're a little kid, it's a badge of distinction. You show the autographs to your schoolmates and they make a fuss and ask what the stars are really like in person. But as you get older, you're aware that people think it's kinda weird, systematically chasing after actors to get them to sign their names on pieces of paper.

So you talk about it less and show the autographs to fewer and fewer people. It becomes a kind of dirty secret. Eventually you're really at ease showing your book only to other collectors, like, "Look, I got Sterling Hayden and you didn't." And that's when the element of shame begins to take hold. When you're waiting outside hotels and restaurants or covering plays, you're always looking over your shoulder in case you run into someone from work or from your neighborhood and you duck if you see them first because you don't want to have to explain what you're doing there. Shame. But you can't stop. It's like an addiction. Collecting time is the only time you really feel alive. The older you get, the greater the feeling of shame. And the dread of what lies ahead.

Back in New York there was an old biddy, skin like leather, always dressed in black, carrying a huge handbag. Her name was Mildred—Old Mildred we always called her—and they said she'd been collecting autographs since before Rudolph Valentino could tango, but she always told the stars she was asking for their signatures "for the children at the library." That was the shame talking. And I think the longer we all collected, the more scared we were that we'd wind up like Old Mildred.

So now through the glass of my movie theater's booth I'm facing a total stranger who's very interested in my adventures as an autograph collector.

"When you saw Roy Darnell getting out of his car, was he alone?" Sgt. Marshak asks.

"Uh-huh."

"What happened then?"

"We walked to the movie house together."

"Did you see him meet anyone when you got there?"

"He said hello to a lot of people."

"But was he *with* anybody?"

"Look, he's my favorite and all, but I didn't keep my eye on him all the time. I was covering the screening for other celebs, too."

"So for all you know, he might have been at *A Star Is Born* alone?"

I shrug. The less said, the better.

"There's a woman who goes to the Academy with him sometimes."

It's not a question, so I don't say anything.

"Was she there the other night?"

"Who?"

"The woman he's with sometimes. Hey, you know, Reva. Your friends told me you got her autograph recently, was it the other night?"

I shake my head no. My armpits are getting sweaty.

"And you took a picture of the two of them, was it when the Hitchcock movies were playing?"

I nod yes. "But the photos didn't come out. Whole roll got spoiled."

"What's the woman's name?"

I'm fingering the locket, gotta stop doing that. "I don't remember. She was nobody."

He sighs. Frustrated. Tough on him. "Can I see your autograph book?"

I stare at him. Does he have the right to ask that? Doesn't he need a warrant or something? But if I make a big deal of this, it'll only make it worse. Okay, let's try it this way. While I fish around in my purse, he comes around to the back of the booth. I bring out my autograph book and open the door a crack and hold it out.

But he doesn't take it.

"Nice looking album," he says. "But I'd like to see your crumb book."

How's he know about crumb books? Those big-mouth kids! If I show him that one, then he's gonna identify her for sure. In my good book every signer is a star and there's a little photo of them pasted on the page so there's no need to write their names. But in my crumb book, photos often aren't available and so I draw a line with a ruler on the bottom of the page and print each name. So I won't forget who they are. And besides, Kim Rafferty has very legible handwriting.

I take back my good book, drop it into my purse, and pretend to dig around for my crumb book, playing for time, knowing that when I hand it to the cop it's an act of betrayal. This man has come to hurt Roy and I don't want to help him in any way, but I have no choice. He's gathering information that'll enable him to close in on Roy and he wants me to be his Judas. My fingers are touching the crumb book, Sgt. Marshak is impatiently holding his hand out, almost snapping his fingers, and I'm about to give it to him when a car screeches up to the curb in front of us, and I do mean *screeches*. There's a red police light perched on the roof. Flashing. A big guy with a walrus mustache behind the wheel and he leans across and yells:

"Arzy! Get in! Quick!"

"Hold on a minute, Harry, I'll be right with you."

"*Now*, dammit, we ain't got a minute!"

"I'll see you later, Reva," Sgt. Marshak tosses to me, but he's already on the run, jumping into the car. They race off. I don't know where they're going, but I'm glad he's gone. It feels like maybe I've bought Roy some time.

30

Arzy & Harry

The G-force of Harry Tigner's takeoff jams Arzy back against the seat. Like all mobile cops, Arzy has long since mastered the art of carrying on a conversation while simultaneously listening to police radio calls. Decoding despite the static. Digesting almost subconsciously.

"Where's the blaze?" Arzy asks.

Hearing the crackling reports of a high-speed chase in progress.

"They've got him on the run," Harry says.

"Who?"

"That remains to be seen. But it sounds like the Hollywood Hills Burglar has spread his wings west to Beverly Hills."

Crackle-crackle. Subject heading west on Sunset. All available cars respond.

Harry careens up through Brentwood to Sunset Boulevard.

"Sounds like the same M.O. as our guy. Broke into a house in Holmby Hills. Tripped the silent alarm. Security company rent-a-cop got there first. Spooked the perp. Who took off—in a little black T-Bird."

Harry takes his eyes off the road an instant to register Arzy's reaction.

"You think—?"

"We should be so lucky."

Crackle-crackle. Suspect has turned north into Beverly Glen.

"Go for the Bel Air west gate," Arzy shouts.

"You got it," Harry agrees. He takes the turn north on two wheels.

"Doesn't make sense for it to be Roy. We've been figuring him as a hitchhiker, riding on the real burglar's rep."

"Diversion maybe?"

"Doesn't feel like his style."

"Hey, we catch him, we'll ask him." Harry grins wolfishly as he negotiates the curves up through the mountain streets like he's at Le Mans. "C'mon, Arzy, bad guys aren't always logical. Could be Roy's in a panic."

"I thought he was in a T-Bird."

He gets a laugh from Harry. Rare thing.

Crackle-crackle. Suspect car approaching Mulholland.

"Hey, Arz. What was so special back there at the movies? Dispatch said where you were but not why."

"That kid in the booth, I think she can give us a line on a gal Darnell was dating. Even before the murder. An actress."

"Named Kim Rafferty," Harry says. "I got all that. I was coming out to get you so we could grab a cup of coffee and compare notes. When the burglary call sounded."

"We talking about the same gal? She's—"

"She's the one who set up Roy for the transom photos. Sleazo P.I. gave me copies, they're in the back seat. Same face is on a billboard on the Strip. I just came from interviewing her at her apartment."

"And?"

"Definitely strange bedfellows. Roy started seriously dating her after the sting. How's that for an acquired taste? Took her to the *Trapeze* premiere, where they had a hassle with Addie. But she backs up Roy's alibi a hundred percent. She was sitting with him all through the movie the other night at the Academy."

"And?"

"And she's fuckin' lying." He tosses another wolfish grin. "Love'll make you do that sometimes."

They're at the crest of the mountain, and Harry takes the right turn onto Mulholland in a sliding power glide. Going east. There's hardly any traffic on the narrow road. The police radio is telling them that the suspect car is on Mulholland. Going west. Headlights appear around the curve in the road. Coming closer. Long enough to register the red gumball flashing on Harry's roof. The car makes a screeching U-turn and races away. With Harry in hot pursuit. Arzy calling it in on the radio.

"Mud on the license plates," Harry says. "But it's a black Bird."

"Half the phonies in Southern California are driving black T-Birds," Arzy says. "But that's a great paint job. Could be him."

The T-Bird has more power than the police Chevy, but the winding road cuts down his advantage. There are steep mountainous drops on both sides of Mulholland, covered by brush, with occasional boulders jutting upward. Far below, the lights of the San Fernando Valley floor stretch out into the distance. Now both cars hit a straightaway. The T-Bird speeds up, widening the gap.

But up ahead, there's a police roadblock. The T-Bird spots it and veers to go down onto a dirt road, but he's going too fast and takes the turn too wide. He misses the dirt road. The T-Bird hurtles off the asphalt, out into space, arcs downward, crashing and bouncing off rocks as it rolls over and over, coming to a stop against a boulder midway down the hillside.

Harry and Arzy brake to a halt, jump out of their car. Harry grabs a fire extinguisher and Arzy a nightstick-size flashlight as they begin to scamper, slide, and tumble down toward the destroyed T-Bird, resting on its roof. Above them, other cops arrive at the crest of the hill, stand watching, and the scream of more approaching sirens is heard.

It's treacherous negotiating this steep descent in near darkness. "Miracle that car hasn't exploded," Harry gasps as he tears his trouser leg on a rusted half-concealed car fender. Remnant of a past disaster.

"No sign of movement down there," Arzy says. They're approaching the wreck site. Arzy shines his flashlight on the upside-down sports car. The driver is still inside. Motionless. The two detectives yank at the driver's door, pull it open. The body of a man falls out onto the ground. Face down. Arzy holds the flashlight, as Harry kneels and turns the man over. They both stare at him. "Now who do we have here?" Harry asks.

31

There's a shouting match going on in my living room. I'm having an argument with someone who doesn't even exist and the worst part is he's winning.

"'Go, go, GO!' Those were your exact goddamn words," I say, "as in get the flock out of there!"

Schmuck, I didn't mean go to Barstow, Jack Havoc says. *I meant drive away a block or so, so we can watch. See what's going on between your fan and your friend the cop and—*

"—and risk getting spotted! That's dumb. Safer to get out of the entire neighborhood!"

I'm wearing a hole in the carpet with my pacing. He's sitting as cool as Cary Grant in the big easy chair, smoking and flicking ashes on the carpet to emphasize his points. I'd kill him if I could. Without a blink.

But now you don't know if little Reva spilled her guts and gave him the locket and told him she found it after the screening in the back of your car with the rest of Addie's so-called stolen stuff—

"C'mon, if she did that, they'd be here already pounding on the door—"

I stop. Because someone's knocking on the front door.

"Quick. Get out of the room," I whisper to Jack Havoc.

I won't say a word. I'll just sit quietly.

"Out!"

Can't make me. He smiles and blows a smoke ring.

I go to the front door. "Who's there?"

Muffled voice. Through the door. Female. "It's Kim."

I swing the door open and there she is. Just like I've been imagining. Beautiful. Shiny. Caring. Coming back to me. But scared. She rushes into my arms, pressing her face against my shoulder, holding me very tight. The perfume in her hair is intoxicating. It's the best moment I've had in days.

"Why didn't you answer the door?" she whispers. "I kept knocking."

"Didn't hear you."

"Who were you yelling at?"

"Nobody, I was running some lines. From *Henry V.* Might do it at City Center in New York." Going into declaiming mode. "'Gentlemen in England now abed shall think themselves accursed they were not here and hold their manhoods cheap while's any speaks who fought with us on St. Crispin's Daaaaaay!'"

She laughs. I put my arm around her shoulders.

"So you're alone?"

"Not if you're here."

"But whose car is that?" She points at the rental in my driveway, near her car.

"Loaner from the shop. My T-Bird's in for servicing." Actually it's parked inside my garage, but why open that can of worms?

"I need a drink," she says.

"You came to the right place."

We walk with our arms around each other into the living room. Where Jack Havoc is still sitting. I ignore him. Settle Kim into the couch as if she's a delicate piece of porcelain.

"When'd you get back?" I'm at the bar pouring her drink.

"Just a couple of hours ago. I got all your messages. I would've called you but—"

"Doesn't matter, you're here now." I hand her the drink. Sit down on the couch next to her. "I missed you. A lot. These last few days—"

"I'm so sorry I couldn't be here. But I thought it'd be for the best."

"Then you knew—about Addie?"

"That's why I left. If I stayed I'd have only made it worse for you. And maybe now I have."

Jack Havoc is pretending not to listen. Studying his fingernails.

"There was this detective," Kim says. "He came to my apartment. I was hardly in the door."

"Marshak? Or Tigner?"

"Sergeant Tigner. He wanted to know about us, of course."

"It's okay," I say. I don't want her to be scared. "What'd you tell him?"

"Everything. More or less. How we met. What I did to you. How you found me again. And how I told you Addie hired me. He already knew that. How we began dating. He smirked. I told him it wasn't something dirty. He smirked again. He's a vile person. He wanted to know where I was the night Addie was killed. I told him I was with you at the movies."

Jack Havoc looks up. I keep my eyes focused on Kim's.

"How'd you know I was at the movies that night?"

"The newspapers. They said you were seeing *A Star Is Born*. One of my favorites, thank God, because Sergeant. Tigner asked questions about it. 'Hello, everybody, this is Mrs. Norman Maine.'"

She manages a small smile. I've never loved anyone so much in my life.

"You believed in me that much," I say. "You lied to protect me." My eyes are misting. But Kim looks, well, not scared. Beyond awkward. Terribly embarrassed.

"Roy. I lied—to protect *me.*"

My eyes fly to Jack Havoc—he's gazing away out the window. I look back at Kim.

"I couldn't just say I was at home alone with a migraine. Which is the truth. From the way Sergeant Tigner's questions were going, I mean, Roy, he treated me like I'm the Devil Woman who'll kill her own grandma for a buck. He was hinting that while you were surrounded by a theater full of people, I was out knocking on Addie's door—"

"But they keep saying it was a burglar who got surprised in the act!"

"No, no, Sergeant Tigner says they know it was an inside job, and Addie probably let her killer in the front door, someone she knew, like me. I got terrified, Roy. I needed an alibi. So I used you. Again." She brushes her hand against her cheek, maybe there's a tear. "You won't tell on me, will you?"

"No, I won't tell," I say.

"That's why I rushed over here, to try to beat them, before they checked with you, so you would know what I told 'em. I couldn't trust the phone."

That's why she came.

"How are you going to explain why you never mentioned before that I was with you?"

"I'll just tell 'em I was being a gentleman. Wanted to keep you out of it, in any way, as long as I could."

She smiles. "That sounds good. Thank you."

"Kim—" I start. Hesitant. To his credit, Jack Havoc gets up and walks out of the room. "As far as you and I go, since the last time we saw each other, I've been doing a lot of thinking—"

"You're not the problem, Roy, I am. I wish we could make it together, because in so many ways you're a terrific guy. But we started off with a lie, and there've been too many lies since then—we'd never get out from under."

"So as far as the future goes—there's no future."

She shakes her head.

Well, if you don't ask, you don't know.

We sit on the couch. Huddling together. Holding hands. Sipping our drinks. In silence. When the drinks are gone, I walk her to her car. We kiss in the driveway. So sweet. Then she's gone. And I know it's forever.

I turn. Jack Havoc is standing in the open doorway.

I'm sorry, kid, he says. *I really am.*

Falling asleep that night is easy. All it takes is guzzling a third of a bottle of vodka and smoking half a joint. Staying asleep is harder. I give up all the tossing and fitful dozing shortly before dawn and go stand under the shower for a long time. Another day, another chance to go ambush a teenager who made the mistake of thinking I'm something special.

I'm dressed and sipping my third cup of coffee, dawdling because it's time to go stake out Reva's apartment again, when I'm saved by the bell. The doorbell. I carry my coffee cup with me.

Fric and Frac are on my doorstep. The vaudeville team of Marshak and Tigner. Just like Yogi Berra says, It's déjà vu all over again.

"Hey," I ask. "Didn't we do this early-morning scene already?"

Arzy smiles. Harry never smiles. It's not in his contract.

"Can we come in, Mr. Darnell?" Tigner says. The man who can make polite sound pugnacious.

"To search and seize?" I figure they're here to check out Kim's alibi.

"We'll settle for coffee if there's any left." Arzy the sweet talker.

They look like they need the coffee. Like they've been up all night. I lead the way into the kitchen. Pour 'em a coupla cups o' java. And wait for the jazz to begin. But they're playing an unexpected tune.

"Do you know a man named Donald Gentry?" Fric says.

That's an easy one. "Never heard of him."

"You eat at Chasen's very often?" Frac says.

"Not much. Once in a while. I'm much more a Romanoff's guy."

Where's this going? They exchange a cop look.

"We'd like you to come with us," Tigner says.

"To lunch? It's a little early." Then: "Let's get this straight. Am I under arrest or something?"

Tigner sighs. He looks like the garbage truck ran over his favorite bloodhound. It's the most passion I've seen him display.

"Why would you think that, Roy?" Arzy gives me choirboy.

Might as well get it out. See what their cards are. "You guys have been all over town asking everybody about me."

"No, you're not under arrest," Arzy assures me. "But we'd like you to come with us. As a favor. Maybe you can help us out again."

"Well, as a matter of fact, I'm kind of busy."

"Please," Tigner adds.

What the hell. He did say, "Please."

We're in their unmarked cop car. Tigner chauffeuring. I'm with Arzy in the back seat. No conversation, just looking out the windows at the passing parade. They don't want to say where we're going, and I'm content to wait and see. Been driving a while. We're on Franklin, past Vine, when Tigner takes a left onto Beachwood. He wends his way up the hill, past old bungalows, newer apartment houses. Looming above us is the HOLLYWOOD sign. We rise closer and I'm impressed by the size of the letters, each propped individually on the mountainside. Legend has it that a young actress back in the '20s or '30s was so depressed by her failure to succeed in Hollywood that she climbed to the top of the sign and jumped to her death. Give me an H.

Tigner signals left and pulls into the driveway of an old Spanish-style apartment court built up against the hill. The regular parking slots are mostly empty, the residents off at work. But there's a police car and a forensic van parked toward the rear. A uniform cop is leaning against the fender of the van, reading the morning edition of the *Examiner.* He lowers the paper, comes to inspect us. Looks in the driver's window. Recognizes Tigner, waves us on. We park and Tigner and Marshak guide me along a narrow path to the center of the court. More Spanish motif, gone ripe. Mossy. Overgrown. Adobe walls flaking. Red tiles above. An occasional one missing makes the roof look gap-toothed. Several of the neighbors clustered together, chatting quietly, like at the site of an accident. They eyeball us to the ground floor entrance of a pool-side apartment. Another uniform cop on duty at the door. Small laminated, lettered card fixed to the door below the bell: Don Gentry. We go inside.

Inside is a surprise. Not seedy as you might expect. Sharp. Still Spanish decor. But high-end stuff. Hand-tooled furniture. Precious fabrics. A large Tamayo original framed over the wood-burning fireplace. Silver candlesticks on the mantel. The two detectives whiz me along into the study. There's a good Miro painting behind the oversize desk. It's flipped back to reveal an open safe. Sparkling goodies cover the surfaces of the desk, the bookcase counter, the coffee table and the leather couches. Baubles, bangles and beads. Cops photographing and cataloguing each and every one. Looks like a fire sale at Tiffany's.

"Mr. Gentry has excellent taste," I say.

"He shopped in all the best places," Arzy says.

"What we'd like you to do," Tigner says, "is go through the things on display. Tell us if you find anything that looks familiar."

"Like it was Addie's?"

He nods. "Take your time. There may not be anything here. Or maybe there is. Either way, let us know."

They step back. Setting me loose. A kid in the toy store. Look at all the shiny stuff. Resplendent stones gleaming in a rainbow of colors: red, blue, green, turquoise, milky white, and purple. Glittering gold, silver, and platinum objects. Rings, pins, necklaces, broaches, cufflinks, money clips, Swiss watches, pearl and diamond earrings, Dunhill cigarette cases and lighters. I go slow, studying each assortment, while my mind is speeding. Doing a hundred-and-fifty on the straight-away. Donald Gentry obviously is the Hollywood Hills serial burglar. The cops have run him to ground. This is his stash.

The $64,000 Question for me is can I find enough trinkets in this treasure trove that match the descriptions I gave Marshak and Tigner earlier of Addie's missing mer-chandise. Because if I can, I'm in the clear. Even if Donald Gentry denies it, who's going to believe him? Of course, one of the other burglary victims might identify the same objects, but, hey, from this kind of confusion I can only gain. After all, the cops are going to be pushing my case, because I can tie Donald Gentry to a murder.

But I've got to be careful.

There's an opal ring pretty close to the one I bought Addie in Hawaii. I examine it, find someone else's initials inside. I put it back. Feel Marshak and Tigner's eyes on me. Move on. By being picky and cautious I eventually pluck out five items from the booty that I think will hold up. I show them to the detectives.

"These were Addie's," I say. Mentally crossing my fingers.

"Had a hunch you'd find something," Tigner says. He doesn't sound glad. He and Arzy swap another cop look. Put their heads together, low talking. Checking a sheet Tigner takes from his inside coat pocket. I wander around the room, taking care to stay away from the 24-carat goods. Arzy appears at my elbow.

"I'll drive you back to your place," he says.

"Okay, lemme hear. Who is Donald Gentry?"

"Was," Arzy corrects me. Keeping his eyes on the road. "Mr. Gentry cashed out last night. Took a header off Mulholland during a car chase. After breaking into a mansion in Holmby Hills. We traced him back here. You saw the loot. Ties him to every Hillside burglary in the last few months. Including, with your ID on Addie's jewelry, the one at your ex-house." Arzy throws a glance my way. "He drove a neat little T-Bird, looked almost like yours."

You wish. "Still doesn't tell me who he is."

"Gentry worked part-time as a parking valet at Chasen's. That's how he got a line on the people he hit. Thursday nights were his favorite. Maid's night off, everybody in Bev Hills eats out. We should have tumbled to that sooner. He'd spot his prospective victims at Chasen's, get their addresses out of the glove compartment. Then next Thursday he'd clock 'em into the restaurant and know he had a couple of hours to operate. Sometimes he even had house keys. Copied them while parking the cars at Chasen's. So he could walk right in when he wanted to. Made those burglaries look like forced entry after the fact. Like at Addie's house."

"How much of the stuff he took did you get back?"

"Half, two-thirds maybe. He fenced the rest. But we're working on that."

"So if Gentry's dead, what happens now?"

"We wrap it up. Orders from headquarters. There'll be a press conference. The big brass will show off the recovered loot for the TV cameras and declare it a win for the department. We tag Gentry for everything. Case solved, investigation closed." He shoots a glance at me. "Good news, huh?"

I nod. Giving him solemn. When I want to do is dance a jig. Shoot off fireworks. I'm in clover.

We're passing the spot on the Strip now where Kim's billboard is. "Pretty girl," Arzy says. "She ought to be in the movies."

Meaning Hollywood? Meaning the Academy Theater? I'm not going to touch that one. Unless he pushes it. He doesn't. We ride quietly together. Beyond the Strip, past the vast rolling lawns and tall sculpted hedges that conceal the dark mansions along Sunset Boulevard.

"I took a TV writing course at UCLA last year," Arzy says. "Know what they taught us were the two most important words for a writer?"

"'How much'?"

Arzy laughs. "Better. *What if.* The professor, he was an old-time screenwriter, wrote *The Prisoner of Zenda.* He said those two words have launched more stories than you can imagine. What if." We stop for the light at Rexford and Sunset. "It means taking something that really happened and turning it inside out. Then projecting that possibility."

He's dying to tell. So I give him the feed line. "Okay, Arzy. What if…"

We're rolling again as Arzy considers.

"What if there's this heavyweight guy, famous, let's say he's a—a big time politician. Being blackmailed. I mean, sucked dry. But he's got a chance to get it all back. All he has to do is bump the blackmailer. Of course, he'll be the first one everyone'll nominate. So he needs an alibi. So what if— he arranges that he's seen entering the er-r Senate Chamber, shakes a lot of hands, then slips off in between, does what has to be done, and slips back in at the end, makes a lot of noise, and hopes nobody can prove he was gone?" Arzy stops in the driveway at my house. "How's that sound to you? As a storyline?"

"Depends. How's your story end?"

"Funny, your pal Wellman asked me the same thing. Well, it's Hollywood, so it has to have a happy ending. The politician skates."

"And the cop?"

"He has the satisfaction of knowing he was just one card away from a royal flush."

Arzy drives off and I go for the front door. As I'm opening it, I hear a gunshot. Sort of. A champagne cork lands at my feet. Here's Jack Havoc behind the bar. With an overflowing bottle wrapped in a towel. Pouring vintage Piper Heidsieck into a pair of my hand-blown Venetian champagne flutes.

A toast, he shouts. *I propose a toast—to Donald Gentry!*

He hands me my wine, we clink glasses and sip. The champagne is icy cold and sparkling. Perfect.

This is the new you, he says. *The old you would've said, It's too early to be drinking. Or, I was saving that bottle of champagne for a special occasion—*

"Which this sure as hell is!" I knock back the rest of my glass. Pour myself another. Top off Jack's glass. "We're celebrating. Our horse came in, along with our ship, our number and—"

—and we won the lottery, beat the bank at Monte Carlo and drew the Get Out Of Jail Free card! We won the game, Roy!

We sprawl on the easy chairs, across from each other. Ice bucket and wine on the coffee table. Plenty more where that came from. Grinning, almost giggling. With delight. With relief. The man who's climbed the steps of the gallows has just been told his services will not be required today.

"You know," I say, "you're the only one in the world I can really talk to about this."

That's why I'm here, kid.

At that moment I love him like the brother I never had.

Then the phone rings.

I pick it up. Figuring it might be a reporter. Maybe the death of Donald Gentry, burglar and murderer, is starting to leak. It's not a reporter. It's a familiar voice. One I didn't expect to hear again.

"Roy? It's Val."

Val Dalton. My agent. My ex-agent. My ex-friend.

"Hey, Val, how are ya?" Hail fellow.

"I'm—so sad about Addie, please accept my deepest condolences. It's horrible. I would have been at the funeral, but I was in London on business. Just got back this morning. And I heard a bulletin on the news that the police caught the man who did it. How are *you?*"

"Trying to stay afloat," I say. Wishing he was still on my team. "It's very thoughtful of you to call." He did the right thing, let him hang up now. Recede into my past. Where I relegated him.

"Actually, there's something else I want to talk to you about. It's kind of awkward, but—I just got a phone call. From Jack Warner. He'd like to see you. At his office. Today."

"Probably ran out of nails for the crucifixion and wants to know where he can buy more." Give a nervous laugh. Val quiet on his end. "What's he want with me?"

"He wouldn't say. But my advice would be to go see him. What do you have to lose?"

"You coming with me?"

"That wouldn't be appropriate. We don't represent you anymore."

"But he called you." Val doesn't say anything. "Okay, I'll get Nate Scanlon and we'll go out to see the old bastard and—"

"He called me because he won't speak to Nate. Hates his guts. He wants to see you alone."

I think it over. I take so long that Val thinks he's been disconnected. "Roy, you still there?"

"Yeah. Fine. I'll go see him. Want me to call you afterward?"

"You don't have to. I'm just relaying a message."

"Thanks, Val." I hang up.

Guess you still don't have an agent, Jack Havoc says.

Jack L. Warner is dressed all in white, except for a black four-in-hand tie and a black carnation in the lapel of his ice cream suit. He looks like Cab Calloway about to sing "Minnie the Moocher." He's hunkered behind the protective barrier of his huge desk. Clutching and stroking a New York Yankees baseball bat.

"Collectors item," he says, although I didn't ask. Spouting his rapid fire, semi-coherent shorthand. "World Series trophy. Old time. Signed by Babe Ruth and Lou Gehrig, that whole crew. Valuable. Americana."

And good for close range defense. He must be remembering the last studio Christmas party when I tried to take a poke at him. They say Zanuck walks around his office swinging a polo mallet. The Colonel has a baseball bat. *C'est la guerre.*

"I'm not a total schmuck, you know," he says. Is he reading my mind?

"Talk about TV, they forget, who introduced sound? Snickering at me, all over town, fuckers at *Variety,* printed my internal memo, 'Please note that NO television sets can be used as props or allowed to be seen on screen in any Warner Brothers motion picture.' Radios, record players, harmonicas and ukuleles, okay, but no TV, not in the living room, not in the bedroom, not in the den, not in the crapper, not nowhere. TV sets are *verboten* and if anybody disobeys, I make it clear I'll can their ass—"

It's a motor mouth monologue. Can't get a word in. And I don't know what the point of any of it is.

"—and why do I do this? Ask yourself? Like to make myself into a laughingstock?" The Colonel thumps the Yankees bat down on the desk. "No, it's because I'm in a fuckin' war! Damn tube, stealing my customers, sitting home on their asses, guzzling beer and watching Lucy, nice girl, never made a dime for us in the movies, and do I think I can win this war? I DO NOT! Holding action. Delaying tactic. I know that. Fight 'em 'til you can co-opt 'em. On my terms. And sure enough, one day, here's Leonard Goldenson, ABC-TV, he says, 'Colonel, how would your studio like to make shows for us?' And I tell him, 'Well, not really, but if the price is right and you can guarantee me enough of 'em, then maybe we can talk.' Convince him, if I do this, doing him a favor. Giving him that slick Warner Bros. kind of movie-making for his crummy little tube—"

The Colonel rises and comes around the desk. Giving the bat a few test swats. If he comes near me, I'm going to bash him with the big metal ashtray next to me. But he moves to the window overlooking the studio street.

"Actually, ABC, saving my life. Enormous factory here in Burbank. Standstill. Nobody using it. Fuckin' directors, wanna shoot movies only on location, location, LOCATION!" Sounding like a real estate broker. "England, France, Italy, Timbuktu. Anywhere but Stage 28. Empty sound stages. I'm losing money. Hand over fist. But—"

He positions himself in front of the window. Like Casey at the plate. Wiggles his ass. Waits for the invisible pitch—and knocks it out of the park. Doffs a make believe cap to the crowd. Triumphant.

"But now I got TV to pay the bills! Made the first deal, made the best deal. Give 'em *Maverick, Sugarfoot, 77 Sunset Strip, Cheyenne, Hawaiian Eye, Jack Havoc.* Now it's okay by me to see a TV set in one of our movies, 'cuz it'll be showing a Warner Brothers TV show."

He pauses. Gleams his full denture smile at me. Waiting for a round of applause. Maybe he's totally lost it.

"Well, Colonel, that was—damn shrewd of you."

"Bet your ass. I'm a survivor, Roy. Are you?"

Now he asks? Sonuvabitch blackballed me. Left me sliced and diced in the gutter.

"Are you a survivor?" the Colonel repeats.

"Remains to be seen," I say.

"That's what they say at funerals." He guffaws like he got off a Milton Berle one-liner. Leans the bat against the wall. "C'mon, kid, gotta go to lunch. That's not an offer. Walk me to the commissary. Eating with Gromyko, the Russki asshole from the U.N. Like to give him a boot in his gazongas, but I'm gonna buy him a sirloin steak and take him on a tour of the lot. Gotta peddle our movies and TV shows in Russia, too, even if they are fuckin' Commies."

We're strolling along the campus-style path between the executive buildings. Down the street between bustling sound stages. A surreal scene that everyone on the lot takes for granted. Cowboys, Indians, dance hall girls, tethered horses, horseshit, an obese teamster snoring in the back of a buckboard, a black-suited agent pitching a young actor-wrangler who's practicing his lassoing on him. As we pass, each and every one of them take notice of Jack L. Warner— and me. He ignores them all. The plantation owner doesn't have to fraternize with the slaves.

"Buried a couple of my brothers," he says out of nowhere. "Decided then, only other funeral I'm going to is my own. Period. Might not even go to that one." Bigger guffaw. "Too damn depressing. Makes you think about what you don't want to think about. But take my wife, hey, I sound like Henny Youngman, 'Take my wife, please.' Anyway, my wife, she goes to funerals, better manners than me. She was at Addie's funeral, and she came back and told me about you giving this eulogy, that what you call it? Better than Georgie Jessel, she said. That's all she could talk about. You made her cry, so now she won't stop noodging me, so that's why I hadda see you."

"I don't really underst—" I manage to squeeze in before the Colonel is off again.

"I grew up in New York. Lemme tell you, I was the tough-est, meanest *momser* in the borough of Manhattan. Play by my own rules. Fair fight is any fight I win. Except I never kicked a man when he was down. Oh, maybe if he was a wiseass and asking for it, but you know what I mean."

"Not yet," I say.

"We had a beef, you and me, we squared off, took our best shots, hey, I won. Kicked you halfway to Canarsie. You're dead meat on the West Coast. Can we agree on that?"

I could hit him. But I'm curious where this is going. "Okay, we can agree on that."

"So, just to get my wife off my back, so she won't keep noodging, I'm declaring a whaddayacallit, an armistice. You lost your wife, you're handling it like a man, I respect that. So. Helping hand. Christian thing to do. Even though I'm Jewish. Maybe we'll fight again some other time. But this time, it's over. You wanna make movies, go make movies."

"Nobody will hire me."

"Go ask 'em again. Maybe they changed their minds." We're in front of the commissary. Near the private entrance to the Blue Room. "Give you something else to think about, kiddo. You can walk away clean. Today. But the sets are still standing on Stage 11. You give me two more years as Jack Havoc and right now I'll double your salary, quadruple it next year. Cash bonuses up front when we go to syndication, for all episodes produced. During hiatus you can make a movie wherever you want, for Zanuck, for Goldwyn, watch out for that cocksucker Harry Cohn, and listen, no loanout fee, you keep all the money. Maybe I'll even have a movie you want to do. Match best offer you get." His grin outshines Doug Sr. "Only proviso is, either way, don't go around town telling people I did something nice. I got a reputation to protect."

He struts off to break bread with Andrei Gromyko. But he calls back to me. "Hey, forgot to say. Cops killed that asshole burglar! Mazel Tov!"

Blessed is the Colonel, Jack Havoc says. *He taketh away and now he hath given back.*

We're on Stage 11. The main *Jack Havoc* sound stage. Stage 12 next door is for the "swing" sets, the temporary sets built for a particular episode, then dismantled and carted away. But Stage 11 contains the permanent standing sets for the show. Permanent, of course, being a relative term. If your TV ratings dipped, the sets and the show and you could be gone overnight.

When we enter, the only light on Stage 11 is from a security stanchion on the floor near the entrance. I go to the electric panel, as familiar to me as the fuse box in my own house, and throw the lever, turning on the house lights. Still gloomy. No one here except Jack Havoc and me. But everything looks the same. My mobile dressing room. With my name still on the door in the center of the big gold star. I have a momentary scary thought.

"Hey, how's everybody in town going to know I'm not blackballed anymore? The Colonel's gotta make some phone calls to—"

He fixed all that just by walking down the studio street with you. In public. Word will be all over town. You are officially back among the living.

Jack Havoc strides forward with that pouter-pigeon shoulders-back-follow-your-chest walk I developed for him. Surveying his territory. The standing sets for the show are Jack Havoc's New York penthouse apartment, the lobby of his East Side building, and the elegant interior of his favorite saloon. It's only been a couple of weeks since I was here, but the sets seem smaller. Like going back to high school and the desks have shrunk.

Jack Havoc feels completely at home.

He reclines comfortably on the Italian suede sofa in the living room of the penthouse apartment. Legs crossed, arms outstretched on the top of the sofa like he's embracing the entire room. Then he strolls onto the balcony. Looks off as if the backdrop is real and he's actually gazing at the lights of the city. He wanders over to the café society saloon set. Perches on his favorite barstool, the one on the far end, back to the wall. Where he can see everything and everybody.

God, I missed this place, he says.

"Yeah. Lots of memories. Most of 'em bad."

But not all. Good times, too.

"Remind me."

C'mon, you enjoyed being the main man.

"That was an illusion. I was a hired hand."

Not anymore. You heard the Colonel. Comin' back a winner. What you want you got.

"If I come back."

If? What're you talking about? Why wouldn't you?

"I don't know. Feels like going backwards. Was that what this was all about? Just a negotiating ploy to get a raise?"

You're not thinking straight, Roy. The Colonel needs you and now he knows it. He's offering you the bird in the hand plus the two in the bush. Get filthy rich out of TV and be a movie star, too.

"Well, feels like once I'm out—stay out. Move on. Keep my options open. If John Huston asks me to go to Africa with him, I don't want to have to say, 'You gotta wait, Johnny, I can't go until my hiatus.' I want to be able to say 'Yes.'"

But what about me?

That's a puzzler. "What about—who?"

Me. Jack Havoc. Being back here on the lot, I just realized. If you walk away from Warners, I don't exist. No more Jack Havoc. I'm over. I'm dead.

"Now who's talking crazy? You'll be with me wherever I go."

But I won't be me. I'm just asking you, Roy—think it over before you decide. Sure, the Colonel pissed you off. But now he'll give you free rein. Want to get rid of Viola, and Killer Lomax too? Just wave a pinkie and they're gone.

"Yeah, I guess. But—"

Okay, okay, just think about it, huh? We got a lot to think about.

"Meaning what?"

Now it's his turn to look puzzled. *C'mon, pal, you know what's left on the agenda.*

"Been a busy day. Suppose you tell me."

Little Reva.

"Don't start that again. Everything's copacetic now. The cops are happy, the Colonel's happy. So why do we have to—"

That's why. Because we have to.

"Marshak said it's over."

He said he was one card away from a royal flush. Reva's that card. As long as she can sing her little song about your comings and goings at the movies during the time Addie was cashing out—

"She wouldn't. I mean, who'd even believe her anymore when—"

With that fuckin' locket to verify the story? Marshak would eat it up.

"They're having a press conference. That officially closes the book!"

There's no statute of limitations on murder.

I hear him. I don't like it. But I hear him.

She's got to go, he says.

"She's got to go," I say.

32

Reva

They ought to give me a medal for sitting in this hot ticket booth all day long since the noon show. Of course, I've got an electric fan on the floor. Basically it just stirs the hot air around, but I've rigged up my own version of an air conditioner. I filled two empty jumbo popcorn boxes from the concession stand with ice and put them on the floor with the fan blowing across them. Every little bit helps.

I'm wearing my best outfit today because I went to apply for a job as a mailroom messenger at Twentieth Century Fox. That's usually a guy's job, so I didn't want to wear a skirt, and my usual dungarees seemed too informal, so that left the wool slacks that fit me like a dream, but they're still wool.

Hey, I think maybe I got the job. Fingers crossed. Wouldn't that be cool? Being on a movie lot every day and getting paid for it.

Our theater started playing a new double feature today. *Picnic* and *The Proud and Profane*. The posters both look the same. Bill Holden with his shirt off standing over Kim Novak in one and Deborah Kerr in the other like he's about to jump their bones. Business was good for the early shows. Everybody likes Bill Holden. Particularly with his shirt off.

I'm supposed to finish my shift at five, but Connie, my relief, calls in with an emergency. She has to take her mom to the hospital for a gallstone. She finally shows up at eight, but I can use the overtime, and I run into a piece of luck.

Norm, one of the off-duty ushers, drops by to pick up his check, and he offers me a ride home. We walk to his VW bug, and I have the sense that someone's watching, you know, hair on the back of your neck rising, but I've felt like that a lot since that detective came here asking questions I didn't want to answer.

"Know what makes a movie star?" Norm asks. He's not a collector, but he likes analyzing movies. "They never blink. When it's an important moment, you never see them blink."

"Unless it's like Scarlett O'Hara, batting her eye lashes, flirting."

"I'm talking about highly dramatic moments. No blinks. Check it out."

I'd never noticed that before, but as I think back on the high points of my favorite movies, it makes sense to me. Blinking indicates hesitancy or even shiftiness. Not blinking means sincerity or determination. Garbo never blinks. Gable winks, but when the chips are down, he never blinks.

Norm's car radio is on, tuned to KLAC, and now there's a newsbreak. They announce that police have confirmed that the Hollywood Hills burglar, who killed TV star Roy Darnell's wife, has been caught and killed in a high speed chase. I'm stunned. "Didn't you hear that before?" Norm asks. "Been on the radio all day." I'm flooded with relief. I knew Roy didn't do it.

Norm pulls up in front of my apartment house and I get out. As I walk toward the stairs, I enjoy the moment. It's dusk, the time just after the sun's gone down, but before it's totally dark. The palm trees look charcoal black, silhouetted against the last light of the day. I can smell raked-up leaves burning in the backyard incinerators, mingling with some of the cooking smells from the kitchens of the apartment house.

Not ours, though.

Mother always comes home too pooped from the bank to cook, so she nurses a drink or two until I pull some Swanson's dinners out of the freezer. On the evenings when I'm out, she just boozes until she passes out.

I unlock the door and step inside gingerly. Like Fred and Gingerly. When I was a kid, Mother might be hiding behind the door to pounce and pound me for some sin like not making my bed. Tonight the lights are on in the living room, and I saw the car at the curb downstairs, so I know she's come home.

"Mom," I call. But she's not here.

My shoes hurt—my new penny loafers with the stack heels that Mother bought for me—and they make me feel like Li'l Abner. I wore them for the interview at Twentieth because the rest of my shoes are sneakers. Before I can kick them off, I hear shuffling on the landing and Mother enters. Carrying her drink in one hand and the empty garbage can from under the sink in the other hand. She bangs into the doorjamb coming through it. Girlish giggle. Really blasted tonight.

"Why hello. And how's the little princess?"

"Hadda work late."

"Y'coulda phoned. In case I was worried."

I snort. "About what?"

"If maybe the pirates or gypsies or perverts have snatched you off the streets. The places you go and the company you keep."

She's worse than usual. Better get some food in her. "Want the chicken dinner or the Salisbury steak?" I'm at the freezer.

"Surprise me," she says. Shoving the garbage can back under the sink. And giggling again.

"What's so funny?"

"Nothing. Nothing at all. Just how some things seem so damn hard, totally out of control, impossible, but—they don't have to be."

"For instance." Sliding the TV dinners in the oven.

"How I've been begging you, and praying, that you'll finally get over this insane obsession with the autographs. It's just not normal, Reva! There's no room for anything else in your life. Anyway—" pouring herself more booze "—my prayers have been answered." Yet another giggle.

"Hallelujah! And what's the answer?"

"Don't mock. Disrespect." Waving her glass, spilling some booze. "God'll punish you. Not your fault. Head filled with nutsy nonsense. You'll thank me, Reva. Know what the gardeners say, when they're cutting back the rose bushes to a stump? 'Y'gotta be cruel to be kind.' That's what they say. So I decided to treat you with total kindness. You'll see, you'll thank me later, you will."

I feel icy. Standing absolutely still. "What have you done, Mother?"

"Asked you a million times, give it up, a grown-up girl like you, chasing cars like a deranged hooker, making a grotesque display of yourself, consorting with the scum of the earth, in order to spend a few precious seconds with the great stars who don't give a flying fuck about anyone but themselves, and now to make it worse, you're in trouble with the police, not once, but twice in the same week, so what choice did I have?"

"Mother," I repeat, "what have you done?"

"Don't be upset, honey." She's pleading, really scaring me. "This way there's an end to it, it's the only way, now you'll have time to go to dances, meet somebody, have a family, a life—"

I run to my bedroom door and see that the padlock has been clipped off. It's on the floor. She's invaded my space. I push open the door and instantly spot what's wrong. I turn back to her and our gazes interlock.

"Where are my autograph books, Mother?" The entire shelf is empty.

She giggles again. I rush over and grab her arms and shake her and yell in her face, *"Where are they?"* and I can read the fear in her eyes, as she mumbles, "For your own good…"

"The garbage," I guess. "You threw them in the garbage!" She ducks her head, so I've got my answer.

I race out the front door. Her voice following me. "You'll thank me someday." They don't pick up the garbage until tomorrow morning, so there's time, and I take the stairs down two-at-a-time and skitter on the pathway in these stiff new shoes and almost fall on my face, and speed around the corner of the apartment house to the garbage dumpster, and then I see the smoke trailing up into the night sky from the backyard incinerator. Two evenings a week the city allows us to burn. And I know what my mother has done.

I yank open the incinerator door and my reflex urge is to shove my hand inside and save whatever's left, but there's nothing left. Just a pile of ashes, some glowing embers, a few pulsing flames still nibbling on the smoldering covers of my star books, the pages all devoured by the fire, except for a page or two curled into blackened ash. I poke them with a stick and they crumble. I drop the stick and sink to my knees and cover my face with my hands and begin to cry, the kind of tears that rip at your insides and scorch your cheeks. "Mama," I hear myself saying, "you shouldn't have, Mama, why couldn't you leave me alone..."

Then I'm choked with tears and can't speak. I rock back and forth, weeping as if I'll never be able to stop, and I'm not even aware that there's anyone else here until I hear a voice. The voice I know better than any other.

"Reva...what's wrong? Can I help you?"

And I look up at him. Standing there. Alone. As if he's in my dream.

"Hi, Roy," I say. Smiling foolish and bleary through my tears. "What are you doing here?"

"I came to see you," he says. "About something special." And he gives me that smile I love so much on TV, that devil-may-care Jack Havoc smile.

33

Jack Havoc

I'm in the driver's seat now. Not a fuckin' moment too soon. Hey, this is no power grab. Roy wants to step aside. Really does. Wants me to handle this. Finally agreed on that on the ride over. Not a question of guts. I give Roy a lot of shit, but I know he's basically one tough hombre. He just can't do certain things. And I can. No problemo.

See, if Jack Warner had asked me that question, I'd've given him the answer in a mini-second. "Fuckin' right I'm a survivor."

All I've got left now are two hurdles. Getting rid of Reva is the easy one. Talking Roy back into the TV series is gonna be a tad tougher. He's a dreamer, my boy Roy. I want him to realize his dream. Be a big movie star like Bogie. But how's it gonna hurt him to keep me alive for another season or two? He's still on the fence on that score, but after tonight he's gonna owe me big time.

So here we are at last.

In Reva's backyard.

Staked her out at the theater. Tailed her back here. Waited for my moment. Couldn't have hoped for a better shot. Gotta stop her bawling. Make nice. Roy's not the only actor in this family. She tells me what happened. Fuckin' mother burned up her autograph collection. Hey, my heart's not made of stone. I feel for the kid. Watching your dreams go up in smoke.

I soothe her, calm her, tell her I came by to discuss something important, something she may like a lot. Can we go get a cup of coffee? It's that easy. Out of the backyard and into the car. The gods are with me: no one sees us. Now we're really rolling.

She's still whimpering in the front seat. "My memories."

"Hey, Reeve, gotta think of the future," I say. In that warm fuzzy way Roy would. Roy's whispering guidance in my ear when I need it. He's in the back seat, but still on the team.

"What future?" she asks.

"Yours. Since Killer Lomax took off on me, I need some help. Scheduling appointments, keeping track of money, screening calls, handling requests and sorting mail, generally making sure I'm where I'm supposed to be when I'm supposed to—"

"Are you asking me to be your secretary?"

"More like an overall kind of executive assistant, you know, taking charge of my life."

She stares at me. Like Cinderella must've at the Prince when he turned up with the glass slipper.

"I—I never did anything like that," she finally says, "I wouldn't want to mess you up."

"You wouldn't mess me up. You're smart, you're loyal—that's number one, I can trust you, everything else I can show you and you'll pick up real fast."

"Well, if you think so."

"You'd really be doing me a favor."

Kid's got a knockout smile. Radiant. "When would you want me to start?"

"How about now? I've gotta swing past the studio for a second, pick up some things. If you've got the time to go with me."

She says she does.

Then she reaches in her pocket. "Got something of yours." She brings out the jackpot. The locket. "I'm sorry I took it. I wanted to give it back to you. I came by your house, but you weren't there."

I take the locket. "You're probably wondering how I got this—and the other stuff," I say.

She shrugs, like *who cares?* But I know she does.

"I went to Addie's house and found her dead. Who knows who did it? She ran around with a lot of freaks. But I knew I'd be blamed, so I made it look like a robbery."

"I knew it was something like that!" She's so relieved.

See how easy it can be, I beam silently to Roy.

Just don't scare her, he whispers in my ear.

She's chewing my ear off. Won't stop talking. All through the Sepulveda Pass into the Valley. Yak-yak-yak. About her monster mother. No wonder this kid's so fucked up. Be doing her a favor, put her out of her misery. If she doesn't stop telling these mama stories, I'll pull over and do it right here.

Bad attitude, Roy murmurs. *You can't be that way.*

Why not? How should I be?

Like you are on TV. Jack Havoc who cares for the little people.

But what do I say to her?

Just change the subject. Ask her about something else.

"Hey, Reeve, what's up with your father? Where's he?"

Good tip from the Royster. Kid lights up.

"My dad, you'd've liked him. Everybody did. Never yelled, never hit me, just went to work, came home, read the paper, listened to *The Cisco Kid* on the radio. He never said it, but I knew he loved me."

"He, err, passed away?"

"Yeah. Right before we came to California. He was an electrician, worked in the Brooklyn Navy Yard during the war, first real steady money he ever made. We were doing pretty good. Then he fell off a ladder and scrambled his brains."

"Was that the medical diagnosis?"

"That's what my mother called it. He didn't die for a long time. They put him in a Navy hospital on Staten Island. A sanitarium, really. He could remember stuff that happened when I was a baby, but he couldn't always remember what happened an hour ago."

"Like shell shock."

"I guess. I'd go visit him. Took the subway to the Battery for a nickel and then the Staten Island ferry for another nickel. Sail past the Statue of Liberty, over to the hospital."

"You and your mom."

"Well, she only went with me once. She said she was stopping off on the way home after work a few times a week, but I think she was lying. Anyway, on Saturday mornings, I'd go there by myself. On the way over I'd be so excited, coming back I'd always cry." She looks out the window. We're on Ventura Boulevard now, heading for Burbank.

"Sounds grim. Didn't you ever, like, horse around, share a laugh?"

"Not much. Well, there was this one time. We were walking on the hospital grounds with all the other nutcases and their visitors, and I'm telling him all about how I got Red Skelton, who always writes "I dood it" above his autograph, and I thought Dad would be interested, 'cause that was a kind of private joke between us when I was younger, but it doesn't seem to register on him now. All he suddenly says is, 'Doctor.' Which startles me because it's like the first word he's said all morning. And I see this tall guy in a white lab coat with a stethoscope dangling steaming toward us on the path. 'My—doctor,' Daddy says.

"The guy stops in front of us and smiles. 'I'm Dr. Borovac,' he says and I know he's waiting for Dad to make the introductions, but I know how hard that can be for him. So I jump in. What's goin' through my mind in that instant is that the ladylike thing is to say, 'How do you do?' But for some reason, I feel this real urge to say 'Howdy.' Kinda casual and western, you know? Anyway. When I open my mouth what comes out is 'Howdydoodleedo.' The doctor gapes at me. Then, like he understands, he smiles even bigger and says, 'So *this* is your daughter.'"

I explode. Cackling, clutching the wheel. She's laughing along with me. "I could've gone right through the ground straight down to China if there'd been a hole deep enough."

"I bet." Wiping away my laugh tears. "So that's it, huh?"

"Well, there was a little more. The doctor walked off. I kept strolling with Dad. Neither of us talking, because I was ashamed. I was sure my father wanted to make a good impression and I blew it. But then while we were strolling, Dad took my hand. Very unusual. He never was much on touching. And then he put something in my hand. It was this ring he always wore on his pinkie. It was gold and had his initials on it in zircons, 'R.H.,' same as mine, his name was Renko, and he puts the ring on my finger." She wags her index finger. No ring. "It was the only gift he ever gave me. 'Thanks, Dad,' I said, 'I'll wear it always.'"

Reva stops. Looks away out the window. We're on the Barham Pass. "So where's the ring now?"

"Oh, I lost it. Back in New York." She looks sort of funny. *Say something to her,* Roy whispers. *She's hurting.*

"Easy come, easy go," I say. Just like I do on TV every week.

Kinda soft, she repeats. "Yeah, easy come, easy go."

We reach the crest of the Barham Pass and there's the Warner Bros. lot down below. Lockheed's aircraft factory is farther out in Burbank. But in the dark, the two places look alike. Hangar-size sound stages. A water tower as tall as an air traffic controller's flight deck. We're approaching the main car entrance. Opposite a billboard that proclaims, *Warner Bros. Studio—Combining Good Citizenship With Good Picture-Making.*

"Reeve, you need a pass to get on the lot and I didn't think to call—"

"I can wait outside for you."

"No, no, I want you to come in. See the *Jack Havoc* stage. Maybe if you duck down on the floor 'til we get past the gate man."

She does it. Without question. Good kid. I toss a car blanket from the back seat over her and I greet the studio cop on the gate.

"Hey, Teddy, they swipe any sound stages tonight?"

"Not on my watch, Mr. Darnell." He raises the metal bar and waves me through.

As soon as we turn the corner, I give Reva the all-clear and up she pops. Eagerly looks around. We stop in front of Stage 11 and although the entire street is empty, I park in the space marked ROY DARNELL ONLY. Usually when they give you the boot off the lot, they paint over your name even before you're out the front gate. It's a Hollywood tradition.

So why'd the Colonel keep my name here? Roy mutters.

Maybe he had 'em put it back today—after he made you the new offer.

Jumpin' the gun, isn't he? Devious old fucker.

Keep an open mind, Roy. "We'll discuss this later."

"Who are you talking to?" Reva asks.

"Just thinking out loud. Reminding myself. Something I've gotta do."

I open the heavy soundproof door and guide her inside the stage. Only the security light on, but I go to the master switch and announce in a deep Roy Darnell voice, "Let there be light." I throw the switch and the gloom lifts enough so Reva can see the permanent sets. It takes her breath away. She's really in Jack Havoc Land.

"Is it okay to walk there?" Inside the sets.

"You're with me. You can go anywhere you want."

She starts forward. Slowly.

Isn't that cute, Roy? Like she's in Buckingham Palace.

This isn't going to work. It's a bad plan.

Whaddaya mean? It's a great plan. Your number one fan sneaks onto the lot. Who knows how? She goes to the Jack Havoc sound stage. Tragedy strikes. In the dark, something falls on her. Or she trips on one of the cables, bangs her head, all this equipment around. You happen to stop by, discover the body. You call the studio cop. Perfect!

Reva's in the penthouse living room. Examining the bar glasses. Touching her fingertips to the gold embossed initials, "J.H." That's me.

They'll think I did it, Roy says.

Always the fuckin' scaredy-cat. Who? Who'd suspect you?

Marshak and Tigner.

The Keystone Kops! They signed off. I'm telling you, you'll be in the clear. All loose ends neatly tied up, plus a bonus of a million dollars worth of free publicity for the show.

Who cares about that? C'mon, Roy cajoles, *let her live.*

His begging is really steaming me. It's over, kid, end of the line!

Okay, okay, look, Jack. I'll give her this cockamamie job you invented to lure her here tonight. You said she's loyal, we can keep an eye on her, hey, without the locket she's got no proof, it'd be my word against hers that I ever left the theater, and she'd never do anything to hurt me or—

You're not coming back to the TV show, are you?

What's that got to do with—

I knew it. You selfish scumbag! Everybody does for you and you never do for anybody but Roy. So worried about her, how about me? I'm your best friend, Roy. Let me live! Without this show on the air, I vanish. Poof! Three months from now I'm forgotten. Dead. Kaput. Less than dust. Not gonna happen. You're gonna do this for me.

Okay, okay, let's cut a deal. I'll do the series, but you let her go.

That's cute. Think you're dealing with a putz? I know what goes on inside your head, Roy. You're just bullshitting me. I'll cut her loose, and you'll still walk away from Jack Havoc.

I wouldn't. I swear I wouldn't.

Too late, baby. We're going all the way.

I won't let you!

Try and stop me. I'm stronger than you are, Roy.

"Can I ask you a question?" Reva's voice. Where the hell is she? Okay, there: standing in the saloon set, behind the bar. "When they shoot you here talking to someone, you know, that funny angle—where do they put the camera?"

"Good question. Let me come over there and show you." Roy steps in my way. To block me.

I walk right over him as if he's not even there.

34

Reva

Tell you the truth, I'm not that knocked out being on the *Jack Havoc* set.

I've snuck onto movie sets before, so the novelty is gone. I know there are fronts that don't have backs and generally things don't look as good as they do on film and that's all they care about. But I'm making a fuss examining the sets because Roy keeps watching me from the sidelines like I'm a kid on my first visit to Disneyland.

That's not how I want him to see me. I want him to realize I'm not a kid and I'm hip to the business and he's not making a mistake offering me this great new job. That's why I'm asking him this technical question.

And here he comes, walking out of the shadows beyond the set. As he steps into the saloon there's a minor transformation. Roy's posture changes and he becomes Jack Havoc. The lion returning to his native habitat. Master of all he surveys. Actors are incredible.

"Now," he smiles across the bar at me, "you're asking about what we call The Hiring Scene. Somebody, usually a pretty girl, slinks into the saloon to ask for Jack Havoc's help. We try to make it look a little more interesting by shooting from down here—" he pats the bar top "—straight up at me and the chick."

"But I've seen the camera. It's won't fit in that small a space."

He looks over his shoulder as if to see if anyone's listening. Then leans forward. "Gonna betray a trade secret, Reva, but you can't tell anyone."

He waits until I nod. "Won't tell a soul."

"Good. Know how I'm usually drinking a dry martini? With an extra olive in the martini? Well, the camera—it's inside the second olive."

I stare at him.

"That's why you'll never see me pound the bar for service. Because that'd make waves in the martini glass and the camera would bob around and spoil my close-up. Do you believe that?"

"No," I blurt.

"Good girl! Neither do I," he says, and he laughs. So I laugh, too. Glad I passed the test. Though I feel a bit jerky. I didn't know Roy likes to tease.

"The way we make that shot is to pull out a chunk of the bar. This place is built to come apart at the seams at a moment's notice."

"Sounds like my mother."

He chuckles. I made him chuckle. He raises the flap door next to me at the end of the bar. "Ready to come out of there?"

"Said the Spider to the Fly?" Try for another chuckle. Get a smile.

"Now that's a story we never did for *Let's Pretend.* Too gory, I guess."

I step out from behind the bar. He lowers the flap door behind me. But doesn't move aside, so I'm boxed in and can't go any further.

"What was your favorite fairy tale on the show?" he asks.

"*Hansel and Gretel.* I always wished I had a brother around my own age to play with."

"Want to know my favorite? *Little Red Riding Hood.* Had everything. Sex, violence, humor, suspense, spunky little heroine, great villain." He lets loose a Big Bad Wolf basso growl. Then in a tiny girl voice, "What big teeth you have, Grandma."

"The Man of a Thousand Voices," I say.

"That's me. Nine-hundred ninety-eight to go."

I wish he'd step aside. I feel jammed. Something's been bothering me. One of those memory ticklers. An itch you can't scratch. Suddenly he moves back. Making room for me. He gives a courtly half-bow. I go with it and sweep past him with a regal wave as if we're acting in one of the fairy tale shows.

"Your Highness," he says, "may I take you on a personal tour of my realm?"

He offers his arm. I take it, and he chatters away as we amble back into the penthouse set.

"Nobody ever asks how Jack Havoc can afford to live in a snazzy place like this. Particularly since I never seem to collect a fee from any of the people I help. The rumor is—I sell drugs on the side." He gives me that roguish Jack Havoc wink.

"Hey, don't make fun of Jack Havoc," I say.

"Why not? What's so special about him?"

"C'mon. You know. You created him."

"I want to know what you see. Tell me."

I hesitate. Is this another test? Take a deep breath. Take a chance. "Look, I know Jack's a made-up person, but—we all wish he were real. That there was someone around in our lives who's strong who'd watch out for us."

His smile fades. "Don't be so sure about old Jack. That's what he does for one hour on Friday nights. You don't know what he does the rest of the week."

"I'm sure. I've seen every show. Bet I know him as well as you do."

"Bet you don't." For a split second he gets this weird look. Then he gestures at the floor-to-ceiling bookcases with a set of the Great Books series that turns out to be the hand-tooled covers only. Elegant pieces of pottery and blown glass art objects perch on the other shelves. "My set decorator and I have exquisite taste," he boasts.

I reach for a glass figurine of a woman with her arms upraised. "And the winner of the award for Best Actor In The World is—Roy Darnell."

He takes the "award" and grips it by the glass woman's torso. "I want to thank the members of the Academy and also my landlord, my tailor, my orthodontist, my lawyer, my ex-wife, my ex-agent, and most of all—my fans, who made it all possible."

Roy grins in mock triumph and lifts the heavy glass figure aloft. Responding to the cue, I applaud him vigorously. He acknowledges the applause by swinging the heavy glass figure downward, right past my head, across his waist in an elaborate bow. Then he puts it back onto the shelf.

"That's the first award anyone ever gave me," he says.

He guides me to the fireplace. There's a vivid abstract oil painting hanging above it. "Move back a couple of steps and focus on the brightest colors in the painting," he suggests. I do it. "Now scrunch your eyes shut, I'll tell you when to open 'em, and you'll really see something. Don't open 'em yet."

So I'm standing there with my eyes closed, smiling in anticipation at the wonder Roy's about to show me. Colors pinwheeling inside my head. That's when the memory tickler kicks in. Sparked maybe by talking in the car about Daddy's ring, just before Roy asked me to hide on the floor to get past the gate man. What I remember is the night in the stage door alley at *Streetcar,* when Tamar the mugger led me off, like a lamb to the slaughter, "Want to go backstage? C'mon with me, I'll take you."

My eyes pop open. I'm startled to see Roy is so close to me that he's a bit out of focus. Like the extreme close-ups of Monty and Liz at the big party in *A Place In The Sun.* He's staring at my forehead. A gentle smile.

"You've got a wisp of hair that's loose—"

He reaches for the wisp and smooths it down on my temple, then pats my cheek.

"You're a pretty girl."

"No, I'm not." I feel embarrassed.

"Sure you are. Look—"

He puts his hands on my shoulders and slowly turns me so I'm facing a mirror on the other wall. I look in the mirror. What I see is a portrait of Roy and me. He's standing right behind me. We look great together. His hands still on my shoulders. And I—well, he's right, I look pretty. Never looked this pretty before. I smile at myself in the mirror and behind me Roy gets a faraway look in his eyes.

"Easy come, easy go," he murmurs.

His right hand comes down off my shoulder and for a second I think he's going to cop a feel and I close my eyes again. But instead his palm covers my mouth and nose and clamps my head against his chest, as snug as a vise, and my eyes open again, in fact they're bugging, as I stare at my reflection in the mirror. I can't breathe, I can't yell, but I can see Roy's face, so close to mine, still with that dreamy look, as he whispers in my ear. "Relax, Reva, just relax, make it easy for both of us."

I struggle, but he holds me easily. I'm gasping for air and getting none. If I don't do something real soon I'm going to pass out, so I lift my foot and kick backward with all the force I can muster. The stack heel of my new puddle-stomper shoe connects with his shinbone and I scrape down with the sharp edge of my heel. He shrieks and lets loose of me. I whirl and see him clutching his leg, hopping around in pain on one foot like Fred MacMurray in a screwball comedy. I do what Carole Lombard would do. I shove my hands against his chest. He goes over backwards onto the sandalwood coffee table with the inlaid mosaic top. Table legs buckle, tiles shatter, the table collapses. I'm clutching my throat and sucking in all the oxygen I can swallow. He's spread-eagled on top of the wreckage and hooting with laughter.

Yeah, laughter.

"Broke the fuckin' table. Prop man's gonna go crazy looking for a duplicate. They'll probably take it out of my salary. No, I'll blame it all on you, Reva. Rabid fan runs amok."

"Why are you doing this, Roy?"

"Don't call me Roy!"

He's on all fours scrambling to get up and he cuts his hand on some of the broken tiles. That strikes him even funnier. Holding up his bloody palm. "Starting to look just like Addie's house around here!"

That tells me everything I need to know.

I'm already on the run before he lurches to his feet.

"Don't leave, sweetie," he calls, "the party's really starting to cook."

He's coming after me. Loping in a half-crouch to favor his wounded leg. Lon Chaney, Jr. as *The Wolfman*. I'm out of the penthouse and racing for the exit door to the studio street. He disappears into the gloom beyond the sets. I'm not that far from the exit. I'm going to make it, I'm way ahead of him, I'll scream bloody murder as soon as I'm outside, attract the studio cops, just a little farther, almost there—when I stumble over a strut supporting the back of a set wall and sprawl headlong on the floor. Lucky thing, too. There's a false window above me looking into the lobby set and I catch a glimpse of Roy galloping by. He doesn't notice me lying prone in the semi-darkness. But the shortcut he's taken totally blocks my escape route. He's already at the exit door, standing guard like a hockey goalie.

One of my shoes kicked off when I stumbled, and I slip off the other shoe and barefoot away as quietly as I can from the exit into the semi-darkness. I don't know where to go and I think I hear him behind me and I'm getting frantic. When I see the ladder. Leading up into the rafters. I don't want to go up there, but there's nowhere else.

I begin climbing and it's all going fine. As I rise, I can see Roy is still guarding the door, scrutinizing the area below for signs of movement. His back is to me; he's calling "Reva, come out, come out, wherever you are." Then I brush against an object wedged in a niche in the wall. It's an empty Coke bottle some sloppy asshole left up here. It goes tumbling down and smashes on the cement floor. Roy turns, sees the shattered glass on the floor, his gaze swings upward and like radar we make eye contact.

He winks. And begins to stroll. Not rush, not even speed walk. Just strolls toward the ladder.

I'm making use of the time, climbing faster, upward to I-don't-know-where as long as it's away from him.

Down below as he starts up the ladder, he begins singing. The words float upward. He knows they're familiar to me. "Cream of Wheat, it's so good to eat, we eat it every day-y-y." Then he switches to his announcer's voice, "Cream of Wheat brings you—*Let's Pretend.*"

I'm getting splinters in my hands, but I don't care. I just keep scurrying higher and higher. A squirrel seeking the safety of the top branch. Or maybe there's a magical escape hatch waiting for me up there. When I glance down, I'm alarmed at how fast he's closing the distance between us, his big hands claiming rungs at twice my rate, swinging him up like an athlete working on the bars. Loudly regaling me all the while.

"Our story today is—*Little Red Riding Hood.*" He goes into Little Red Riding Hood's voice: "Here I am in the deep, dark forest, on my way to my sick Grandma's house." Then the announcer's voice again: "What she doesn't know is that the Big Bad Wolf has already devoured her Grandma."

He emits a ferocious howl that echoes off the roof of the sound stage and raises my hackles. I'm trying to shut him out, concentrate on escape. He's ascending so fast, but there's a catwalk up above me...

I hear Red Riding Hood's voice: "Here's Grandma's cottage now, I'll just go inside and give her this get-well basket of goodies. Oh, she's in bed resting. Hi, Grandma!" Now he does the Big Bad Wolf-pretending-to-be-Grandma's voice: "Hello, sweetheart, glad you could come see me."

I reach the catwalk; it's a narrow footbridge extending diagonally over the sound stage. I glance down. From up here the sets are as small as a dollhouse. And he's still coming, so I run out across the catwalk, as I hear Red Riding Hood's voice...

"My, what big eyes you have, Grandma."

And he's on the catwalk too. So I race onward, and he's following me, doing his ferocious wolf howl and shaking the handrails of the catwalk so hard that I'm afraid I'll fall off. I'm whimpering with terror as I reach the far end of the catwalk. No escape hatch. Just another ladder. Not going down. Going up. Higher.

I climb. It's like a nightmare. Straining but not getting anywhere. My heart is pounding. Sweat running down my face, stinging my eyes. I can't see anything except the next rung above. I'm too scared to look back because I don't want to know how close he is and I'm getting dizzy and as I lift my foot to climb a step higher the fingers of his hand lock around my ankle. I look down and he's smiling toothily up at me. He's right, he's not Roy anymore. He's someone else only vaguely familiar. The diseased *Picture of Dorian Gray* finally out of the closet. It's Jack Havoc gone psycho, his features twisted, eyes glaring evil.

"What big teeth you have," he says as Little Red Riding Hood.

"The better to eat you with!" the Big Bad Wolf bellows.

And he yanks my leg so that I'm torn away from the ladder.

I'm floating in the air. Then I look down. That's a mistake; it's like in one of the *Tom and Jerry* cartoons when Tom walks off the cliff and he's okay until he looks down and that's when he starts to plummet. Now I'm a skydiver without a chute. Hurtling through empty space. Until I stop. With a tremendous jolt. I've landed on my back on the catwalk.

But the trip's not over. The catwalk tilts precariously from the impact and I'm sliding backward, trying to grab something before I go over the side. There's nothing. I go over. But as I do I manage to grasp one of the guide wires with my right hand. My body is dangling over the cement floor far below. My left hand claws the air in search of another handhold.

And, like Dracula swooping down for the kill, I can see him scooting down the ladder onto the catwalk. Toward me. I'm still swaying in the void, clinging to the guide wire with one hand, desperately waving the other. He's walking closer. I can't get away. Pearl White in *The Perils of Pauline*. Tied to the railroad tracks and here comes the Super Chief. He's right above me. Looking down. From where he's standing, he could kick me in the head or stomp on my fingers. Knock me loose. Finish me off. Or just stand there and watch.

Because one by one, my clenched fingers are starting to open.

"For God's sake, Roy!" I yell up at him.

Just as I lose my grip on the guide wire, his arm shoots out and grabs my left wrist. Pulls me up onto the catwalk. Gentle smile. A Roy smile. I grab hold of a post along the handrail. Hug it tight. Stare at him. "Thank you," I whisper.

He turns around abruptly. As if someone behind him said something.

He moves off a couple of steps, his back is to me, but I can see his hands gesticulating, imploring: "Jack, I begged you not to scare her." It's Roy's voice.

But it's Jack Havoc's voice that answers.

"Look, none of us are proud of the way this is going."

"Then why can't we just stop?"

"Forgive and forget?" Jack Havoc tosses over his shoulder: "Can you do that, Reva?"

"I—don't know."

"See, Roy, there's an honest kid. She doesn't know."

He turns to me and it's Roy's face again.

"Reva, say you'll never tell a soul, promise him!"

Before I can answer, the wild Jack Havoc gleam comes back into his eyes. "Sorry, Roy, I can't live with the uncertainty."

He lunges for me, but he stumbles—it's as if someone deliberately tripped him. He tries to regain his balance, but he can't. He plunges headlong over the handrail, giving the catwalk another terrible shake. I hear him scream as he falls, but I cling to the post during the crazy swaying. Then I hear a sickening thud down below and the screaming stops. When I look over the side, I see his shattered body in the center of the penthouse set. Jack's come home. His arms and legs are twisted and contorted. Like a broken doll's.

part three

"Twinkle, twinkle, little star,
How I wonder what you are…"

—Ann Taylor

35

Roy

It's late winter here in Woodland Hills, but there's sunshine almost every day. We're located in the Valley, off the 101 Freeway, a bit this side of the Ventura county line. The worst of the L.A. rains are usually over by mid-March, and through my window I can see the new foliage sprouting again as lush as the hills of Wales (*How Green Was My Valley* was shot nearby on the Fox Ranch) or the greenery of Sherwood Forest (Errol Flynn made *Robin Hood* just down the road). But Lake Sherwood is now Westlake Village, a major suburban residential community. And Woodland Hills is known, if at all, as the site of the Motion Picture Country Home.

The place where I live.

Look around. Pretty nice, huh? Like an elegant condominium country club. Emerald lawns. Immaculately tended putting greens. Tennis, shuffleboard, a huge swimming pool and spa. Private cottages. Mary Astor, one of the sex queens of the '30s, used to ride a big-wheeled tricycle along the sloping pathways, and I'd sit on my porch and watch her still-gorgeous ass as she rolled by, pumping those pedals. She's gone now. We have our own private theater. The major studios show us many of the new flicks and, of course, we run a lot of oldies. There's a recreation hall, our own hospital, state of the art, let me tell you, and a restaurant—since everyone here had something to do with the Business, we call it the Commissary. Big, cheerful place with food they

say is as tasty as Spago. We provide our own dinner entertainment sometimes. Johnny Weissmuller, still living in the
past, used to enjoy stripping off his shirt, climbing up on his
table, thumping his chest and giving his patented *Tarzan*
yodel until the male nurses schlepped him down. He's gone
now. It's been quiet lately.

I used to have a fair number of visitors. Bogie and Betty
came around in the beginning, but he's gone now, and Betty
moved back to New York. Nate Scanlon was a regular every
Sunday. He played golf in Calabasas, and he'd drop by afterward. Until Nate had a stroke on the golf course and wound
up in the cottage down the row from mine. He's gone now.
Merle Heifetz, my P.R. friend from Warners, was good for
five, six visits a year. Until he retired and moved to Rancho
Santa Fe, but I still get Christmas cards from him.

Kim? Well, she came once, took a good look at me, and
said, "Sorry, honey, I can't cut it," and that was the last of
her. Jack Warner used to drive out now and then to donate
a new building, and he'd always stop by for a few minutes.
He's gone now. Arzy Marshak was a regular for a long time.
"You sly sonuvabitch," he'd say to me with a shit-eating
grin, "you got away with it, didn't you?" Arzy's gone now,
too, not *gone,* just pulled the pin and went to live in Col-
orado. Last time I heard from him he was the Sheriff of
Ouray County. Ride 'em cowboy!

Who does that leave? You got it. Reva. Ever-ready, ever-
steady, ever-lovin' Reva. Guess I ought to fill you in on the
gory details. Some of this I can only give you secondhand
because I was out of things for a while. But that night, when
they scraped me off the sound stage floor—yeah, I can joke
about it now—I was in no condition to answer questions. So
it was up to Reva to carry the conversational ball. She told
the cops what happened. I read about it later in back copies
of the *L.A. Times.*

She told them how, because she was president of my fan
club, I had stopped by her apartment to offer her a job.
When she accepted we drove out to the studio to pick up
some files. While we were visiting the set, I showed her

around. We climbed up the ladder to the catwalk to get a scenic bird's-eye view of the place. She said she tripped and fell off and I leaned over, at great risk to my own life, to save her, which I did, but in the process I lost my own balance and plunged to the ground. She made me sound like a hero, and with that tear-stained, innocent-looking face, who wouldn't believe her?

Certainly not the police or the public. I became a terrific running story, everyone hanging on the daily bulletins from City of Hope Hospital. Roy Darnell Still On Critical List. Hero Actor's Condition Improving. More Surgery Scheduled For Roy. Mayor Visits Hospital, Presents Roy Darnell With Citizen's Medal Of Valor For Saving Life Of Young Fan. After Successful Multiple Surgeries, Roy Darnell Transferred To Motion Picture Country Home.

A success story, that's me.

The wonder is that with all the damage my body sustained, and let me tell you, that'd fill a medical textbook, my face was unmarked. It was the way I hit the ground. Probably actor's instinct. Your face is your fortune. Protect it at all costs.

At first I was a hot item at the Country Home. A celebrity among celebrities. The prettiest staff and permanent residents would fuss over me, vying for the privilege of pushing my chair. But you know how it is, new faces arrive and they get all the attention. After a while I was just another guy around here. Not that I'm neglected; I get all the care and feeding I can handle. Although about eating, there's a fluky thing. As a result of the fall, I lost my sense of taste. For food, that is. Something got knocked loose, I guess, but I'm still a good judge of women and movies. And though people don't talk to me much anymore, I still get a kick out of listening to all the industry gossip. We've got retired script supervisors, makeup and wardrobe people, camera crew veterans, as well as actors, writers, producers, and directors. The average age is somewhere between sixty-five and death—that's a local joke.

For a while after I came here I still wasn't doing very well physically. Then things leveled off, and I've been on this kind of plateau ever since. Don't get better, don't get worse. I went through a period of deep depression until I came to terms with it. I mean, I wanted to die. Fortunately—or unfortunately—I wasn't in a position to do anything about it. Then I became resigned, I guess that's the word, resigned to my situation.

Not that it hasn't been interesting, hanging around like this. If I'd died back then I would've missed a lot. The moon landing. The Kennedy Years. The Beatles. The Flower Generation. The Vietnam War. Watergate. My Lai. The rise of feminism. The fall of Communism. Hard to believe that Ronnie Reagan, who I used to beat regularly at tennis, became President. Or that Frank Sinatra's gone. Or Princess Grace and Princess Di. Or that the World Trade Center towers are gone. Or that movie stars are being paid more than twenty million dollars a picture now. I really missed that boat. But I made it through into the new millennium.

Anyway. Back to Reva. She's here every weekend, bless her, like clockwork. Goes wheeling around the campus with me, gabbing away even though I never answer. Recently she did an absolutely fantastic thing. She waged a letter campaign, getting friends of hers all over the country to mail in requests to the Nickelodeon cable channel, asking Nick At Nite to rerun the original episodes of *Jack Havoc*. It worked!

Now Reva drives out here for an extra visit every time the show is on and proudly pushes me into the rec hall where the whole crowd watches on the big screen TV and cheers. It feels good. I've been here so long that most of the people didn't know who or what I was. Even the cute young nurses ooh and aah over Jack Havoc. Last night one of them said, "You were definitely a stud muffin, honey," and kissed me on the cheek.

While we're on the subject of Jack Havoc.

He's gone now.

Guess he died in the fall.

At least he's never been inside my head since then.

Although I'm a living testimonial to the skills and persistence of modern medicine, and I'm generally sedated enough so that I don't feel much pain, I am nevertheless what most people would describe as a vegetable. I'm a quadriplegic in a wheelchair who can't walk, speak, stand, or otherwise care for myself. The Man of a Thousand Voices reduced to none. The only things I can do unassisted are swallow, breathe, listen, and think. Oh yeah, I can also blink my eyes. Good for a yes/no exchange, but hard to hold a real discussion. The only good thing is I don't ever get migraines anymore.

Somebody once told me that no one who comes to L.A. ever leaves. Like all those who pursue the Hollywood Dream, I discovered that the thing you think you have been promised isn't necessarily what you get. It's Bogie's joke. *Pincus fuctus.* But I survived. Don't ask me why. Maybe it's my punishment.

I got life.

36

Reva

When I was a little kid living in Brooklyn I went to the Biltmore Theater one Saturday and saw Danny Kaye in *The Kid From Brooklyn*. In a lot of ways I still feel like that little kid, but last week I had to decide whether to take early retirement on my social security pension. I decided to keep on working three more years until I'm sixty-five.

Remember that job I applied for as a messenger at Twentieth Century Fox? Well, they hired me, and I've been there ever since. I'm a department head now, in charge of scheduling all the set construction crews, both features and TV. The salary is good and the perks are great, medical coverage and a 401K pension, plus weekly screenings on the lot. Also, I manage to finagle tickets to the premieres and publicity parties for our jumbo epics. Occasionally I see a familiar face among the fans at the premieres. When they see me, the few that remember me start to shout from the bleachers, "Revahhh, Revaahhh!" And the others who never knew me join in anyway, because I'm told I'm something of a legend among the collectors.

I still look more or less the same, still wearing my hair in a pageboy. I dress better, like a grownup business person. If you get close enough you can see the years, but at a glance from a distance, I look pretty good. Pert. Not pretty. I only looked pretty that one time for that one moment when he made me look in the mirror. But, as the kids say, that was then and this is now.

Mother died in 1967 of cirrhosis of the liver. I'd moved out and gotten my own apartment long before. I'm still in that same apartment, off of Overland near Pico, close to the studio. I drive a fifteen-year-old Mercedes two-seater, the kind Audrey Hepburn and Albert Finney used to scoot around Europe in *Two For The Road,* a Fox picture, incidentally. I bought the car used from one of the studio production managers and have babied it ever since. I take good care of my things. I never got married. Just too busy, I guess.

I don't have many friends. A few from Fox, plus Podolsky, of course. Don't have time for more. I work long hours, and there's always so much to do for Roy after work. Shopping, planning, keeping up. Underwear and socks wear out, there are birthday presents, Christmas presents, April Fools' Day presents, Easter presents, Fourth of July presents, and Thanksgiving Day presents to search for. I always try to be a bit offbeat and original, and he appreciates the effort. The Country Home does a terrific job providing the basics, but he deserves some of the frills, too, after all he's been through.

So, for instance, I buy him a yearly subscription to *Daily Variety,* and I tip one of the nurses extra to set the trade paper up for him each morning on a special reading board and turn the pages every few minutes. Then when he's done, the trades are donated to the other residents, which doesn't hurt Roy's popularity around there. Tell the truth, though, he's not very popular. No one's mean to him, they just don't pay any attention to him. Because he can't respond, people tend to assume he can't understand. But he can. He understands everything that's going on. And that's where I try to help out.

Since Nick At Nite started rerunning the *Jack Havoc* shows, fan mail has begun to arrive again. I've had a supply of 8x10 glossies made up and I sign them. No problem. I know that signature as well as my own. Podolsky says I could have a stamp made, but this way it's more personal. "To Debbie, with best wishes from Roy Darnell."

You're probably asking yourself how I came to terms with what happened between us on that night. When the cops and the press first talked to me, protecting his reputation was an automatic reaction. I never liked anyone speaking badly of him, all that Roy the Bad Boy stuff. But inside myself I was totally confused. I never told anyone else what really happened that night, not even Podolsky. It's our secret. Roy's and mine. He had tried to murder me. But he had also saved my life. Both things were true. It was like Dr. Jekyll and Mr. Hyde. I did a lot of reading about split personalities, and he came up like a poster boy for schizoid behavior. I blame Addie for addling his mind—the first time I said that to him, he laughed, well, he can't move those facial muscles, but I could see in his eyes that he thought it was funny—but he *was* addled by Addie's treatment of him. Off his nut. But he came back that night. And he's been okay ever since. I can see that in his eyes, too.

I drive out there every Saturday and Sunday. He's always sitting in his wheelchair, looking toward the parking lot for the first glimpse of me. When we're together, I talk to him incessantly and probably inanely. He seems to like it. The first time I came to visit I brought flowers. I could see his surprise that I'd come at all. That was the day we worked out the wigwag system with blinks for yes and no and even for spelling out a few words. He looked at the big bouquet of flowers and then blinked out: a-m-i-d-e-a-d? I laughed and I could see the flicker of pleasure in his eyes.

Remember the ending of that old tearjerker *An Affair To Remember?* When Cary Grant finds out that the reason Deborah Kerr didn't meet him on top of the Empire State Building was because she had become a cripple? I always wondered what happened after that. I found out. They lived happily ever after. Well, anyway, they did the best they could.

We have our little rituals. I always give him a shave when I come out. They do it on the other days, of course, but he likes the way I do it best. And I cut his hair. Just recently, when I suggested doing the part on the other side, he was nervous, but I persuaded him to let me try it and it turned out great. I've been leaving his hair a little thicker and longer on the crown because it's sparse back there. I haven't told him, why make him worry about getting bald? It may seem silly to worry about appearances, I know that other people just see him as this basket case propped up in a wheelchair. But to me, he's still the shaggy-haired guy who walked out onto the stage of the *Let's Pretend* theater in a black windbreaker and wrinkled pants and work boots. I thought he was a stagehand. I didn't realize he was Prince Charming.

That's what I miss the most. The sound of his voice. But it's not gone. When I concentrate, I can still hear it in my head. I found out the same thing about my autograph books. They're not gone, either. I can still turn the pages of the ones that were burned, using my mind like a Rolodex.

Podolsky wound up working for the Motion Picture Academy Library. Whatever researchers are looking for, he knows where to find it. He's been thanked in the dedication section of so many books about the movies. Podolsky is still a collector, but now he collects videotapes and DVDs by the hundreds. He says he realized that when he was going after autographs, what he really wanted to have was the movies themselves. And with modern technology, now he can.

It was different with me.

So what is the significance of this autograph thing, after all? I've thought about that a lot. Guess it's a kind of proof that you actually saw these great people. Proof to who? Well, that's a little harder to say. Maybe just proof to ourselves that we really exist and we really matter, too, even if it's only through flashes of reflected glory. We wanted so much to be part of that beautiful, exciting, romantic world we saw up on the screen.

I know I tend to see reality in terms of the movies and that's limited and I guess immature. But things worked out so much better than I could have ever dreamed. In fact, I told Podolsky recently that my life turned out to be even better than a movie. I really meant it. And that's the ultimate thing I could have wished for. So maybe I never got Garbo, but there's more to life than that.

I got Roy.

about the author

Jerry Ludwig began his work in the star-studded world of film as a teenager collecting autographs in New York. After a career in journalism, Ludwig became a publicist for Burt Lancaster's independent company, and went on to work on everything from *Murder, She Wrote* to *West Side Story* with everyone from Barbara Hershey to Marlon Brando. His work in the film business has earned him several awards and dozens more nominations.

Ludwig's most recent Hollywood credits include writing and producing *Dash and Lilly*, an A&E TV movie. Ludwig won the Writers Guild of America award for Best Teleplay, and the picture was nominated for nine TV Academy Emmy Awards, as well as nominations from the Humanitas Prize, Golden Globes, and Producers Guild of America.

Jerry Ludwig and his wife Tobi, an artist, live in Rancho Mirage, California, where he is currently working on his next novel about Hollywood.